Dear Philip

with lots of love and many
happy huntings of the snark
and other monsters!

Christmas 1996

P.S. This is from me, SANTA.
Even though you've announced
that I do not exist
I can still give your present
an
extra
little
twist.

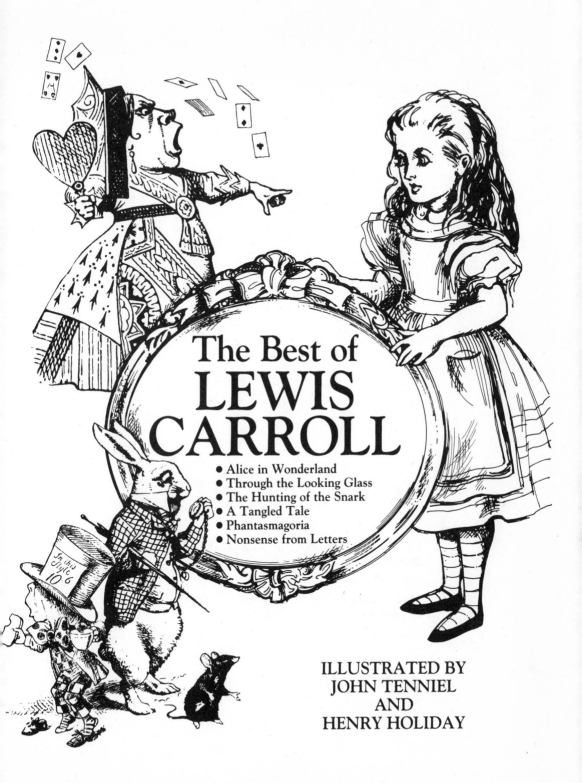

The Best of
LEWIS CARROLL

- Alice in Wonderland
- Through the Looking Glass
- The Hunting of the Snark
- A Tangled Tale
- Phantasmagoria
- Nonsense from Letters

ILLUSTRATED BY
JOHN TENNIEL
AND
HENRY HOLIDAY

CASTLE

TABLE OF CONTENTS

PAGE

ALICE IN WONDERLAND

All in the golden afternoon
  Full leisurely we glide;
For both our oars, with little skill,
  By little arms are plied,
While little hands make vain pretence
  Our wanderings to guide.

Ah, cruel Three! In such an hour
  Beneath such dreamy weather,
To beg a tale of breath too weak
  To stir the tiniest feather!
Yet what can one poor voice avail
  Against three tongues together?

Imperious Prima flashes forth
  Her edict "to begin it"—
In gentler tone Secunda hopes
  "There will be nonsense in it!"—
While Tertia interrupts the tale
  Not more than once a minute.

Anon, to sudden silence won,
  In fancy they pursue
The dream-child moving through a land
  Of wonders wild and new,
In friendly chat with bird or beast—
  And half believe it true.

And ever, as the story drained
   The wells of fancy dry,
And faintly strove that weary one
   To put the subject by,
"The rest next time—" "It is next time!"
   The happy voices cry.

Thus grew the tale of Wonderland:
   Thus slowly, one by one,
Its quaint events were hammered out—
   And now the tale is done,
And home we steer, a merry crew,
   Beneath the setting sun.

Alice! a childish story take,
   And with a gentle hand
Lay it where Childhood's dreams are twined
   In Memory's mystic band,
Like pilgrim's wither'd wreath of flowers
   Pluck'd in a far-off land.

CHAPTER I

DOWN THE RABBIT-HOLE

ALICE was beginning to get very tired of sitting by her sister on the bank, and of having nothing to do: once or twice she had peeped into the book her sister was reading, but it had no pictures or conversations in it, "and what is the use of a book," thought Alice, "without pictures or conversations?"

So she was considering in her own mind (as well as she could, for the hot day made her feel very sleepy and stupid) whether the pleasure of making a daisy-chain would be worth the trouble of getting up and picking the daisies, when suddenly a White Rabbit with pink eyes ran close by her.

5

There was nothing so *very* remarkable in that; nor did Alice think it so *very* much out of the way to hear the Rabbit say to itself, "Oh dear! Oh dear! I shall be too late!" (when she thought it over afterwards, it occurred to her that she ought to have wondered at this, but at the time it all seemed quite natural); but when the Rabbit actually *took a watch out of its waistcoat-pocket*, and looked at it, and then hurried on, Alice started to her feet, for it flashed across her mind that she had never before seen a rabbit with either a waistcoat-pocket, or a watch to take out of it, and burning with curiosity, she ran across the field after it, and fortunately was just in time to see it pop down a large rabbit-hole under the hedge.

In another moment down went Alice after it, never once considering how in the world she was to get out again.

The rabbit-hole went straight on like a tunnel for some way, and then dipped suddenly down, so suddenly that Alice had not a moment to think about stopping herself before she found herself falling down a very deep well.

Either the well was very deep, or she fell very slowly, for she had plenty of time as she went down to look about her, and to wonder what was going to happen next. First, she tried to look down and make out what she was coming to, but it was too dark to see anything; then she looked at the sides of the well, and noticed that they were filled with cupboards and bookshelves: here and there she saw maps and pictures hung upon pegs. She took down a jar from one of the shelves as she passed; it was labelled "ORANGE MARMALADE," but to her great disappointment it was empty: she did not like to drop the jar for fear of killing somebody, so managed to put it into one of the cupboards as she fell past it.

"Well!" thought Alice to herself. "After such a fall as this, I shall think nothing of tumbling downstairs! How brave they'll all think me at home! Why, I wouldn't say anything about it, even if I fell off the top of the house!" (Which was very likely true.)

Down, down, down. Would the fall *never* come to an end? "I wonder how many miles I've fallen by this time?" she said aloud. "I must be getting somewhere near the centre of the earth. Let me see: that would be four thousand miles down, I think—" (for, you see, Alice had learnt several things of this sort in her lessons in the schoolroom, and though this was not a *very* good opportunity for showing off her knowledge, as there was no one to listen to her, still it was good practice to say it over) "—yes, that's about the right distance—but then I wonder what Latitude or Longitude I've got to?" (Alice had no idea what Latitude was, or Longitude either, but thought they were nice grand words to say.)

Presently she began again. "I wonder if I shall fall right *through* the earth! How funny it'll seem to come out among the people that walk with their heads downwards! The Antipathies, I think—" (she was rather glad there *was* no one listening this time, as it didn't sound at all the right word) "—but I shall have to ask them what the name of the country is, you know. Please, Ma'am, is this New Zealand or Australia?" (and she tried to curtsey as she spoke—fancy *curtseying* as you're falling through the air! Do you think you could manage it?) "And what an ignorant little girl she'll think me! No, it'll never do to ask; perhaps I shall see it written up somewhere."

Down, down, down. There was nothing else to do, so Alice soon began talking again. "Dinah'll miss me very much to-night, I should think!" (Dinah was the cat.) "I hope they'll remember her saucer of milk at tea-time. Dinah, my dear, I wish you were down here with me! There are no mice in the air, I'm afraid, but you might catch a bat, and that's very like a mouse, you know. But do cats eat bats, I wonder?" And here Alice began to get rather sleepy, and went on saying to herself, in a dreamy sort of way, "Do cats eat bats? Do cats eat bats?" and sometimes, "Do bats eat cats?" for, you see, as she couldn't answer either question, it didn't much matter which way she put it. She felt that she was dozing off, and had just begun to dream that she was walking hand in hand with Dinah, and saying to her very earnestly, "Now, Dinah, tell me the truth: did you ever eat a bat?" when suddenly, thump thump! down she came upon a heap of dry leaves, and the fall was over.

Alice was not a bit hurt, and she jumped up on to her feet in a moment: she looked up, but it was all dark overhead; before

her was another long passage, and the White Rabbit was still in sight, hurrying down it. There was not a moment to be lost: away went Alice like the wind, and was just in time to hear it say, as it turned a corner, "Oh my ears and whiskers, how late it's getting!" She was close behind it when she turned the corner, but the Rabbit was no longer to be seen: she found herself in a long, low hall, which was lit up by a row of lamps hanging from the roof.

There were doors all round the hall, but they were all locked; and when Alice had been all the way down one side and up the other, trying every door, she walked sadly down the middle, wondering how she was ever to get out again.

Suddenly she came upon a little three-legged table, all made of solid glass; there was nothing on it except a tiny golden key, and Alice's first thought was that it might belong to one of the doors of the hall; but, alas! either the locks were too large, or the key was too small, but at any rate it would not open any of them. However, the second time round, she came upon a low curtain she had not noticed before, and behind it was a little door about fifteen inches high:

she tried the little golden key in the lock, and to her great delight it fitted!

Alice opened the door and found that it led into a small passage, not much larger than a rat-hole: she knelt down and looked along the passage into the loveliest garden you ever saw. How she longed to get out of that dark hall, and wander about among those beds of bright flowers and those cool fountains, but she could not even get her head through the doorway; "and even if my head would go through," thought poor Alice, "it would be of very little use without my shoulders. Oh, how I wish I could shut up like a telescope! I think I could, if I only knew how to begin." For, you see, so many out-of-the-way things had happened lately that Alice had begun to think that very few things indeed were really impossible.

There seemed to be no use in waiting by the little door, so she went back to the table, half hoping she might find another key on it, or at any rate a book of rules for shutting people up like telescopes: this time she found a little bottle on it ("which certainly was not here before," said Alice), and round its neck a paper label, with the words "DRINK ME" beautifully printed on it in large letters.

It was all very well to say "Drink me," but the wise little Alice was not going to do *that* in a hurry. "No, I'll look first," she said, "and see whether it's marked '*poison*' or not"; for she had read several nice little histories about children who had got burnt, and eaten up by wild beasts, and many other unpleasant things, all because they *would* not remember the simple rules their friends had taught them: such as, that a red-hot poker will burn you if you hold it too long; and that, if you cut your finger *very* deeply with a knife, it usually bleeds; and she had never forgotten that, if you drink much from a bottle marked "poison," it is almost certain to disagree with you, sooner or later.

However, this bottle was *not* marked "poison," so Alice ventured to taste it, and finding it very nice (it had, in fact, a sort of mixed flavour of cherry-tart, custard, pine-apple, roast turkey, toffee, and hot buttered toast), she very soon finished it off.

"What a curious feeling!" said Alice. "I must be shutting up like a telescope."

.   .   .   .

And so it was indeed: she was now only ten inches high, and her face brightened up at the thought that she was now the right size for going through the little door into that lovely garden. First, however, she waited for a few minutes to see if she was going to shrink any further: she felt a little nervous about this; "for it might end, you know," said Alice, "in my going out altogether, like a candle. I wonder what I should be like then?" And she tried to fancy what the flame of a candle is like after it is blown out, for she could not remember ever having seen such a thing.

After a while, finding that nothing more happened, she decided on going into the garden at once; but, alas for poor Alice! when she got to the door, she found she had forgotten the little golden key, and when she went back to the table for it, she found she could not possibly reach it: she could see it quite plainly through the glass, and she tried her best to climb up one of the table-legs, but it was too slippery; and when she had tired herself out with trying, the poor little thing sat down and cried.

"Come, there's no use in crying like that!" said Alice to herself, rather sharply. "I advise you to leave off this minute!" She generally gave herself very good advice (though she very seldom followed it), and sometimes she scolded herself so severely as to bring tears into her eyes; and once she remembered trying to box her own ears for having cheated herself in a game of croquet she was playing against herself, for this curious child was very fond of pretending to be two people. "But it's no use now," thought poor Alice, "to pretend to be two people! Why, there's hardly enough of me left to make *one* respectable person!"

Soon her eye fell on a little glass box that was lying under the table: she opened it, and found in it a very small cake, on which the words "EAT ME" were beautifully marked in currants. "Well, I'll eat it," said Alice, "and if it makes me larger, I can reach the key; and if it makes me smaller, I can creep under the door; so either way I'll get into the garden, and I don't care which happens!"

She ate a little bit, and said anxiously to herself, "Which way? Which way?" holding her hand on the top of her head to feel which way it was growing, and she was quite surprised to find that she remained the same size: to be sure, this generally happens when one eats cake, but Alice had got so much into the way of expecting nothing but out-of-the-way things to happen, that it seemed quite dull and stupid for life to go on in the common way.

So she set to work, and very soon finished off the cake.

CHAPTER II

POOL OF TEARS

"Curiouser and curiouser!" cried Alice (she was so much surprised, that for the moment she quite forgot how to speak good English); "now I'm opening out like the largest telescope that ever was! Good-bye, feet!" (for when she looked down at her feet, they seemed to be almost out of sight, they were getting so far off) "Oh, my poor little feet, I wonder who will put on your shoes and stockings for you now, dears? I'm sure *I* shan't be able! I shall be a great deal too far off to trouble myself about you: you must manage the best way you can—but I must be kind to them," thought Alice, "or perhaps they won't walk the way I want to go! Let me see: I'll give them a new pair of boots every Christmas."

And she went on planning to herself how she would manage it. "They must go by the carrier," she thought; "and how funny it'll seem, sending presents to one's own feet! And how odd the directions will look!

> *Alice's Right Foot, Esq.*
> *Hearthrug,*
> *near the Fender*
> *(with Alice's love).*

Oh dear, what nonsense I'm talking!"

Just then her head struck against the roof of the hall: in fact she was now more than nine feet high, and she at once took up the little golden key and hurried off to the garden door.

Poor Alice! It was as much as she could do, lying down on one side, to look through into the garden with one eye; but to get through was more hopeless than ever: she sat down and began to cry again.

"You ought to be ashamed of yourself," said Alice, "a great girl like you" (she might well say this), "to go on crying in this way! Stop this moment, I tell you!" But she went on all the same, shedding gallons of tears, until there was a large pool all round her, about four inches deep and reaching half down the hall.

After a time she heard a little pattering of feet in the distance, and she hastily dried her eyes to see what was coming. It was the White Rabbit returning, splendidly dressed, with a pair of white kid gloves in one hand and a large fan in the other: he came trotting along in a great hurry, muttering to himself as he came, "Oh! the Duchess, the Duchess! Oh! won't she be savage if I've kept her waiting!" Alice felt so desperate that she was ready to ask help of anyone; so, when the Rabbit came near her, she began, in a low, timid voice, "If you please, sir——" The Rabbit started violently, dropped the white kid gloves and the fan, and scurried away into the darkness as hard as he could go.

Alice took up the fan and gloves, and, as the hall was very

hot, she kept fanning herself all the time she went on talking:
"Dear, dear! How queer everything is to-day! And yesterday
things went on just as usual. I wonder if I've been changed
in the night? Let me think: was I the same when I got up
this morning? I almost think I can remember feeling a little
different. But if I'm not the same, the next question is, Who
in the world am I? Ah, *that's* the great puzzle!" And she
began thinking over all the children she knew that were of

the same age as herself, to see if she could have been changed for any of them.

"I'm sure I'm not Ada," she said, "for her hair goes in such long ringlets, and mine doesn't go in ringlets at all; and I'm sure I can't be Mabel, for I know all sorts of things, and she, oh! she knows such a very little! Besides, *she's* she, and *I'm* I, and—oh dear, how puzzling it all is! I'll try if I know all the things I used to know. Let me see: four times five is twelve, and four times six is thirteen, and four times seven is—oh dear! I shall never get to twenty at that rate! However, the Multiplication Table doesn't signify: let's try Geography. London is the capital of Paris, and Paris is the capital of Rome, and Rome—no, *that's* all wrong, I'm certain! I must have been changed for Mabel! I'll try and say 'How doth the little——'" and she crossed her hands on her lap as if she were saying lessons, and began to repeat it, but her voice sounded hoarse and strange, and the words did not come the same as they used to do:

> *"How doth the little crocodile*
> *Improve his shining tail,*
> *And pour the waters of the Nile*
> *On every golden scale!*
>
> *"How cheerfully he seems to grin,*
> *How neatly spread his claws,*
> *And welcomes little fishes in*
> *With gently smiling jaws!*

"I'm sure those are not the right words," said poor Alice, and her eyes filled with tears again as she went on, "I must be Mabel after all, and I shall have to go and live in that poky little house, and have next to no toys to play with, and oh! ever so many lessons to learn! No, I've made up my mind about it; if I'm Mabel, I'll stay down here! It'll be no use their putting their heads down and saying 'Come up again, dear!' I shall only look up and say 'Who am I then? Tell me that first, and then, if I like being that person, I'll come up: if not, I'll stay down here till I'm somebody else' —but, oh dear!" cried Alice, with a sudden burst of tears, "I do wish they *would* put their heads down! I am so *very* tired of being all alone here!"

As she said this she looked down at her hands, and was surprised to see that she had put on one of the Rabbit's little white kid gloves while she was talking. "How *can* I have done that?" she thought. "I must be growing small again." She got up and went to the table to measure herself by it, and found that, as nearly as she could guess, she was now about two feet high, and was going on shrinking rapidly: she soon found out that the cause of this was the fan she was holding, and she dropped it hastily, just in time to avoid shrinking away altogether.

"That *was* a narrow escape!" said Alice, a good deal frightened at the sudden change, but very glad to find herself still in existence; "and now for the garden!" and she ran with all speed back to the little door; but, alas! the little door was shut again, and the little golden key was lying on the glass table as before, "and things are worse than ever," thought the poor child, "for I never was so small as this before, never! And I declare it's too bad, that it is."

As she said these words her foot slipped, and in another moment, splash! she was up to her chin in salt water. Her first idea was that she had somehow fallen into the sea, "and in that case I can go back by railway," she said to herself. (Alice had been to the seaside once in her life, and had come to the general conclusion that wherever you go to on the English coast you find a number of bathing machines in the sea, some children digging in the sand with wooden spades, then a row of lodging houses, and behind them a railway station.) However, she soon made out that she was in the

pool of tears which she had wept when she was nine feet
high.

"I wish I hadn't cried so much!" said Alice, as she swam
about, trying to find her way out. "I shall be punished for it

now, I suppose, by being drowned in my own tears! That
will be a queer thing, to be sure! However, everything is
queer to-day."

Just then she heard something splashing about in the pool
a little way off, and she swam nearer to make out what it
was: at first she thought it must be a walrus or hippopotamus,
but then she remembered how small she was now, and she
soon made out that it was only a mouse that had slipped in
like herself.

"Would it be of any use now," thought Alice, "to speak
to this mouse? Everything is so out-of-the-way down here,
that I should think very likely it can talk: at any rate, there's
no harm in trying." So she began: "O Mouse, do you know
the way out of this pool? I am very tired of swimming about
here, O Mouse!" (Alice thought this must be the right way

of speaking to a mouse: she had never done such a thing before, but she remembered having seen in her brother's Latin
Grammar, "A mouse—of a mouse—to a mouse—a mouse—
O mouse!") The Mouse looked at her rather inquisitively,
and seemed to her to wink with one of its little eyes, but it
said nothing.

"Perhaps it doesn't understand English," thought Alice;
"I dare say it's a French mouse, come over with William
the Conqueror." (For, with all her knowledge of history,
Alice had no very clear notion how long ago anything had
happened.) So she began again: "Où est ma chatte?" which
was the first sentence in her French lesson-book. The Mouse
gave a sudden leap out of the water, and seemed to quiver
all over with fright. "Oh, I beg your pardon!" cried Alice
hastily, afraid that she had hurt the poor animal's feelings.
"I quite forgot you didn't like cats."

"Not like cats!" cried the Mouse, in a shrill, passionate
voice. "Would *you* like cats if you were me?"

"Well, perhaps not," said Alice in a soothing tone: "don't
be angry about it. And yet I wish I could show you our cat

Dinah: I think you'd take a fancy to cats if you could only see her. She is such a dear quiet thing," Alice went on, half to herself, as she swam lazily about in the pool, "and she sits purring so nicely by the fire, licking her paws and washing her face—and she is such a nice soft thing to nurse—and she's such a capital one for catching mice—— Oh, I beg your pardon!" cried Alice again, for this time the Mouse was bristling all over, and she felt certain it must be really offended. "We won't talk about her any more if you'd rather not."

"We, indeed!" cried the Mouse, who was trembling down to the end of his tail. "As if *I* would talk on such a subject! Our family always *hated* cats: nasty, low, vulgar things! Don't let me hear the name again!"

"I won't indeed!" said Alice, in a great hurry to change the subject of conversation. "Are you—are you fond—of—of dogs?" The Mouse did not answer, so Alice went on eagerly: "There is such a nice little dog near our house I should like to show you! A little bright-eyed terrier, you know, with oh, such long curly brown hair! And it'll fetch things when you throw them, and it'll sit up and beg for its dinner, and all sorts of things—I can't remember half of them—and it belongs to a farmer, you know, and he says it's so useful, it's worth a hundred pounds! He says it kills all the rats and—oh dear!" cried Alice in a sorrowful tone, "I'm afraid I've offended it again!" For the Mouse was swimming away from her as hard as it could go, and making quite a commotion in the pool as it went.

So she called softly after it, "Mouse dear! Do come back again, and we won't talk about cats or dogs either, if you don't like them!" When the Mouse heard this, it turned round and swam slowly back to her: its face was quite pale (with passion, Alice thought), and it said in a low trembling voice, "Let us get to the shore, and then I'll tell you my history, and you'll understand why it is I hate cats and dogs."

It was high time to go, for the pool was getting quite crowded with the birds and animals that had fallen into it: there were a Duck and a Dodo, a Lory and an Eaglet, and several other curious creatures. Alice led the way, and the whole party swam to the shore.

CHAPTER III

A CAUCUS-RACE AND A LONG TALE

They were indeed a queer-looking party that assembled on the bank—the birds with draggled feathers, the animals with their fur clinging close to them, and all dripping wet, cross, and uncomfortable.

The first question of course was, how to get dry again: they had a consultation about this, and after a few minutes it seemed quite natural to Alice to find herself talking familiarly with them, as if she had known them all her life. Indeed, she had quite a long argument with the Lory, who at last turned sulky, and would only say, "I am older than you, and must know better"; and this Alice would not allow without knowing how old it was, and, as the Lory positively refused to tell its age, there was no more to be said.

At last the Mouse, who seemed to be a person of authority among them, called out, "Sit down, all of you, and listen to me! *I'll* soon make you dry enough!" They all sat down at once, in a large ring, with the Mouse in the middle. Alice kept her eyes anxiously fixed on it, for she felt sure she would catch a bad cold if she did not get dry very soon.

"Ahem!" said the Mouse with an important air. "Are you all ready? This is the driest thing I know. Silence all round, if you please! 'William the Conqueror, whose cause was favoured by the pope, was soon submitted to by the English, who wanted leaders, and had been of late much accustomed to usurpation and conquest. Edwin and Morcar, the earls of Mercia and Northumbria——' "

"Ugh!" said the Lory, with a shiver.

"I beg your pardon!" said the Mouse, frowning, but very politely. "Did you speak?"

"Not I!" said the Lory hastily.

"I thought you did," said the Mouse. "I proceed. 'Edwin and Morcar, the earls of Mercia and Northumbria, declared for him: and even Stigand, the patriotic Archbishop of Canterbury, found it advisable——' "

"Found *what?*" said the Duck.

"Found *it*," the Mouse replied rather crossly: "of course you know what 'it' means."

"I know what 'it' means well enough, when *I* find a thing," said the Duck: "it's generally a frog or a worm. The question is, what did the archbishop find?"

The Mouse did not notice this question, but hurriedly went

on, " '—found it advisable to go with Edgar Atheling to meet William and offer him the crown. William's conduct at first was moderate. But the insolence of his Normans——' How are you getting on now, my dear?" it continued, turning to Alice as it spoke.

"As wet as ever," said Alice in a melancholy tone: "it doesn't seem to dry me at all."

"In that case," said the Dodo solemnly, rising to its feet, "I move that the meeting adjourn, for the immediate adoption of more energetic remedies——"

"Speak English!" said the Eaglet. "I don't know the meaning of half those long words, and, what's more, I don't believe you do either!" And the Eaglet bent down its head to hide a smile: some of the other birds tittered audibly.

"What I was going to say," said the Dodo in an offended tone, "was, that the best thing to get us dry would be a Caucus-race."

"What *is* a Caucus-race?" said Alice; not that she much wanted to know, but the Dodo had paused as if it thought that *somebody* ought to speak, and no one else seemed inclined to say anything.

"Why," said the Dodo, "the best way to explain it is to do it." (And, as you might like to try the thing yourself some winter day, I will tell you how the Dodo managed it.)

First it marked out a race-course, in a sort of circle ("the exact shape doesn't matter," it said), and then all the party were placed along the course, here and there. There was no "One, two, three, and away," but they began running when they liked, and left off when they liked, so that it was not easy to know when the race was over. However, when they had been running half an hour or so, and were quite dry again, the Dodo suddenly called out "The race is over!" and they all crowded round it, panting, and asking, "But who has won?"

This question the Dodo could not answer without a great deal of thought, and it sat for a long time with one finger pressed upon its forehead (the position in which you usually see Shakespeare, in the pictures of him), while the rest waited in silence. At last the Dodo said, "*Everybody* has won, and all must have prizes."

"But who is to give the prizes?" quite a chorus of voices asked.

"Why, *she*, of course," said the Dodo, pointing to Alice with one finger; and the whole party at once crowded round her, calling out in a confused way, "Prizes! Prizes!"

Alice had no idea what to do, and in despair she put her hand in her pocket, and pulled out a box of comfits (luckily the salt water had not got into it), and handed them round as prizes. There was exactly one apiece all round.

"But she must have a prize herself, you know," said the Mouse.

"Of course," the Dodo replied very gravely. "What else have you got in your pocket?" he went on, turning to Alice.

"Only a thimble," said Alice sadly.

"Hand it over here," said the Dodo.

Then they all crowded round her once more, while the Dodo solemnly presented the thimble, saying, "We beg your acceptance of this elegant thimble"; and, when it had finished this short speech, they all cheered.

Alice thought the whole thing very absurd, but they all looked so grave that she did not dare to laugh; and, as she could not think of anything to say, she simply bowed, and took the thimble, looking as solemn as she could.

The next thing was to eat the comfits: this caused some noise and confusion, as the large birds complained that they could not taste theirs, and the small ones choked and had to be patted on the back. However, it was over at last, and they sat down again in a ring, and begged the Mouse to tell them something more.

"You promised to tell me your history, you know," said Alice, "and why it is you hate—C and D," she added in a whisper, half afraid that it would be offended again.

"Mine is a long and a sad tale!" said the Mouse, turning to Alice and sighing.

"It *is* a long tail, certainly," said Alice, looking down with wonder at the Mouse's tail; "but why do you call it sad?" And she kept on puzzling about it while the Mouse was speaking, so that her idea of the tale was something like this—

Fury said to a
mouse, That he
met in the
house,
"Let us
both go
to law:
I will
prosecute
you. Come, I'll
take no denial;
We must
have a trial:
For really
this morning
I've nothing
to do."
Said the
mouse to the
cur, "Such a
trial,
dear Sir,
With no
jury or
judge,
would be
wasting
our breath."
"I'll be judge,
I'll be jury,"
Said
cunning
old Fury:
"I'll
try the
whole
cause,
and
condemn
you
to
death."

"You are not attending!" said the Mouse to Alice severely. "What are you thinking of?"

"I beg your pardon," said Alice very humbly: "you had got to the fifth bend, I think?"

"I had *not!*" cried the Mouse angrily.

"A knot!" said Alice, always ready to make herself useful, and looking anxiously about her. "Oh, do let me help to undo it!"

"I shall do nothing of the sort," said the Mouse, getting up and walking away. "You insult me by talking such nonsense!"

"I didn't mean it!" pleaded poor Alice. "But you're so easily offended, you know!"

The Mouse only growled in reply.

"Please come back and finish your story!" Alice called after it. And the others all joined in chorus, "Yes, please do!" but the Mouse only shook its head impatiently and walked a little quicker.

"What a pity it wouldn't stay!" sighed the Lory, as soon as it was quite out of sight; and an old Crab took the opportunity of saying to her daughter, "Ah, my dear! Let this be a lesson to you never to lose *your* temper!" "Hold your tongue, Ma!" said the young Crab, a little snappishly. "You're enough to try the patience of an oyster!"

"I wish I had our Dinah here, I know I do!" said Alice aloud, addressing nobody in particular. "She'd soon fetch it back!"

"And who is Dinah, if I might venture to ask the question?" said the Lory.

Alice replied eagerly, for she was always ready to talk about her pet: "Dinah's our cat. And she's such a capital one for catching mice, you can't think! And oh, I wish you could see her after the birds! Why, she'll eat a little bird as soon as look at it!"

This speech caused a remarkable sensation among the

party. Some of the birds hurried off at once: one old Magpie began wrapping itself up very carefully, remarking, "I really must be getting home; the night-air doesn't suit my throat!" and a Canary called out in a trembling voice to its children, "Come away, my dears! It's high time you were all in bed!" On various pretexts they all moved off, and Alice was soon left alone.

"I wish I hadn't mentioned Dinah!" she said to herself in a melancholy tone. "Nobody seems to like her, down here, and I'm sure she's the best cat in the world! Oh, my dear Dinah! I wonder if I shall ever see you any more!" And here poor Alice began to cry again, for she felt very lonely and low-spirited. In a little while, however, she again heard a little pattering of footsteps in the distance, and she looked up eagerly, half hoping that the Mouse had changed his mind, and was coming back to finish his story.

CHAPTER IV

THE RABBIT SENDS IN A LITTLE BILL

It was the White Rabbit, trotting slowly back again, and looking anxiously about as it went, as if it had lost something; and she heard it muttering to itself, "The Duchess! The Duchess! Oh my dear paws! Oh my fur and whiskers! She'll get me executed, as sure as ferrets are ferrets! Where *can* I have dropped them, I wonder?" Alice guessed in a moment that it was looking for the fan and the pair of white kid gloves, and she very good-naturedly began hunting about for them, but they were nowhere to be seen—everything seemed to have changed since her swim in the pool, and the great hall, with the glass table and the little door, had vanished completely.

Very soon the Rabbit noticed Alice, as she went hunting

about, and called out to her in an angry tone, "Why, Mary
Ann, what *are* you doing out here? Run home this moment,
and fetch me a pair of gloves and a fan! Quick, now!" And
Alice was so much frightened that she ran off at once in the
direction it pointed to, without trying to explain the mistake
it had made.

"He took me for his housemaid," she said to herself as
she ran. "How surprised he'll be when he finds out who I
am! But I'd better take him his fan and gloves—that is, if
I can find them." As she said this, she came upon a neat little
house, on the door of which was a bright brass plate with the
name "W. Rabbit" engraved upon it. She went in without
knocking, and hurried upstairs, in great fear lest she should
meet the real Mary Ann, and be turned out of the house
before she had found the fan and gloves.

"How queer it seems," Alice said to herself, "to be going
messages for a rabbit. I suppose Dinah'll be sending me on
messages next!" And she began fancying the sort of thing
that would happen: " 'Miss Alice! Come here directly, and
get ready for your walk!' 'Coming in a minute, nurse! But
I've got to watch this mouse-hole till Dinah comes back, and
see that the mouse doesn't get out.' Only I don't think,"
Alice went on, "that they'd let Dinah stop in the house if it
began ordering people about like that!"

By this time she had found her way into a tidy little room
with a table in the window, and on it (as she had hoped) a
fan and two or three pairs of tiny white kid gloves: she took
up the fan and a pair of the gloves, and was just going to
leave the room, when her eye fell upon a little bottle that
stood near the looking-glass. There was no label this time
with the words "drink me," but nevertheless she uncorked
it and put it to her lips. "I know *something* interesting is sure
to happen," she said to herself, "whenever I eat or drink
anything; so I'll just see what this bottle does. I do hope it'll

make me grow large again, for really I'm quite tired of being such a tiny little thing!"

It did so indeed, and much sooner than she had expected: before she had drunk half the bottle, she found her head pressing against the ceiling, and had to stoop to save her neck

from being broken. She hastily put down the bottle, saying to herself, "That's quite enough—I hope I shan't grow any more.—As it is, I can't get out at the door—I do wish I hadn't drunk quite so much!"

Alas! it was too late to wish that! She went on growing, and growing, and very soon had to kneel down on the floor: in another minute there was not even room for this, and she tried the effect of lying down with one elbow against the door, and the other arm curled round her head. Still she went on growing, and, as a last resource, she put one arm out of the window, and one foot up the chimney, and said to herself, "Now I can do no more, whatever happens. What *will* become of me?"

Luckily for Alice, the little magic bottle had now had its full effect, and she grew no larger: still it was very uncomfortable, and, as there seemed to be no sort of chance of her ever getting out of the room again, no wonder she felt unhappy.

"It was much pleasanter at home," thought poor Alice, "when one wasn't always growing larger and smaller, and being ordered about by mice and rabbits. I almost wish I hadn't gone down that rabbit-hole—and yet—and yet—it's rather curious, you know, this sort of life! I do wonder what *can* have happened to me! When I used to read fairy-tales, I fancied that kind of thing never happened, and now here I am in the middle of one! There ought to be a book written about me, that there ought! And when I grow up, I'll write one—but I'm grown up now," she added in a sorrowful tone; "at least there's no room to grow up any more *here*."

"But then," thought Alice, "shall I *never* get any older than I am now? That'll be a comfort, one way—never to be an old woman—but then—always to have lessons to learn! Oh, I shouldn't like *that!*"

"Oh, you foolish Alice!" she answered herself. "How can you learn lessons in here? Why, there's hardly room for *you*, and no room at all for any lesson-books!"

And so she went on, taking first one side and then the other, and making quite a conversation of it altogether; but after a few minutes she heard a voice outside, and stopped to listen.

"Mary Ann! Mary Ann!" said the voice. "Fetch me my gloves this moment!" Then came a little pattering of feet on the stairs. Alice knew it was the Rabbit coming to look for her, and she trembled till she shook the house, quite forgetting that she was now about a thousand times as large as the Rabbit, and had no reason to be afraid of it.

Presently the Rabbit came up to the door, and tried to open it; but, as the door opened inwards, and Alice's elbow was pressed hard against it, that attempt proved a failure. Alice heard it say to itself, "Then I'll go round and get in at the window."

"*That* you won't!" thought Alice, and, after waiting till she fancied she heard the Rabbit just under the window, she suddenly spread out her hand, and made a snatch in the air. She did not get hold of anything, but she heard a little shriek and a fall, and a crash of broken glass, from which she concluded that it was just possible it had fallen into a cucumber-frame, or something of the sort.

Next came an angry voice—the Rabbit's—"Pat! Pat! Where are you?" And then a voice she had never heard before, "Sure then I'm here! Digging for apples, yer honour!"

"Digging for apples, indeed!" said the Rabbit angrily. "Here! Come and help me out of *this!*" (Sounds of more broken glass.)

"Now tell me, Pat, what's that in the window?"

"Sure, it's an arm, yer honour!" (He pronounced it "arrum.")

"An arm, you goose! Who ever saw one that size? Why, it fills the whole window!"

"Sure, it does, yer honour: but it's an arm for all that."

"Well, it's got no business there, at any rate: go and take it away!"

There was a long silence after this, and Alice could only hear whispers now and then; such as, "Sure, I don't like it, yer honour, at all, at all!" "Do as I tell you, you coward!" and at last she spread out her hand again, and made another snatch in the air. This time there were *two* little shrieks, and more sounds of broken glass. "What a number of cucumber-frames there must be!" thought Alice. "I wonder what they'll do next! As for pulling me out of the window, I only wish they *could!* I'm sure *I* don't want to stay in here any longer!"

She waited for some time without hearing anything more: at last came a rumbling of little cart-wheels, and the sound of a good many voices all talking together: she made out the words: "Where's the other ladder?—Why, I hadn't to bring but one; Bill's got the other.—Bill! Fetch it here, lad!—Here, put 'em up at this corner.—No, tie 'em together first—they don't reach half high enough yet.—Oh! they'll do well enough; don't be particular.—Here, Bill! catch hold of this rope.—Will the roof bear!—Mind that loose slate.—Oh, it's coming down! Heads below!" (a loud crash)—"Now, who did that?—It was Bill, I fancy.—Who's to go down the chimney?—Nay, *I* shan't! *You* do it!—*That* I won't, then!—Bill's to go down.—Here, Bill! the master says you've got to go down the chimney!"

"Oh! So Bill's got to come down the chimney, has he?" said Alice to herself. "Why, they seem to put everything upon Bill! I wouldn't be in Bill's place for a good deal: this fire-place is narrow, to be sure; but I *think* I can kick a little!"

She drew her foot as far down the chimney as she could, and waited till she heard a little animal (she couldn't guess of what sort it was) scratching and scrambling about in the chimney close above her: then, saying to herself, "This is Bill," she gave one sharp kick, and waited to see what would happen next.

The first thing she heard was a general chorus of, "There goes Bill!" then the Rabbit's voice alone—"Catch him, you by the hedge!" then silence, and then another confusion of voices—"Hold up his head.—Brandy now.—Don't choke him.—How was it, old fellow? What happened to you? Tell us all about it!"

At last came a little feeble, squeaking voice ("That's Bill," thought Alice), "Well, I hardly know.—No more, thank ye; I'm better now—but I'm a deal too flustered to tell you—all I know is, something comes at me like a Jack-in-the-box, and up I goes like a sky-rocket!"

"So you did, old fellow!" said the others.

"We must burn the house down!" said the Rabbit's voice. And Alice called out as loud as she could, "If you do, I'll set Dinah at you!"

There was a dead silence instantly, and Alice thought to herself, "I wonder what they *will* do next! If they had any sense, they'd take the roof off." After a minute or two, they began moving about again, and Alice heard the Rabbit say, "A barrowful will do, to begin with."

"A barrowful of *what?*" thought Alice. But she had not long to doubt, for the next moment a shower of little pebbles came rattling in at the window, and some of them hit her in the face. "I'll put a stop to this," she said to herself, and shouted out, "You'd better not do that again!" which produced another dead silence.

Alice noticed with some surprise that the pebbles were all turning into little cakes as they lay on the floor, and a bright idea came into her head. "If I eat one of these cakes," she thought, "it's sure to make *some* change in my size; and, as it can't possibly make me larger, it must make me smaller, I suppose."

So she swallowed one of the cakes, and was delighted to find that she began shrinking directly. As soon as she was small enough to get through the door, she ran out of the house, and found quite a crowd of little animals and birds waiting outside. The poor little Lizard, Bill, was in the middle, being held up by two guinea-pigs, who were giving it something out of a bottle. They all made a rush at Alice the moment she appeared; but she ran off as hard as she could, and soon found herself safe in a thick wood.

"The first thing I've got to do," said Alice to herself, as she wandered about in the wood, "is to grow to my right size again; and the second thing is to find my way into that lovely garden. I think that will be the best plan."

It sounded an excellent plan, no doubt, and very neatly and simply arranged; the only difficulty was, that she had

not the smallest idea how to set about it; and, while she was
peering about anxiously among the trees, a little sharp bark
just over her head made her look up in a great hurry.

An enormous puppy was looking down at her with large
round eyes, and feebly stretching out one paw, trying to
touch her. "Poor little thing!" said Alice, in a coaxing tone,

and she tried hard to whistle to it; but she was terribly frightened all the time at the thought that it might be hungry, in which case it would be very likely to eat her up in spite of all her coaxing.

Hardly knowing what she did, she picked up a little bit of stick, and held it out to the puppy; whereupon the puppy jumped into the air off all its feet at once, with a yelp of delight and rushed at the stick, and made believe to worry it; then Alice dodged behind a great thistle, to keep herself from being run over; and, the moment she appeared on the other side, the puppy made another rush at the stick, and tumbled head over heels in its hurry to get hold of it; then Alice, thinking it was very like having a game of play with a cart-horse, and expecting every moment to be trampled under its feet, ran round the thistle again; then the puppy began a series of short charges at the stick, running a very little way forwards each time and a long way back, and barking hoarsely all the while, till at last it sat down a good way off, panting, with its tongue hanging out of its mouth, and its great eyes half shut.

This seemed to Alice a good opportunity for making her escape; so she set off at once, and ran till she was quite tired and out of breath, and till the puppy's bark sounded quite faint in the distance.

"And yet what a dear little puppy it was!" said Alice, as she leant against a buttercup to rest herself, and fanned herself with one of the leaves. "I should have liked teaching it tricks very much, if—if I'd only been the right size to do it! Oh dear! I'd nearly forgotten that I've got to grow up again! Let me see—how *is* it to be managed? I suppose I ought to eat or drink something or other; but the great question is, what?"

The great question certainly was, what? Alice looked all round her at the flowers and the blades of grass, but she could not see anything that looked like the right thing to eat or drink under the circumstances. There was a large mushroom growing near her, about the same height as herself; and, when she had looked under it, and on both sides of it, and behind it, it occurred to her that she might as well look and see what was on the top of it.

She stretched herself up on tiptoe, and peeped over the edge of the mushroom, and her eyes immediately met those of a large blue caterpillar, that was sitting on the top with its arms folded, quietly smoking a long hookah, and taking not the smallest notice of her or of anything else.

CHAPTER V

ADVICE FROM A CATERPILLAR

THE Caterpillar and Alice looked at each other for some time in silence: at last the Caterpillar took the hookah out of its mouth, and addressed her in a languid, sleepy voice.

"Who are *you?*" said the Caterpillar.

This was not an encouraging opening for a conversation. Alice replied, rather shyly, "I—I hardly know, sir, just at present—at least I know who I *was* when I got up this morning, but

I think I must have been changed several times since then."

"What do you mean by that?" said the Caterpillar sternly. "Explain yourself!"

"I can't explain *myself*, I'm afraid, sir," said Alice, "because I'm not myself, you see."

"I don't see," said the Caterpillar.

"I'm afraid I can't put it more clearly," Alice replied very politely, "for I can't understand it myself to begin with; and being so many different sizes in a day is very confusing."

"It isn't," said the Caterpillar.

"Well, perhaps you haven't found it so yet," said Alice; "but when you have to turn into a chrysalis—you will some day, you know—and then after that into a butterfly, I should think you'll feel it a little queer, won't you?"

"Not a bit," said the Caterpillar.

"Well, perhaps your feelings may be different," said Alice; "all I know is, it would feel very queer to *me*."

"You!" said the Caterpillar contemptuously. "Who are *you?*"

Which brought them back again to the beginning of the conversation. Alice felt a little irritated at the Caterpillar's making such *very* short remarks, and she drew herself up and said, very gravely, "I think you ought to tell me who *you* are, first."

"Why?" said the Caterpillar.

Here was another puzzling question; and as Alice could not think of any good reason, and as the Caterpillar seemed to be in a *very* unpleasant state of mind, she turned away.

"Come back!" the Caterpillar called after her. "I've something important to say!"

This sounded promising, certainly: Alice turned and came back again.

"Keep your temper," said the Caterpillar.

"Is that all?" said Alice, swallowing down her anger as well as she could.

"No," said the Caterpillar.

Alice thought she might as well wait, as she had nothing else to do, and perhaps after all it might tell her something worth hearing. For some minutes it puffed away without speaking, but at last it unfolded its arms, took the hookah out of its mouth again, and said, "So you think you're changed, do you?"

"I'm afraid I am, sir," said Alice; "I can't remember things as I used—and I don't keep the same size for ten minutes together!"

"Can't remember *what* things?" said the Caterpillar.

"Well, I've tried to say, 'How doth the little busy bee,' but it all came different!" Alice replied in a very melancholy voice.

"Repeat 'You are old, Father William,'" said the Caterpillar.

Alice folded her hands, and began:

"You are old, Father William," the young man said,
 "And your hair has become very white;
And yet you incessantly stand on your head—
 Do you think, at your age, it is right?"

"In my youth," Father William replied to his son,
 "I feared it might injure the brain;
But, now that I'm perfectly sure I have none,
 Why, I do it again and again."

"You are old," said the youth, "as I mentioned before,
 And have grown most uncommonly fat;
Yet you turned a back-somersault in at the door—
 Pray, what is the reason of that?"

"In my youth," said the sage, as he shook his grey locks,
  "I kept all my limbs very supple
By the use of this ointment—one shilling the box—
  Allow me to sell you a couple?"

"You are old," said the youth, "and your jaws are too weak
  For anything tougher than suet;
Yet you finished the goose, with the bones and the beak—
  Pray, how did you manage to do it?"

"In my youth," said his father, "I took to the law,
  And argued each case with my wife;
And the muscular strength, which it gave to my jaw,
  Has lasted the rest of my life."

"You are old," said the youth, "one would hardly suppose
That your eye was as steady as ever;
Yet you balanced an eel on the end of your nose—
What made you so awfully clever?"

"I have answered three questions, and that is enough,"
Said his father; "don't give yourself airs!
Do you think I can listen all day to such stuff?
Be off, or I'll kick you downstairs!"

"That is not said right," said the Caterpillar.

"Not *quite* right, I'm afraid," said Alice, timidly; "some of the words have got altered."

"It is wrong from beginning to end," said the Caterpillar decidedly, and there was silence for some minutes.

The Caterpillar was the first to speak.

"What size do you want to be?" it asked.

"Oh, I'm not particular as to size," Alice hastily replied; "only one doesn't like changing so often, you know."

"I *don't* know," said the Caterpillar.

Alice said nothing: she had never been so much contradicted in all her life before, and she felt that she was losing her temper.

"Are you content now?" said the Caterpillar.

"Well, I should like to be a *little* larger, sir, if you wouldn't mind," said Alice: "three inches is such a wretched height to be."

"It is a very good height indeed!" said the Caterpillar angrily, rearing itself upright as it spoke (it was exactly three inches high).

"But I'm not used to it!" pleaded poor Alice in a piteous tone. And she thought to herself, "I wish the creatures wouldn't be so easily offended!"

"You'll get used to it in time," said the Caterpillar; and it put the hookah into its mouth and began smoking again.

This time Alice waited patiently until it chose to speak again. In a minute or two the Caterpillar took the hookah out of its mouth and yawned once or twice, and shook itself. Then it got down off the mushroom and crawled away into the grass, merely remarking as it went, "One side will make you grow taller, and the other side will make you grow shorter."

"One side of *what?* The other side of *what?*" thought Alice to herself.

"Of the mushroom," said the Caterpillar, just as if she had asked it aloud; and in another moment it was out of sight.

Alice remained looking thoughtfully at the mushroom for a minute, trying to make out which were the two sides of it; and as it was perfectly round, she found this a very difficult question. However, at last she stretched her arms round it as far as they would go, and broke off a bit of the edge with each hand.

"And now which is which?" she said to herself, and nib-

bled a little of the right-hand bit to try the effect: the next
moment she felt a violent blow underneath her chin: it had
struck her foot!

She was a good deal frightened by this very sudden
change, but she felt that there was no time to be lost, as she
was shrinking rapidly; so she set to work at once to eat some
of the other bit. Her chin was pressed so closely against her
foot, that there was hardly room to open her mouth; but she
did it at last, and managed to swallow a morsel of the left-
hand bit.

.   .   .   .

"Come, my head's free at last!" said Alice in a tone of
delight, which changed into alarm in another moment, when
she found that her shoulders were nowhere to be found: all
she could see, when she looked down, was an immense length
of neck, which seemed to rise like a stalk out of a sea of
green leaves that lay far below her.

"What *can* all that green stuff be?" said Alice. "And where
have my shoulders got to? And oh, my poor hands, how is it
I can't see you?" She was moving them about as she spoke,
but no result seemed to follow, except a little shaking among
the distant green leaves.

As there seemed to be no chance of getting her hands up to
her head, she tried to get her head down to them, and was
delighted to find that her neck would bend about easily in any
direction, like a serpent. She had just succeeded in curving it
down into a graceful zigzag, and was going to dive in among
the leaves, which she found to be nothing but the tops of the
trees under which she had been wandering, when a sharp hiss
made her draw back in a hurry: a large pigeon had flown into
her face, and was beating her violently with its wings.

"Serpent!" screamed the pigeon.

"I'm *not* a serpent!" said Alice indignantly. "Let me
alone!"

"Serpent, I say again!" repeated the Pigeon, but in a more

subdued tone, and added with a kind of sob, "I've tried every way, and nothing seems to suit them!"

"I haven't the least idea what you're talking about," said Alice.

"I've tried the roots of trees, and I've tried banks, and I've tried hedges," the Pigeon went on, without attending to her; "but those serpents! There's no pleasing them!"

Alice was more and more puzzled, but she thought there was no use in saying anything more till the Pigeon had finished.

"As if it wasn't trouble enough hatching the eggs," said the Pigeon; "but I must be on the look-out for serpents night and day! Why, I haven't had a wink of sleep these three weeks!"

"I'm very sorry you've been annoyed," said Alice, who was beginning to see its meaning.

"And just as I'd taken the highest tree in the wood," continued the Pigeon, raising its voice to a shriek, "and just as I was thinking I should be free of them at last, they must needs come wriggling down from the sky! Ugh, Serpent!"

"But I'm *not* a serpent, I tell you!" said Alice. "I'm a— I'm a——"

"Well! *What* are you?" said the Pigeon. "I can see you're trying to invent something!"

"I—I'm a little girl," said Alice, rather doubtfully as she remembered the number of changes she had gone through, that day.

"A likely story indeed!" said the Pigeon in a tone of the deepest contempt. "I've seen a good many little girls in my time, but never *one* with such a neck as that! No, no! You're a serpent; and there's no use denying it. I suppose you'll be telling me next that you never tasted an egg!"

"I *have* tasted eggs, certainly," said Alice, who was a very truthful child; "but little girls eat eggs quite as much as serpents do, you know."

"I don't believe it," said the Pigeon; "but if they do, why, then, they're a kind of serpent, that's all I can say."

This was such a new idea to Alice, that she was quite silent for a minute or two, which gave the Pigeon the opportunity of adding, "You're looking for eggs, I know *that* well enough; and what does it matter to me whether you're a little girl or a serpent?"

"It matters a good deal to *me*," said Alice hastily; "but I'm not looking for eggs, as it happens; and if I was, I shouldn't want *yours:* I don't like them raw."

"Well, be off, then!" said the Pigeon in a sulky tone, as it settled down again into its nest. Alice crouched down among the trees as well as she could, for her neck kept getting entangled among the branches, and every now and then she had to stop and untwist it. After a while she remembered that she held the pieces of mushroom in her hands, and she set to work very carefully, nibbling first at one and then at the other, and growing sometimes taller and sometimes shorter, until she had succeeded in bringing herself down to her usual height.

It was so long since she had been anything near the right size, that it felt quite strange at first; but she got used to it in a few minutes, and began talking to herself, as usual. "Come, there's half my plan done now! How puzzling all these changes are! I'm never sure what I'm going to be, from one minute to another! However, I've got back to my right size: the next thing is to get into that beautiful garden—how *is* that to be done, I wonder?" As she said this, she came suddenly upon an open place, with a little house in it about four feet high. "Whoever lives there," thought Alice, "it'll never do to come upon them *this* size: why, I should frighten them out of their wits!" So she began nibbling at the right-hand bit again, and did not venture to go near the house till she had brought herself down to nine inches high.

CHAPTER VI

PIG AND PEPPER

FOR a minute or two she stood looking at the house, and wondering what to do next, when suddenly a footman in livery came running out of the wood—(she considered him

to be a footman because he was in livery: otherwise, judging by his face only, she would have called him a fish)—and rapped loudly at the door with his knuckles. It was opened

by another footman in livery, with a round face, and large
eyes like a frog; and both footmen, Alice noticed, had pow-
dered hair that curled all over their heads. She felt very
curious to know what it was all about, and crept a little way
out of the wood to listen.

The Fish-Footman began by producing from under his
arm a great letter, nearly as large as himself, and this he
handed over to the other, saying, in a solemn tone, "For the
Duchess. An invitation from the Queen to play croquet."
The Frog-Footman repeated, in the same solemn tone, only
changing the order of the words a little, "From the Queen.
An invitation for the Duchess to play croquet."

Then they both bowed low, and their curls got entangled
together.

Alice laughed so much at this, that she had to run back
into the wood for fear of their hearing her; and, when she
next peeped out, the Fish-Footman was gone, and the other
was sitting on the ground near the door, staring stupidly up
into the sky.

Alice went timidly up to the door, and knocked.

"There's no sort of use in knocking," said the Footman,
"and that for two reasons. First, because I'm on the same
side of the door as you are; secondly, because they're making
such a noise inside, no one could possibly hear you." And
certainly there was a most extraordinary noise going on
within—a constant howling and sneezing, and every now and
then a great crash, as if a dish or kettle had been broken to
pieces.

"Please, then," said Alice, "how am I to get in?"

"There might be some sense in your knocking," the Footman went on without attending to her, "if we had the door
between us. For instance, if you were *inside*, you might knock,
and I could let you out, you know." He was looking up into
the sky all the time he was speaking, and this Alice thought
decidedly uncivil. "But perhaps he can't help it," she said to

herself; "his eyes are so *very* nearly at the top of his head. But at any rate he might answer questions.—How am I to get in?" she repeated, aloud.

"I shall sit here," the Footman remarked, "till to-morrow——"

At this moment the door of the house opened, and a large plate came skimming out, straight at the Footman's head: it just grazed his nose, and broke to pieces against one of the trees behind him.

"—or next day, maybe," the Footman continued in the same tone, exactly as if nothing had happened.

"How am I to get in?" asked Alice again, in a louder tone.

"*Are* you to get in at all?" said the Footman. "That's the first question, you know."

It was, no doubt: only Alice did not like to be told so. "It's really dreadful," she muttered to herself, "the way all the creatures argue. It's enough to drive one crazy!"

The Footman seemed to think this a good opportunity for repeating his remark, with variations. "I shall sit here," he said, "on and off, for days and days."

"But what am *I* to do?" said Alice.

"Anything you like," said the Footman, and began whistling.

"Oh, there's no use in talking to him," said Alice desperately: "he's perfectly idiotic!" And she opened the door and went in.

The door led right into a large kitchen, which was full of smoke from one end to the other: the Duchess was sitting on a three-legged stool in the middle, nursing a baby; the cook was leaning over the fire, stirring a large cauldron which seemed to be full of soup.

"There's certainly too much pepper in that soup!" Alice said to herself, as well as she could for sneezing.

There was certainly too much of it in the air. Even the Duchess sneezed occasionally; and the baby was sneezing and howling alternately without a moment's pause. The only things in the kitchen that did not sneeze, were the cook, and a large cat which was sitting on the hearth and grinning from ear to ear.

"Please, would you tell me," said Alice a little timidly, for she was not quite sure whether it was good manners for her to speak first, "why your cat grins like that?"

"It's a Cheshire cat," said the Duchess, "and that's why. Pig!"

She said the last word with such sudden violence that Alice quite jumped; but she saw in another moment that it was addressed to the baby, and not to her, so she took courage, and went on again:

"I didn't know that Cheshire cats always grinned; in fact, I didn't know that cats *could* grin."

"They all can," said the Duchess; "and most of 'em do."

"I don't know of any that do," Alice said very politely, feeling quite pleased to have got into a conversation.

"You don't know much," said the Duchess; "and that's a fact."

Alice did not at all like the tone of this remark, and thought it would be as well to introduce some other subject of conversation. While she was trying to fix on one, the cook took the cauldron of soup off the fire, and at once set to work throwing everything within her reach at the Duchess and the baby—the fire-irons came first; then followed a shower of saucepans, plates, and dishes. The Duchess took no notice of them even when they hit her; and the baby was howling so much already, that it was quite impossible to say whether the blows hurt it or not.

"Oh, *please* mind what you're doing!" cried Alice, jumping up and down in an agony of terror. "Oh, there goes his *precious* nose"; as an unusually large saucepan flew close by it, and very nearly carried it off.

"If everybody minded their own business," the Duchess said in a hoarse growl, "the world would go round a deal faster than it does."

"Which would *not* be an advantage," said Alice, who felt very glad to get an opportunity of showing off a little of her knowledge. "Just think what work it would make with the day and night! You see the earth takes twenty-four hours to turn round on its axis——"

"Talking of axes," said the Duchess, "chop off her head!"

Alice glanced rather anxiously at the cook, to see if she meant to take the hint; but the cook was busily engaged in stirring the soup, and did not seem to be listening, so she ventured to go on again: "Twenty-four hours, I *think*; or is it twelve? I——"

"Oh, don't bother *me*," said the Duchess; "I never could abide figures!" And with that she began nursing her child again, singing a sort of lullaby to it as she did so, and giving it a violent shake at the end of every line:

> *"Speak roughly to your little boy,*
> *And beat him when he sneezes:*
> *He only does it to annoy,*
> *Because he knows it teases."*

CHORUS
(In which the cook and the baby joined)
"Wow! wow! wow!"

While the Duchess sang the second verse of the song, she kept tossing the baby violently up and down, and the poor little thing howled so, that Alice could hardly hear the words:

> *"I speak severely to my boy,*
> *I beat him when he sneezes;*
> *For he can thoroughly enjoy*
> *The pepper when he pleases!"*

CHORUS
"Wow! wow! wow!"

"Here! you may nurse it a bit, if you like!" the Duchess said to Alice, flinging the baby at her as she spoke. "I must go and get ready to play croquet with the Queen," and she hurried out of the room. The cook threw a frying-pan after her as she went out, but it just missed her.

Alice caught the baby with some difficulty, as it was a queer-shaped little creature, and held out its arms and legs in all directions, "just like a star-fish," thought Alice. The poor little thing was snorting like a steam-engine when she caught it, and kept doubling itself up and straightening itself out again, so that altogether, for the first minute or two, it was as much as she could do to hold it.

As soon as she had made out the proper way of nursing it (which was to twist it up into a sort of knot, and then keep  tight hold of its right ear and left foot, so as to prevent its undoing itself), she carried it out into the open air. "If I don't take this child away with me," thought Alice, "they're sure to kill it in a day or two: wouldn't it be murder to leave it behind?" She said the last words out loud, and the little thing grunted in reply (it had left off sneezing by this time). "Don't grunt," said Alice; "that's not at all a proper way of expressing yourself."

The baby grunted again, and Alice looked very anxiously into its face to see what was the matter with it. There could be no doubt that it had a *very* turn-up nose, much more like a snout than a real nose; also its eyes were getting extremely small for a baby: altogether Alice did not like the look of the thing at all. "But perhaps it was only sobbing," she thought, and looked into its eyes again, to see if there were any tears.

No, there were no tears. "If you're going to turn into a pig, my dear," said Alice, seriously, "I'll have nothing more to do with you. Mind now!" The poor little thing sobbed again (or grunted, it was impossible to say which), and they went on for some while in silence.

Alice was just beginning to think to herself, "Now, what am I to do with this creature when I get it home?" when it grunted again, so violently that she looked down into its face in some alarm. This time there could be *no* mistake about it: it was neither more nor less than a pig, and she felt that it would be quite absurd for her to carry it any further.

So she set the little creature down, and felt quite relieved to see it trot away quietly into the wood. "If it had grown up," she said to herself, "it would have made a dreadfully ugly child: but it makes rather a handsome pig, I think." And she began thinking over other children she knew, who might do very well as pigs, and was just saying to herself, "If one only knew the right way to change them——" when she was a little startled by seeing the Cheshire Cat sitting on a bough of a tree a few yards off.

The Cat only grinned when it saw Alice. It looked good-natured, she thought: still it had *very* long claws and a great many teeth, so she felt that it ought to be treated with respect.

"Cheshire Puss," she began, rather timidly, as she did not at all know whether it would like the name: however, it only grinned a little wider. "Come, it's pleased so far," thought Alice, and she went on: "Would you tell me, please, which way I ought to go from here?"

"That depends a good deal on where you want to get to," said the Cat.

"I don't much care where——" said Alice.

"Then it doesn't matter which way you go," said the Cat.

"—so long as I get *somewhere*," Alice added as an explanation.

"Oh, you're sure to do that," said the Cat, "if you only walk long enough."

Alice felt that this could not be denied, so she tried another question: "What sort of people live about here?"

"In *that* direction," the Cat said, waving its right paw round, "lives a Hatter: and in *that* direction," waving the other paw, "lives a March Hare. Visit either you like: they're both mad."

"But I don't want to go among mad people," Alice remarked.

"Oh, you can't help that," said the Cat: "we're all mad here. I'm mad. You're mad."

"How do you know I'm mad?" said Alice.

"You must be," said the Cat, "or you wouldn't have come here."

Alice didn't think that proved it at all; however, she went on: "And how do you know that you're mad?"

"To begin with," said the Cat, "a dog's not mad. You grant that?"

"I suppose so," said Alice.

"Well, then," the Cat went on, "you see a dog growls when it's angry, and wags its tail when it's pleased. Now *I* growl when I'm pleased, and wag my tail when I'm angry. Therefore I'm mad."

"*I* call it purring, not growling," said Alice.

"Call it what you like," said the Cat. "Do you play croquet with the Queen to-day?"

"I should like it very much," said Alice, "but I haven't been invited yet."

"You'll see me there," said the Cat, and vanished.

Alice was not much surprised at this, she was getting so used to queer things happening. While she was looking at the place where it had been, it suddenly appeared again.

"By the by, what became of the baby?" said the Cat. "I'd nearly forgotten to ask."

"It turned into a pig," Alice quietly said, just as if it had come back in a natural way.

"I thought it would," said the Cat, and vanished again.

Alice waited a little, half expecting to see it again, but it did not appear, and after a minute or two she walked on in the direction in which the March Hare was said to live. "I've seen hatters before," she said to herself; "the March Hare will be much the most interesting, and perhaps, as this is May, it won't be raving mad—at least not so mad as it was in March." As she said this, she looked up, and there was the Cat again, sitting on a branch of a tree.

"Did you say pig, or fig?" said the Cat.

"I said pig," replied Alice; "and I wish you wouldn't keep appearing and vanishing so suddenly: you make one quite giddy."

"All right," said the Cat; and this time it vanished quite slowly, beginning with the end of the tail, and ending with the grin, which remained some time after the rest of it had gone.

"Well! I've often seen a cat without a grin," thought Alice; "but a grin without a cat! It's the most curious thing I ever saw in all my life!"

She had not gone much farther before she came in sight of the house of the March Hare: she thought it must be the right house, because the chimneys were shaped like ears and the roof was thatched with fur. It was so large a house, that she did not like to go nearer till she had nibbled some more of the left-hand bit of mushroom, and raised herself to about two feet high: even then she walked up towards it rather timidly, saying to herself, "Suppose it should be raving mad after all! I almost wish I'd gone to see the Hatter instead!"

CHAPTER VII

A MAD TEA-PARTY

THERE was a table set out under a tree in front of the house, and the March Hare and the Hatter were having tea at it: a Dormouse was sitting between them, fast asleep, and the other two were resting their elbows on it, and talking over its head. "Very uncomfortable for the Dormouse," thought Alice; "only, as it's asleep, I suppose it doesn't mind."

The table was a large one, but the three were all crowded together at one corner of it. "No room! No room!" they cried out when they saw Alice coming. "There's *plenty* of room!" said Alice indignantly, and she sat down in a large arm-chair at one end of the table.

"Have some wine," the March Hare said in an encouraging tone.

Alice looked all round the table, but there was nothing on it but tea. "I don't see any wine," she remarked.

"There isn't any," said the March Hare.

"Then it wasn't very civil of you to offer it," said Alice angrily.

"It wasn't very civil of you to sit down without being invited," said the March Hare.

"I didn't know it was *your* table," said Alice; "it's laid for a great many more than three."

"Your hair wants cutting," said the Hatter. He had been looking at Alice for some time with great curiosity, and this was his first speech.

"You shouldn't make personal remarks," Alice said with some severity; "it's very rude."

The Hatter opened his eyes very wide on hearing this; but all he *said* was, "Why is a raven like a writing-desk?"

"Come, we shall have some fun now!" thought Alice.

"I'm glad they've begun asking riddles.—I believe I can guess that," she added aloud.

"Do you mean that you think you can find out the answer to it?" said the March Hare.

"Exactly so," said Alice.

"Then you should say what you mean," the March Hare went on.

"I do," Alice hastily replied; "at least—at least I mean what I say—that's the same thing, you know."

"Not the same thing a bit!" said the Hatter. "You might just as well say that 'I see what I eat' is the same thing as 'I eat what I see'!"

"You might just as well say," added the March Hare, "that 'I like what I get' is the same thing as 'I get what I like'!"

"You might just as well say," added the Dormouse, who seemed to be talking in his sleep, "that 'I breathe when I sleep' is the same thing as 'I sleep when I breathe'!"

"It *is* the same thing with you," said the Hatter, and here the conversation dropped, and the party sat silent for a minute, while Alice thought over all she could remember about ravens and writing-desks, which wasn't much.

The Hatter was the first to break the silence. "What day of the month is it?" he said, turning to Alice: he had taken his watch out of his pocket, and was looking at it uneasily, shaking it every now and then, and holding it to his ear.

Alice considered a little, and then said, "The fourth."

"Two days wrong!" sighed the Hatter. "I told you butter wouldn't suit the works!" he added, looking angrily at the March Hare.

"It was the *best* butter," the March Hare meekly replied.

"Yes, but some crumbs must have got in as well," the Hatter grumbled: "you shouldn't have put it in with the bread-knife."

The March Hare took the watch and looked at it gloomily: then he dipped it into his cup of tea, and looked at it again: but he could think of nothing better to say than his first remark, "It was the *best* butter, you know."

Alice had been looking over his shoulder with some curiosity. "What a funny watch!" she remarked. "It tells the day of the month, and doesn't tell what o'clock it is!"

"Why should it?" muttered the Hatter. "Does *your* watch tell you what year it is?"

"Of course not," Alice replied very readily: "but that's because it stays the same year for such a long time together."

"Which is just the case with *mine*," said the Hatter.

Alice felt dreadfully puzzled. The Hatter's remark seemed to have no meaning in it, and yet it was certainly English. "I don't quite understand," she said, as politely as she could.

"The Dormouse is asleep again," said the Hatter, and he poured a little hot tea upon its nose.

The Dormouse shook its head impatiently, and said, without opening its eyes, "Of course, of course; just what I was going to remark myself."

"Have you guessed the riddle yet?" the Hatter said, turning to Alice again.

"No, I give it up," Alice replied: "what's the answer?"

"I haven't the slightest idea," said the Hatter.

"Nor I," said the March Hare.

Alice sighed wearily. "I think you might do something better with the time," she said, "than waste it asking riddles with no answers."

"If you knew Time as well as I do," said the Hatter, "you wouldn't talk about wasting *it*. It's *him*."

"I don't know what you mean," said Alice.

"Of course you don't!" the Hatter said, tossing his head contemptuously. "I dare say you never even spoke to Time!"

"Perhaps not," Alice cautiously replied: "but I know I have to beat time when I learn music."

"Ah! that accounts for it," said the Hatter. "He won't stand beating. Now, if you only kept on good terms with him, he'd do almost anything you liked with the clock. For instance, suppose it were nine o'clock in the morning, just time to begin lessons: you'd only have to whisper a hint to Time, and round goes the clock in a twinkling! Half-past one, time for dinner!"

("I only wish it was," the March Hare said to itself in a whisper.)

"That would be grand, certainly," said Alice thoughtfully: "but then—I shouldn't be hungry for it, you know."

"Not at first, perhaps," said the Hatter: "but you could keep it to half-past one as long as you liked."

"Is that the way *you* manage?" Alice asked.

The Hatter shook his head mournfully. "Not I!" he replied. "We quarrelled last March—just before *he* went mad, you know—" (pointing with his teaspoon at the March

Hare) "—it was at the great concert given bv the Queen of Hearts, and I had to sing

"Twinkle, twinkle, little bat!
How I wonder what you're at!

You know the song, perhaps?"
"I've heard something like it," said Alice.

"It goes on, you know," the Hatter continued, "in this way:

"Up above the world you fly,
Like a tea-tray in the sky.
            Twinkle, twinkle——"

Here the Dormouse shook itself, and began singing in its sleep, "Twinkle, twinkle, twinkle, twinkle——" and went on so long that they had to pinch it to make it stop.

"Well, I'd hardly finished the first verse," said the Hatter, "when the Queen jumped up and bawled out, 'He's murdering the time! Off with his head!' "

"How dreadfully savage!" exclaimed Alice.

"And ever since that," the Hatter went on in a mournful tone, "he won't do a thing I ask! It's always six o'clock now."

A bright idea came into Alice's head. "Is that the reason so many tea-things are put out here?" she asked.

"Yes, that's it," said the Hatter with a sigh: "it's always tea-time, and we've no time to wash the things between whiles."

"Then you keep moving round, I suppose?" said Alice.

"Exactly so," said the Hatter: "as the things get used up."

"But what hapens when you come to the beginning again?" Alice ventured to ask.

"Suppose we change the subject," the March Hare interrupted, yawning. "I'm getting tired of this. I vote the young lady tells us a story."

"I'm afraid I don't know one," said Alice, rather alarmed at the proposal.

"Then the Dormouse shall!" they both cried. "Wake up, Dormouse!" And they pinched it on both sides at once.

The Dormouse slowly opened his eyes. "I wasn't asleep," he said in a hoarse, feeble voice: "I heard every word you fellows were saying."

"Tell us a story!" said the March Hare.

"Yes, please do!" pleaded Alice.

"And be quick about it," added the Hatter, "or you'll be asleep again before it's done."

"Once upon a time there were three little sisters," the Dormouse began in a great hurry; "and their names were Elsie, Lacie, and Tillie; and they lived at the bottom of a well——"

"What did they live on?" said Alice, who always took a great interest in questions of eating and drinking.

"They lived on treacle," said the Dormouse, after thinking a minute or two.

"They couldn't have done that, you know," Alice gently remarked; "they'd have been ill."

"So they were," said the Dormouse; "*very* ill."

Alice tried to fancy to herself what such an extraordinary way of living would be like, but it puzzled her too much, so she went on: "But why did they live at the bottom of a well?"

"Take some more tea," the March Hare said to Alice, very earnestly.

"I've had nothing yet," Alice replied in an offended tone, "so I can't take more."

"You mean you can't take *less*," said the Hatter: "it's very easy to take *more* than nothing."

"Nobody asked *your* opinion," said Alice.

"Who's making personal remarks now?" the Hatter asked triumphantly.

Alice did not quite know what to say to this: so she helped herself to some tea and bread-and-butter, and then turned to the Dormouse, and repeated her question: "Why did they live at the bottom of a well?"

The Dormouse again took a minute or two to think about it, and then said, "It was a treacle-well."

"There's no such thing!" Alice was beginning very angrily, but the Hatter and the March Hare went "Sh! sh!" and the Dormouse sulkily remarked, "If you can't be civil, you'd better finish the story for yourself."

"No, please go on!" Alice said. "I won't interrupt again. I dare say there may be *one*."

"One, indeed!" said the Dormouse indignantly. However, he consented to go on: "And so these three little sisters—they were learning to draw, you know——"

"What did they draw?" said Alice, quite forgetting her promise.

"Treacle," said the Dormouse, without considering at all this time.

"I want a clean cup," interrupted the Hatter: "let's all move one place on."

He moved on as he spoke, and the Dormouse followed him: the March Hare moved into the Dormouse's place, and Alice rather unwillingly took the place of the March Hare. The Hatter was the only one who got any advantage from the change: and Alice was a good deal worse off, as the March Hare had just upset the milk-jug into his plate.

Alice did not wish to offend the Dormouse again, so she began very cautiously: "But I don't understand. Where did they draw the treacle from?"

"You can draw water out of a water-well," said the Hatter; "so I should think you could draw treacle out of a treacle-well—eh, stupid?"

"But they were *in* the well," Alice said to the Dormouse, not choosing to notice this last remark.

"Of course they were," said the Dormouse; "—well in."

This answer so confused poor Alice, that she let the Dormouse go on for some time without interrupting it.

"They were learning to draw," the Dormouse went on, yawning and rubbing its eyes, for it was getting very sleepy; "and they drew all manner of things—everything that begins with an M——"

"Why with an M?" said Alice.

"Why not?" said the March Hare.

Alice was silent.

The Dormouse had closed its eyes by this time, and was going off into a doze; but, on being pinched by the Hatter, it woke up again with a little shriek, and went on: "—that begins with an M, such as mouse-traps, and the moon, and memory, and muchness—you know you say things are 'much of a muchness'—did you ever see such a thing as a drawing of a muchness?"

"Really, now you ask me," said Alice, very much confused, "I don't think——"

"Then you shouldn't talk," said the Hatter.

This piece of rudeness was more than Alice could bear: she got up in great disgust, and walked off; the Dormouse fell asleep instantly, and neither of the others took the least notice of her going, though she looked back once or twice,

half hoping that they would call after her: the last time she saw them, they were trying to put the Dormouse into the teapot.

"At any rate I'll never go *there* again!" said Alice as she picked her way through the wood. "It's the stupidest tea-party I ever was at in all my life!"

Just as she said this, she noticed that one of the trees had a door leading right into it. "That's very curious!" she thought. "But everything's curious to-day. I think I may as well go in at once." And in she went.

Once more she found herself in the long hall, and close

to the little glass table. "Now, I'll manage better this time," she said to herself, and began by taking the little golden key, and unlocking the door that led into the garden. Then she set to work nibbling at the mushroom (she had kept a piece of it in her pocket) till she was about a foot high: then she walked down the little passage: and *then*—she found herself at last in the beautiful garden, among the bright flower-beds and the cool fountains.

CHAPTER VIII

THE QUEEN'S CROQUET-GROUND

A LARGE rose-tree stood near the entrance of the garden: the roses growing on it were white, but there were three gardeners at it, busily painting them red. Alice thought this a very curious thing, and she went nearer to watch them, and just as she came up to them she heard one of them say, "Look out now, Five! Don't go splashing paint over me like that!"

"I couldn't help it," said Five, in a sulky tone. "Seven jogged my elbow."

On which Seven looked up and said, "That's right, Five! Always lay the blame on others!"

"*You'd* better not talk!" said Five. "I heard the Queen say only yesterday you deserved to be beheaded!"

"What for?" said the one who had first spoken.

"That's none of *your* business, Two!" said Seven.

"Yes, it *is* his business!" said Five. "And I'll tell him—it was for bringing the cook tulip-roots instead of onions."

Seven flung down his brush, and had just begun, "Well, of all the unjust things——" when his eye chanced to fall upon Alice, as she stood watching them, and he checked himself suddenly: the others looked round also, and all of them bowed low.

"Would you tell me," said Alice, a little timidly, "why you are painting those roses?"

Five and Seven said nothing, but looked at Two. Two began in a low voice, "Why, the fact is, you see, Miss, this here ought to have been a *red* rose-tree, and we put a white one in by mistake; and if the Queen was to find it out, we should all have our heads cut off, you know. So you see, Miss, we're doing our best, afore she comes, to——" At this moment, Five, who had been anxiously looking across the garden, called out, "The Queen! The Queen!" and the three gardeners instantly threw themselves flat upon their faces. There was a sound of many footsteps, and Alice looked round, eager to see the Queen.

First came ten soldiers carrying clubs; these were all shaped like the three gardeners, oblong and flat, with their hands and feet at the corners: next the ten courtiers; these were ornamented all over with diamonds, and walked two and two, as the soldiers did. After these came the royal children; there were ten of them, and the little dears came jumping merrily along hand in hand, in couples; they were all ornamented with hearts. Next came the guests, mostly Kings and Queens, and among them Alice recognised the White Rabbit: it was talking in a hurried, nervous manner, smiling at everything that was said, and went by without noticing her. Then followed the Knave of Hearts, carrying the King's crown on a crimson velvet cushion; and, last of all this grand procession, came THE KING AND QUEEN OF HEARTS.

Alice was rather doubtful whether she ought not to lie down on her face like the three gardeners, but she could not remember ever having heard of such a rule at processions; "and besides, what would be the use of a procession," thought she, "if people had all to lie down upon their faces, so that they couldn't see it?" So she stood still where she was, and waited.

When the procession came opposite to Alice, they all stopped and looked at her, and the Queen said severely, "Who is this?" She said it to the Knave of Hearts, who only bowed and smiled in reply.

"Idiot!" said the Queen, tossing her head impatiently; and, turning to Alice, she went on, "What's your name, child?"

"My name is Alice, so please your Majesty," said Alice very politely; but she added to herself, "Why, they're only a pack of cards, after all. I needn't be afraid of them!"

"And who are *these?*" said the Queen, pointing to the three gardeners who were lying round the rose-tree; for, you see, as they were lying on their faces, and the pattern on their backs was the same as the rest of the pack, she could not tell whether they were gardeners, or soldiers, or courtiers, or three of her own children.

"How should *I* know? said Alice, surprised at her own courage. "It's no business of *mine.*"

The Queen turned crimson with fury, and, after glaring at her for a moment like a wild beast, screamed, "Off with her head! Off——"

"Nonsense!" said Alice, very loudly and decidedly, and the Queen was silent.

The King laid his hand upon her arm, and timidly said, "Consider, my dear: she is only a child!"

The Queen turned angrily away from him, and said to the knave, "Turn them over!"

The Knave did so, very carefully, with one foot.

"Get up!" said the Queen, in a shrill, loud voice, and the three gardeners instantly jumped up, and began bowing to the King, the Queen, the royal children, and everybody else.

"Leave off that!" screamed the Queen. "You make me

giddy." And then, turning to the rose-tree, she went on, "What *have* you been doing here?"

"May it please your Majesty," said Two, in a very humble tone, going down on one knee as he spoke, "we were try-ing——"

"*I* see!" said the Queen, who had meanwhile been examin-ing the roses. "Off with their heads!" and the procession moved on, three of the soldiers remaining behind to execute the unfortunate gardeners, who ran to Alice for protection.

"You shan't be beheaded!" said Alice, and she put them into a large flower-pot that stood near. The three soldiers wandered about for a minute or two, looking for them, and then quietly marched off after the others.

"Are their heads off?" shouted the Queen.

"Their heads are gone, if it please your Majesty!" the soldiers shouted in reply.

"That's right!" shouted the Queen. "Can you play cro-quet?"

The soldiers were silent, and looked at Alice, as the ques-tion was evidently meant for her.

"Yes!" shouted Alice.

"Come on, then!" roared the Queen, and Alice joined the procession, wondering very much what would happen next.

"It's—it's a very fine day!" said a timid voice at her side. She was walking by the White Rabbit, who was peeping anxiously into her face.

"Very," said Alice: "where's the Duchess?"

"Hush! Hush!" said the Rabbit in a low, hurried tone. He looked anxiously over his shoulder as he spoke, and then raised himself upon tiptoe, put his mouth close to her ear, and whispered, "She's under sentence of execution."

"What for?" said Alice.

"Did you say, 'What a pity!'?" the Rabbit asked.

"No, I didn't," said Alice: "I don't think it's at all a pity. I said, 'What for?'"

"She boxed the Queen's ears——" the Rabbit began. Alice gave a little scream of laughter. "Oh, hush!" the Rabbit whispered in a frightened tone. "The Queen will hear you! You see she came rather late, and the Queen said——"

"Get to your places!" shouted the Queen in a voice of thunder, and people began running about in all directions, tumbling up against each other; however, they got settled down in a minute or two, and the game began.

Alice thought she had never seen such a curious croquet-ground in all her life; it was all ridges and furrows; the balls were live hedge-hogs, the mallets live flamingoes, and the soldiers had to double themselves up and to stand upon their hands and feet, to make the arches.

The chief difficulty Alice found at first was in managing her flamingo: she succeeded in getting its body tucked away, comfortably enough, under her arm, with its legs hanging down, but generally, just as she had got its neck nicely straightened out, and was going to give the hedgehog a blow with its head, it *would* twist itself round and look up in her face, with such a puzzled expression that she could not help bursting out laughing: and when she had got its head down, and was going to begin again, it was very provoking to find that the hedge-hog had unrolled itself, and was in the act of crawling away: besides all this, there was generally a ridge or furrow in the way wherever she wanted to send the hedgehog to, and, as the doubled-up soldiers were always getting up and walk-ing off to other parts of the ground, Alice soon came to the conclusion that it was a very difficult game indeed.

The players all played at once without waiting for turns, quarrelling all the while, and fighting for the hedgehogs; and in a very short time the Queen was in a furious passion, and went stamping about, and shouting, "Off with his head!" or "Off with her head!" about once in a minute.

Alice began to feel very uneasy: to be sure she had not as yet had any dispute with the Queen, but she knew that it might happen any minute, "and then," thought she, "what would become of me? They're dreadfully fond of beheading people here; the great wonder is that there's anyone left alive!"

She was looking about for some way of escape, and won-dering whether she could get away without being seen, when she noticed a curious appearance in the air: it puzzled her very much at first, but, after watching it a minute or two, she made it out to be a grin, and she said to herself, "It's the Cheshire Cat: now I shall have somebody to talk to."

"How are you getting on?" said the Cat, as soon as there was mouth enough for it to speak with.

Alice waited till the eyes appeared, and then nodded. "It's no use speaking to it," she thought, "till its ears have come, or at least one of them." In another minute the whole head appeared, and then Alice put down her flamingo, and began an account of the game, feeling very glad she had someone to listen to her. The Cat seemed to think that there was enough of it now in sight, and no more of it appeared.

"I don't think they play at all fairly," Alice began, in rather a complaining tone, "and they all quarrel so dreadfully one can't hear oneself speak—and they don't seem to have any rules in particular; at least, if there are, nobody attends to them—and you've no idea how confusing it is all the things being alive; for instance, there's the arch I've got to go through next walking about at the other end of the ground—and I should have croqueted the Queen's hedge-hog just now, only it ran away when it saw mine coming!"

"How do you like the Queen?" said the Cat in a low voice.

"Not at all," said Alice: "she's so extremely——" Just then she noticed that the Queen was close behind her listening: so she went on, "—likely to win, that it's hardly worth while finishing the game."

The Queen smiled and passed on.

"Who *are* you talking to?" said the King, coming up to Alice, and looking at the Cat's head with great curiosity.

"It's a friend of mine—a Cheshire Cat," said Alice: "allow me to introduce it."

"I don't like the look of it at all," said the King: "however, it may kiss my hand if it likes."

"I'd rather not," the Cat remarked.

"Don't be impertinent," said the King, "and don't look at me like that!" He got behind Alice as he spoke.

"A cat may look at a king," said Alice. "I've read that in some book, but I don't remember where."

"Well, it must be removed," said the King very decidedly, and he called to the Queen, who was passing at the moment, "My dear! I wish you would have this cat removed!"

The Queen had only one way of settling all difficulties, great or small. "Off with his head!" she said, without even looking round.

"I'll fetch the executioner myself," said the King eagerly, and he hurried off.

Alice thought she might as well go back and see how the game was going on, as she heard the Queen's voice in the distance, screaming with passion. She had already heard her sentence three of the players to be executed for having missed their turns, and she did not like the look of things at all, as the game was in such confusion that she never knew whether it was her turn or not. So she went in search of her hedgehog.

The hedgehog was engaged in a fight with another hedge-hog, which seemed to Alice an excellent opportunity for croqueting one of them with the other: the only difficulty was, that her flamingo was gone across to the other side of the garden, where Alice could see it trying in a helpless sort of way to fly up into one of the trees.

By the time she had caught the flamingo and brought it back, the fight was over, and both the hedgehogs were out of sight: "but it doesn't matter much," thought Alice, "as all the arches are gone from this side of the ground." So she tucked it under her arm, that it might not escape again, and went back for a little more conversation with her friend.

When she got back to the Cheshire Cat, she was surprised to find quite a large crowd collected round it: there was a dispute going on between the executioner, the King, and the Queen, who were all talking at once, while all the rest were quite silent, and looked very uncomfortable.

The moment Alice appeared, she was appealed to by all three to settle the question, and they repeated their arguments to her, though, as they all spoke at once, she found it very hard to make out exactly what they said.

The executioner's argument was, that you couldn't cut off a head unless there was a body to cut it off from: that he had never had to do such a thing before, and he wasn't going to begin at *his* time of life.

The King's argument was, that anything that had a head could be beheaded, and that you weren't to talk nonsense.

The Queen's argument was, that if something wasn't done

about it in less than no time, she'd have everybody executed, all round. (It was this last remark that had made the whole party look so grave and anxious.)

Alice could think of nothing else to say but, "It belongs to the Duchess: you'd better ask *her* about it."

"She's in prison," the Queen said to the executioner: "fetch her here." And the executioner went off like an arrow.

The Cat's head began fading away the moment he was

gone, and, by the time he had come back with the Duchess, it had entirely disappeared; so the King and the executioner ran wildly up and down looking for it, while the rest of the party went back to the game.

CHAPTER IX

THE MOCK TURTLE'S STORY

"You can't think how glad I am to see you again, you dear old thing!" said the Duchess, as she tucked her arm affectionately into Alice's, and they walked off together.

Alice was very glad to find her in such a pleasant temper, and thought to herself that perhaps it was only the pepper that had made her so savage when they met in the kitchen.

"When *I'm* a Duchess," she said to herself (not in a very hopeful tone though), "I won't have any pepper in my kitchen *at all*. Soup does very well without. Maybe it's always pepper that makes people hot-tempered," she went on, very much pleased at having found out a new kind of rule, "and vinegar that makes them sour—and camomile that makes them bitter—and—and barley-sugar and such things that make children sweet-tempered. I only wish people knew *that*: then they wouldn't be so stingy about it, you know——"

She had quite forgotten the Duchess by this time, and was a little startled when she heard her voice close to her ear. "You're thinking about something, my dear, and that makes you forget to talk. I can't tell you just now what the moral of that is, but I shall remember it in a bit."

"Perhaps it hasn't one," Alice ventured to remark.

"Tut, tut, child!" said the Duchess. "Everything's got a moral, if only you can find it." And she squeezed herself up closer to Alice's side as she spoke.

Alice did not much like her keeping so close to her: first, because the Duchess was *very* ugly; and secondly, because she was exactly the right height to rest her chin upon Alice's shoulder, and it was an uncomfortably sharp chin. However, she did not like to be rude, so she bore it as well as she could. "The game seems to be going on rather better now," she said.

" 'Tis so," said the Duchess: "and the moral of it is —'Oh, 'tis love, 'tis love, that makes the world go round!' "

"Somebody said," 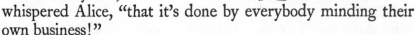 whispered Alice, "that it's done by everybody minding their own business!"

"Ah, well! It means much the same thing," said the Duchess, digging her sharp little chin into Alice's shoulder as she added, "and the moral of *that* is—'Take care of the sense, and the sounds will take care of themselves.' "

"How fond she is of finding morals in things!" Alice thought to herself.

"I dare say you're wondering why I don't put my arm round your waist," the Duchess said after a pause: "the reason is, that I'm doubtful about the temper of your flamingo. Shall I try the experiment?"

"He might bite," Alice cautiously replied, not feeling at all anxious to have the experiment tried.

"Very true," said the Duchess: "flamingoes and mustard both bite. And the moral of that is—'Birds of a feather flock together.' "

"Only mustard isn't a bird," Alice remarked.

"Right, as usual," said the Duchess: "what a clear way you have of putting things!"

"It's a mineral, I *think*," said Alice.

"Of course it is," said the Duchess, who seemed ready to agree to everything that Alice said; "there's a large mustard-mine near here. And the moral of that is—'The more there is of mine, the less there is of yours.' "

"Oh, I know!" exclaimed Alice, who had not attended to this last remark. "It's a vegetable. It doesn't look like one, but it is."

"I quite agree with you," said the Duchess; "and the moral of that is—'Be what you would seem to be'—or if you'd like it put more simply—'Never imagine yourself not to be otherwise than what it might appear to others that what you were or might have been was not otherwise than what you had been would have appeared to them to be otherwise.' "

"I think I should understand that better," Alice said very politely, "if I had it written down: but I'm afraid I can't quite follow it as you say it."

"That's nothing to what I could say if I chose," the Duchess replied, in a pleased tone.

"Pray don't trouble yourself to say it any longer than that," said Alice.

"Oh, don't talk about trouble!" said the Duchess. "I make you a present of everything I've said as yet."

"A cheap sort of present!" thought Alice. "I'm glad

they don't give birthday presents like that!" But she did
not venture to say it out loud.

"Thinking again?" the Duchess asked with another dig
of her sharp little chin.

"I've a right to think," said Alice sharply, for she was
beginning to feel a little worried.

"Just about as much right," said the Duchess, "as pigs
have to fly; and the m——"

But here, to Alice's great surprise, the Duchess's voice
died away, even in the middle of her favourite word "moral,"
and the arm that was linked into hers began to tremble.
Alice looked up, and there stood the Queen in front of
them with her arms folded, frowning like a thunderstorm.

"A fine day, your Majesty!" the Duchess began in a low,
weak voice.

"Now, I give you fair warning," shouted the Queen,
stamping on the ground as she spoke; "either you or your
head must be off, and that in about half no time! Take your
choice!"

The Duchess took her choice, and was gone in a moment.

"Let's go on with the game," the Queen said to Alice;
and Alice was too much frightened to say a word, but slowly
followed her back to the croquet-ground.

The other guests had taken advantage of the Queen's ab-
sence, and were resting in the shade: however, the moment
they saw her, they hurried back to the game, the Queen
merely remarking that a moment's delay would cost them
their lives.

All the time they were playing the Queen never left off
quarrelling with the other players, and shouting, "Off with
his head!" or "Off with her head!" Those whom she sen-
tenced were taken into custody by the soldiers, who of course
had to leave off being arches to do this, so that by the end
of half an hour or so there were no arches left, and all the

players, except the King, the Queen, and Alice, were in custody and under sentence of execution.

Then the Queen left off, quite out of breath, and said to Alice, "Have you seen the Mock Turtle yet?"

"No," said Alice. "I don't even know what a Mock Turtle is."

"It's the thing Mock Turtle Soup is made from," said the Queen.

"I never saw one, or heard of one," said Alice.

"Come on, then," said the Queen, "and he shall tell you his history."

As they walked off together, Alice heard the King say in a low voice, to the company generally, "You are all pardoned." "Come, *that's* a good thing!" she said to herself, for she had felt quite unhappy at the number of executions the Queen had ordered.

They very soon came upon a Gryphon, lying fast asleep in the sun. (If you don't know what a Gryphon is, look at the picture.) "Up, lazy thing!" said the Queen, "and take

this young lady to see the Mock Turtle, and to hear his history. I must go back, and see after some executions I have ordered," and she walked off, leaving Alice alone with the Gryphon. Alice did not quite like the look of the creature, but on the whole she thought it would be quite as safe to stay with it as to go after that savage Queen: so she waited.

The Gryphon sat up and rubbed its eyes: then it watched the Queen till she was out of sight: then it chuckled. "What fun!" said the Gryphon, half to itself, half to Alice.

"What *is* the fun?" said Alice.

"Why, *she*," said the Gryphon. "It's all her fancy, that: they never executes nobody, you know. Come on!"

"Everybody says 'come on!' here," thought Alice, as she went slowly after it: "I never was so ordered about in all my life, never!"

They had not gone far before they saw the Mock Turtle in the distance, sitting sad and lonely on a little ledge of rock, and, as they came nearer, Alice could hear him sighing as if his heart would break. She pitied him deeply. "What is his sorrow?" she asked the Gryphon, and the Gryphon answered, very nearly in the same words as before, "It's all his fancy, that: he hasn't got no sorrow, you know. Come on!"

So they went up to the Mock Turtle, who looked at them with large eyes full of tears, but said nothing.

"This here young lady," said the Gryphon, "she wants for to know your history, she do."

"I'll tell it her," said the Mock Turtle in a deep, hollow tone: "sit down, both of you, and don't speak a word till I've finished."

So they sat down, and nobody spoke for some minutes. Alice thought to herself, "I don't see how he can *ever* finish, if he doesn't begin." But she waited patiently.

"Once," said the Mock Turtle at last, with a deep sigh, "I was a real Turtle."

These words were followed by a very long silence, broken
only by an occasional exclamation of "Hjckrrh!" from the
Gryphon, and the constant heavy sobbing of the Mock Turtle.

Alice was very nearly getting up and saying. "Thank you,
sir, for your interesting story," but she could not help thinking there *must* be more to come, so she sat still and said
nothing.

"When we were little," the Mock Turtle went on at last, more calmly, though still sobbing a little now and then, "we went to school in the sea. The master was an old Turtle—we used to call him Tortoise——"

"Why did you call him Tortoise, if he wasn't one?" Alice asked.

"We called him Tortoise because he taught us," said the Mock Turtle angrily: "really you are very dull!"

"You ought to be ashamed of yourself for asking such a simple question," added the Gryphon; and then they both sat silent and looked at poor Alice, who felt ready to sink into the earth. At last the Gryphon said to the Mock Turtle, "Drive on, old fellow! Don't be all day about it!" and he went on in these words:

"Yes, we went to school in the sea, though you mayn't believe it——"

"I never said I didn't!" interrupted Alice.

"You did," said the Mock Turtle.

"Hold your tongue!" added the Gryphon, before Alice could speak again. The Mock Turtle went on:

"We had the best of educations—in fact, we went to school every day——"

"*I've* been to a day-school, too," said Alice: "you needn't be so proud as all that."

"With extras?" asked the Mock Turtle a little anxiously.

"Yes," said Alice, "we learned French and music."

"And washing?" said the Mock Turtle.

"Certainly not!" said Alice indignantly.

"Ah! then yours wasn't a really good school," said the Mock Turtle in a tone of great relief. "Now at *ours* they had at the end of the bill, 'French, music *and washing*—extra.' "

"You couldn't have wanted it much," said Alice; "living at the bottom of the sea."

"I couldn't afford to learn it," said the Mock Turtle with a sigh. "I only took the regular course."

"What was that?" inquired Alice.

"Reeling and Writing, of course, to begin with," the Mock Turtle replied; "and then the different branches of Arithmetic—Ambition, Distraction, Uglification, and Derision."

"I never heard of 'Uglification,'" Alice ventured to say. "What is it?"

The Gryphon lifted up both its paws in surprise. "What! Never heard of uglifying!" it exclaimed. "You know what to beautify is, I suppose?"

"Yes," said Alice doubtfully: "it means—to—make—anything—prettier."

"Well, then," the Gryphon went on, "if you don't know what to uglify is, you *must* be a simpleton."

Alice did not feel encouraged to ask any more questions about it, so she turned to the Mock Turtle, and said, "What else had you to learn?"

"Well, there was Mystery," the Mock Turtle replied, counting off the subjects on his flappers, "—Mystery, ancient and modern, with Seaography: then Drawling—the Drawling-master was an old conger-eel, that used to come once a week: *he* taught us Drawling, Stretching, and Fainting in Coils."

"What was *that* like?" said Alice.

"Well, I can't show it you myself," the Mock Turtle said: "I'm too stiff. And the Gryphon never learnt it."

"Hadn't time," said the Gryphon: "I went to the Classical master, though. He was an old crab, *he* was."

"I never went to him," the Mock Turtle said with a sigh: "he taught Laughing and Grief, they used to say."

"So he did, so he did," said the Gryphon, sighing in his turn; and both creatures hid their faces in their paws.

"And how many hours a day did you do lessons?" said Alice, in a hurry to change the subject.

"Ten hours the first day," said the Mock Turtle: "nine the next, and so on."

"What a curious plan!" exclaimed Alice.

"That's the reason they're called lessons," the Gryphon remarked: "because they lessen from day to day."

This was quite a new idea to Alice, and she thought it over a little before she made her next remark. "Then the eleventh day must have been a holiday?"

"Of course it was," said the Mock Turtle.

"And how did you manage on the twelfth?" Alice went on eagerly.

"That's enough about lessons," the Gryphon interrupted in a very decided tone: "tell her something about the games now."

CHAPTER X

THE LOBSTER QUADRILLE

THE Mock Turtle sighed deeply, and drew the back of one flapper across his eyes. He looked at Alice, and tried to speak, but, for a minute or two, sobs choked his voice. "Same as if he had a bone in his throat," said the Gryphon: and it set to work shaking him and punching him in the back. At last the Mock Turtle recovered his voice, and, with tears running down his cheeks, went on again:

"You may not have lived much under the sea——" ("I haven't," said Alice) "and perhaps you were never even introduced to a lobster——" (Alice began to say, "I once tasted——" but checked herself hastily, and said, "No, never") "—so you can have no idea what a delightful thing a Lobster Quadrille is!"

"No, indeed," said Alice. "What sort of a dance is it?"

"Why," said the Gryphon, "you first form into a line along the sea-shore——"

"Two lines!" cried the Mock Turtle. "Seals, turtles, and so

on; then, when you've cleared the jelly-fish out of the way——"

"*That* generally takes some time," interrupted the Gryphon.

"——you advance twice——"

"Each with a lobster as a partner!" cried the Gryphon.

"Of course," the Mock Turtle said: "advance twice, set to partners——"

"——change lobsters, and retire in same order," continued the Gryphon.

"Then, you know," the Mock Turtle went on, "you throw the——"

"The lobsters!" shouted the Gryphon, with a bound into the air.

"——as far out to sea as you can——"

"Swim after them!" screamed the Gryphon.

"Turn a somersault in the sea!" cried the Mock Turtle, capering wildly about.

"Change lobsters again!" yelled the Gryphon.

"Back to land again, and—that's all the first figure," said the Mock Turtle, suddenly dropping his voice; and the two creatures, who had been jumping about like mad things, sat down again very sadly and quietly, and looked at Alice.

"It must be a very pretty dance," said Alice, timidly.

"Would you like to see a little of it?" said the Mock Turtle.

"Very much indeed," said Alice.

"Let's try the first figure!" said the Mock Turtle to the Gryphon. "We can do without lobsters, you know. Which shall sing?"

"Oh, *you* sing," said the Gryphon. "I've forgotten the words."

So they began solemnly dancing round and round Alice, every now and then treading on her toes when they passed too close, and waving their forepaws to mark the time, while the Mock Turtle sang this, very slowly and sadly:

"Will you walk a little faster?" said a whiting to a snail.
"There's a porpoise close behind us, and he's treading on my
tail.
See how eagerly the lobsters and the turtles all advance!

They are waiting on the shingle—will you come and join the
dance?
  Will you, won't you, will you, won't you, will you join the
  dance?
  Will you, won't you, will you, won't you, won't you join the
  dance?

"You can really have no notion how delightful it will be,
When they take us up and throw us, with the lobsters, out to
     sea!"
But the snail replied "Too far, too far!" and gave a look
     askance—
Said he thanked the whiting kindly, but he would not join the
     dance.
     Would not, could not, would not, could not, would not join
        the dance.
     Would not, could not, would not, could not, could not join
        the dance.

"What matters it how far we go?" his scaly friend replied.
"There is another shore, you know, upon the other side.
The further off from England the nearer is to France—
Then turn not pale, beloved snail, but come and join the dance.
     Will you, won't you, will you, won't you, will you join the
        dance?
     Will you, won't you, will you, won't you, won't you join the
        dance?"

"Thank you, it's a very interesting dance to watch," said Alice, feeling very glad that it was over at last: "and I do so like that curious song about the whiting!"

"Oh, as to the whiting," said the Mock Turtle, "they—you've seen them, of course?"

"Yes," said Alice, "I've often seen them at dinn——" she checked herself hastily.

"I don't know where Dinn may be," said the Mock Turtle, "but if you've seen them so often, of course you know what they're like."

"I believe so," Alice replied thoughtfully. "They have their tails in their mouths—and they're all over crumbs."

"You're wrong about the crumbs," said the Mock Turtle:

"crumbs would all wash off in the sea. But they *have* their tails in their mouths; and the reason is——" here the Mock Turtle yawned and shut his eyes. "Tell her about the reason and all that," he said to the Gryphon.

"The reason is," said the Gryphon, "that they *would* go with the lobsters to the dance. So they got thrown out to sea. So they had to fall a long way. So they got their tails fast in their mouths. So they couldn't get them out again. That's all."

"Thank you," said Alice, "it's very interesting. I never knew so much about a whiting before."

"I can tell you more than that, if you like," said the Gryphon. "Do you know why it's called a whiting?"

"I never thought about it," said Alice. "Why?"

"*It does the boots and shoes,*" the Gryphon replied very solemnly.

Alice was thoroughly puzzled. "Does the boots and shoes!" she repeated in a wondering tone.

"Why, what are *your* shoes done with?" said the Gryphon. "I mean, what makes them so shiny?"

Alice looked down at them, and considered a little before she gave her answer. "They're done with blacking, I believe."

"Boots and shoes under the sea," the Gryphon went on in a deep voice, "are done with whiting. Now you know."

"And what are they made of?" Alice asked in a tone of great curiosity.

"Soles and eels, of course," the Gryphon replied rather impatiently: "any shrimp could have told you that."

"If I'd been the whiting," said Alice, whose thoughts were still running on the song, "I'd have said to the porpoise, 'Keep back, please: we don't want *you* with us!'"

"They were obliged to have him with them," the Mock Turtle said: "no wise fish would go anywhere without a porpoise."

"Wouldn't it really?" said Alice in a tone of great surprise.

"Of course not," said the Mock Turtle: "why, if a fish came to *me*, and told me he was going on a journey, I should say, 'With what porpoise?'"

"Don't you mean 'purpose'?" said Alice.

"I mean what I say," the Mock Turtle replied in an offended tone. And the Gryphon added, "Come, let's hear some of *your* adventures."

"I could tell you my adventures—beginning from this morning," said Alice a little timidly: "but it's no use going back to yesterday, because I was a different person then."

"Explain all that," said the Mock Turtle.

"No, no! The adventures first," said the Gryphon in an impatient tone: "explanations take such a dreadful time."

So Alice began telling them her adventures from the time when she first saw the White Rabbit. She was a little nervous about it just at first, the two creatures got so close to her, one on each side, and opened their eyes and mouths so *very* wide, but she gained courage as she went on. Her listeners were perfectly quiet till she got to the part about her repeating "You are old, Father William," to the Caterpillar, and the words all coming different, and then the Mock Turtle drew a long breath, and said, "That's very curious."

"It's all about as curious as it can be," said the Gryphon.

"It all came different!" the Mock Turtle repeated thoughtfully. "I should like to hear her repeat something now. Tell her to begin." He looked at the Gryphon as if he thought it had some kind of authority over Alice.

"Stand up and repeat ''Tis the voice of the sluggard,'" said the Gryphon.

"How the creatures order one about, and make one repeat lessons!" thought Alice. "I might as well be at school at once." However, she got up, and began to repeat it, but her head was so full of the Lobster Quadrille, that she hardly knew what she was saying, and the words came very queer indeed:

" 'Tis the voice of the Lobster; I heard him declare,
'You have baked me too brown, I must sugar my hair.'
As a duck with its eyelids, so he with his nose
Trims his belt and his buttons, and turns out his toes.
When the sands are all dry, he is gay as a lark,
And will talk in contemptuous tone of the Shark:
But, when the tide rises and sharks are around,
His voice has a timid and tremulous sound."

"That's different from what *I* used to say when I was a child," said the Gryphon.

"Well, I never heard it before," said the Mock Turtle; "but it sounds uncommon nonsense."

Alice said nothing; she had sat down with her face in her hands, wondering if anything would *ever* happen in a natural way again.

"I should like to have it explained," said the Mock Turtle.

"She can't explain it," hastily said the Gryphon. "Go on to the next verse."

"But about his toes?"

the Mock Turtle persisted. "How *could* he turn them out with his nose, you know?"

"It's the first position in dancing," Alice said; but was dreadfully puzzled by it all, and longed to change the subject.

"Go on with the next verse," the Gryphon repeated: "it begins with the words, 'I passed by his garden.'"

Alice did not dare to disobey, though she felt sure it would all come wrong, and she went on in a trembling voice:

"I passed by his garden, and marked, with one eye,
How the Owl and the Panther were sharing a pie:
The Panther took pie-crust, and gravy, and meat,
While the Owl had the dish as its share of the treat.
When the pie was all finished, the Owl, as a boon,
Was kindly permitted to pocket the spoon:
While the Panther received knife and fork with a growl,
And concluded the banquet by——"

"What *is* the use of repeating all that stuff," the Mock Turtle interrupted, "if you don't explain it as you go on? It's by far the most confusing thing *I* ever heard!"

"Yes, I think you'd better leave off," said the Gryphon: and Alice was only too glad to do so.

"Shall we try another figure of the Lobster Quadrille?" the Gryphon went on. "Or would you like the Mock Turtle to sing you a song?"

"Oh, a song, please, if the Mock Turtle would be so kind," Alice replied, so eagerly that the Gryphon said, in a rather offended tone, "Hm! No accounting for tastes! Sing her 'Turtle Soup,' will you, old fellow?"

The Mock Turtle sighed deeply, and began, in a voice sometimes choked with sobs, to sing this:

"Beautiful Soup, so rich and green,
Waiting in a hot tureen!
Who for such dainties would not stoop?
Soup of the evening, beautiful Soup!
Soup of the evening, beautiful Soup!
*   Beau—ootiful Soo—oop!*
*   Beau—ootiful Soo—oop!*
Soo—oop of the e—e—evening,
*   Beautiful, beautiful Soup!*

"Beautiful Soup! Who cares for fish,
Game, or any other dish?
Who would not give all else for two p
ennyworth only of beautiful Soup?
Pennyworth only of beautiful Soup?
*   Beau—ootiful Soo—oop!*
*   Beau—ootiful Soo—oop!*
Soo—oop of the e—e—evening,
*   Beautiful, beauti—*FUL SOUP!*"*

"Chorus again!" cried the Gryphon, and the Mock Turtle had just begun to repeat it, when a cry of "The trial's beginning!" was heard in the distance.

"Come on!" cried the Gryphon, and, taking Alice by the hand, it hurried off, without waiting for the end of the song.

"What trial is it?" Alice panted as she ran; but the Gryphon only answered, "Come on!" and ran the faster, while more and more faintly came, carried on the breeze that followed them, the melancholy words:

"Soo—oop of the e—e—evening,
*   Beautiful, beautiful Soup!"*

CHAPTER XI

WHO STOLE THE TARTS?

THE King and Queen of Hearts were seated on their throne when they arrived, with a great crowd assembled about them —all sorts of little birds and beasts, as well as the whole pack of cards: the Knave was standing before them, in chains, with a soldier on each side to guard him; and near the King was the White Rabbit, with a trumpet in one hand, and a scroll of parchment in the other. In the very middle of the court was a table, with a large dish of tarts upon it: they looked so good that it made Alice quite hungry to look at them— "I wish they'd get the trial done," she thought, "and hand round the refreshments!" But there seemed to be no chance of this, so she began looking about her, to pass away the time.

Alice had never been in a court of justice before, but she had read about them in books, and she was quite pleased to find that she knew the name of nearly everything there. "That's the judge," she said to herself, "because of his great wig."

The judge, by the way, was the King; and as he wore his crown over the wig (look at the frontispiece if you want to see how he did it), he did not look at all comfortable, and it was certainly not becoming.

"And that's the jury-box," thought Alice, "and those twelve creatures" (she was obliged to say "creatures," you see, because some of them were animals, and some were birds), "I suppose they are the jurors." She said this last word two or three times over to herself, being rather proud of it: for she thought, and rightly too, that very few little girls of her age knew the meaning of it at all. However, "jurymen" would have done just as well.

The twelve jurors were all writing very busily on slates.

"What are they all doing?" Alice whispered to the Gryphon. "They can't have anything to put down yet, before the trial's begun."

"They're putting down their names," the Gryphon whispered in reply, "for fear they should forget them before the end of the trial."

"Stupid things!" Alice began in a loud, indignant voice, but she stopped hastily, for the White Rabbit cried out,

"Silence in the court!" and the King put on his spectacles and looked anxiously round, to see who was talking.

Alice could see, as well as if she were looking over their

shoulders, that all the jurors were writing down "stupid things!" on their slates, and she could even make out that one of them didn't know how to spell "stupid," and that he had to ask his neighbour to tell him. "A nice muddle their slates will be in before the trial's over!" thought Alice.

One of the jurors had a pencil that squeaked. This, of course, Alice could *not* stand, and she went round the court and got behind him, and very soon found an opportunity of taking it away. She did it so quickly that the poor little juror (it was Bill, the Lizard) could not make out at all what had become of it; so, after hunting all about for it, he was obliged to write with one finger for the rest of the day; and this was of very little use, as it left no mark on the slate.

"Herald, read the accusation!" said the King.

On this the White Rabbit blew three blasts on the trumpet, and then unrolled the parchment scroll, and read as follows:

> *"The Queen of Hearts, she made some tarts,*
> *All on a summer day:*
> *The Knave of Hearts, he stole those tarts,*
> *And took them quite away!"*

"Consider your verdict," the King said to the jury.

"Not yet, not yet!" the Rabbit hastily interrupted. "There's a great deal to come before that!"

"Call the first witness," said the King; and the White Rabbit blew three blasts on the trumpet, and called out, "First witness!"

The first witness was the Hatter. He came in with a tea-cup in one hand and a piece of bread-and-butter in the other. "I beg pardon, your Majesty," he began, "for bringing these in: but I hadn't quite finished my tea when I was sent for."

"You ought to have finished," said the King. "When did you begin?"

The Hatter looked at the March Hare, who had followed

him into the court, arm-in-arm with the Dormouse. "Fourteenth of March, I *think* it was," he said.

"Fifteenth," said the March Hare.

"Sixteenth," added the Dormouse.

"Write that down," the King said to the jury, and the jury eagerly wrote down all three dates on their slates, and then added them up, and reduced the answer to shillings and pence.

"Take off your hat," the King said to the Hatter.

"It isn't mine," said the Hatter.

. . "*Stolen!*" the King exclaimed, turning to the jury, who instantly made a memorandum of the fact.

"I keep them to sell," the Hatter added as an explanation: "I've none of my own. I'm a hatter."

Here the Queen put on her spectacles, and began staring hard at the Hatter, who turned pale and fidgeted.

"Give your evidence," said the King, "and don't be nervous, or I'll have you executed on the spot."

This did not seem to encourage the witness at all: he kept shifting from one foot to the other, looking uneasily at the Queen, and in his confusion he bit a large piece out of his teacup instead of the bread-and-butter.

Just at this moment Alice felt a very curious sensation, which puzzled her a good deal until she made out what it was: she was beginning to grow larger again, and she thought at first she would get up and leave the court; but on second thoughts she decided to remain where she was as long as there was room for her.

"I wish you wouldn't squeeze so," said the Dormouse, who was sitting next to her. "I can hardly breathe."

"I can't help it," said Alice very meekly: "I'm growing."

"You've no right to grow *here*," said the Dormouse.

"Don't talk nonsense," said Alice more boldly: "you know you're growing too."

"Yes, but *I* grow at a reasonable pace," said the Dormouse:

"not in that ridiculous fashion." And he got up very sulkily and crossed over to the other side of the court.

All this time the Queen had never left off staring at the Hatter, and, just as the Dormouse crossed the court, she said

to one of the officers of the court, "Bring me the list of the singers in the last concert!" on which the wretched Hatter trembled so, that he shook both his shoes off.

"Give your evidence," the King repeated angrily, "or I'll have you executed, whether you're nervous or not."

"I'm a poor man, your Majesty," the Hatter began, in a trembling voice, "and I hadn't begun my tea—not above a week or so—and what with the bread-and-butter getting so thin—and the twinkling of the tea——"

"The twinkling of the *what?*" said the King.

"It *began* with the tea," the Hatter replied.

"Of course twinkling begins with a T!" said the King sharply. "Do you take me for a dunce? Go on!"

"I'm a poor man," the Hatter went on, "and most things twinkled after that—only the March Hare said——"

"I didn't!" the March Hare interrupted in a great hurry.

"You did!" said the Hatter.

"I deny it!" said the March Hare.

"He denies it," said the King: "leave out that part."

"Well, at any rate, the Dormouse said——" the Hatter went on, looking anxiously round to see if he would deny it too: but the Dormouse denied nothing, being fast asleep.

"After that," continued the Hatter, "I cut some more bread-and-butter——"

"But what did the Dormouse say?" one of the jury asked.

"That I can't remember," said the Hatter.

"You *must* remember," remarked the King, "or I'll have you executed."

The miserable Hatter dropped his teacup and bread-and-butter, and went down on one knee. "I'm a poor man, your Majesty," he began.

"You're a *very* poor *speaker*," said the King.

Here one of the guinea-pigs cheered, and was immediately suppressed by the officers of the court. (As that is rather a hard word, I will just explain to you how it was done. They had a large canvas bag, which tied up at the mouth with strings: into this they slipped the guinea-pig, head first, and then sat upon it.)

"I'm glad I've seen that done," thought Alice. "I've so often read in the newspapers, at the end of trials, 'There was some attempt at applause, which was immediately suppressed by the officers of the court,' and I never understood what it meant till now."

"If that's all you know about it, you may stand down," continued the King.

"I can't go no lower," said the Hatter: "I'm on the floor, as it is."

"Then you may *sit* down," the King replied.

Here the other guinea-pig cheered, and was suppressed.

"Come, that finishes the guinea-pigs!" thought Alice. "Now we shall get on better."

"I'd rather finish my tea," said the Hatter, with an anxious look at the Queen, who was reading the list of singers.

"You may go," said the King; and the Hatter hurriedly left the court, without even waiting to put his shoes on.

"—and just take his head off outside," the Queen added to one of the officers; but the Hatter was out of sight before the officer could get to the door.

"Call the next witness!" said the King.

The next witness was the Duchess's cook. She carried the pepper-box in her hand, and Alice guessed who it was, even before she got into the court, by the way the people near the door began sneezing all at once.

"Give your evidence," said the King.

"Shan't," said the cook.

The King looked anxiously at the White Rabbit, who said in a low voice, "Your Majesty must cross-examine *this* witness."

"Well, if I must, I must," the King said with a melancholy air, and, after folding his arms and frowning at the cook till his eyes were nearly out of sight, he said in a deep voice, "What are tarts made of?"

"Pepper, mostly," said the cook.

"Treacle," said a sleepy voice behind her.

"Collar that Dormouse," the Queen shrieked out. "Behead that Dormouse! Turn that Dormouse out of court! Suppress him! Pinch him! Off with his whiskers!"

For some minutes the whole court was in confusion, getting the Dormouse turned out, and, by the time they had settled down again, the cook had disappeared.

"Never mind!" said the King, with an air of great relief. "Call the next witness." And, he added in an undertone to the Queen, "Really, my dear, *you* must cross-examine the next witness. It quite makes my forehead ache!"

Alice watched the White Rabbit as he fumbled over the list, feeling very curious to see what the next witness would be like, "—for they haven't got much evidence *yet*," she said to herself. Imagine her surprise when the White Rabbit read out, at the top of his shrill little voice, the name "Alice!"

CHAPTER XII

ALICE'S EVIDENCE

"Here!" cried Alice, quite forgetting in the flurry of the moment how large she had grown in the last few minutes, and she jumped up in such a hurry that she tipped over the jury-box with the edge of her skirt, upsetting all the jurymen on to the heads of the crowd below, and there they lay sprawling about, reminding her very much of a globe of gold-fish she had accidentally upset the week before.

"Oh, I *beg* your pardon!" she exclaimed in a tone of great dismay, and began picking them up again as quickly as she could, for the accident of the gold-fish kept running in her head, and she had a vague sort of idea that they must be collected at once and put back into the jury-box, or they would die.

"The trial cannot proceed," said the King in a very grave voice, "until all the jurymen are back in their proper places —*all*," he repeated with great emphasis, looking hard at Alice as he said so.

Alice looked at the jury-box, and saw that, in her haste, she had put the Lizard in head downwards, and the poor little thing was waving its tail about in a melancholy way, being quite unable to move. She soon got it out again, and put it right; "not that it signifies much," she said to herself; "I should think it would be *quite* as much use in the trial one way up as the other."

As soon as the jury had a little recovered from the shock of being upset, and their slates and pencils had been found and handed back to them, they set to work very diligently to write out a history of the accident, all except the Lizard, who seemed too much overcome to do anything but sit with its mouth open, gazing up into the roof of the court.

"What do you know about this business?" the King said to Alice.

"Nothing," said Alice.

"Nothing *whatever?*" persisted the King.

"Nothing whatever," said Alice.

"That's very important," the King said, turning to the jury. They were just beginning to write this down on their slates, when the White Rabbit interrupted: "*Un*important, your Majesty means, of course," he said in a very respectful tone, but frowning and making faces at him as he spoke.

"*Un*important, of course, I meant," the King hastily said, and went on to himself in an undertone, "important—unimportant—unimportant—important——" as if he were trying which word sounded best.

Some of the jury wrote it down "important," and some "unimportant." Alice could see this, as she was near enough to look over their slates; "but it doesn't matter a bit," she thought to herself.

At this moment the King, who had been for some time busily writing in his notebook, called out "Silence!" and read out from his book, "Rule Forty-two. *All persons more than a mile high to leave the court.*"

Everybody looked at Alice.

"*I'm* not a mile high," said Alice.

"You are," said the King.

"Nearly two miles high," added the Queen.

"Well, I shan't go, at any rate," said Alice: "besides, that's not a regular rule: you invented it just now."

"It's the oldest rule in the book," said the King.

"Then it ought to be Number One," said Alice.

The King turned pale, and shut his notebook hastily. "Consider your verdict," he said to the jury, in a low trembling voice.

"There's more evidence to come yet, please your Majesty," said the White Rabbit, jumping up in a great hurry: "this paper has just been picked up."

"What's in it?" said the Queen.

"I haven't opened it yet," said the White Rabbit, "but it seems to be a letter, written by the prisoner to—to somebody."

"It must have been that," said the King, "unless it was written to nobody, which isn't usual, you know."

"Who is it directed to?" said one of the jurymen.

"It isn't directed at all," said the White Rabbit; "in fact, there's nothing written on the *outside*." He unfolded the paper as he spoke, and added, "It isn't a letter, after all: it's a set of verses."

"Are they in the prisoner's handwriting?" asked another of the jurymen.

"No, they're not," said the White Rabbit, "and that's the queerest thing about it." (The jury all looked puzzled.)

"He must have imitated somebody else's hand," said the King. (The jury all brightened up again.)

"Please your Majesty," said the Knave, "I didn't write it, and they can't prove I did: there's no name signed at the end."

"If you didn't sign it," said the King, "that only makes the matter worse. You *must* have meant some mischief, or else you'd have signed your name like an honest man."

There was a general clapping of hands at this: it was the first really clever thing the King had said that day.

"That *proves* his guilt," said the Queen.

"It proves nothing of the sort!" said Alice. "Why, you don't even know what they're about!"

"Read them," said the King.

The White Rabbit put on his spectacles. "Where shall I begin, please your Majesty?" he asked.

"Begin at the beginning," the King said gravely, "and go on till you come to the end; then stop."

These were the verses the White Rabbit read:

> "*They told me you had been to her,*
> *And mentioned me to him:*
> *She gave me a good character,*
> *But said I could not swim.*
>
> *He sent them word I had not gone*
> *(We know it to be true):*
> *If she should push the matter on,*
> *What would become of you?*
>
> *I gave her one, they gave him two,*
> *You gave us three or more;*
> *They all returned from him to you,*
> *Though they were mine before.*
>
> *If I or she should chance to be*
> *Involved in this affair,*
> *He trusts to you to set them free,*
> *Exactly as we were.*
>
> *My notion was that you had been*
> *(Before she had this fit)*
> *An obstacle that came between*
> *Him, and ourselves, and it.*

*Don't let him know she
    liked them best,
For this must ever be
A secret, kept from all the
    rest,
Between yourself and
    me."*

"That's the most impor-
tant piece of evidence
we've heard yet," said the
King, rubbing his hands;
"so now let the jury——"

"If any one of them can
explain it," said Alice (she
had grown so large in the
last few minutes that she

wasn't a bit afraid of interrupting him), "I'll give him six-
pence. *I* don't believe there's an atom of meaning in it."

The jury all wrote down on their slates, "*She* doesn't
believe there's an atom of meaning in it," but none of them
attempted to explain the paper.

"If there's no meaning in it," said the King, "that saves

a world of trouble, you know, as we needn't try to find any. And yet I don't know," he went on, spreading out the verses on his knee, and looking at them with one eye; "I seem to see some meaning in them, after all. '—said I could not swim——' you can't swim, can you?" he added, turning to the Knave.

The Knave shook his head sadly. "Do I look like it?" he said. (Which he certainly did *not*, being made entirely of cardboard.)

"All right, so far," said the King, and he went on muttering over the verses to himself: "'We know it to be true——' that's the jury, of course—'I gave her one, they gave him two——' why, that must be what he did with the tarts, you know——"

"But it goes on, 'they all returned from him to you,'" said Alice.

"Why, there they are!" said the King triumphantly, pointing to the tarts on the table. "Nothing can be clearer than *that*. Then again—'before she had this fit——' you never had fits, my dear, I think?" he said to the Queen.

"Never!" said the Queen furiously, throwing an inkstand at the Lizard as she spoke. (The unfortunate little Bill had left off writing on his slate with one finger, as he found it made no mark; but he now hastily began again, using the ink, that was trickling down his face, as long as it lasted.)

"Then the words don't *fit* you," said the King, looking round the court with a smile. There was a dead silence.

"It's a pun!" the King added in an offended tone, and everybody laughed.

"Let the jury consider their verdict," the King said, for about the twentieth time that day.

"No, no!" said the Queen. "Sentence first—verdict afterwards."

"Stuff and nonsense!" said Alice loudly. "The idea of having the sentence first!"

"Hold your tongue!" said the Queen, turning purple.

"I won't!" said Alice.

"Off with her head!" the Queen shouted at the top of her voice. Nobody moved.

"Who cares for you?" said Alice (she had grown to her full size by this time). "You're nothing but a packs of cards!"

At this the whole pack rose up into the air, and came flying down upon her: she gave a little scream, half of fright and half of anger, and tried to beat them off, and found herself lying on the bank, with her head in the lap of her sister, who was gently brushing away some dead leaves that had fluttered down from the trees upon her face.

"Wake up, Alice dear!" said her sister. "Why, what a long sleep you've had!"

"Oh, I've had such a curious dream!" said Alice, and she told her sister, as well as she could remember them, all these strange Adventures of hers that you have just been reading about; and when she had finished, her sister kissed her, and said, "It *was* a curious dream, dear, certainly: but now run in to your tea; it's getting late." So Alice got up and ran off, thinking while she ran, as well she might, what a wonderful dream it had been.

But her sister sat still just as she left her, leaning her head on her hand, watching the setting sun, and thinking of little Alice and all her wonderful Adventures, till she too began dreaming after a fashion, and this was her dream:

First, she dreamed of little Alice herself, and once again the tiny hands were clasped upon her knee, and the bright eager eyes were looking up into hers—she could hear the very tones of her voice, and see that queer little toss of her head to keep back the wandering hair that *would* always get into her eyes—and still as she listened, or seemed to listen, the whole place around her became alive with the strange creatures of her little sister's dream.

The long grass rustled at her feet as the White Rabbit hurried by—the frightened Mouse splashed his way through the neighbouring pool—she could hear the rattle of the tea-cups as the March Hare and his friends shared their never-ending meal, and the shrill voice of the Queen ordering off her unfortunate guests to execution—once more the pig-baby was sneezing on the Duchess's knee, while plates and dishes crashed around it—once more the shriek of the Gryphon, the squeaking of the Lizard's slate-pencil, and the choking of the suppressed guinea-pigs, filled the air, mixed up with the distant sobs of the miserable Mock Turtle.

So she sat on with closed eyes, and half believed herself in Wonderland, though she knew she had but to open them again, and all would change to dull reality—the grass would be only rustling in the wind, and the pool rippling to the waving of the reeds—the rattling teacups would change to the tinkling sheep-bells, and the Queen's shrill cries to the voice of the shepherd boy—and the sneeze of the baby, the shriek of the Gryphon, and all the other queer noises, would change (she knew) to the confused clamour of the busy farm-yard—while the lowing of the cattle in the distance would take the place of the Mock Turtle's heavy sobs.

Lastly, she pictured to herself how this same little sister of hers would, in the after-time, be herself a grown woman; and how she would keep, through all her riper years, the simple and loving heart of her childhood: and how she would gather about her other little children, and make *their* eyes bright and eager with many a strange tale, perhaps even with the dream of Wonderland of long ago: and how she would feel with all their simple sorrows, and find a pleasure in all their simple joys, remembering her own child-life, and the happy summer days.

PHANTASMAGORIA

DYSCOMFYTURE

As one who strives a hill to climb,
   Who never climbed before:
Who finds it, in a little time,
Grow every moment less sublime,
   And votes the thing a bore:

Yet, having once begun to try,
   Dares not desert his quest,
But, climbing, ever keeps his eye
On one small hut against the sky
   Wherein he hopes to rest:

Who climbs till nerve and force are spent,
   With many a puff and pant:
Who still, as rises the ascent,
In language grows more violent,
   Although in breath more scant:

Who, climbing, gains at length the place
   That crowns the upward track:
And, entering with unsteady pace,
Receives a buffet in the face
   That lands him on his back:

And feels himself, like one in sleep,
   Glide swiftly down again,
A helpless weight, from steep to steep,
Till, with a headlong giddy sweep,
   He drops upon the plain—

So I, that had resolved to bring
   Conviction to a ghost,
And found it quite a different thing
From any human arguing,
   Yet dared not quit my post.

POETA FIT, NON NASCITUR

"How shall I be a poet?
   How shall I write in rhyme?
You told me once 'the very wish
   Partook of the sublime.'
Then tell me how! Don't put me off
   With your 'another time'!"

The old man smiled to see him,
   To hear his sudden sally;
He liked the lad to speak his mind
   Enthusiastically;
And thought, "There's no hum-drum in him,
   Nor any shilly-shally."

"And would you be a poet
   Before you've been to school?
Ah, well! I hardly thought you
   So absolute a fool.
First learn to be spasmodic—
   A very simple rule.

"For first you write a sentence,
   And then you chop it small;
Then mix the bits, and sort them out
   Just as they chance to fall:
The order of the phrases makes
   No difference at all.

"Then, if you'd be impressive,
   Remember what I say,
That abstract qualities begin
   With capitals alway:
The True, the Good, the Beautiful—
   Those are the things that pay!

"Next, when you are describing
   A shape, or sound, or tint,
Don't state the matter plainly,
   But put it in a hint;
And learn to look at all things
   With a sort of mental squint."

"For instance, if I wished, Sir,
   Of mutton-pies to tell,
Should I say, 'dreams of fleecy flocks
   Pent in a wheaten cell'?"
"Why, yes," the old man said: "that phrase
   Would answer very well.

"Then fourthly, there are epithets
   That suit with any word—
As well as Harvey's Reading Sauce
   With fish, or flesh, or bird—
Of these, 'wild,' 'lonely,' 'weary,' 'strange,'
   Are much to be preferred."

"And will it do, oh, will it do
   To take them in a lump—
As 'the wild man went his weary way
   To a strange and lonely pump'?"
"Nay, nay! You must not hastily
   To such conclusions jump.

"Such epithets, like pepper,
    Give zest to what you write;
And, if you strew them sparely,
    They whet the appetite;
But if you lay them on too thick,
    You spoil the matter quite!

"Last, as to the arrangement:
    Your reader, you should show him,
Must take what information he
    Can get, and look for no im-
mature disclosure of the drift
    And purpose of your poem.

"Therefore, to test his patience—
    How much he can endure—
Mention no places, names, or dates,
    And evermore be sure
Throughout the poem to be found
    Consistently obscure.

"First fix upon the limit
    To which it shall extend:
Then fill it up with 'Padding'
    (Beg some of any friend):
Your great SENSATION-STANZA
    You place towards the end."

"And what is a Sensation,
    Grandfather, tell me, pray?
I think I never heard the word
    So used before to-day:
Be kind enough to mention one
    'Exempli gratiâ.'"

And the old man, looking sadly
  Across the garden-lawn,
Where here and there a dew-drop
  Yet glittered in the dawn,
Said, "Go to the Adelphi,
  And see the 'Colleen Bawn.'

"The word is due to Boucicault—
  The theory is his,
Where Life becomes a Spasm,
  And History a Whiz:
If that is not Sensation,
  I don't know what it is.

"Now try your hand, ere Fancy
  Have lost its present glow——"
"And then," his grandson added,
  "We'll publish it, you know:
Green cloth—gold-lettered at the back—
  In duodecimo!"

Then proudly smiled that old man
  To see the eager lad
Rush madly for his pen and ink
  And for his blotting-pad—
But, when he thought of *publishing*,
  His face grew stern and sad.

A SEA DIRGE

There are certain things—as, a spider, a ghost,
  The income-tax, gout, an umbrella for three—
That I hate, but the thing that I hate the most
  Is a thing they call the Sea.

Pour some salt water over the floor—
  Ugly I'm sure you'll allow it to be:
Suppose it extended a mile or more;
  That's very like the Sea.

Beat a dog till it howls outright—
  Cruel, but all very well for a spree:
Suppose that he did so day and night;
  That would be like the Sea.

I had a vision of nursery-maids;
  Tens of thousands passed by me—
All leading children with wooden spades,
  And this was by the Sea.

Who invented those spades of wood?
  Who was it cut them out of the tree?
None, I think, but an idiot could—
  Or one that loved the Sea.

It is pleasant and dreamy, no doubt, to float
  With "thought as boundless, and souls as free":
But, suppose you are very unwell in the boat,
  How do you like the Sea?

There is an insect that people avoid
  (Whence is derived the verb "to flee").
Where have you been by it most annoyed?
  In lodgings by the Sea.

If you like your coffee with sand for dregs,
  A decided hint of salt in your tea,
And a fishy taste in the very eggs—
  By all means choose the Sea.

And if, with these dainties to drink and eat,
   You prefer not a vestige of grass or tree,
And a chronic state of wet in your feet,
   Then—I recommend the Sea.

For *I* have friends who dwell by the coast—
   Pleasant friends they are to me!
It is when I am with them I wonder most
   That anyone likes the Sea.

They take me a walk: though tired and stiff,
   To climb the heights I madly agree:
And, after a tumble or so from the cliff,
   They kindly suggest the Sea.

I try the rocks, and I think it cool
   That they laugh with such an excess of glee,
As I heavily slip into every pool
   That skirts the cold, cold Sea.

YE CARPETTE KNYGHTE

I have a horse—a ryghte goode horse—
   Ne doe I envye those
Who scoure ye playne yn headye course
   Tyll soddayne on theyre nose
They lyghte wyth unexpected force—
   Yt ys—a horse of clothes.

I have a saddel—"Say'st thou soe?
   Wyth styrruppes, Knyghte, to boote?"
I sayde not that—I answere "Noe"—
   Yt lacketh such, I woote:
Yt ys a mutton-saddel, loe!
   Parte of ye fleecye brute.

I have a bytte—a ryghte goode bytte—
   As shall bee seene yn tyme.
Ye jawe of horse yt wyll not fytte;
   Yts use ys more sublyme.
Fayre Syr, how deemest thou of yt?
   Yt ys—thys bytte of rhyme.

ATALANTA IN CAMDEN-TOWN

Ay, 'twas here, on this spot,
   In that summer of yore,
Atalanta did not
   Vote my presence a bore,
Nor reply to my tenderest talk, "She had heard all that
   nonsense before."

She'd the brooch I had bought
   And the necklace and sash on,
And her heart, as I thought,
   Was alive to my passion;
And she'd done up her hair in the style that the Empress
   had brought into fashion.

I had been to the play
   With my pearl of a Peri—
But, for all I could say,
   She declared she was weary,
That "the place was so crowded and hot, and she couldn't
   abide that Dundreary."

Then I thought, "Lucky boy!
   'Tis for *you* that she whimpers!"
And I noted with joy

Those sensational simpers:
And I said, "This is scrumptious!"—a phrase I had learned
from the Devonshire shrimpers.

And I vowed, " 'Twill be said
I'm a fortunate fellow,
When the breakfast is spread,
When the topers are mellow,
When the foam of the bride-cake is white, and the fierce
orange-blossoms are yellow!"

O that languishing yawn!
O those eloquent eyes!
I was drunk with the dawn
Of a splendid surmise—
I was stung by a look, I was slain by a tear, by a tempest
of sighs.

Then I whispered, "I see
The sweet secret thou keepest,
And the yearning for ME
That thou wistfully weepest!
And the question is 'License or Banns?' though undoubtedly
Banns are the cheapest."

"Be my Hero," said I,
"And let *me* be Leander!"
But I lost her reply—
Something ending with "gander"—
For the omnibus rattled so loud that no mortal could quite
understand her.

THE PROFESSOR'S SONG: THE LITTLE MAN
THAT HAD A LITTLE GUN

In stature the Manlet was dwarfish—
  No burly big Blunderbore he:
And he wearily gazed on the crawfish
  His Wifelet had dressed for his tea.
"Now reach me, sweet Atom, my gunlet,
  And hurl the old shoelet for luck!
Let me hie to the bank of the runlet,
    And shoot thee a Duck!"

She has reached him his minikin gunlet:
  She has hurled the old shoelet for luck:
She is busily baking a bunlet
  To welcome him home with his Duck.
On he speeds, never wasting a wordlet,
  Though thoughtlets cling, closely as wax,
To the spot where the beautiful birdlet
    So quietly quacks:

Where the Lobsterlet lurks, and the Crablet
  So slowly and sleepily crawls:
Where the Dolphin's at home, and the Dablet
  Pays long ceremonious calls:
Where the Grublet is sought by the Froglet:
  Where the Frog is pursued by the Duck:
Where the Ducklet is chased by the Doglet—
    So runs the world's luck!

He has loaded with bullet and powder:
　His footfall is noiseless as air:
But the Voices grow louder and louder,
　And bellow, and bluster, and blare.
They bristle before him and after,
　They flutter above and below,
Shrill shriekings of lubberly laughter,
　　Weird wailings of woe!

They echo without him, within him:
　They thrill through his whiskers and beard:
Like a teetotum seeming to spin him,
　With sneers never hitherto sneered.
"Avengement," they cry, "on our Foelet!
　Let the Manikin weep for our wrongs!
Let us drench him, from toplet to toelet,
　　With Nursery-Songs!

"He shall muse upon 'Hey! Diddle! Diddle!'
　On the Cow that surmounted the Moon:
He shall rave of the Cat and the Fiddle,
　And the Dish that eloped with the Spoon:
And his soul shall be sad for the Spider,
　When Miss Muffet was sipping her whey,
That so tenderly sat down beside her,
　　And scared her away!

"The music of Midsummer-madness
　Shall sting him with many a bite,
Till, in rapture of rollicking sadness,
　He shall groan with a gloomy delight:
He shall swathe him, like mists of the morning,
　In platitudes luscious and limp,
Such as deck, with a deathless adorning,
　　The Song of the Shrimp!

"When the Ducklet's dark doom is decided,
  We shall trundle him home in a trice:
And the banquet so plainly provided,
  Shall round into rosebuds and rice:
In a blaze of pragmatic invention
  He shall wrestle with Fate and shall reign:
But he has not a friend fit to mention,
    So hit him again!"

He has shot it, the delicate darling!
  And the voices have ceased from their strife:
Not a whisper of sneering or snarling,
  As he carries it home to his Wife:
Then, cheerily champing the bunlet
  His spouse was so skilful to bake,
He hies him once more to the runlet,
    To fetch her the Drake!

DOLL SONG

Matilda Jane, you never look
At any toy or picture-book:
I show you pretty things in vain—
You must be blind, Matilda Jane.

I ask you riddles, tell you tales,
But *all* our conversation fails:
You *never* answer me again—
I fear you're dumb, Matilda Jane:

Matilda, darling, when I call,
You never seem to hear at all:
I shout with all my might and main—
But you're *so* deaf, Matilda Jane!

Matilda Jane, you needn't mind:
For though you're deaf, and dumb, and blind,
There's *someone* loves you, it is plain—
And that is *me*, Matilda Jane!

KING FISHER SONG

King Fisher courted Lady Bird—
  Sing Beans, sing Bones, sing Butterflies!
"Find me my match," he said,
"With such a noble head—
With such a beard, as white as curd—
  With such expressive eyes!"

"Yet pins have heads," said Lady Bird—
Sing Prunes, sing Prawns, sing Primrose-Hill!
  "And, where you stick them in,
  They stay, and thus a pin
Is very much to be preferred
  To one that's never still!"

"Oysters have beards," said Lady Bird—
Sing Flies, sing Frogs, sing Fiddle-strings!
  "I love them, for I know
  They never chatter so:
They would not say a single word—
  Not if you crowned them Kings!"

"Needles have eyes," said Lady Bird—
Sing Cats, sing Corks, sing Cowslip-tea!
  "And they are sharp—just what
  Your Majesty is *not:*
So get you gone—'tis too absurd
  To come a-courting *me!*"

THERE BE THREE BADGERS ON A
MOSSY STONE

There be three Badgers on a mossy stone,
  Beside a dark and covered way:
Each dreams himself a monarch on his throne,
  And so they stay and stay—
Though their old Father languishes alone,
  They stay and stay and stay.

There be three Herrings loitering around,
  Longing to share that mossy seat:
Each Herring tries to sing what she has found
  That makes Life seem so sweet.
Thus, with a grating and uncertain sound,
  They bleat and bleat and bleat.

The Mother-Herring, on the salt sea wave,
  Sought vainly for her absent ones:
The Father-Badger, writing in a cave,
  Shrieked out, "Return, my sons!
You shall have buns," he shrieked, "if you'll behave!
  Yea, buns and buns and buns!"

"I fear," said she, "your sons have gone astray?
  My daughters left me while I slept."
"Yes'm," the Badger said: "It's as you say."
  "They should be better kept."
Thus the poor parents talked the time away,
  And wept and wept and wept.

THE GARDENER'S SONG

He thought he saw an Elephant
    That practised on a fife:
He looked again, and found it was
    A letter from his wife.
"At length I realise," he said,
    "The bitterness of life!"

He thought he saw a Buffalo
    Upon the chimney-piece:
He looked again, and found it was
    His Sister's Husband's Niece.
"Unless you leave this house," he said,
    "I'll send for the police!"

He thought he saw a Rattlesnake
    That questioned him in Greek:
He looked again, and found it was
    The Middle of Next Week.
"The one thing I regret," he said,
    "Is that it cannot speak!"

He thought he saw a Banker's Clerk
    Descending from the bus:
He looked again, and found it was
    A Hippopotamus:
"If this should stay to dine," he said,
    "There won't be much for us!"

He thought he saw a Kangaroo
   That worked a coffee-mill:
He looked again, and found it was
   A Vegetable-Pill.
"Were I to swallow this," he said,
   "I should be very ill!"

He thought he saw a Coach-and-Four
   That stood beside his bed:
He looked again, and found it was
   A Bear without a head.
"Poor thing," he said, "poor silly thing!
   It's waiting to be fed!"

He thought he saw an Albatross
   That fluttered round the lamp:
He looked again, and found it was
   A Penny-Postage-Stamp.
"You'd best be getting home," he said;
   "The nights are very damp!"

He thought he saw a Garden-Door
   That opened with a key:
He looked again, and found it was
   A Double Rule of Three:
"And all its mystery," he said,
   "Is clear as day to me!"

He thought he saw an Argument
   That proved he was the Pope:
He looked again, and found it was
   A Bar of Mottled Soap.
"A fact so dread," he faintly said,
   "Extinguishes all hope!"

THE PIG-TALE

Little Birds are drinking
  Warily and well,
    Hid in mossy cell:
Hid, I say, by waiters
Gorgeous in their gaiters—
    I've a Tale to tell.

Little Birds are feeding
  Justices with jam,
    Rich in frizzled ham;
Rich, I say, in oysters
Haunting shady cloisters—
    That is what I am.

Little Birds are teaching
  Tigresses to smile,
    Innocent of guile:
Smile, I say, not smirkle—
Mouth a semicircle,
    That's the proper style.

Little Birds are sleeping
  All among the pins,
    Where the loser wins:
Where, I say, he sneezes
When and how he pleases—
    So the Tale begins.

There was a Pig that sat alone
  Beside a ruined Pump:
By day and night he made his moan—
It would have stirred a heart of stone
To see him wring his hoofs and groan,
  Because he could not jump.

A certain Camel heard him shout—
    A Camel with a hump.
"Oh, is it Grief, or is it Gout?
What is this bellowing about?"
That Pig replied, with quivering snout,
    "Because I cannot jump!"

That Camel scanned him, dreamy-eyed.
    "Methinks you are too plump.
I never knew a Pig so wide—
That wobbled so from side to side—
Who could, however much he tried,
    Do such a thing as *jump!*

"Yet mark those trees, two miles away,
    All clustered in a clump:
If you could trot there twice a day,
Nor ever pause for rest or play,
In the far future—who can say?—
    You may be fit to jump."

That Camel passed and left him there
    Beside the ruined Pump.
Oh, horrid was that Pig's despair!
His shrieks of anguish filled the air,
He wrung his hoofs, he rent his hair,
    Because he could not jump.

There was a Frog that wandered by—
    A sleek and shining lump:
Inspected him with fishy eye,
And said, "O Pig, what makes you cry?"
And bitter was the Pig's reply,
    "Because I cannot jump!"

That Frog he grinned a grin of glee,
  And hit his chest a thump.
"O Pig," he said, "be ruled by me,
And you shall see what you shall see.
This minute for a trifling fee,
  I'll teach you how to jump!

"You may be faint from many a fall,
  And bruised by many a bump:
But if you persevere through all,
And practise first on something small,
Concluding with a ten-foot wall,
  You'll find that you *can* jump!"

That Pig looked up with joyful start:
  "O Frog, you *are* a trump!
Your words have healed my inward smart—
Come, name your fee, and do your part:
Bring comfort to a broken heart,
  By teaching me to jump!"

"My fee shall be a mutton-chop,
  My goal this ruined Pump.
Observe with what an airy flop
I plant myself upon the top!
Now bend your knees and take a hop,
  For that's the way to jump!"

Uprose that Pig, and rushed, full whack,
  Against the ruined Pump:
Rolled over like an empty sack,
And settled down upon his back,
While all his bones at once went "Crack!"
  It was a fatal jump.

Little Birds are writing
   Interesting books,
    To be read by cooks:
Read, I say, not roasted—
Letterpress, when toasted,
   Loses its good looks.

Little Birds are playing
   Bagpipes on the shore,
    Where the tourists snore:
"Thanks!" they cry; " 'Tis thrilling!
Take, oh, take this shilling!
   Let us have no more!"

Little Birds are bathing
   Crocodiles in cream,
    Like a happy dream:
Like, but not so lasting—
Crocodiles, when fasting,
   Are not all they seem!

That Camel passed, as Day grew dim
   Around the ruined Pump.
"O broken heart! O broken limb!
It needs," that Camel said to him,
"Something more fairy-like and slim,
   To execute a jump!"

That Pig lay still as any stone,
   And could not stir a stump:
Nor ever, if the truth were known,
Was he again observed to moan,
Nor ever wring his hoofs and groan,
   Because he could not jump.

That Frog made no remark, for he
  Was dismal as a dump:
He knew the consequence must be
That he would never get his fee—
And still he sits, in miserie,
  Upon that ruined Pump!

    Little Birds are choking
      Baronets with bun,
       Taught to fire a gun:
    Taught, I say, to splinter
    Salmon in the winter—
      Merely for the fun.

    Little Birds are hiding
      Crimes in carpet-bags,
       Blessed by happy stags:
    Blessed, I say, though beaten—
    Since our friends are eaten
      When the memory flags.

    Little Birds are tasting
      Gratitude and gold,
       Pale with sudden cold:
    Pale, I say, and wrinkled—
    When the bells have tinkled,
      And the Tale is told.

WHAT TOTTLES MEANT

"One thousand pounds per annum
Is not so bad a figure come!"
Cried Tottles. "And I tell you, flat,
A man may marry well on that!

To say 'the Husband needs the Wife'
Is *not* the way to represent it.
The crowning joy of Woman's life
Is Man!" said Tottles (and he meant it).

The blissful Honeymoon is past:
The Pair have settled down at last:
Mamma-in-law their home will share,
And make their Happiness her Care.
"Your income is an ample one:
Go it, my children!" (And they went it.)
"I *rayther* think this kind of fun
Won't last!" said Tottles (and he meant it).

They took a little country-box—
A box at Covent Garden also:
They lived a life of double knocks,
Acquaintances began to call so:
Their London house was much the same
(It took three hundred, clear, to rent it):
"Life is a very jolly game!"
Cried happy Tottles (and he meant it).

"Contented with a frugal lot"
(He always used that phrase at Gunter's),
He bought a handy little yacht—
A dozen serviceable hunters—
The fishing of a Highland Loch—
A sailing-boat to circumvent it—
"The sounding of that Gaelic 'och'
Beats me!" cried Tottles (and he meant it).

But oh, the worst of human ills
(Poor Tottles found) are "little bills!"
And, with no balance in the bank,
What wonder that his spirits sank?
Still, as the money flowed away,
He wondered how on earth she spent it.
"You cost me twenty pounds a day,
At least," cried Tottles (and he meant it).

She sighed. "Those Drawing-rooms, you know!
I really never thought about it:
Mamma declared we ought to go—
We should be Nobodies without it.
That diamond-circlet for my brow—
I quite believed that *she* had sent it,
Until the bill came in just now——"
"Viper!" cried Tottles (and he meant it).

Poor Mrs. T. could bear no more:
She fainted flat upon the floor;
Mamma-in-law, with anguish wild,
Seeks, all in vain, to rouse her child.
"Quick! Take this box of smelling-salts!
Don't scold her, James, or you'll repent it;
She's a *dear* girl, with all her faults——"
"She *is*," groaned Tottles (and he meant it).

"I was a donkey," Tottles cried,
"To choose your daughter for my bride!
'Twas *you* that bid us cut a dash!
'Tis *you* have brought us to this smash!
You don't suggest a single thing
That can in any way prevent it—
Then what's the use of arguing?
Shut up!" cried Tottles (and he meant it).

"And now the mischief's done, perhaps
You'll kindly go and pack your traps?
Since *two* (your daughter and your son)
Are Company but *three* are none.
A course of saving we'll begin:
When change is needed, *I'll* invent it:
Don't think to put your finger in
This pie!" cried Tottles (and he meant it).

See now this couple settled down
In quiet lodgings, out of town:
Submissively the tearful wife
Accepts a plain and humble life:
Yet begs one boon on bended knee:
"My ducky-darling, don't resent it!
Mamma might come for two or three——"
"Never!" yelled Tottles. And he meant it.

HIAWATHA'S PHOTOGRAPHING

(In an age of imitation, I can claim no special merit for
this slight attempt at doing what is known to be so easy. Any
fairly practised writer, with the slightest ear for rhythm,
could compose, for hours together, in the easy running metre
of "The Song of Hiawatha." Having, then, distinctly stated
that I challenge no attention in the following little poem to
its merely verbal jingle, I must beg the candid reader to con-
fine his criticism to its treatment of the subject.)

From his shoulder Hiawatha
Took the camera of rosewood,
Made of sliding, folding rosewood;
Neatly put it all together.

In its case it lay compactly,
Folded into nearly nothing;
But he opened out the hinges,
Pushed and pulled the joints and hinges,
Till it looked all squares and oblongs,
Like a complicated figure
In the Second Book of Euclid.

This he perched upon a tripod—
Crouched beneath its dusky cover—
Stretched his hand, enforcing silence—
Said, "Be motionless, I beg you!"
Mystic, awful was the process.

All the family in order
Sat before him for their pictures:
Each in turn, as he was taken,
Volunteered his own suggestions,
His ingenious suggestions.

First the Governor, the Father:
He suggested velvet curtains
Looped about a massy pillar;
And the corner of a table,
Of a rosewood dining-table.
He would hold a scroll of something,
Hold it firmly in his left-hand;
He would keep his right-hand buried
(Like Napoleon) in his waistcoat;
He would contemplate the distance
With a look of pensive meaning,
As of ducks that die in tempests.

Grand, heroic was the notion:
Yet the picture failed entirely:
Failed, because he moved a little,
Moved, because he couldn't help it.

Next his better half took courage;
She would have her picture taken.

She came dressed beyond description,
Dressed in jewels and in satin
Far too gorgeous for an empress.
Gracefully she sat down sideways,
With a simper scarcely human,
Holding in her hand a bouquet
Rather larger than a cabbage.
All the while that she was sitting,
Still the lady chattered, chattered,
Like a monkey in the forest.
"Am I sitting still?" she asked him.
"Is my face enough in profile?
Shall I hold the bouquet higher?
Will it come into the picture?"
And the picture failed completely.

Next the Son, the Stunning-Cantab:
He suggested curves of beauty,
Curves pervading all his figure,
Which the eye might follow onward,
Till they centred in the breast-pin,
Centred in the golden breast-pin.
He had learnt it all from Ruskin
(Author of "The Stones of Venice,"
"Seven Lamps of Architecture,"
"Modern Painters," and some others);
And perhaps he had not fully
Understood his author's meaning;
But, whatever was the reason,
All was fruitless, as the picture
Ended in an utter failure.

Next to him the eldest daughter:
She suggested very little,
Only asked if he would take her
With her look of "passive beauty."

Her idea of passive beauty
Was a squinting of the left-eye,
Was a drooping of the right-eye,
Was a smile that went up sideways
To the corner of the nostrils.
   Hiawatha, when she asked him,
Took no notice of the question,
Looked as if he hadn't heard it,
But, when pointedly appealed to,
Smiled in his peculiar manner,
Coughed and said it "didn't matter,"
Bit his lip and changed the subject.
   Nor in this was he mistaken,
As the picture failed completely.
   So in turn the other sisters.
Last, the youngest son was taken:
Very rough and thick his hair was,
Very round and red his face was,
Very dusty was his jacket,
Very fidgety his manner.
And his overbearing sisters
Called him names he disapproved of:
Called him Johnny, "Daddy's Darling,"
Called him Jacky, "Scrubby School-boy."
And so awful was the picture,
In comparison the others
Seemed, to one's bewildered fancy,
To have partially succeeded.
   Finally my Hiawatha
Tumbled all the tribe together,
("Grouped" is not the right expression),
And, as happy chance would have it,
Did at last obtain a picture
Where the faces all succeeded:

Each came out a perfect likeness.
    Then they joined and all abused it,
Unrestrainedly abused it,
As the worst and ugliest picture
They could possibly have dreamed of;
"Giving one such strange expressions—
Sullen, stupid, pert expressions.
Really anyone would take us
(Anyone that did not know us)
For the most unpleasant people!"
(Hiawatha seemed to think so,
Seemed to think it not unlikely.)
All together rang their voices,
Angry, loud, discordant voices,
As of dogs that howl in concert,
As of cats that wail in chorus.
    But my Hiawatha's patience,
His politeness and his patience,
Unaccountably had vanished,
And he left that happy party.
Neither did he leave them slowly,
With the calm deliberation
Of a photographic artist:
But he left them in a hurry,
Left them in a mighty hurry,
Stating in emphatic language
What he'd be before he'd stand it.
Hurriedly he packed his boxes:
Hurriedly the porter trundled
On a barrow all his boxes:
Hurriedly he took his ticket,
Hurriedly the train received him:
Thus departed Hiawatha.

THE THREE VOICES

The First Voice

He trilled a carol fresh and free,
He laughed aloud for very glee:
There came a breeze from off the sea:

It passed athwart the glooming flat—
It fanned his forehead as he sat—
It lightly bore away his hat,

All to the feet of one who stood
Like maid enchanted in a wood,
Frowning as darkly as she could.

With huge umbrella, lank and brown,
Unerringly she pinned it down,
Right through the centre of the crown.

Then, with an aspect cold and grim,
Regardless of its battered rim,
She took it up and gave it him.

Awhile like one in dreams he stood,
Then faltered forth his gratitude
In words just short of being rude:

For it had lost its shape and shine,
And it had cost him four-and-nine,
And he was going out to dine.

"To dine!" she sneered in acid tone,
"To bend thy being to a bone
Clothed in a radiance not its own!"

The tear-drop trickled to his chin:
There was a meaning in her grin
That made him feel on fire within.

"Term it not 'radiance,'" said he:
" 'Tis solid nutriment to me.
Dinner is Dinner: Tea is Tea."

And she: "Yea so? Yet wherefore cease?
Let thy scant knowledge find increase.
Say, 'Men are Men, and Geese are Geese.'"

He moaned: he knew not what to say.
The thought, "That I could get away!"
Strove with the thought, "But I must stay!"

"To dine!" she shrieked in dragon-wrath.
"To swallow wines all foam and froth!
To simper at a table-cloth!

"Say, can thy noble spirit stoop
To join the gormandising troop
Who find a solace in the soup?

"Canst thou desire or pie or puff?
Thy well-bred manners were enough,
Without such gross material stuff."

"Yet well-bred men," he faintly said,
"Are not unwilling to be fed:
Nor are they well without the bread."

Her visage scorched him ere she spoke:
"There are," she said, "a kind of folk
Who have no horror of a joke.

"Such wretches live: they take their share
Of common earth and common air:
We come across them here and there:

"We grant them—there is no escape—
A sort of semi-human shape
Suggestive of the man-like Ape."

"In all such theories," said he,
"One fixed exception there must be.
That is, the Present Company."

Baffled, she gave a wolfish bark:
He, aiming blindly in the dark,
With random shaft had pierced the mark.

She felt that her defeat was plain,
Yet madly strove with might and main
To get the upper hand again.

Fixing her eyes upon the beach,
As though unconscious of his speech,
She said, "Each gives to more than each."

He could not answer yea or nay:
He faltered, "Gifts may pass away,"
Yet knew not what he meant to say.

"If that be so," she straight replied,
"Each heart with each doth coincide.
What boots it? For the world is wide."

"The world is but a Thought," said he:
"The vast unfathomable sea
Is but a Notion—unto me."

And darkly fell her answer dread
Upon his unresisting head,
Like half a hundredweight of lead:

"The Good and Great must ever shun
That reckless and abandoned one
Who stoops to perpetrate a pun.

"The man that smokes—that reads the *Times*—
That goes to Christmas Pantomimes—
Is capable of *any* crimes!"

He felt it was his turn to speak,
And, with a shamed and crimson cheek,
Moaned, "This is harder than bezique!"

But when she asked him, "Wherefore so?"
He felt his very whiskers glow,
And frankly owned, "I do not know."

While, like broad waves of golden grain,
Or sunlit hues on cloistered pane,
His colour came and went again.

Pitying his obvious distress,
Yet with a tinge of bitterness,
She said, "The More exceeds the Less."

"A truth of such undoubted weight,"
He urged, "and so extreme in date,
It were superfluous to state."

Roused into sudden passion, she
In tone of cold malignity:
"To others, yea: but not to thee."

But when she saw him quail and quake,
And when he urged, "For pity's sake!"
Once more in gentle tone she spake.

"Thought in the mind doth still abide:
That is by Intellect supplied,
And within that Idea doth hide:

"And he that yearns the truth to know,
Still further inwardly may go,
And find Idea from Notion flow:

"And thus the chain, that sages sought,
Is to a glorious circle wrought,
For Notion hath its source in Thought."

So passed they on with even pace:
Yet gradually one might trace
A shadow growing on his face.

The Second Voice

They walked beside the wave-worn beach;
Her tongue was very apt to teach,
And now and then he did beseech

She would abate her dulcet tone,
Because the talk was all her own,
And he was dull as any drone.

She urged, "No cheese is made of chalk":
And ceaseless flowed her dreary talk,
Tuned to the footfall of a walk.

Her voice was very full and rich,
And, when at length she asked him, "Which?"
It mounted to its highest pitch.

He a bewildered answer gave,
Drowned in the sullen moaning wave,
Lost in the echoes of the cave.

He answered her he knew not what:
Like shaft from bow at random shot,
He spoke, but she regarded not.

She waited not for his reply,
But with a downward leaden eye
Went on as if he were not by:

Sound argument and grave defence,
Strange questions raised on "Why?" and "Whence?"
And wildly tangled evidence.

When he, with racked and whirling brain,
Feebly implored her to explain,
She simply said it all again.

Wrenched with an agony intense,
He spoke, neglecting Sound and Sense,
And careless of all consequence:

"Mind—I believe—is Essence—Ent—
Abstract—that is—an Accident—
Which we—that is to say—I meant——"

When with quick breath and cheeks all flushed,
At length his speech was somewhat hushed,
She looked at him and he was crushed.

It needed not her calm reply:
She fixed him with a stony eye,
And he could neither fight nor fly

While she dissected, word by word,
His speech, half guessed at and half heard,
As might a cat a little bird.

Then, having wholly overthrown
His views, and stripped them to the bone,
Proceeded to unfold her own.

"Shall Man be Man? And shall he miss
 Of other thoughts no thought but this,
Harmonious dews of sober bliss?

"What boots it? Shall his fevered eye
Through towering nothingness descry
The grisly phantom hurry by?

"And hear dumb shrieks that fill the air;
See mouths that gape, and eyes that stare
And redden in the dusky glare?

"The meadows breathing amber light,
The darkness toppling from the height,
The feathery train of granite Night?

"Shall he, grown grey among his peers,
Through the thick curtain of his tears
Catch glimpses of his earlier years,

"And hear the sounds he knew of yore,
Old shufflings on the sanded floor,
Old knuckles tapping at the door?

"Yet still before him, as he flies,
One pallid form shall ever rise,
And, bodying forth in glassy eyes

"The vision of a vanished good,
Low peering through the tangled wood,
Shall freeze the current of his blood."

Still from each fact, with skill uncouth
And savage rapture, like a tooth
She wrenched some slow reluctant truth;

Till, like a silent water-mill,
When summer suns have dried the rill,
She reached a full stop, and was still.

Dead calm succeeded to the fuss,
As when the loaded omnibus
Has reached the railway terminus:

When, for the tumult of the street,
Is heard the engine's stifled beat,
The velvet tread of porters' feet.

With glance that ever sought the ground,
She moved her lips without a sound,
And every now and then she frowned.

He gazed upon the sleeping sea,
And joyed in its tranquillity,
And in that silence dread, but she

To muse a little space did seem,
Then, like the echo of a dream,
Harped back upon her threadbare theme.

Still an attentive ear he lent
But could not fathom what she meant:
She was not deep nor eloquent.

He marked the ripple on the sand:
The even swaying of her hand
Was all that he could understand.

He saw in dreams a drawing-room,
Where thirteen wretches sat in gloom,
Waiting—he thought he knew for whom:

He saw them drooping here and there,
Each feebly huddled on a chair,
In attitudes of blank despair:

Oysters were not more mute than they,
For all their brains were pumped away,
And they had nothing more to say—

Save one, who groaned, "Three hours are gone!"
Who shrieked, "We'll wait no longer, John!
Tell them to set the dinner on!"

The vision passed: the ghosts were fled:
He saw once more that woman dread:
He heard once more the words she said.

He left her, and he turned aside:
He sat and watched the coming tide
Across the shores so newly dried.

He wondered at the waters clear,
The breeze that whispered in his ear,
The billows heaving far and near,

And why he had so long preferred
To hang upon her every word:
"In truth," he said, "it was absurd."

The Third Voice

Not long this transport held its place:
Within a little moment's space
Quick tears were raining down his face.

His heart stood still, aghast with fear;
A wordless voice, nor far nor near,
He seemed to hear and not to hear.

"Tears kindle not the doubtful spark.
If so, why not? Of this remark
The bearings are profoundly dark."

"Her speech," he said, "hath caused this pain.
Easier I count it to explain
The jargon of the howling main,

"Or, stretched beside some babbling brook,
To con, with inexpressive look,
An unintelligible book."

Low spake the voice within his head,
In words imagined more than said,
Soundless as ghost's intended tread:

"If thou art duller than before,
Why quitted'st thou the voice of lore?
Why not endure, expecting more?"

"Rather than that," he groaned aghast,
"I'd writhe in depths of caverns vast,
Some loathly vampire's rich repast."

" 'Twere hard," it answered, "themes immense
To coop within the narrow fence
That rings *thy* scant intelligence."

"Not so," he urged, "nor once alone:
But there was something in her tone
That chilled me to the very bone.

"Her style was anything but clear,
And most unpleasantly severe;
Her epithets were very queer.

"And yet, so grand were her replies,
I could not choose but deem her wise;
I did not dare to criticise;

"Nor did I leave her, till she went
So deep in tangled argument
That all my powers of thought were spent."

A little whisper inly slid,
"Yet truth is truth: you know you did";
A little wink beneath the lid.

And, sickened with excess of dread,
Prone to the dust he bent his head,
And lay like one three-quarters dead.

The whisper left him—like a breeze
Lost in the depths of leafy trees—
Left him by no means at his ease.

Once more he weltered in despair,
With hands, through denser-matted hair,
More tightly clenched than then they were.

When, bathed in Dawn of living red,
Majestic frowned the mountain-head,
"Tell me my fault," was all he said.

When, at high Noon, the blazing sky
Scorched in his head each haggard eye,
Then keenest rose his weary cry.

And when at Eve the unpitying sun
Smiled grimly on the solemn fun,
"Alack," he sighed, "what *have* I done?"

But saddest, darkest was the sight,
When the cold grasp of leaden Night
Dashed him to earth and held him tight.

Tortured, unaided, and alone,
Thunders were silence to his groan,
Bagpipes sweet music to its tone:

"What? Ever thus, in dismal round,
Shall Pain and Mystery profound
Pursue me like a sleepless hound,

"With crimson-dashed and eager jaws,
Me, still in ignorance of the cause,
Unknowing what I broke of laws?"

The whisper to his ear did seem
Like echoed flow of silent stream,
Or shadow of forgotten dream;

The whisper trembling in the wind,
"Her fate with thine was intertwined,"
So spake it in his inner mind:

"Each orbed on each a baleful star:
Each proved the other's blight and bar:
Each unto each was best, most far:

"Yea, each to each was worse than foe:
Thou, a scared dullard, gibbering low,
AND SHE, AN AVALANCHE OF WOE!"

TEMA CON VARIAZIONI

Why is it that Poetry has never yet been subjected to that
process of Dilution which has proved so advantageous to her
sister-art, Music? The Diluter gives us first a few notes of
some well-known Air, then a dozen bars of his own, then a
few more notes of the Air, and so on alternately: thus saving the listener, if not from all risk of recognising the melody
at all, at least from the too-exciting transports which it might
produce in a more concentrated form. The process is termed
"setting" by Composers, and anyone that has ever experi-
enced the emotion of being unexpectedly set down in a heap
of mortar, will recognise the truthfulness of this happy
phrase.

For truly, just as the supreme Epicure lingers lovingly
over a morsel of supreme Venison—whose very fibre seems to
murmur "Excelsior!"—yet swallows, ere returning to the

toothsome dainty, great mouthfuls of oatmeal-porridge and winkles: and just as the perfect Connoisseur in Claret permits himself but one delicate sip, and then tosses off a pint or more of boarding-school beer: so also—

I never loved a dear Gazelle—
Nor anything that cost me much:
High prices profit those who sell,
But why should I be fond of such?

To glad me with his soft black eye,
My son comes trotting home from school;
He's had a fight, but can't tell why—
He always was a little fool!

But, when he came to know me well,
He kicked me out, her testy Sire:
And when I stained my hair, that Belle
Might note the change, and thus admire

And love me, it was sure to dye
A muddy green, or staring blue:
Whilst one might trace, with half an eye,
The still-triumphant carrot through.

THE LANG COORTIN'

The ladye she stood at her lattice high,
    Wi' her doggie at her feet;
Through the lattice she can spy
    The passers in the street.

"There's one that standeth at the door,
    And tirleth at the pin:
Now speak and say, my popinjay,
    If I sall let him in."

Then up and spake the popinjay
    That flew abune her head:
"Gae let him in that tirls the pin:
    He cometh thee to wed."

O when he cam' the parlour in,
    A woeful man was he!
"And dinna ye ken your lover agen,
    Sae well that loveth thee?"

"And how wad I ken ye loved me, Sir?
    That have been sae lang away?
And how wad I ken ye loved me, Sir?
    Ye never telled me sae."

Said—"Ladye dear," and the salt, salt tear
    Cam' rinnin' doon his cheek,
"I have sent thee tokens of my love
    This many and many a week.

"O didna ye get the rings, Ladye,
    The rings o' the gowd sae fine?
I wot that I have sent to thee
    Four score, four score and nine."

"They cam' to me," said that fair ladye.
    "Wow, they were flimsie things!"
Said—"that chain o' gowd, my doggie to howd,
    It is made of thae selfsame rings."

"And didna ye get the locks, the locks,
　The locks o' my ain black hair,
Whilk I sent by post, whilk I sent by box,
　Whilk I sent by the carrier?"

"They cam' to me," said that fair ladye;
　"And I prithee send nae mair!"
Said—"that cushion sae red, for my doggie's head,
　It is stuffed wi' thae locks o' hair."

"And didna ye get the letter, Ladye,
　Tied wi' a silken string,
Whilk I sent to thee frae the far countrie,
　A message of love to bring?"

"It cam' to me frae the far countrie
　Wi' its silken strings and a';
But it wasna prepaid," said that high-born maid,
　"Sae I gar'd them tak' it awa'."

"O ever alack that ye sent it back,
　It was written sae clerkly and well!
Now the message it brought, and the boon that it sought,
　I must even say it mysel'."

Then up and spake the popinjay,
　Sae wisely counselled he:
"Now say it in the proper way:
　Gae doon upon thy knee!"

The lover he turned baith red and pale,
　Went doon upon his knee:
"O Ladye, hear the waesome tale
　That must be told to thee!

"For five lang years, and five lang years,
  I coorted thee by looks;
By nods and winks, by smiles and tears,
  As I had read in books.

"For ten lang years, O weary hours!
  I coorted thee by signs;
By sending game, by sending flowers,
  By sending Valentines.

"For five lang years, and five lang years,
  I have dwelt in the far countrie,
Till that thy mind should be inclined
  Mair tenderly to me.

"Now thirty years are gane and past,
  I am come frae a foreign land:
I am come to tell thee my love at last—
  O Ladye, gie me thy hand!"

The ladye she turned not pale nor red,
  But she smiled a pitiful smile:
"Sic' a coortin' as yours, my man," she said,
  "Takes a lang and a weary while!"

And out and laughed the popinjay,
  A laugh of bitter scorn:
"A coortin' done in sic' a way,
  It ought not to be borne!"

Wi' that the doggie barked aloud,
  And up and doon he ran,
And tugged and strained his chain o' gowd,
  All for to bite the man.

"O hush thee, gentle popinjay!
O hush thee, doggie dear!
There is a word I fain wad say,
It needeth he should hear!"

Aye louder screamed that ladye fair
To drown her doggie's bark:
Ever the lover shouted mair
To make the ladye hark:

Shrill and more shrill the popinjay
Upraised his angry squall:
I trow the doggie's voice that day
Was louder than them all!

The serving-men and serving-maids
Sat by the kitchen fire:
They heard sic' a din the parlour within
As made them much admire.

Out spake the boy in buttons
(I ween he wasna thin),
"Now wha will tae the parlour gae,
And stay this deadlie din?"

And they have taen a kerchief,
Casted their kevils in,
For wha wad tae the parlour gae,
And stay that deadlie din.

When on that boy the kevil fell
To stay the fearsome noise,
"Get in," they cried, "whate'er betide,
Thou prince of button-boys!"

Syne, he has taen a supple cane
  To swinge that dog sae fat:
The doggie yowled, the doggie howled
  The louder aye for that.

Syne, he has taen a mutton-bane—
  The doggie ceased his noise,
And followed doon the kitchen stair
  That prince of button-boys!

Then sadly spake that ladye fair,
  Wi' a frown upon her brow:
"O dearer to me is my sma' doggie
  Than a dozen sic' as thou!

"Nae use, nae use for sighs and tears:
  Nae use at all to fret:
Sin' ye've bided sae well for thirty years,
  Ye may bide a wee langer yet!"

Sadly, sadly he crossed the floor
  And tirlèd at the pin:
Sadly went he through the door
  Where sadly he cam' in.

"O gin I had a popinjay
  To fly abune my head,
To tell me what I ought to say,
  I had by this been wed.

"O gin I find anither ladye,"
  He said wi' sighs and tears,
"I wot my coortin' sall not be
  Anither thirty years:

"For gin I find a ladye gay,
　　Exactly to my taste,
I'll pop the question, aye or nay,
　　In twenty years at maist."

THROUGH THE LOOKING-GLASS

AND WHAT ALICE FOUND THERE

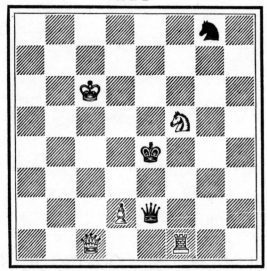

White Pawn (Alice) to play, and win in eleven moves.

1. Alice meets R. Q.	1. R. Q. to K. R.'s 4th
2. Alice through Q.'s 3rd (*by railway*) to Q.'s 4th (*Tweedledum and Tweedledee*)	2. W. Q. to Q. B.'s 4th (*after shawl*)
3. Alice meets W. Q. (*with shawl*)	3. W. Q. to Q. B.'s 5th (*becomes sheep*)
4. Alice to Q.'s 5th (*shop, river, shop*)	4. W. Q. to K. B.'s 8th (*leaves egg on shelf*)
5. Alice to Q.'s 6th (*Humpty Dumpty*)	5. W. Q. to Q. B.'s 8th (*flying from R. Kt.*)
6. Alice to Q.'s 7th (*forest*)	6. R. Kt. to K.'s 2nd (ch.)
7. W. Kt. takes R. Kt.	7. W. Kt. to K. B.'s 5th
8. Alice to Q.'s 8th (*coronation*)	8. R. Q. to K.'s sq. (*examination*)
9. Alice becomes Queen	9. Queens castle
10. Alice castles (*feast*)	10. W. Q. to Q. R. 6th (*soup*)
11. Alice takes R. Q. & wins	

PREFACE

As THE chess-problem, given on the opposite page, has puzzled some of my readers, it may be well to explain that it is correctly worked out, so far as the *moves* are concerned. The *alternation* of Red and White is perhaps not so strictly observed as it might be, and the "castling" of the three Queens is merely a way of saying that they entered the palace: but the "check" of the White King at move 6, the capture of the Red Knight at move 7, and the final "checkmate" of the Red King, will be found, by anyone who will take the trouble to set the pieces and play the moves as directed, to be strictly in accordance with the laws of the game.

The new words, in the poem "Jabberwocky," have given rise to some differences of opinion as to their pronunciation: so it may be well to give instructions on *that* point also. Pronounce "slithy" as if it were the two words "sly, the": make the "g" *hard* in "gyre" and "gimble": and pronounce "rath" to rhyme with "bath."

Child of the pure unclouded brow
    And dreaming eyes of wonder!
Though time be fleet, and I and thou
    Are half a life asunder,
Thy loving smile will surely hail
The love-gift of a fairy-tale.

I have not seen thy sunny face,
    Nor heard thy silver laughter;
No thought of me shall find a place
    In thy young life's hereafter—
Enough that now thou wilt not fail
To listen to my fairy-tale.

A tale begun in other days,
    When summer suns were glowing—
A simple chime, that served to time
    The rhythm of our rowing—
Whose echoes live in memory yet,
Though envious years would say "forget."

Come, hearken then, ere voice of dread,
    With bitter tidings laden,
Shall summon to unwelcome bed
    A melancholy maiden!
We are but older children, dear,
Who fret to find our bedtime near.

Without, the frost, the blinding snow,
    The storm-wind's moody madness—

Within, the firelight's ruddy glow
  And childhood's nest of gladness.
The magic words shall hold thee fast:
Thou shalt not heed the raving blast.

And though the shadow of a sigh
  May tremble through the story,
For "happy summer days" gone by,
  And vanish'd summer glory—
It shall not touch with breath of bale
The pleasance of our fairy-tale.

CHAPTER I

LOOKING-GLASS HOUSE

ONE thing was certain, that the *white* kitten had had nothing to do with it:—it was the black kitten's fault entirely. For the white kitten had been having its face washed by the old cat for the last quarter of an hour (and bearing it pretty well, considering); so you see that it *couldn't* have had any hand in the mischief.

The way Dinah washed her children's faces was this: first she held the poor thing down by its ear with one paw, and then with the other paw she rubbed its face all over, the wrong way, beginning at the nose: and just now, as I said, she was hard at work on the white kitten, which was lying quite still and trying to purr—no doubt feeling that it was all meant for its good.

But the black kitten had been finished with earlier in the afternoon, and so, while Alice was sitting curled up in a corner of the great arm-chair, half talking to herself and half asleep, the kitten had been having a grand game of romps with the ball of worsted Alice had been trying to wind up, and had been rolling it up and down till it had all come undone again; and there it was, spread over the hearth-rug, all knots and tangles, with the kitten running after its own tail in the middle.

"Oh, you wicked, wicked little thing!" cried Alice, catching up the kitten, and giving it a little kiss to make it understand that it was in disgrace. "Really, Dinah ought to have taught you better manners! You *ought*, Dinah, you know you ought!" she added, looking reproachfully at the old cat, and speaking in as cross a voice as she could manage— and then she scrambled back into the arm-chair, taking the kitten and worsted with her, and began winding up the ball again. But she didn't get on very fast, as she was talking all the time, sometimes to the kitten, and sometimes to herself. Kitty sat very demurely on her knee, pretending to watch the progress of the winding, and now and then putting out one paw and gently touching the ball, as if it would be glad to help if it might.

"Do you know what to-morrow is, Kitty?" Alice began. "You'd have guessed if you'd been up in the window with me—only Dinah was making you tidy, so you couldn't. I was watching the boys getting in sticks for the bonfire—and it wants plenty of sticks, Kitty! Only it got so cold, and it snowed so, they had to leave off. Never mind, Kitty, we'll go and see the bonfire to-morrow." Here Alice wound two or three turns of the worsted round the kitten's neck, just to see how it would look: this led to a scramble, in which the ball rolled down upon the floor, and yards and yards of it got unwound again.

"Do you know, I was so angry, Kitty," Alice went on, as soon as they were comfortably settled again, "when I saw all the mischief you had been doing, I was very nearly opening the window, and putting you out into the snow! And you'd have deserved it, you little mischievous darling! What have you got to say for yourself? Now don't interrupt me!" she went on, holding up one finger. "I'm going to tell you all

your faults. Number one: you squeaked twice while Dinah was washing your face this morning. Now you can't deny it, Kitty, for I heard you! What's that you say?" (pretending that the kitten was speaking). "Her paw went into your eye? Well, that's *your* fault, for keeping your eyes open—if you'd shut them tight up, it wouldn't have happened. Now don't make any more excuses, but listen! Number two: you pulled Snowdrop away by the tail just as I had put down the saucer of milk before her! What, you were thirsty, were you? How do you know she wasn't thirsty too? Now for number three: you unwound every bit of the worsted while I wasn't looking!

"That's three faults, Kitty, and you've not been punished for any of them yet. You know I'm saving up all your punishments for Wednesday week.—Suppose they had saved up all *my* punishments!" she went on, talking more to herself than the kitten. "What *would* they do at the end of a year? I should be sent off to prison, I suppose, when the day came. Or—let me see—suppose each punishment was to be going without a dinner: then, when the miserable day came, I should have to go without fifty dinners at once! Well, I shouldn't mind *that* much! I'd far rather go without them than eat them!

"Do you hear the snow against the window panes, Kitty? How nice and soft it sounds! Just as if someone was kissing the window all over outside. I wonder if the snow *loves* the trees and fields, that it kisses them so gently? And then it covers them up snug, you know, with a white quilt; and perhaps it says, 'Go to sleep, darlings, till the summer comes again.' And when they wake up in the summer, Kitty, they dress themselves all in green, and dance about—whenever the wind blows—oh, that's very pretty!" cried Alice, dropping the ball of worsted to clap her hands. "And I do so *wish* it was true! I'm sure the woods look sleepy in the autumn, when the leaves are getting brown.

"Kitty, can you play chess? Now, don't smile, my dear, I'm asking it seriously. Because, when we were playing just now, you watched just as if you understood it: and when I said 'Check!' you purred! Well, it *was* a nice check, Kitty, and really I might have won, if it hadn't been for that nasty Knight, that came wriggling down among my pieces. Kitty, dear, let's pretend——" And here I wish I could tell you half the things Alice used to say, beginning with her favourite phrase, "Let's pretend." She had had quite a long argument with her sister only the day before—all because Alice had begun with, "Let's pretend we're kings and queens"; and her sister, who liked being very exact, had argued that they couldn't, because there were only two of them, and Alice had been reduced at last to say, "Well, *you* can be one of them then, and *I'll* be all the rest." And once she had really frightened her old nurse by shouting suddenly in her ear, "Nurse! Do let's pretend that I'm a hungry hyæna, and you're a bone!"

But this is taking us away from Alice's speech to the kitten. "Let's pretend that you're the Red Queen, Kitty! Do you know, I think, if you sat up and folded your arms, you'd look exactly like her. Now do try, there's a dear!" And Alice got the Red Queen off the table, and set it up before the kitten as a model for it to imitate: however, the thing didn't succeed, principally, Alice said, because the kitten wouldn't fold its arms properly. So, to punish it, she held it up to the Looking-glass, that it might see how sulky it was—"and if you're not good directly," she added, "I'll put you through into Looking-glass House. How would you like *that?*

"Now, if you'll only attend, Kitty, and not talk so much, I'll tell you all my ideas about Looking-glass House. First, there's the room you can see through the glass—that's just the same as our drawing-room, only the things go the other way. I can see all of it when I get upon a chair—all but the bit just behind the fire-place. Oh! I do so wish I could see *that* bit! I want so much to know whether they've a fire in the winter: you never *can* tell, you know, unless our fire smokes, and then smoke comes up in that room too—but that may be only pretence, just to make it look as if they had a fire. Well then, the books are something like our books, only the words go the wrong way; I know that, because I've held

up one of our books to the glass, and then they hold up one in the other room.

"How would you like to live in Looking-glass House, Kitty? I wonder if they'd give you milk, there? Perhaps Looking-glass milk isn't good to drink.—But oh, Kitty! now

we come to the passage. You can just see a little *peep* of the passage in Looking-glass House, if you leave the door of our drawing-room wide open: and it's very like our passage as far as you can see, only you know it may be quite different on beyond. Oh, Kitty! how nice it would be if we could only get through into Looking-glass House! I'm sure it's got, oh! such beautiful things in it! Let's pretend there's a way of getting through into it somehow, Kitty. Let's pretend the glass has got soft like gauze, so that we can get through. Why, it's turning into a sort of mist now, I declare! It'll be easy enough to get through——" She was up on the chimney-piece while she said this, though she hardly knew how she had got there. And certainly the glass *was* beginning to melt away, just like a bright silvery mist.

In another moment Alice was through the glass, and had jumped lightly down into the Looking-glass room. The very first thing she did was to look whether there was a fire in the fire-place, and she was quite pleased to find that there was a real one, and blazing away as brightly as the one she had left behind. "So I shall be as warm here as I was in the old room," thought Alice: "warmer, in fact, because there'll be no one here to scold me away from the fire. Oh, what fun it'll be, when they see me through the glass in here, and can't get at me!"

Then she began looking about, and noticed that what could be seen from the old room was quite common and uninterest-ing, but that all the rest was as different as possible. For instance, the pictures on the wall next the fire seemed to be all alive, and the very clock on the chimney-piece (you know you can only see the back of it in the Looking-glass) had got the face of a little old man, and grinned at her.

"They don't keep this room so tidy as the other," Alice thought to herself, as she noticed several of the chessmen down in the hearth among the cinders: but in another mo-ment, with a little "Oh!" of surprise, she was down on her hands and knees watching them. The chessmen were walking about, two and two!

"Here are the Red King and the Red Queen," Alice said (in a whisper, for fear of frightening them), "and there are the White King and the White Queen sitting on the edge of the shovel—and here are two Castles walking arm in arm—I don't think they can hear me," she went on, as she put her head closer down, "and I'm nearly sure they can't see me. I feel as if I were invisible——"

Here something began squeaking on the table, and made Alice turn her head just in time to see one of the White Pawns roll over and begin kicking: she watched it with great curiosity to see what would happen next.

"It is the voice of my child!" the White Queen cried out, as she rushed past the King, so violently that she knocked him over among the cinders. "My precious Lily! My imperial kitten!" and she began scrambling wildly up the side of the fender.

"Imperial fiddlestick!" said the King, rubbing his nose, which had been hurt by the fall. He had a right to be a *little* annoyed, for he was covered with ashes from head to foot.

Alice was very anxious to be of use, and, as the poor little Lily was nearly screaming herself into a fit, she hastily picked up the Queen and set her upon the table by the side of her noisy little daughter.

The Queen gasped, and sat down: the rapid journey through the air had quite taken away her breath, and for a minute or two she could do nothing but hug the little Lily in silence. As soon as she had recovered her breath a little, she called out to the White King, who was sitting sulkily among the ashes, "Mind the volcano!"

"What volcano?" said the King, looking up anxiously into the fire, as if he thought that was the most likely place to find one.

"Blew—me—up," panted the Queen, who was still a little out of breath. "Mind you come up—the regular way—don't get blown up!"

Alice watched the White King as he slowly struggled up from bar to bar, till at last she said, "Why, you'll be hours and hours getting to the table, at that rate. I'd far better help you, hadn't I?" But the King took no notice of the question: it was quite clear that he could neither hear her nor see her.

So Alice picked him up very gently, and lifted him across more slowly than she had lifted the Queen, that she mightn't take his breath away: but, before she put him on the table, she thought she might as well dust him a little, he was so covered with ashes.

She said afterwards that she had never seen in all her life such a face as the King made, when he found himself held in the air by an invisible hand, and being dusted: he was far too much astonished to cry out, but his eyes and his mouth went on getting larger and larger, and rounder and rounder, till her hand shook so with laughing that she nearly let him drop upon the floor.

"Oh! *please* don't make such faces, my dear!" she cried out, quite forgetting that the King couldn't hear her. "You make me laugh so that I can hardly hold you! And don't keep your mouth so wide open! All the ashes will get into it—there, now I think you're tidy enough!" she added, as she smoothed his hair, and set him down very carefully upon the table near the Queen.

The King immediately fell flat on his back, and lay perfectly still; and Alice was a little alarmed at what she had done, and went round the room to see if she could find any water to throw over him. However, she could find nothing but a bottle of ink, and when she got back with it she found he had recovered, and he and the Queen were talking together in a frightened whisper—so low, that Alice could hardly hear what they said.

The King was saying, "I assure you, my dear, I turned cold to the very ends of my whiskers!"

To which the Queen replied, "You haven't got any whiskers."

"The horror of that moment," the King went on, "I shall never, *never* forget!"

"You will, though," the Queen said, "if you don't make a memorandum of it."

Alice looked on with great interest as the King took an enormous memorandum-book out of his pocket, and began writing. A sudden thought struck her, and she took hold of the end of the pencil, which came some way over his shoulder, and began writing for him.

The poor King looked puzzled and unhappy, and struggled with the pencil for some time without saying anything; but Alice was too strong for him, and at last he panted out, "My dear! I really *must* get a thinner pencil. I can't manage this one a bit; it writes all manner of things that I don't intend——"

"What manner of things?" said the Queen, looking over the book (in which Alice had put, "The White Knight is sliding down the poker. He balances very badly"). "That's not a memorandum of *your* feelings!"

There was a book lying near Alice on the table, and while she sat watching the White King (for she was still a little anxious about him, and had the ink all ready to throw over him, in case he fainted again), she turned over the leaves, to find some part that she could read, "—for it's all in some language I don't know," she said to herself.

It was like this:

ЈАВВЕКМОСКҮ

'Twas brillig, and the slithy toves
Did gyre and gimble in the wabe;
All mimsy were the borogoves,
And the mome raths outgrabe.

She puzzled over this for some time, but at last a bright thought struck her. "Why, it's a Looking-glass book, of course! And if I hold it up to a glass, the words will all go the right way again."

This was the poem that Alice read:

JABBERWOCKY

'Twas brillig, and the slithy toves
    Did gyre and gimble in the wabe;
All mimsy were the borogoves,
    And the mome raths outgrabe.

"Beware the Jabberwock, my son!
    The jaws that bite, the claws that catch!
Beware the Jubjub bird, and shun
    The frumious Bandersnatch!"

He took his vorpal sword in hand:
    Long time the manxome foe he sought—
So rested he by the Tumtum tree,
    And stood awhile in thought.

And as in uffish thought he stood,
    The Jabberwock, with eyes of flame,
Came whiffling through the tulgey wood,
    And burbled as it came!

One, two! One, two! And through and through
    The vorpal blade went snicker-snack!
He left it dead, and with its head
    He went galumphing back.

"And hast thou slain the Jabberwock?
  Come to my arms, my beamish boy!
O frabjous day! Callooh! Callay!"
  He chortled in his joy.

'Twas brillig, and the slithy toves
  Did gyre and gimble in the wabe;
All mimsy were the borogoves,
  And the mome raths outgrabe.

"It seems very pretty," she said when she had finished it, "but it's *rather* hard to understand!" (You see she didn't like to confess, even to herself, that she couldn't make it out at all.) "Somehow it seems to fill my head with ideas—only I don't exactly know what they are! However, *somebody* killed *something:* that's clear, at any rate——"

"But oh!" thought Alice, suddenly jumping up, "if I don't make haste I shall have to go back through the Looking-glass, before I've seen what the rest of the house is like! Let's have a look at the garden first!" She was out of the room in a moment, and ran downstairs—or, at least, it wasn't exactly running, but a new invention for getting downstairs quickly and easily, as Alice said to herself. She just kept the tips of her fingers on the hand-rail, and floated gently down without even touching the stairs with her feet; then she floated on through the hall, and would have gone straight out at the door in the same way, if she hadn't caught hold of the door-post. She was getting a little giddy with so much floating in the air, and was rather glad to find herself walking again in the natural way.

CHAPTER II

THE GARDEN OF LIVE FLOWERS

"I SHOULD see the garden far better," said Alice to herself, "if I could get to the top of that hill: and here's a path that leads straight to it—at least, no, it doesn't do that——" (after going a few yards along the path, and turning several sharp corners), "but I suppose it will at last. But how curiously it twists! It's more like a corkscrew than a path! Well, *this* turn goes to the hill, I suppose—no, it doesn't! This goes straight back to the house! Well then, I'll try it the other way."

And so she did: wandering up and down, and trying turn after turn, but always coming back to the house, do what she would. Indeed, once, when she turned a corner rather more quickly than usual, she ran against it before she could stop herself.

"It's no use talking about it," Alice said, looking up at the house and pretending it was arguing with her. "I'm *not* going in again yet. I know I should have to get through the Looking-glass again—back into the old room—and there'd be an end of all my adventures!"

So, resolutely turning her back upon the house, she set out once more down the path, determined to keep straight on till she got to the hill. For a few minutes all went on well, and she was just saying, "I really *shall* do it this time——" when the path gave a sudden twist and shook itself (as she described it afterwards), and the next moment she found herself actually walking in at the door.

"Oh, it's too bad!" she cried. "I never saw such a house for getting in the way! Never!"

However, there was the hill full in sight, so there was

nothing to be done but start again. This time she came upon a large flower-bed, with a border of daisies, and a willow-tree growing in the middle.

"O Tiger-lily," said Alice, ad-

dressing herself to one that was waving gracefully about in the wind, "I *wish* you could talk!"

"We *can* talk," said the Tiger-lily: "when there's anybody worth talking to."

Alice was so astonished that she couldn't speak for a minute: it quite seemed to take her breath away. At length, as the Tiger-lily only went on waving about, she spoke again, in a timid voice—almost in a whisper: "And can *all* the flowers talk?"

"As well as *you* can," said the Tiger-lily. "And a great deal louder."

"It isn't manners for us to begin, you know," said the Rose, "and I really was wondering when you'd speak! Said I to myself, 'Her face has got *some* sense in it, though it's not a clever one!' Still, you're the right colour, and that goes a long way."

"I don't care about the colour," the Tiger-lily remarked. "If only her petals curled up a little more, she'd be all right."

Alice didn't like being criticised, so she began asking questions: "Aren't you sometimes frightened at being planted out here, with nobody to take care of you?"

"There's the tree in the middle," said the Rose. "What else is it good for?"

"But what could it do, if any danger came?" Alice asked.

"It could bark," said the Rose.

"It says, 'Bough-wough!'" cried a Daisy: "that's why its branches are called boughs!"

"Didn't you know *that?*" cried another Daisy, and here they all began shouting together, till the air seemed quite full of little shrill voices. "Silence, every one of you!" cried the Tiger-lily, waving itself passionately from side to side, and trembling with excitement. "They know I can't get at them!" it panted, bending its quivering head towards Alice, "or they wouldn't dare do it!"

"Never mind!" Alice said in a soothing tone, and stooping down to the daisies, who were just beginning again, she whispered, "If you don't hold your tongues, I'll pick you!"

There was silence in a moment, and several of the pink daisies turned white.

"That's right!" said the Tiger-lily. "The daisies are worst

of all. When one speaks, they all begin together, and it's enough to make one wither to hear the way they go on!"

"How is it you can all talk so nicely?" Alice said, hoping to get it into a better temper by a compliment. "I've been in many gardens before, but none of the flowers could talk."

"Put your hand down, and feel the ground," said the Tiger-lily. "Then you'll know why."

Alice did so. "It's very hard," she said, "but I don't see what that has to do with it."

"In most gardens," the Tiger-lily said, "they make the beds too soft—so that the flowers are always asleep."

This sounded a very good reason, and Alice was quite pleased to know it. "I never thought of that before!" she said.

"It's *my* opinion you never think *at all*," the Rose said in a rather severe tone.

"I never saw anybody that looked stupider," a Violet said, so suddenly that Alice quite jumped; for it hadn't spoken before.

"Hold *your* tongue!" cried the Tiger-lily. "As if *you* ever saw anybody! You keep your head under the leaves, and snore away there till you know no more what's going on in the world, than if you were a bud!"

"Are there any more people in the garden besides me?" Alice said, not choosing to notice the Rose's last remark.

"There's one other flower in the garden that can move about like you," said the Rose. "I wonder how you do it——" ("You're always wondering," said the Tiger-lily), "but she's more bushy than you are."

"Is she like me?" Alice asked eagerly, for the thought crossed her mind, "There's another little girl in the garden somewhere!"

"Well, she has the same awkward shape as you," the Rose said: "but she's redder—and her petals are shorter, I think."

"Her petals are done up close, almost like a dahlia," the Tiger-lily interrupted: "not tumbled about anyhow, like yours."

"But that's not *your* fault," the Rose added kindly: "you're beginning to fade, you know—and then one can't help one's petals getting a little untidy."

Alice didn't like this idea at all: so, to change the subject, she asked, "Does she ever come out here?"

"I dare say you'll see her soon," said the Rose. "She's one of the thorny kind."

"Where does she wear the thorns?" Alice asked with some curiosity.

"Why, all round her head, of course," the Rose replied. "I was wondering *you* hadn't got some too. I thought it was the regular rule."

"She's coming!" cried the Larkspur. "I hear her footstep, thump, thump, along the gravel-walk!"

Alice looked round eagerly, and found that it was the Red Queen. "She's grown a good deal!" was her first remark. She had indeed: when Alice first found her in the ashes, she had been only three inches high—and here she was, half a head taller than Alice herself!

"It's the fresh air that does it," said the Rose: "wonderfully fine air it is, out here."

"I think I'll go and meet her," said Alice, for, though the flowers were very interesting, she felt that it would be far grander to have a talk with a real Queen.

"You can't possibly do that," said the Rose: "*I* should advise you to walk the other way."

This sounded nonsense to Alice, so she said nothing, but set off at once towards the Red Queen. To her surprise, she lost sight of her in a moment, and found herself walking in at the front-door again.

A little provoked, she drew back and, after looking everywhere for the Queen (whom she spied out at last, a long way off), she thought she would try the plan, this time, of walking in the opposite direction.

It succeeded beautifully. She had not been walking a minute before she found herself face to face with the Red Queen, and full in sight of the hill she had been so long aiming at.

"Where do you come from?" said the Red Queen. "And where are you going? Look up, speak nicely, and don't twiddle your fingers all the time."

Alice attended to all these directions, and explained, as well as she could, that she had lost her way.

"I don't know what you mean by *your* way," said the Queen: "all the ways about here belong to *me*—but why did you come out here at all?" she added in a kinder tone. "Curtsey while you're thinking what to say. It saves time."

Alice wondered a little at this, but she was too much in awe of the Queen to disbelieve it. "I'll try it when I go home," she thought to herself, "the next time I'm a little late for dinner."

"It's time for you to answer now," the Queen said, looking at her watch: "open your mouth a *little* wider when you speak, and always say 'your Majesty.' "

"I only wanted to see what the garden was like, your Majesty——"

"That's right," said the Queen, patting her on the head, which Alice didn't like at all: "though, when you say 'garden,' *I've* seen gardens, compared with which this would be a wilderness."

Alice didn't dare to argue the point, but went on: "——and I thought I'd try and find my way to the top of that hill——"

"When you say 'hill,' " the Queen interrupted, "*I* could show you hills, in comparison with which you'd call that a valley."

"No, I shouldn't," said Alice, surprised into contradicting her at last: "a hill *can't* be a valley, you know. That would be nonsense——"

The Red Queen shook her head. "You may call it 'nonsense' if you like," she said, "but *I've* heard nonsense, compared with which that would be as sensible as a dictionary!"

Alice curtseyed again, as she was afraid from the Queen's tone that she was a *little* offended: and they walked on in silence till they got to the top of the little hill.

For some minutes Alice stood without speaking, looking out in all directions over the country—and a most curious country it was. There were a number of little brooks running across from side to side, and the ground between was divided up into squares by a number of hedges, that reached from brook to brook.

"I declare it's marked out just like a large chess-board!" Alice said at last. "There ought to be some men moving about somewhere—and so there are!" she added in a tone of delight, and her heart began to beat quick with excitement as she went on: "It's a great game of chess that's being played—all over the world—if this *is* the world at all, you know. Oh, what fun it is! How I *wish* I was one of them! I wouldn't mind being a Pawn, if only I might join—though of course I should *like* to be a Queen, best."

She glanced rather shyly at the real Queen as she said this, but her companion only smiled pleasantly, and said, "That's easily managed. You can be the White Queen's Pawn, if you like, as Lily's too young to play; and you're in the Second Square to begin with: when you get into the Eighth Square you'll be a Queen——" Just at this moment, somehow or other, they began to run.

Alice never could quite make out, in thinking it over afterwards, how it was that they began: all she remembers is, that they were running hand in hand, and the Queen went so fast that it was all she could do to keep up with her: and still the Queen kept crying "Faster!" but Alice felt she *could not* go faster, though she had no breath to say so.

The most curious part of the thing was, that the trees and the other things round them never changed their places at all: however fast they went, they never seemed to pass anything. "I wonder if all the things move along with us?" thought poor puzzled Alice. And the Queen seemed to guess her thoughts, for she cried, "Faster! Don't try to talk!"

Not that Alice had any idea of doing *that*. She felt as if she would never be able to talk again, she was getting so out of breath: and still the Queen cried, "Faster! Faster!" and dragged her along. "Are we nearly there?" Alice managed to pant out at last.

"Nearly there!" the Queen repeated. "Why, we passed it ten minutes ago! Faster!" And they ran on for a time in silence, with the wind whistling in Alice's ears, and almost blowing her hair off her head, she fancied.

"Now! Now!" cried the Queen. "Faster! Faster!" And they went so fast that at last they seemed to skim through the air, hardly touching the ground with their feet, till suddenly, just as Alice was getting quite exhausted, they stopped, and she found herself sitting on the ground, breathless and giddy.

The Queen propped her against a tree, and said kindly, "You may rest a little now."

Alice looked round her in great surprise. "Why, I do believe we've been under this tree all the time! Everything's just as it was!"

"Of course it is," said the Queen: "what would you have it?"

"Well, in *our* country," said Alice, still panting a little, "you'd generally get to somewhere else—if you ran very fast for a long time, as we've been doing."

"A slow sort of country!" said the Queen. "Now, *here*, you see, it takes all the running *you* can do, to keep in the same place. If you want to get somewhere else, you must run at least twice as fast as that!"

"I'd rather not try, please!" said Alice. "I'm quite content to stay here—only I *am* so hot and thirsty!"

"I know what *you'd* like!" the Queen said good-naturedly, taking a little box out of her pocket. "Have a biscuit?"

Alice thought it would not be civil to say, "No," though it wasn't at all what she wanted. So she took it, and ate it as well as she could: and it was *very* dry; and she thought she had never been so nearly choked in all her life.

"While you're refreshing yourself," said the Queen, "I'll just take the measurements." And she took a ribbon out of her pocket, marked in inches, and began measuring out the ground, and sticking little pegs in here and there.

"At the end of two yards," she said, putting in a peg to mark the distance, "I shall give you your directions—have another biscuit?"

"No, thank you," said Alice: "one's *quite* enough!"

"Thirst quenched, I hope?" said the Queen.

Alice did not know what to say to this, but luckily the

Queen did not wait for an answer, but went on: "At the end of *three* yards I shall repeat them—for fear of your forgetting them. At the end of *four*, I shall say good-bye. And at the end of *five*, I shall go!"

She had got all the pegs put in by this time, and Alice looked on with great interest as she returned to the tree, and then began slowly walking down the row.

At the two-yard peg she faced round, and said, "A pawn goes two squares in its first move. So you'll go *very* quickly through the Third Square—by railway, I should think—and you'll find yourself in the Fourth Square in no time. Well, *that* square belongs to Tweedledum and Tweedledee— the Fifth is mostly water—the Sixth belongs to Humpty Dumpty.—But you make no remark?"

"I—I didn't know I had to make one—just then," Alice faltered out.

"You *should* have said," the Queen went on in a tone of grave reproof, " 'It's extremely kind of you to tell me all this'—however, we'll suppose it said—the Seventh Square is all forest—however, one of the Knights will show you the way—and in the Eighth Square we shall be Queens together, and it's all feasting and fun!" Alice got up and curtseyed, and sat down again.

At the next peg the Queen turned again, and said, "Speak in French when you can't think of the English for a thing— turn out your toes as you walk—and remember who you are!" She did not wait for Alice to curtsey this time, but walked on quickly to the next peg, where she turned to say "good-bye," and then hurried on to the last.

How it happened, Alice never knew, but exactly as she came to the last peg, she was gone. Whether she vanished into the air, or ran quickly into the wood ("and she *can* run very fast!" thought Alice), there was no way of guessing, but she was gone, and Alice began to remember that she was a Pawn, and that it would soon be time to move.

CHAPTER III

LOOKING-GLASS INSECTS

OF course the first thing to do was to make a grand survey of the country she was going to travel through. "It's something very like learning geography," thought Alice, as she stood on tiptoe in hopes of being able to see a little further. "Principal rivers—there *are* none. Principal mountains—I'm on the only one, but I don't think it's got any name. Principal towns—why, what *are* those creatures, making honey down there? They can't be bees—nobody ever saw bees a mile off, you know——" and for some minutes she stood silent, watching one of them that was bustling about among the flowers, poking its proboscis into them, "just as if it was a regular bee," thought Alice.

However, this was anything but a regular bee: in fact, it was an elephant—as Alice soon found out, though the idea quite took her breath away at first. "And what enormous flowers they must be!" was her next idea. "Something like cottages with the roofs taken off, and stalks put to them—and what quantities of honey they must make! I think I'll go down and—no, I won't go *just* yet," she went on, checking herself just as she was beginning to run down the hill, and trying to find some excuse for turning shy so suddenly. "It'll never do to go down among them without a good long branch to brush them away—and what fun it'll be when they ask me how I liked my walk. I shall say—'Oh, I liked it well enough——' (here came the favourite little toss of the head), 'only it was so dusty and hot, and the elephants did tease so!'"

"I think I'll go down the other way," she said after a pause: "and perhaps I may visit the elephants later on. Besides, I do so want to get into the Third Square!"

So with this excuse she ran down the hill and jumped over the first of the six little brooks.

.   .   .   .

"Tickets, please!" said the Guard, putting his head in at the window. In a moment everybody was holding out a ticket: they were about the same size as the people, and quite seemed to fill the carriage.

"Now then! Show your ticket, child!" the Guard went on, looking angrily at Alice. And a great many voices all said together ("like the chorus of a song," thought Alice), "Don't keep him waiting, child! Why, his time is worth a thousand pounds a minute!"

"I'm afraid I haven't got one," Alice said in a frightened tone: "there wasn't a ticket-office where I came from." And again the chorus of voices went on: "There wasn't room for one where she came from. The land there is worth a thousand pounds an inch!"

"Don't make excuses," said the Guard: "you should have bought one from the engine-driver." And once more the chorus of voices went on with, "The man that drives the engine. Why, the smoke alone is worth a thousand pounds a puff!"

Alice thought to herself, "Then there's no use in speaking." The voices didn't join in this time, as she hadn't spoken, but, to her great surprise, they all *thought* in chorus (I hope you understand what *thinking in chorus* means—for I must confess that *I* don't), "Better say nothing at all. Language is worth a thousand pounds a word!"

"I shall dream about a thousand pounds to-night, I know I shall!" thought Alice.

All this time the Guard was looking at her, first through a telescope, then through a microscope, and then through an

opera-glass. At last he said, "You're travelling the wrong
way," and shut up the window and went away.

"So young a child," said the gentleman sitting opposite to
her (he was dressed in white paper), "ought to know which
way she's going, even if she doesn't know her own name!"

A Goat, that was sitting next to the gentleman in white,
shut his eyes and said in a loud voice, "She ought to know her
way to the ticket-office, even if she doesn't know her alphabet!"

There was a Beetle sitting next the Goat (it was a very
queer set of passengers altogether), and, as the rule seemed
to be that they should all speak in turn, *he* went on with,
"She'll have to go back from here as luggage!"

Alice couldn't see who was sitting beyond the Beetle, but
a hoarse voice spoke next. "Change engines——" it said, and
there it choked and was obliged to leave off.

"It sounds like a horse," Alice thought to herself. And an extremely small voice, close to her ear, said, "*You might make a joke on that—something about 'horse' and 'hoarse,' you know.*"

Then a very gentle voice in the distance said, "She must be labelled, 'Lass, with care,' you know——"

And after that other voices went on ("What a number of people there are in the carriage!" thought Alice), saying, "She must go by post, as she's got a head on her——" "She must be sent as a message by the telegraph——" "She must draw the train herself the rest of the way——," and so on.

But the gentleman dressed in white paper leaned forwards and whispered in her ear, "Never mind what they all say, my dear, but take a return-ticket every time the train stops."

"Indeed I shan't!" Alice said rather impatiently. "I don't belong to this railway journey at all—I was in a wood just now—and I wish I could get back there!"

"*You might make a joke on* that," said the little voice close to her ear: "*something about 'you* would *if you could,'* you *know.*"

"Don't tease so," said Alice, looking about in vain to see where the voice came from; "if you're so anxious to have a joke made, why don't you make one yourself?"

The little voice sighed deeply: it was *very* unhappy, evidently, and Alice would have said something pitying to comfort it, "if it would only sigh like other people!" she thought. But this was such a wonderfully small sigh, that she wouldn't have heard it at all, if it hadn't come *quite* close to her ear. The consequence of this was that it tickled her ear very much, and quite took off her thoughts from the unhappiness of the poor little creature.

"*I know you are a friend,*" the little voice went on; "*a dear friend, and an old friend. And you won't hurt me, though I am an insect.*"

"What kind of insect?" Alice inquired a little anxiously.

What she really wanted to know was, whether it could sting or not, but she thought this wouldn't be quite a civil question to ask.

"*What, then you don't*——" the little voice began, when it was drowned by a shrill scream from the engine, and everybody jumped up in alarm, Alice among the rest.

The Horse, who had put his head out of the window, quietly drew it in and said, "It's only a brook we have to jump over." Everybody seemed satisfied with this, though Alice felt a little nervous at the idea of trains jumping at all. "However, it'll take us into the Fourth Square, that's some comfort!" she said to herself. In another moment she felt the carriage rise straight up into the air, and in her fright she caught at the thing nearest to her hand, which happened to be the Goat's beard.

.   .   .   .

But the beard seemed to melt away as she touched it, and she found herself sitting quietly under a tree—while the Gnat (for that was the insect she had been talking to) was balancing itself on a twig just over her head, and fanning her with its wings.

It certainly was a *very* large Gnat: "about the size of a chicken," Alice thought. Still, she couldn't feel nervous with it, after they had been talking together so long.

"—then you don't like all insects?" the Gnat went on, as quietly as if nothing had happened.

"I like them when they can talk," Alice said. "None of them ever talk, where *I* come from."

"What sort of insects do you rejoice in, where *you* come from?" the Gnat inquired.

"I don't *rejoice* in insects at all," Alice explained, "because I'm rather afraid of them—at least the large kinds. But I can tell you the names of some of them."

"Of course they answer to their names?" the Gnat remarked carelessly.

"I never knew them do it."

"What's the use of their having names," the Gnat said, "if they won't answer to them?"

"No use to *them*," said Alice, "but it's useful to the people that name them, I suppose. If not, why do things have names at all?"

"I can't say," said the Gnat. "In the wood down there, they've got no names—however, go on with your list of insects."

"Well, there's the Horse-fly," Alice began, counting off the names on her fingers.

"All right," said the Gnat: "half-way up that bush, you'll see a Rocking-horse-fly, if you look. It's made entirely of wood, and gets about by swinging itself from branch to branch."

"What does it live on?" Alice asked, with great curiosity.

"Sap and sawdust," said the Gnat. "Go on with the list."

Alice looked at the Rocking-horse-fly with great interest, and made up her mind that it must have been just repainted, it looked so bright and sticky; and then she went on:

"And there's the Dragon-fly."

"Look on the branch above your head," said the Gnat, "and there you'll find a Snap-dragon-fly. Its body is made of plum-pudding, its wings of holly-leaves, and its head is a raisin burning in brandy."

"And what does it live on?" Alice asked, as before.

"Frumenty and mince-pie," the Gnat replied; "and it makes its nest in a Christmas-box."

"And then there's the Butterfly," Alice went on, after she had taken a good look at the insect with its head on fire, and had thought to herself, "I wonder if that's the reason insects are so fond of flying into candles—because they want to turn into Snap-dragon-flies!"

"Crawling at your feet," said the Gnat (Alice drew her feet back in some alarm), "you may observe a Bread-and-butter-fly. Its wings are thin slices of bread-and-butter, its body is a crust, and its head is a lump of sugar."

"And what does *it* live on?"

"Weak tea with cream in it."

A new difficulty came into Alice's head. "Supposing it couldn't find any?" she suggested.

"Then it would die, of course."

"But that must happen very often," Alice remarked thoughtfully.

"It always happens," said the Gnat.

After this, Alice was silent for a minute or two, pondering. The Gnat amused itself meanwhile by humming round and round her head: at last it settled again and remarked, "I suppose you don't want to lose your name?"

"No, indeed," Alice said, a little anxiously.

"And yet I don't know," the Gnat went on in a careless tone: "only think how convenient it would be if you could manage to go home without it! For instance, if the governess wanted to call you to your lessons, she would call out, 'Come here——,' and there she would have to leave off, because there wouldn't be any name for her to call, and of course you wouldn't have to go, you know."

"That would never do, I'm sure," said Alice: "the governess would never think of excusing me lessons for that. If she couldn't remember my name, she'd call me 'Miss!' as the servants do."

"Well, if she said 'Miss,' and didn't say anything more," the Gnat remarked, "of course you'd miss your lessons. That's a joke. I wish *you* had made it."

"Why do you wish *I* had made it?" Alice asked. "It's a very bad one."

But the Gnat only sighed deeply, while two large tears came rolling down its cheeks.

"You shouldn't make jokes," Alice said, "if it makes you so unhappy."

Then came another of those melancholy little sighs, and this time the poor Gnat really seemed to have sighed itself away, for, when Alice looked up, there was nothing whatever to be seen on the twig, and, as she was getting quite chilly with sitting still so long, she got up and walked on.

She very soon came to an open field, with a wood on the other side of it: it looked much darker than the last wood, and Alice felt a *little* timid about going into it. However, on second thoughts, she made up her mind to go on: "for I certainly won't go *back*," she thought to herself, and this was the only way to the Eighth Square.

"This must be the wood," she said thoughtfully to herself, "where things have no names. I wonder what'll become of *my* name when I go in? I shouldn't like to lose it at all—because they'd have to give me another, and it would be almost certain to be an ugly one. But then the fun would be, trying to find the creature that had got my old name! That's just like the advertisements, you know, when people lose dogs —'answers to the name of "Dash": had on a brass collar' —just fancy calling everything you met 'Alice,' till one of them answered! Only they wouldn't answer at all, if they were wise."

She was rambling on in this way when she reached the wood: it looked very cool and shady. "Well, at any rate it's a great comfort," she said as she stepped under the trees, "after being so hot, to get into the—into the—into *what?*"

she went on, rather surprised at not being able to think of the word. "I mean to get under the—under the—under *this*, you know!" putting her hand on the trunk of the tree. "What *does* it call itself? I do believe it's got no name—why, to be sure it hasn't!"

She stood silent for a minute, thinking: then she suddenly began again. "Then it really *has* happened, after all! And now, who am I? I *will* remember, if I can! I'm determined to do it!" But being determined didn't help her much, and all she could say, after a great deal of puzzling, was, "L, I *know* it begins with L!"

Just then a Fawn came wandering by: it looked at Alice with its large gentle eyes, but didn't seem at all frightened. "Here then! Here then!" Alice said, as she held out her hand and tried to stroke it; but it only started back a little, and then stood looking at her again. "What do you call yourself?" the Fawn said at last. Such a soft sweet voice it had!

"I wish I knew!" thought poor Alice. She answered, rather sadly, "Nothing, just now."

"Think again," it said: "that won't do."

Alice thought, but nothing came of it. "Please, would you tell me what *you* call yourself?" she said timidly. "I think that might help a little."

"I'll tell you, if you'll come a little further on," the Fawn said. "I can't remember here."

So they walked on together through the wood, Alice with her arms clasped lovingly round the soft neck of the Fawn, till they came out into another open field, and here the Fawn gave a sudden bound into the air, and shook itself free from Alice's arms. "I'm a Fawn!" it cried out in a voice of delight. "And, dear me, you're a human child!" A sudden look of alarm came into its beautiful brown eyes, and in another moment it had darted away at full speed.

Alice stood looking after it, almost ready to cry with vexation at having lost her dear little fellow-traveller so sud-

denly. "However, I know my name now," she said: "that's *some* comfort. Alice—Alice—I won't forget it again. And now, which of these finger-posts ought I to follow, I wonder?"

It was not a difficult question to answer, as there was only one road, and the finger-posts both pointed along it. "I'll settle it," Alice said to herself, "when the road divides and they point different ways."

But this did not seem likely to happen. She went on and on, a long way, but wherever the road divided there were sure to be two finger-posts pointing the same way, one marked, "TO TWEEDLEDUM'S HOUSE," and the other, "TO THE HOUSE OF TWEEDLEDEE."

"I do believe," said Alice at last, "that they live in the same house! I wonder I never thought of that before.— But I can't stay there long. I'll just call and say, 'How d'ye do?' and ask them the way out of the wood. If I could only get to the Eighth Square before it gets dark!" So she wandered on, talking to herself as she went, till, on turning a sharp corner, she came upon two fat little men, so suddenly that she could not help starting back, but in another moment she recovered herself, feeling sure that they must be—

CHAPTER IV

TWEEDLEDUM AND TWEEDLEDEE

THEY were standing under a tree, each with an arm round the other's neck, and Alice knew which was which in a moment, because one of them had "DUM" embroidered on his collar, and the other "DEE." "I suppose they've each got 'TWEEDLE' round at the back of the collar," she said to herself.

They stood so still that she quite forgot they were alive, and she was just looking round to see if the word "TWEEDLE" was written at the back of each collar, when she was startled by a voice coming from the one marked "DUM."

"If you think we're wax-works," he said, "you ought to pay, you know. Wax-works weren't made to be looked at for nothing. Nohow!"

"Contrariwise," added the one marked "DEE," "if you think we're alive, you ought to speak."

"I'm sure I'm very sorry," was all Alice could say; for the words of the old song kept ringing through her head like the ticking of a clock, and she could hardly help saying them out loud:

Tweedledum and Tweedledee
    Agreed to have a battle;
For Tweedledum said Tweedledee
    Had spoiled his nice new rattle.

Just then flew down a monstrous crow,
    As black as a tar-barrel;
Which frightened both the heroes so,
    They quite forgot their quarrel.

"I know what you're thinking about," said Tweedledum: "but it isn't so, nohow."

"Contrariwise," continued Tweedledee, "if it was so, it might be; and if it were so, it would be: but as it isn't, it ain't. That's logic."

"I was thinking," Alice said very politely, "which is the best way out of this wood: it's getting so dark. Would you tell me, please?"

But the fat little men only looked at each other and grinned.

They looked so exactly like a couple of great schoolboys, that Alice couldn't help pointing her finger at Tweedledum, and saying; "First Boy!"

"Nohow!" Tweedledum cried out briskly, and instantly shut his mouth up again with a snap.

"Next Boy!" said Alice, passing on to Tweedledee, though she felt quite certain he would only shout out, "Contrariwise!" and so he did.

"You've begun wrong!" cried Tweedledum. "The first thing in a visit is to say 'How d'ye do?' and shake hands!" And here the two brothers gave each other a hug, and then they held out the two hands that were free, to shake hands with her.

Alice did not like shaking hands with either of them first, for fear of hurting the other one's feelings; so, as the best way out of the difficulty, she took hold of both hands at once: the next moment they were dancing round in a ring. This seemed quite natural (she remembered afterwards), and she was not even surprised to hear music playing: it seemed to come from the tree under which they were dancing, and it was done (as well as she could make it out) by the branches rubbing one across the other, like fiddles and fiddlesticks.

"But it certainly *was* funny" (Alice said afterwards, when she was telling her sister the history of all this), "to find myself singing 'Here we go round the mulberry bush.' I don't know when I began it, but somehow I felt as if I'd been singing it a long long time!"

The other two dancers were fat, and very soon out of breath. "Four times round is enough for one dance," Tweedledum panted out, and they left off dancing as suddenly as they had begun: the music stopped at the same moment.

Then they let go of Alice's hands, and stood looking at her for a minute: there was a rather awkward pause, as Alice didn't know how to begin a conversation with people she had just been dancing with. "It would never do to say, 'How d'ye do?' *now*," she said to herself: "we seem to have got beyond that, somehow!"

"I hope you're not much tired?" she said at last.

"Nohow. And thank you *very* much for asking," said Tweedledum.

"So *much* obliged!" added Tweedledee. "You like poetry?"

"Ye-es, pretty well—*some* poetry," Alice said doubtfully. "Would you tell me which road leads out of the wood?"

"What shall I repeat to her?" said Tweedledee, looking round at Tweedledum with great solemn eyes, and not noticing Alice's question.

" 'The Walrus and the Carpenter' is the longest," Tweedledum replied, giving his brother an affectionate hug.

Tweedledee began instantly:

"The sun was shining——"

Here Alice ventured to interrupt. "If it's *very* long," she said, as politely as she could, "would you tell me first which road——"

Tweedledee smiled gently, and began again:

> *"The sun was shining on the sea,*
> *Shining with all his might:*
> *He did his very best to make*
> *The billows smooth and bright—*
> *And this was odd, because it was*
> *The middle of the night.*

"The moon was shining sulkily,
Because she thought the sun
Had got no business to be there
After the day was done—
'It's very rude of him,' she said,
'To come and spoil the fun!'

"The sea was wet as wet could be,
The sands were dry as dry.
You could not see a cloud, because
No cloud was in the sky:
No birds were flying overhead—
There were no birds to fly.

"The Walrus and the Carpenter
Were walking close at hand;
They wept like anything to see
Such quantities of sand:
'If this were only cleared away,'
They said, 'it would be grand!'

" 'If seven maids with seven mops
Swept it for half a year,
Do you suppose,' the Walrus said,
'That they could get it clear?'
'I doubt it,' said the Carpenter,
And shed a bitter tear.

" 'O Oysters, come and walk with us!'
The Walrus did beseech.
'A pleasant walk, a pleasant talk,
Along the briny beach:
We cannot do with more than four,
To give a hand to each.'

"The eldest Oyster looked at him,
  But never a word he said:
The eldest Oyster winked his eye,
  And shook his heavy head—
Meaning to say he did not choose
  To leave the oyster-bed.

"But four young Oysters hurried up,
  All eager for the treat:
Their coats were brushed, their faces washed,
  Their shoes were clean and neat—
And this was odd, because, you know,
  They hadn't any feet.

"Four other Oysters followed them,
  And yet another four;
And thick and fast they came at last,
  And more, and more, and more—
All hopping through the frothy waves,
  And scrambling to the shore.

"*The Walrus and the Carpenter*
Walked on a mile or so,
And then they rested on a rock
Conveniently low:

And all the little Oysters stood
And waited in a row.

" '*The time has come,*' *the Walrus said,*
'*To talk of many things:*
Of shoes—and ships—and sealing-wax—
Of cabbages—and kings—
And why the sea is boiling hot—
And whether pigs have wings.'

" '*But wait a bit,*' *the Oysters cried,*
'*Before we have our chat;*
For some of us are out of breath,
And all of us are fat!'
'*No hurry!*' *said the Carpenter.*
They thanked him much for that.

" 'A loaf of bread,' the Walrus said,
  'Is what we chiefly need:
Pepper and vinegar besides
  Are very good indeed—
Now if you're ready, Oysters dear,
  We can begin to feed.'

" 'But not on us!' the Oysters cried,
  Turning a little blue.
'After such kindness, that would be
  A dismal thing to do!'
'The night is fine,' the Walrus said.
  'Do you admire the view?

" 'It was so kind of you to come!
  And you are very nice!'
The Carpenter said nothing but
  'Cut us another slice:
I wish you were not quite so deaf—
  I've had to ask you twice!'

" 'It seems a shame,' the Walrus said,
  'To play them such a trick,
After we've brought them out so far,
  And made them trot so quick!'
The Carpenter said nothing but.
  'The butter's spread too thick!'

" 'I weep for you,' the Walrus said: .
  'I deeply sympathise.'
With sobs and tears he sorted out
  Those of the largest size,
Holding his pocket-handkerchief
  Before his streaming eyes.

" 'O Oysters,' said the Carpenter,
  'You've had a pleasant run!
Shall we be trotting home again?'
  But answer came there none—
And this was scarcely odd, because
  They'd eaten every one."

"I like the Walrus best," said Alice: "because you see he was a *little* sorry for the poor oysters."

"He ate more than the Carpenter, though," said Tweedledee. "You see he held his handkerchief in front, so that the Carpenter couldn't count how many he took: contrariwise."

"That was mean!" Alice said indignantly. "Then I like the Carpenter best—if he didn't eat so many as the Walrus."

"But he ate as many as he could get," said Tweedledum.

This was a puzzler. After a pause, Alice began, "Well! They were *both* very unpleasant characters——" Here she checked herself in some alarm, at hearing something that sounded to her like the puffing of a large steam-engine in the wood near them, though she feared it was more likely to be a wild beast. "Are there any lions or tigers about here?" she asked timidly.

"It's only the Red King snoring," said Tweedledee.

"Come and look at him!" the brothers cried, and they each took one of Alice's hands, and led her up to where the King was sleeping.

"Isn't he a *lovely* sight?" said Tweedledum.

Alice couldn't say honestly that he was. He had a tall red night-cap on, with a tassel, and he was lying crumpled up into a sort of untidy heap, and snoring loud—"fit to snore his head off!" as Tweedledum remarked.

"I'm afraid he'll catch cold with lying on the damp grass," said Alice, who was a very thoughtful little girl.

"He's dreaming now," said Tweedledee: "and what do you think he's dreaming about?"

Alice said, "Nobody can guess that."

"Why, about *you!*" Tweedledee exclaimed, clapping his hands triumphantly. "And if he left off dreaming about you, where do you suppose you'd be?"

"Where I am now, of course," said Alice.

"Not you!" Tweedledee retorted contemptuously. "You'd be nowhere. Why, you're only a sort of thing in his dream!"

"If that there King was to wake," added Tweedledum, "you'd go out—bang!—just like a candle!"

"I shouldn't!" Alice exclaimed indignantly. "Besides, if *I'm* only a sort of thing in his dream, what are *you*, I should like to know?"

"Ditto," said Tweedledum.

"Ditto, ditto!" cried Tweedledee.

He shouted this so loud that Alice couldn't help saying, "Hush! You'll be waking him, I'm afraid, if you make so much noise."

"Well, it's no use *your* talking about waking him," said Tweedledum, "when you're only one of the things in his dream. You know very well you're not real."

"I *am* real!" said Alice, and began to cry.

"You won't make yourself a bit realer by crying," Tweedledee remarked: "there's nothing to cry about."

"If I wasn't real," Alice said—half laughing through her tears, it all seemed so ridiculous—"I shouldn't be able to cry."

"I hope you don't suppose those are real tears?" Tweedledum interrupted in a tone of great contempt.

"I know they're talking nonsense," Alice thought to herself: "and it's foolish to cry about it." So she brushed away her tears, and went on as cheerfully as she could, "At any rate I'd better be getting out of the wood, for really it's coming on very dark. Do you think it's going to rain?"

Tweedledum spread a large umbrella over himself and his brother, and looked up into it. "No, I don't think it is," he said: "at least—not under *here*. Nohow."

"But it may rain *outside*?"

"It may—if it chooses," said Tweedledee: "we've no objection. Contrariwise."

"Selfish things!" thought Alice, and she was just going to say, "Good night," and leave them, when Tweedledum sprang out from under the umbrella, and seized her by the wrist.

"Do you see *that?*" he said, in a voice choking with passion,

and his eyes grew large and yellow all in a moment, as he pointed with a trembling finger at a small white thing lying under the tree.

"It's only a rattle," Alice said, after a careful examination of the little white thing. "Not a rattle-*snake*, you know," she added hastily, thinking that he was frightened; "only an old rattle—quite old and broken."

"I knew it was!" cried Tweedledum, beginning to stamp about wildly and tear his hair. "It's spoilt, of course!" Here he looked at Tweedledee, who immediately sat down on the ground, and tried to hide himself under the umbrella.

Alice laid her hand upon his arm, and said in a soothing tone, "You needn't be so angry about an old rattle."

"But it isn't old!" Tweedledum cried, in a greater fury than ever. "It's new, I tell you—I bought it yesterday—my nice *new* RATTLE!" and his voice rose to a perfect scream.

All this time Tweedledee was trying his best to fold up the umbrella, with himself in it: which was such an extraor-

dinary thing to do, that it quite took off Alice's attention from
the angry brother. But he couldn't quite succeed, and it ended
in his rolling over, bundled up in the umbrella, with only his
head out: and there he lay, opening and shutting his mouth
and his large eyes—"looking more like a fish than anything
else," Alice thought.

"Of course you agree to have a battle?" Tweedledum said
in a calmer tone.

"I suppose so," the other sulkily replied, as he crawled
out of the umbrella: "only *she* must help us to dress up, you
know."

So the two brothers went off hand-in-hand into the wood,
and returned in a minute with their arms full of things—such
as bolsters, blankets, hearth-rugs, table-cloths, dish-covers, and
coal-scuttles. "I hope you're a good hand at pinning and tying
strings?" Tweedledum remarked. "Every one of these things
has to go on, somehow or other."

Alice said afterwards she had never seen such a fuss made

about anything in all her life—the way those two bustled about—and the quantity of things they put on—and the trouble they gave her in tying strings and fastening buttons— "Really they'll be more like bundles of old clothes than anything else, by the time they're ready!" she said to herself, as she arranged a bolster round the neck of Tweedledee, "to keep his head from being cut off," as he said.

"You know," he added very gravely, "it's one of the most serious things that can possibly happen to one in a battle— to get one's head cut off."

Alice laughed loud, but managed to turn it into a cough, for fear of hurting his feelings.

"Do I look very pale?" said Tweedledum, coming up to have his helmet tied on. (He *called* it a helmet, though it certainly looked much more like a saucepan.)

"Well—yes—a *little*," Alice replied gently.

"I'm very brave generally," he went on in a low voice: "only to-day I happen to have a headache."

"And *I've* got a toothache!" said Tweedledee, who had overheard the remark. "I'm far worse than you!"

"Then you'd better not fight to-day," said Alice, thinking it a good opportunity to make peace.

"We *must* have a bit of a fight, but I don't care about going on long," said Tweedledum. "What's the time now?"

Tweedledee looked at his watch, and said, "Half-past four."

"Let's fight till six, and then have dinner," said Tweedledum.

"Very well," the other said, rather sadly: "and *she* can watch us—only you'd better not come *very* close," he added: "I generally hit everything I can see—when I get really excited."

"And *I* hit everything within reach," cried Tweedledum, "whether I can see it or not!"

Alice laughed. "You must hit the *trees* pretty often, I should think," she said.

Tweedledum looked round him with a satisfied smile. "I don't suppose," he said, "there'll be a tree left standing, for ever so far round, by the time we've finished!"

"And all about a rattle!" said Alice, still hoping to make them a *little* ashamed of fighting for such a trifle.

"I shouldn't have minded it so much," said Tweedledum, "if it hadn't been a new one."

"I wish the monstrous crow would come!" thought Alice.

"There's only one sword, you know," Tweedledum said to his brother: "but you can have the umbrella—it's quite as sharp. Only we must begin quick. It's getting as dark as it can."

"And darker," said Tweedledee.

It was getting dark so suddenly that Alice thought there must be a thunderstorm coming on. "What a thick black cloud that is!" she said. "And how fast it comes! Why, I do believe it's got wings!"

"It's the crow!" Tweedledum cried out in a shrill voice of alarm: and the two brothers took to their heels and were out of sight in a moment.

Alice ran a little way into the wood, and stopped under a large tree. "It can never get at me *here*," she thought: "it's far too large to squeeze itself in among the trees. But I wish it wouldn't flap its wings so—it makes quite a hurricane in the wood—here's somebody's shawl being blown away!"

CHAPTER V

WOOL AND WATER

She caught the shawl as she spoke, and looked about for the owner: in another moment the White Queen came running wildly through the wood, with both arms stretched out wide, as if she were flying, and Alice very civilly went to meet her with the shawl.

"I'm very glad I happened to be in the way," Alice said, as she helped her to put on her shawl again.

The White Queen only looked at her in a helpless frightened sort of way, and kept repeating something in a whisper to herself that sounded like, "Bread-and-butter, bread-and-butter," and Alice felt that if there was to be any conversation at all, she must manage it herself. So she began rather timidly: "Am I addressing the White Queen?"

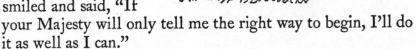

"Well, yes, if you call that a-dressing," the Queen said. "It isn't *my* notion of the thing, at all."

Alice thought it would never do to have an argument at the very beginning of their conversation, so she smiled and said, "If your Majesty will only tell me the right way to begin, I'll do it as well as I can."

"But I don't want it done at all!" groaned the poor Queen. "I've been a-dressing myself for the last two hours."

It would have been all the better, as it seemed to Alice, if only she had got someone else to dress her, she was so dreadfully untidy. "Every single thing's crooked," Alice thought to herself, "and she's all over pins!—May I put your shawl a little more straight for you?" she added aloud.

"I don't know what's the matter with it!" the Queen said, in a melancholy voice. "It's out of temper, I think. I've pinned it here, and I've pinned it there, but there's no pleasing it!"

"It *can't* go straight, you know, if you pin it all on one side," Alice said, as she gently put it right for her; "and, dear me, what a state your hair is in!"

"The hair-brush has got entangled in it!" the Queen said with a sigh. "And I lost the comb yesterday."

Alice carefully released the brush, and did her best to get the hair into order. "Come, you look rather better now!" she said, after altering most of the pins. "But really you should have a lady's-maid!"

"I'm sure I'll take you with pleasure!" the Queen said. "Twopence a week, and jam every other day."

Alice couldn't help laughing, as she said, "I don't want you to hire *me*—and I don't care for jam."

"It's very good jam," said the Queen.

"Well, I don't want any *to-day*, at any rate."

"You couldn't have it if you *did* want it," the Queen said. "The rule is, jam to-morrow and jam yesterday—but never jam to-day."

"It *must* come sometimes to 'jam to-day,'" Alice objected.

"No, it can't," said the Queen. "It's jam every *other* day: to-day isn't any *other* day, you know."

"I don't understand you," said Alice. "It's dreadfully confusing!"

"That's the effect of living backwards," the Queen said kindly: "it always makes one a little giddy at first——"

"Living backwards!" Alice repeated in great astonishment. "I never heard of such a thing!"

"—But there's one great advantage in it, that one's memory works both ways."

"I'm sure *mine* only works one way," Alice remarked. "I can't remember things before they happen."

"It's a poor sort of memory that only works backwards," the Queen remarked.

"What sort of things do *you* remember best?" Alice ventured to ask.

"Oh, things that happened the week after next," the Queen replied in a careless tone. "For instance, now," she went on, sticking a large piece of plaster on her finger as she spoke, "there's the King's Messenger. He's in prison now, being punished: and the trial doesn't even begin till next Wednesday: and of course the crime comes last of all."

"Suppose he never commits the crime?" said Alice.

"That would be all the better, wouldn't it?" the Queen said, as she bound the plaster round her finger with a bit of ribbon.

Alice felt there was no denying *that*. "Of course it would be all the better," she said: "but it wouldn't be all the better his being punished."

"You're wrong *there*, at any rate," said the Queen: "were *you* ever punished?"

"Only for faults," said Alice.

"And you were all the better for it, I know!" the Queen said triumphantly.

"Yes, but then I *had* done the things I was punished for," said Alice: "that makes all the difference."

"But if you *hadn't* done them," the Queen said, "that would have been better still; better, and better, and better!" Her voice went higher with each "better," till it got quite to a squeak at last.

Alice was just beginning to say, "There's a mistake somewhere——," when the Queen began screaming, so loud that she had to leave the sentence unfinished. "Oh, oh, oh!" shouted the Queen, shaking her hand about as if she wanted to shake it off. "My finger's bleeding! Oh, oh, oh, oh!"

Her screams were so exactly like the whistle of a steam-engine, that Alice had to hold both her hands over her ears.

"What *is* the matter?" she said, as soon as there was a chance of making herself heard. "Have you pricked your finger?"

"I haven't pricked it *yet,*" the Queen said, "but I soon shall —oh, oh, oh!"

"When do you expect to do it?" Alice asked, feeling very much inclined to laugh.

"When I fasten my shawl again," the poor Queen groaned out: "the brooch will come undone directly. Oh, oh!" As she said the words the brooch flew open, and the Queen clutched wildly at it, and tried to clasp it again.

"Take care!" cried Alice. "You're holding it all crooked!" And she caught at the brooch; but it was too late: the pin had slipped, and the Queen had pricked her finger.

"That accounts for the bleeding, you see," she said to Alice with a smile. "Now you understand the way things happen here."

"But why don't you scream now?" Alice asked, holding her hands ready to put over her ears again.

"Why, I've done all the screaming already," said the

Queen. "What would be the good of having it all over again?"

By this time it was getting light. "The crow must have flown away, I think," said Alice: "I'm so glad it's gone. I thought it was the night coming on."

"I wish *I* could manage to be glad!" the Queen said. "Only I never can remember the rule. You must be very happy, living in this wood, and being glad whenever you like!"

"Only it is so *very* lonely here!" Alice said in a melancholy voice; and at the thought of her loneliness two large tears came rolling down her cheeks.

"Oh, don't go on like that!" cried the poor Queen, wringing her hands in despair. "Consider what a great girl you are. Consider what a long way you've come to-day. Consider what o'clock it is. Consider anything, only don't cry!"

Alice could not help laughing at this, even in the midst of her tears. "Can *you* keep from crying by considering things?" she asked.

"That's the way it's done," the Queen said with great decision: "nobody can do two things at once, you know. Let's consider your age to begin with—how old are you?"

"I'm seven and a half exactly."

"You needn't say 'exactually,' " the Queen remarked: "I can believe it without that. Now I'll give *you* something to believe. I'm just one hundred and one, five months and a day."

"I can't believe *that!*" said Alice.

"Can't you?" the Queen said in a pitying tone. "Try again: draw a long breath, and shut your eyes."

Alice laughed. "There's no use trying," she said: "one *can't* believe impossible things."

"I dare say you haven't had much practice," said the Queen. "When I was your age, I always did it for half an hour a day. Why, sometimes I've believed as many as six impossible things before breakfast. There goes the shawl again!"

The brooch had come undone as she spoke, and a sudden gust of wind blew her shawl across a little brook. The Queen spread out her arms again, and went flying after it, and this time succeeded in catching it for herself. "I've got it!" she cried in a triumphant tone. "Now you shall see me pin it on again, all by myself!"

"Then I hope your finger is better now?" Alice said very politely, as she crossed the little brook after the Queen.

.   .   .   .

"Oh, much better!" cried the Queen, her voice rising into a squeak as she went on. "Much be-etter! Be-etter! Be-e-e-etter! Be-e-ehh!" The last word ended in a long bleat, so like a sheep that Alice quite started.

She looked at the Queen, who seemed to have suddenly wrapped herself up in wool. Alice rubbed her eyes, and looked again. She couldn't make out what had happened at all. Was she in a shop? And was that really—was it really a *sheep* that was sitting on the other side of the counter? Rub as she would, she could make nothing more of it: she was in a little dark shop, leaning with her elbows on the counter, and opposite to her was an old Sheep, sitting in an arm-chair knitting, and every now and then leaving off to look at her through a great pair of spectacles.

"What is it you want to buy?" the Sheep said at last, looking up for a moment from her knitting.

"I don't *quite* know yet," Alice said very gently. "I should like to look all round me first, if I might."

"You may look in front of you, and on both sides, if you like," said the Sheep; "but you can't look *all* round you—unless you've got eyes at the back of your head."

But these, as it happened, Alice had *not* got; so she contented herself with turning round, looking at the shelves as she came to them.

The shop seemed to be full of all manner of curious things —but the oddest part of it all was, that whenever she looked

hard at any shelf, to make out exactly what it had on it, that particular shelf was always quite empty: though the others round it were crowded as full as they could hold.

"Things flow about so here!" she said at last in a plaintive tone, after she had spent a minute or so in vainly pursuing a large bright thing, that looked sometimes like a doll and sometimes like a work-box, and was always in the shelf next above the one she was looking at. "And this one is the most provoking of all—but I'll tell you what——" she added, as a sudden thought struck her, "I'll follow it up to the very top shelf of all. It'll puzzle it to go through the ceiling, I expect!"

But even this plan failed: the "thing" went through the ceiling as quietly as possible, as if it were quite used to it.

"Are you a child or a teetotum?" the Sheep said, as she took up another pair of needles. "You'll make me giddy soon, if you go on turning round like that." She was now working with fourteen pairs at once, and Alice couldn't help looking at her in great astonishment.

"How *can* she knit with so many?" the puzzled child thought to herself. "She gets more and more like a porcupine every minute!"

"Can you row?" the Sheep asked, handing her a pair of knitting-needles as she spoke.

"Yes, a little—but not on land—and not with needles——" Alice was beginning to say, when suddenly the needles turned into oars in her hands, and she found they were in a little boat, gliding along between banks: so there was nothing for it but to do her best.

"Feather!" cried the Sheep, as she took up another pair of needles.

This didn't sound like a remark that needed any answer, so Alice said nothing, but pulled away. There was something very queer about the water, she thought, as every now and then the oars got fast in it, and would hardly come out again.

"Feather! Feather!" the Sheep cried again, taking more needles. "You'll be catching a crab directly."

"A dear little crab!" thought Alice. "I should like that."

"Didn't you hear me say 'Feather'?" the Sheep cried angrily, taking up quite a bunch of needles.

"Indeed I did," said Alice: "you've said it very often—and very loud. Please, where *are* the crabs?"

"In the water, of course!" said the Sheep, sticking some of the needles into her hair, as her hands were full. "Feather, I say!"

"*Why* do you say 'Feather' so often?" Alice asked at last, rather vexed. "I'm not a bird!"

"You are," said the Sheep; "you're a little goose."

This offended Alice a little, so there was no more conversation for a minute or two, while the boat glided gently on, sometimes among beds of weeds (which made the oars stick fast in the water, worse than ever), and sometimes under trees, but always with the same tall riverbanks frowning over their heads.

"Oh, please! There are some scented rushes!" Alice cried in a sudden transport of delight. "There really are—and *such* beauties!"

"You needn't say 'please' to *me* about 'em," the Sheep said, without looking up from her knitting: "I didn't put 'em there, and I'm not going to take 'em away."

"No, but I meant—please, may we wait and pick some?" Alice pleaded. "If you don't mind stopping the boat for a minute."

"How am *I* to stop it?" said the Sheep. "If you leave off rowing, it'll stop of itself."

So the boat was left to drift down the stream as it would, till it glided gently in among the waving rushes. And then the little sleeves were carefully rolled up, and the little arms were plunged in elbow-deep, to get hold of the rushes a good long way down before breaking them off—and for a while Alice forgot all about the Sheep and the knitting, as she bent over the side of the boat, with just the ends of her tangled hair dipping into the water—while with bright eager eyes she caught at one bunch after another of the darling scented rushes.

"I only hope the boat won't tipple over!" she said to herself. "Oh, *what* a lovely one! Only I couldn't quite reach it." And it certainly *did* seem a little provoking ("almost as if it happened on purpose," she thought) that, though she managed to pick plenty of beautiful rushes as the boat glided by, there was always a more lovely one that she couldn't reach.

"The prettiest are always farther!" she said at last, with a sigh at the obstinacy of the rushes in growing so far off, as, with flushed cheeks and dripping hair and hands, she scrambled back into her place, and began to arrange her new-found treasures.

What mattered it to her just then that the rushes had begun to fade, and to lose all their scent and beauty, from the very moment that she picked them? Even real scented rushes, you know, last only a very little while—and these, being dream-rushes, melted away almost like snow, as they lay in heaps at her feet—but Alice hardly noticed this, there were so many other curious things to think about.

They hadn't gone much farther before the blade of one of the oars got fast in the water and *wouldn't* come out again (so Alice explained it afterwards), and the consequence was that the handle of it caught her under the chin, and, in spite of a series of little shrieks of "Oh, oh, oh!" from poor Alice, it swept her straight off the seat, and down among the heap of rushes.

However, she wasn't a bit hurt, and was soon up again: the Sheep went on with her knitting all the while, just as if nothing had happened. "That was a nice crab you caught!" she remarked, as Alice got back into her place, very much relieved to find herself still in the boat.

"Was it? I didn't see it," said Alice, peeping cautiously over the side of the boat into the dark water. "I wish it hadn't let go—I should so like a little crab to take home with me!" But the Sheep only laughed scornfully, and went on with her knitting.

"Are there many crabs here?" said Alice.

"Crabs, and all sorts of things," said the Sheep: "plenty of choice, only make up your mind. Now, what *do* you want to buy?"

"To buy!" Alice echoed in a tone that was half astonished and half frightened—for the oars, and the boat, and the river, had vanished all in a moment, and she was back again in the little dark shop.

"I should like to buy an egg, please," she said timidly. "How do you sell them?"

"Fivepence farthing for one—twopence for two," the Sheep replied.

"Then two are cheaper than one?" Alice said in a surprised tone, taking out her purse.

"Only, you *must* eat them both, if you buy two," said the Sheep.

"Then I'll have *one*, please," said Alice, as she put the money down on the counter. For she thought to herself, "They mightn't be at all nice, you know."

The Sheep took the money, and put it away in a box: then she said, "I never put things into people's hands—that would never do—you must get it for yourself." And so saying, she went off to the other end of the shop, and set the egg upright on a shelf.

"I wonder *why* it wouldn't do?" thought Alice, as she groped her way among the tables and chairs, for the shop was very dark towards the end. "The egg seems to get farther away the more I walk towards it. Let me see, is this a chair? Why, it's got branches, I declare! How very odd to find trees growing here! And actually here's a little brook! Well, this is the very queerest shop I ever saw!"

.   .   .   .

So she went on, wondering more and more at every step, as everything turned into a tree the moment she came up to it, and she quite expected the egg to do the same.

CHAPTER VI

HUMPTY DUMPTY

HOWEVER, the egg only got larger and larger, and more and more human: when she had come within a few yards of it, she saw that it had eyes and a nose and mouth; and when she had come close to it, she saw clearly that it was HUMPTY DUMPTY himself. "It can't be anybody else!" she said to herself. "I'm as certain of it, as if his name were written all over his face!"

It might have been written a hundred times, easily, on that enormous face. Humpty Dumpty was sitting with his legs crossed, like a Turk, on the top of a high wall—such a narrow one that Alice quite wondered how he could keep his balance—and, as his eyes were steadily fixed in the opposite direction, and he didn't take the least notice of her, she thought he must be a stuffed figure.

"And how exactly like an egg he is!" she said aloud, standing with her hands ready to catch him, for she was every moment expecting him to fall.

"It's *very* provoking," Humpty Dumpty said after a long silence, looking away from Alice as he spoke, "to be called an egg—*very!*"

"I said you *looked* like an egg, Sir," Alice gently explained. "And some eggs are very pretty, you know," she added, hoping to turn her remark into a sort of compliment.

"Some people," said Humpty Dumpty, looking away from her as usual, "have no more sense than a baby!"

Alice didn't know what to say to this: it wasn't at all like conversation, she thought, as he never said anything to *her*; in fact, his last remark was evidently addressed to a tree— so she stood and softly repeated to herself:

> *"Humpty Dumpty sat on a wall:*
> *Humpty Dumpty had a great fall.*
> *All the King's horses and all the King's men*
> *Couldn't put Humpty Dumpty in his place again."*

"That last line is much too long for the poetry," she added, almost out loud, forgetting that Humpty Dumpty would hear her.

"Don't stand chattering to yourself like that," Humpty Dumpty said, looking at her for the first time, "but tell me your name and your business."

"My *name* is Alice, but——"

"It's a stupid name enough!" Humpty Dumpty interrupted impatiently. "What does it mean?"

"*Must* a name mean something?" Alice asked doubtfully.

"Of course it must," Humpty Dumpty said with a short laugh: "*my* name means the shape I am—and a good handsome shape it is, too. With a name like yours, you might be any shape, almost."

"Why do you sit out here all alone?" said Alice, not wishing to begin an argument.

"Why, because there's nobody with me!" cried Humpty Dumpty. "Did you think I didn't know the answer to *that?* Ask another."

"Don't you think you'd be safer down on the ground?" Alice went on, not with any idea of making another riddle, but simply in her good-natured anxiety for the queer creature. "That wall is so *very* narrow!"

"What tremendously easy riddles you ask!" Humpty Dumpty growled out. "Of course I don't think so! Why, if ever I *did* fall off—which there's no chance of—but *if* I did——" Here he pursed up his lips, and looked so solemn and grand that Alice could hardly help laughing. "*If I did fall,*" he went on, "*the King has promised me*—ah, you may turn pale, if you like! You didn't think I was going to say that, did you? *The King has promised me—with his own mouth—to—to*——"

"To send all his horses and all his men," Alice interrupted, rather unwisely.

"Now I declare that's too bad!" Humpty Dumpty cried, breaking into a sudden passion. "You've been listening at doors—and behind trees—and down chimneys—or **you** couldn't have known it!"

"I haven't, indeed!" Alice said very gently. "It's in a book."

"Ah, well! They may write such things in a *book*," Humpty Dumpty said in a calmer tone. "That's what you call a History of England, that is. Now, take a good look at me! I'm one that has spoken to a King, *I* am: may-hap you'll never see such an-other: and to show you I'm not proud, you may shake hands with me!" And he grinned al-most from ear to ear, as he leant forwards (and as nearly as pos-sible fell off the wall in doing so) and offered Alice his hand. She watched him a little anxiously as she took it. "If he smiled much more, the ends of his mouth might meet behind," she thought: "and then I don't know what would happen to his head! I'm afraid it would come off!"

"Yes, all his horses and all his men," Humpty Dumpty went on. "They'd pick me up again in a minute, *they* would!

However, this conversation is going on a little too fast: let's go back to the last remark but one."

"I'm afraid I can't quite remember it," Alice said very politely.

"In that case we may start fresh," said Humpty Dumpty, "and it's my turn to choose a subject——" ("He talks about it just as if it was a game!" thought Alice.) "So here's a question for you: How old did you say you were?"

Alice made a short calculation, and said, "Seven years and six months."

"Wrong!" Humpty Dumpty exclaimed triumphantly. "You never said a word like it."

"I thought you meant, 'How old *are* you?'" Alice explained.

"If I'd meant that, I'd have said it," said Humpty Dumpty.

Alice didn't want to begin another argument, so she said nothing.

"Seven years and six months!" Humpty Dumpty repeated thoughtfully. "An uncomfortable sort of age. Now if you'd asked *my* advice, I'd have said, 'Leave off at seven'—but it's too late now."

"I never ask advice about growing," Alice said indignantly.

"Too proud?" the other inquired.

Alice felt even more indignant at this suggestion. "I mean," she said, "that one can't help growing older."

"*One* can't, perhaps," said Humpty Dumpty, "but *two* can. With proper assistance, you might have left off at seven."

"What a beautiful belt you've got on!" Alice suddenly remarked. (They had had quite enough of the subject of age, she thought: and if they were really to take turns in choosing subjects, it was her turn now.) "At least," she corrected herself on second thoughts, "a beautiful cravat, I should have said—no, a belt, I mean—oh, I *beg* your pardon!" she added in dismay, for Humpty Dumpty looked thoroughly offended, and she began to wish she hadn't chosen that subject. "If only I knew," she thought to herself, "which was neck and which was waist!"

Evidently Humpty Dumpty was very angry, though he said nothing for a minute or two. When he *did* speak again, it was in a deep growl.

"It is a—*most—provoking*—thing," he said at last, "when a person doesn't know a cravat from a belt!"

"I know it's very ignorant of me," Alice replied, in so humble a tone that Humpty Dumpty relented.

"It's a cravat, child, and a beautiful one, as you say. It's a present from the White King and Queen. There now!"

"Is it really?" said Alice, quite pleased to find she *had* chosen a good subject, after all.

"They gave it me," Humpty Dumpty continued thoughtfully, as he crossed one knee over the other and clasped his hands round it, "—for an un-birthday present."

"I beg your pardon?" Alice said with a puzzled air.

"I'm not offended," said Humpty Dumpty.

"I mean, what *is* an un-birthday present?"

"A present given when it isn't your birthday, of course."

Alice considered a little. "I like birthday presents best," she said at last.

"You don't know what you're talking about!" cried Humpty Dumpty. "How many days are there in a year?"

"Three hundred and sixty-five," said Alice.

"And how many birthdays have you?"

"One."

"And if you take one from three hundred and sixty-five, what remains?"

"Three hundred and sixty-four, of course."

Humpty Dumpty looked doubtful. "I'd rather see that done on paper," he said.

Alice couldn't help smiling as she took out her memorandum-book, and worked the sum for him:

$$
\begin{array}{r}
3\,6\,5 \\
1 \\
\hline
3\,6\,4 \\
\hline
\end{array}
$$

Humpty Dumpty took the book, and looked at it very carefully. "That *seems* to be done right——" he began.

"You're holding it upside down!" Alice interrupted.

"To be sure I was!" Humpty Dumpty said gaily, as she turned it round for him. "I thought it looked a little queer. As I was saying, that *seems* to be done right—though I haven't time to look it over thoroughly just now—and that shows that there are three-hundred and sixty-four days when you might get un-birthday presents——"

"Certainly," said Alice.

"And only *one* for birthday presents, you know. There's glory for you!"

"I don't know what you mean by 'glory,' " Alice said.

Humpty Dumpty smiled contemptuously. "Of course you don't—till I tell you. I meant 'there's a nice knock-down argument for you!' "

"But 'glory' doesn't mean 'a nice knock-down argument,' " Alice objected.

"When *I* use a word," Humpty Dumpty said in rather a scornful tone, "it means just what I choose it to mean—neither more nor less."

"The question is," said Alice, "whether you *can* make words mean different things."

"The question is," said Humpty Dumpty, "which is to be master—that's all."

Alice was too much puzzled to say anything, so after a minute Humpty Dumpty began again. "They've a temper, some of them—particularly verbs, they're the proudest—adjectives you can do anything with, but not verbs—however, *I* can manage the whole lot! Impenetrability! That's what *I* say!"

"Would you tell me, please," said Alice, "what that means?"

"Now you talk like a reasonable child," said Humpty Dumpty, looking very much pleased. "I meant by 'impenetrability' that we've had enough of that subject, and it would be just as well if you'd mention what you mean to do next, as I suppose you don't intend to stop here all the rest of your life."

"That's a great deal to make one word mean," Alice said in a thoughtful tone.

"When I make a word do a lot of work like that," said Humpty Dumpty, "I always pay it extra."

"Oh!" said Alice. She was too much puzzled to make any other remark.

"Ah, you should see 'em come round me of a Saturday night," Humpty Dumpty went on, wagging his head gravely from side to side: "for to get their wages, you know."

(Alice didn't venture to ask what he paid them with; and so you see I can't tell *you.*)

"You seem very clever at explaining words, Sir," said Alice. "Would you kindly tell me the meaning of the poem 'Jabberwocky'?"

"Let's hear it," said Humpty Dumpty. "I can explain all the poems that ever were invented—and a good many that haven't been invented just yet."

This sounded very hopeful, so Alice repeated the first verse:

" 'Twas brillig, and the slithy toves
Did gyre and gimble in the wabe:
All mimsy were the borogoves,
And the mome raths outgrabe."

"That's enough to begin with," Humpty Dumpty interrupted: "there are plenty of hard words there. 'Brillig'
means four o'clock in the afternoon—the time when you begin *broiling* things for dinner."

"That'll do very well," said Alice: "and 'slithy'?"

"Well, 'slithy' means 'lithe and slimy.' 'Lithe' is the same
as 'active.' You see it's like a portmanteau—there are two
meanings packed up into one word."

"I see it now," Alice remarked thoughtfully: "and what
are 'toves'?"

"Well, 'toves' are something like badgers—they're something like lizards—and they're something like corkscrews."

"They must be very curious creatures."

"They are that," said Humpty Dumpty: "also they make
their nests under sundials—also they live on cheese."

"And what's to 'gyre' and to 'gimble'?"

"To 'gyre' is to go round and round like a gyroscope. To
'gimble' is to make holes like a gimlet."

"And the 'wabe' is the grass plot round a sundial, I suppose?" said Alice, surprised at her own ingenuity.

"Of course it is. It's called 'wabe,' you know, because it
goes a long way before it, and a long way behind it——"

"And a long way beyond it on each side," Alice added.

"Exactly so. Well then, 'mimsy' is 'flimsy and miserable'
(there's another portmanteau for you). And a 'borogove' is
a thin shabby-looking bird with its feathers sticking out all
round—something like a live mop."

"And then 'mome raths'?" said Alice. "If I'm not giving
you too much trouble."

"Well, a 'rath' is a sort of green pig: but 'mome' I'm not

certain about. I think it's short for 'from home'—meaning that they'd lost their way, you know."

"And what does 'outgrabe' mean?"

"Well, 'outgribing' is something between bellowing and whistling, with a kind of sneeze in the middle: however, you'll hear it done, maybe—down in the wood yonder—and when you've once heard it you'll be *quite* content. Who's been repeating all that hard stuff to you?"

"I read it in a book," said Alice. "But I had some poetry repeated to me, much easier than that, by—Tweedledee, I think."

"As to poetry, you know," said Humpty Dumpty, stretching out one of his great hands, "*I* can repeat poetry as well as other folk if it comes to that——"

"Oh, it needn't come to that!" Alice hastily said, hoping to keep him from beginning.

"The piece I'm going to repeat," he went on without noticing her remark, "was written entirely for your amusement."

Alice felt that in that case she really *ought* to listen to it, so she sat down, and said "Thank you" rather sadly.

> "*In winter, when the fields are white,*
> *I sing this song for your delight——*

only I don't sing it," he explained.

"I see you don't," said Alice.

"If you can *see* whether I'm singing or not, you've sharper eyes than most," Humpty Dumpty remarked severely. Alice was silent.

> "*In spring, when woods are getting green,*
> *I'll try and tell you what I mean.*"

"Thank you very much," said Alice.

> "*In summer, when the days are long,*
> *Perhaps you'll understand the song:*
>
> "*In autumn, when the leaves are brown,*
> *Take pen and ink and write it down.*"

"I will, if I can remember it so long," said Alice.

"You needn't go on making remarks like that," Humpty Dumpty said: "they're not sensible, and they put me out.

> *"I sent a message to the fish:*
> *I told them, 'This is what I wish.'*
>
> *"The little fishes of the sea,*
> *They sent an answer back to me.*
>
> *"The little fishes' answer was*
> *'We cannot do it, Sir, because——' "*

"I'm afraid I don't quite understand," said Alice.

"It gets easier further on," Humpty Dumpty replied.

> *"I sent to them again to say,*
> *'It will be better to obey.'*
>
> *"The fishes answered with a grin,*
> *'Why, what a temper you are in!'*
>
> *"I told them once, I told them twice:*
> *They would not listen to advice.*
>
> *"I took a kettle large and new,*
> *Fit for the deed I had to do.*
>
> *"My heart went hop, my heart went thump;*
> *I filled the kettle at the pump.*
>
> *"Then someone came to me and said,*
> *'The little fishes are in bed.'*
>
> *"I said to him, I said it plain,*
> *'Then you must wake them up again.'*

"I said it very loud and clear;
I went and shouted in his ear."

Humpty Dumpty raised his voice almost to a scream as he repeated this verse, and Alice thought with a shudder, "I wouldn't have been the messenger for *anything!*"

"But he was very stiff and proud;
He said, 'You needn't shout so loud!'

"And he was very proud and stiff;
He said, 'I'd go and wake them, if——'

"I took a corkscrew from the shelf:
I went to wake them up myself.

"And when I found the door was locked,
I pulled and pushed and kicked and knocked.

"And when I found the door was shut,
I tried to turn the handle, but——"

There was a long pause.

"Is that all?" Alice timidly asked.

"That's all," said Humpty Dumpty. "Good-bye."

This was rather sudden, Alice thought: but, after such a *very* strong hint that she ought to be going, she felt it would hardly be civil to stay. So she held out her hand. "Good-bye, till we meet again!" she said as cheerfully as she could.

"I shouldn't know you again if we *did* meet," Humpty Dumpty replied in a discontented tone, giving her one of his fingers to shake; "you're so exactly like other people."

"The *face* is what one goes by, generally," Alice remarked in a thoughtful tone.

"That's just what I complain of," said Humpty Dumpty. "Your face is the same as everybody has—the two eyes, so——" (marking their places in the air with his thumb) "nose in the middle, mouth under. It's always the same. Now if you had the two eyes on the same side of the nose, for instance—or the mouth at the top—that would be *some* help."

"It wouldn't look nice," Alice objected. But Humpty Dumpty only shut his eyes and said, "Wait till you've tried."

Alice waited a minute to see if he would speak again, but as he never opened his eyes or took any further notice of her, she said, "Good-bye!" once more, and, on getting no answer to this, she quietly walked away: but she couldn't help saying to herself as she went, "Of all the unsatisfactory——" (she repeated this aloud, as it was a great comfort to have such a long word to say) "of all the unsatisfactory people I *ever* met——" She never finished the sentence, for at this moment a heavy crash shook the forest from end to end.

CHAPTER VII

THE LION AND THE UNICORN

THE next moment soldiers came running through the wood, at first in twos and threes, then ten or twenty together, and at last in such crowds that they seemed to fill the whole forest. Alice got behind a tree, for fear of being run over, and watched them go by.

She thought that in all her life she had never seen soldiers so uncertain on their feet: they were always tripping over something or other, and whenever one went down, several more always fell over him, so that the ground was soon covered with little heaps of men.

Then came the horses. Having four feet, these managed rather better than the foot-soldiers: but even *they* stumbled now and then; and it seem to be a regular rule that, whenever a horse stumbled, the rider fell off instantly. The confusion got worse every moment, and Alice was very glad to get into an open place, where she found the White King seated on the ground, busily writing in his memorandum-book.

"I've sent them all!" the King cried in a tone of delight, on seeing Alice. "Did you happen to meet any soldiers, my dear, as you came through the wood?"

"Yes, I did," said Alice: "several thousand, I should think."

"Four thousand two hundred and seven, that's the exact number," the King said, referring to his book. "I couldn't send all the horses, you know, because two of them are wanted in the game. And I haven't sent the two Messengers,

either. They're both gone to the town. Just look along the road, and tell me if you can see either of them."

"I see nobody on the road," said Alice.

"I only wish *I* had such eyes," the King remarked in a fretful tone. "To be able to see Nobody! And at that distance too! Why, it's as much as *I* can do to see real people, by this light!"

All this was lost on Alice, who was still looking intently along the road, shading her eyes with one hand. "I see somebody now!" she exclaimed at last. "But he's coming very slowly—and what curious attitudes he goes into!" (For the Messenger kept skipping up and down, and wriggling like an eel, as he came along, with his great hands spread out like fans on each side.)

"Not at all," said the King. "He's an Anglo-Saxon Messenger—and those are Anglo-Saxon attitudes. He only does them when he's happy. His name is Haigha." (He pronounced it so as to rhyme with "mayor.")

"I love my love with an H," Alice couldn't help beginning, "because he is Happy. I hate him with an H, because he is Hideous. I fed him with—with—with Ham-sandwiches and Hay. His name is Haigha, and he lives——"

"He lives on the Hill," the King remarked simply, without the least idea that he was joining in the game, while Alice was still hesitating for the name of a town beginning with H. "The other Messenger's called Hatta. I must have *two*, you know—to come and go. One to come, and one to go."

"I beg your pardon?" said Alice.

"It isn't respectable to beg," said the King.

"I only meant that I didn't understand," said Alice. "Why one to come and one to go?"

"Don't I tell you?" the King repeated impatiently. "I must have *two*—to fetch and carry. One to fetch, and one to carry."

At this moment the Messenger arrived: he was far too much out of breath to say a word, and could only wave his hands about, and make the most fearful faces at the poor King.

"This young lady loves you with an H," the King said, introducing Alice in the hope of turning off the Messenger's attention from himself—but it was no use—the Anglo-Saxon attitudes only got more extraordinary every moment, while the great eyes rolled wildly from side to side.

"You alarm me!" said the King. "I feel faint.—Give me a ham-sandwich!"

On which the Messenger, to Alice's great amusement, opened a bag that hung round his neck, and handed a sandwich to the King, who devoured it greedily.

"Another sandwich!" said the King.

"There's nothing but hay left now," the Messenger said, peeping into the bag.

"Hay, then," the King faintly murmured.

Alice was glad to see that it revived him a good deal. "There's nothing like eating hay when you're faint," he remarked to her, as he munched away.

"I should think throwing cold water over you would be better," Alice suggested: "—or some sal volatile."

"I didn't say there was nothing *better*," the King replied. "I said there was nothing *like* it." Which Alice did not venture to deny.

"Who did you pass on the road?" the King went on, holding out his hand to the Messenger for some more hay.

"Nobody," said the Messenger.

"Quite right," said the King: "this young lady saw him too. So of course Nobody walks slower than you."

"I do my best," the Messenger said in a sullen tone. "I'm sure nobody walks much faster than I do!"

"He can't do that," said the King, "or else he'd have been here first. However, now you've got your breath, you may tell us what's happened in the town."

"I'll whisper it," said the Messenger, putting his hands to his mouth in the shape of a trumpet, and stooping so as to get close to the King's ear. Alice was sorry for this, as she wanted to hear the news too. However, instead of whispering, he simply shouted at the top of his voice, "They're at it again!"

"Do you call *that* a whisper!" cried the poor King, jumping up and shaking himself. "If you do such a thing again I'll have you buttered! It went through and through my head like an earthquake!"

"It would have to be a very tiny earthquake!" thought Alice. "Who are at it again?" she ventured to ask.

"Why, the Lion and the Unicorn, of course," said the King.

"Fighting for the crown?"

"Yes, to be sure," said the King: "and the best of the joke is, that it's *my* crown all the while! Let's run and see them." And they trotted off, Alice repeating to herself, as she ran, the words of the old song:

"The Lion and the Unicorn were fighting for the crown:
The Lion beat the Unicorn all round the town.

Some gave them white bread and some gave them brown;
Some gave them plum-cake and drummed them out of
town."

"And does—the one—that wins—get the crown?" she asked, as well as she could, for the long run was putting her quite out of breath.

"Dear me, no!" said the King. "What an idea!"

"Would you—be good enough——" Alice panted out, after running a little farther, "to stop a minute—just to get —one's breath?"

"I'm *good* enough," the King said, "only I'm not strong enough. You see, a minute goes by so fearfully quick. You might as well try to stop a Bandersnatch!"

Alice had no more breath for talking, so they trotted on in silence, till they came in sight of a great crowd, in the middle of which the Lion and Unicorn were fighting. They were in such a cloud of dust, that at first Alice could not make out which was which: but she soon managed to distinguish the Unicorn by his horn.

They placed themselves close to where Hatta, the other Messenger, was standing watching the fight, with a cup of tea in one hand and a piece of bread-and-butter in the other.

"He's only just out of prison, and he hadn't finished his tea when he was sent in," Haigha whispered to Alice: "and they only give them oyster-shells in there—so you see he's very hungry and thirsty. How are you, dear child?" he went on, putting his arm affectionately round Hatta's neck.

Hatta looked round and nodded, and went on with his bread-and-butter.

"Were you happy in prison, dear child?" said Haigha.

Hatta looked round once more, and this time a tear or two trickled down his cheek: but not a word would he say.

"Speak, can't you!" Haigha cried impatiently. But Hatta only munched away, and drank some more tea.

"Speak, won't you!" cried the King. "How are they getting on with the fight?"

Hatta made a desperate effort, and swallowed a large piece of bread-and-butter. "They're getting on very well," he said in a choking voice: "each of them has been down about eighty-seven times."

"Then I suppose they'll soon bring the white bread and the brown?" Alice ventured to remark.

"It's waiting for 'em now," said Hatta: "this is a bit of it as I'm eating."

There was a pause in the fight just then, and the Lion and the Unicorn sat down, panting, while the King called out, "Ten minutes allowed for refreshments!" Haigha and Hatta set to work at once, carrying round trays of white and brown bread. Alice took a piece to taste, but it was *very* dry.

"I don't think they'll fight any more to-day," the King

said to Hatta: "go and order the drums to begin." And Hatta went bounding away like a grasshopper.

For a minute or two Alice stood silently watching him. Suddenly she brightened up. "Look! Look!" she cried, pointing eagerly. "There's the White Queen running across the country! She came flying out of the wood over yonder. —How fast those Queens *can* run!"

"There's some enemy after her, no doubt," the King said, without even looking round. "That wood's full of them."

"But aren't you going to run and help her?" Alice asked, very much surprised at his taking it so quietly.

"No use, no use!" said the King. "She runs so fearfully quick. You might as well try to catch a Bandersnatch! But I'll make a memorandum about her, if you like.—She's a dear good creature," he repeated softly to himself, as he opened his memorandum-book. "Do you spell 'creature' with a double 'e'?"

At this moment the Unicorn sauntered by them, with his hands in his pockets. "I had the best of it this time!" he said to the King, just glancing at him as he passed.

"A little—a little," the King replied, rather nervously. "You shouldn't have run him through with your horn, you know."

"It didn't hurt him," the Unicorn said carelessly, and he was going on, when his eye happened to fall upon Alice: he turned round instantly, and stood for some time looking at her with an air of the deepest disgust.

"What—is—this?" he said at last.

"This is a child!" Haigha replied eagerly, coming in front of Alice to introduce her, and spreading out both his hands towards her in an Anglo-Saxon attitude. "We only found it to-day. It's as large as life, and twice as natural!"

"I always thought they were fabulous monsters!" said the Unicorn. "Is it alive?"

"It can talk," said Haigha solemnly.

The Unicorn looked dreamily at Alice, and said, "Talk, child."

Alice could not help her lips curling up into a smile as she began: "Do you know, I always thought Unicorns were fabulous monsters, too! I never saw one alive before!"

"Well, now that we *have* seen each other," said the Unicorn, "if you'll believe in me, I'll believe in you. Is that a bargain?"

"Yes, if you like," said Alice.

"Come, fetch out the plum-cake, old man!" the Unicorn went on, turning from her to the King. "None of your brown bread for me!"

"Certainly—certainly!" the King muttered, and beckoned to Haigha. "Open the bag!" he whispered. "Quick! Not that one—that's full of hay!"

Haigha took a large cake out of the bag, and gave it to Alice to hold, while he got out a dish and carving-knife. How they all came out of it Alice couldn't guess. It was just like a conjuring trick, she thought.

The Lion had joined them while this was going on: he looked very tired and sleepy, and his eyes were half shut. "What's this!" he said, blinking lazily at Alice, and speaking in a deep hollow tone that sounded like the tolling of a great bell.

"Ah, what *is* it, now?" the Unicorn cried eagerly. "You'll never guess! *I* couldn't."

The Lion looked at Alice wearily. "Are you animal—or vegetable—or mineral?" he said, yawning at every other word.

"It's a fabulous monster!" the Unicorn cried out, before Alice could reply.

"Then hand round the plum-cake, Monster," the Lion said, lying down and putting his chin on his paws. "And sit down, both of you" (to the King and the Unicorn): "fair play with the cake, you know!"

The King was evidently very uncomfortable at having to sit down between the two great creatures: but there was no other place for him.

"What a fight we might have for the crown, *now!*" the Unicorn said, looking slyly up at the crown, which the poor King was nearly shaking off his head, he trembled so much.

"I should win easy," said the Lion.

"I'm not so sure of that," said the Unicorn.

"Why, I beat you all round the town, you chicken!" the Lion replied angrily, half getting up as he spoke.

Here the King interrupted, to prevent the quarrel going on: he was very nervous, and his voice quite quivered. "All round the town?" he said. "That's a good long way. Did you go by the old bridge, or the market-place? You get the best view by the old bridge."

"I'm sure I don't know," the Lion growled out as he lay down again. "There was too much dust to see anything. What a time the Monster is, cutting up that cake!"

Alice had seated herself on the bank of a little brook, with the great dish on her knees, and was sawing away diligently with the knife. "It's very provoking!" she said, in reply to the Lion (she was getting quite used to being called "the Monster").

"I've cut off several slices already, but they will always join on again!"

"You don't know how to manage looking-glass cakes," the Unicorn remarked. "Hand it round first, and cut it afterwards."

This sounded nonsense, but Alice very obediently got up, and carried the dish round, and the cake divided itself into three pieces as she did so. "*Now* cut it up," said the Lion, as she returned to her place with the empty dish.

"I say, this isn't fair!" cried the Unicorn, as Alice sat with the knife in her hand, very much puzzled how to begin. "The Monster has given the Lion twice as much as me!"

"She's kept none for herself, anyhow," said the Lion. "Do you like plum-cake, Monster?"

But, before Alice could answer him, the drums began. Where the noise came from, she couldn't make out:

the air seemed full of it, and it rang through and through her head till she felt quite deafened. She started to her feet, and in her terror she sprang across the brook, and had just time

. . . .

to see the Lion and Unicorn rise to their feet, with angry looks at being interrupted in their feast, before she dropped to her knees, and put her hands over her ears, vainly trying to shut out the dreadful uproar.

"If *that* doesn't 'drum them out of town,' " she thought to herself, "nothing ever will!"

CHAPTER VIII

"IT'S MY OWN INVENTION"

AFTER a while the noise seemed gradually to die away, till all was dead silence, and Alice lifted up her head in some alarm. There was no one to be seen, and her first thought was that she must have been dreaming about the Lion and the Unicorn and those queer Anglo-Saxon Messengers. However, there was the great dish still lying at her feet, on which she had tried to cut the plum-cake, "So I wasn't dreaming, after all," she said to herself, "unless—unless we're all part of the same dream. Only I do hope it's *my* dream, and not the Red King's! I don't like belonging to another person's dream," she went on in a rather complaining tone: "I've a great mind to go and wake him, and see what happens!"

At this moment her thoughts were interrupted by a loud shouting of "Ahoy! Ahoy! Check!" and a Knight, dressed in crimson armour, came galloping down upon her, brandishing a great club. Just as he reached her, the horse stopped suddenly: "You're my prisoner!" the Knight cried, as he tumbled off his horse.

Startled as she was, Alice was more frightened for him than for herself at the moment, and watched him with some anxiety as he mounted again. As soon as he was comfortably in the saddle, he began once more, "You're my——" but here another voice broke in, "Ahoy! Ahoy! Check!" and Alice looked round in some surprise for the new enemy.

This time it was a White Knight. He drew up at Alice's side, and tumbled off his horse just as the Red Knight had done: then he got on again, and the two Knights sat and looked at each other without speaking. Alice looked from one to the other in some bewilderment.

"She's *my* prisoner, you know!" the Red Knight said at last.

"Yes, but then *I* came and rescued her!" the White Knight replied.

"Well, we must fight for her, then," said the Red Knight, as he took up his helmet (which hung from the saddle, and was something the shape of a horse's head), and put it on.

"You will observe the Rules of Battle, of course?" the White Knight remarked, putting on his helmet too.

"I always do," said the Red Knight, and they began banging away at each other with such fury that Alice got behind a tree to be out of the way of the blows.

"I wonder, now, what the Rules of Battle are," she said to herself, as she watched the fight, timidly peeping out from her hiding-place: "one Rule seems to be that, if one Knight hits the other, he knocks him off his horse, and if he misses, he tumbles off himself—and another Rule seems to be that they hold their clubs in their arms, as if they were Punch and Judy. What a noise they make when they tumble. Just like fire-irons falling into the fender! And how quiet the horses are! They let them get on and off them just as if they were tables!"

Another Rule of Battle, that Alice had not noticed, seemed to be that they always fell on their heads, and the

battle ended with their both falling off in this way, side by side: when they got up again, they shook hands, and then the Red Knight mounted and galloped off.

"It was a glorious victory, wasn't it?" said the White Knight, as he came up panting.

"I don't know," Alice said doubtfully. "I don't want to be anybody's prisoner. I want to be a Queen."

"So you will, when you've crossed the next brook," said the White Knight. "I'll see you safe to the end of the wood —and then I must go back, you know. That's the end of my move."

"Thank you very much," said Alice. "May I help you off with your helmet?" It was evidently more than he could manage by himself; however, she managed to shake him out of it at last.

"Now one can breathe more easily," said the Knight, putting back his shaggy hair with both hands, and turning his gentle face and large mild eyes to Alice. She thought she had never seen such a strange-looking soldier in all her life.

He was dressed in tin armour, which seemed to fit him very badly, and he had a queer little deal box fastened across his shoulders upside-down, and with the lid hanging open. Alice looked at it with great curiosity.

"I see you're admiring my little box," the Knight said in a friendly tone. "It's my own invention—to keep clothes and sandwiches in. You see I carry it upside-down, so that the rain can't get in."

"But the things can get *out*," Alice gently remarked. "Do you know the lid's open?"

"I didn't know it," the Knight said, a shade of vexation passing over his face. "Then all the things must have fallen out! And the box is no use without them." He unfastened it as he spoke, and was just going to throw it into the bushes, when a sudden thought seemed to strike him, and he hung it carefully on a tree. "Can you guess why I did that?" he said to Alice.

Alice shook her head.

"In hopes some bees may make a nest in it—then I should get the honey."

"But you've got a bee-hive—or something like one—fastened to the saddle," said Alice.

"Yes, it's a very good bee-hive," the Knight said in a discontented tone, "one of the best kind. But not a single bee has come near it yet. And the other thing is a mouse-trap. I suppose the mice keep the bees out—or the bees keep the mice out, I don't know which."

"I was wondering what the mouse-trap was for," said Alice. "It isn't very likely there would be any mice on the horse's back."

"Not very likely, perhaps," said the Knight; "but, if they *do* come, I don't choose to have them running all about."

"You see," he went on after a pause, "it's as well to be provided for *everything*. That's the reason the horse has anklets round his feet."

"But what are they for?" Alice asked in a tone of great curiosity.

"To guard against the bites of sharks," the Knight replied. "It's an invention of my own. And now help me on. I'll go with you to the end of the wood.—What's that dish for?"

"It's meant for plum-cake," said Alice.

"We'd better take it with us," the Knight said. "It'll come in handy if we find any plum-cake. Help me to get it into this bag."

This took a long time to manage, though Alice held the bag open very carefully, because the Knight was so *very* awkward in putting in the dish: the first two or three times that he tried he fell in himself instead. "It's rather a tight fit, you see," he said, as they got it in at last; "there are so many candlesticks in the bag." And he hung it to the saddle, which was already loaded with bunches of carrots, and fire-irons, and many other things.

"I hope you've got your hair well fastened on?" he continued, as they set off.

"Only in the usual way," Alice said, smiling.

"That's hardly enough," he said anxiously. "You see the wind is so *very* strong here. It's as strong as soup."

"Have you invented a plan for keeping one's hair from being blown off?" Alice inquired.

"Not yet," said the Knight. "But I've got a plan for keeping it from *falling* off."

"I should like to hear it very much."

"First you take an upright stick," said the Knight. "Then you make your hair creep up it, like a fruit-tree. Now the reason hair falls off is because it hangs *down*—things never fall *upwards*, you know. It's my own invention. You may try it if you like."

It didn't sound a comfortable plan, Alice thought, and for a few minutes she walked on in silence, puzzling over the idea, and every now and then stopping to help the poor Knight, who certainly was *not* a good rider.

Whenever the horse stopped (which it did very often), he fell off in front; and whenever it went on again (which it generally did rather suddenly), he fell off behind. Otherwise he kept on pretty well, except that he had a habit of now and then falling off sideways; and as he generally did this on the side on which Alice was walking, she soon found that it was the best plan not to walk *quite* close to the horse.

"I'm afraid you've not had much practice in riding," she ventured to say, as she was helping him up from his fifth tumble.

The Knight looked very much surprised, and a little offended at the remark. "What makes you say that?" he asked, as he scrambled back into the saddle, keeping hold of Alice's hair with one hand, to save himself from falling over on the other side.

"Because people don't fall off quite so often, when they've had much practice."

"I've had plenty of practice," the Knight said very gravely: "plenty of practice."

Alice could think of nothing better to say than, "Indeed?" but she said it as heartily as she could. They went on a little way in silence after this, the Knight with his eyes shut, muttering to himself, and Alice watching anxiously for the next tumble.

"The great art of riding," the Knight suddenly began in a loud voice, waving his right arm as he spoke, "is to keep——" Here the sentence ended as suddenly as it had begun, as the Knight fell heavily on the top of his head exactly in the path where Alice was walking. She was quite frightened this time, and said in an anxious tone, as she picked him up, "I hope no bones are broken?"

"None to speak of," the Knight said, as if he didn't mind breaking two or three of them. "The great art of riding, as I was saying, is—to keep your balance. Like this, you know——"

He let go the bridle, and stretched out both his arms to show Alice what he meant, and this time he fell flat on his back, right under the horse's feet.

"Plenty of practice!" he went on repeating, all the time that Alice was getting him on his feet again. "Plenty of practice!"

"It's too ridiculous!" cried Alice, getting quite out of patience. "You ought to have a wooden horse on wheels, that you ought!"

"Does that kind go smoothly?" the Knight asked in a tone of great interest, clasping his arms round the horse's neck as he spoke, just in time to save himself from tumbling off again.

"Much more smoothly than a live horse," Alice said, with a little scream of laughter, in spite of all she could do to prevent it.

"I'll get one," the Knight said thoughtfully to himself. "One or two—several."

There was a short silence after this; then the Knight went on again: "I'm a great hand at inventing things. Now, I dare say you noticed, the last time you picked me up, that I was looking thoughtful?"

"You *were* a little grave," said Alice.

"Well, just then I was inventing a new way of getting over a gate—would you like to hear it?"

"Very much indeed," Alice said politely.

"I'll tell you how I came to think of it," said the Knight. "You see, I said to myself, 'The only difficulty is with the feet: the *head* is high enough already.' Now, first I put my head on the top of the gate—then the head's high enough—then I stand on my head—then the feet are high enough, you see—then I'm over, you see."

"Yes, I suppose you'd be over when that was done," Alice said thoughtfully: "but don't you think it would be rather hard?"

"I haven't tried it yet," the Knight said gravely: "so I can't tell for certain—but I'm afraid it *would* be a little hard."

He looked so vexed at the idea, that Alice changed the subject hastily. "What a curious helmet you've got!" she said cheerfully. "Is that your invention too?"

The Knight looked down proudly at his helmet, which hung from the saddle. "Yes," he said, "but I've invented a better one than that—like a sugar-loaf. When I used to wear it, if I fell off the horse, it always touched the ground directly. So I had a *very* little way to fall, you see.—But there *was* the danger of falling *into* it, to be sure. That happened to me once—and the worst of it was, before I could get out again, the other White Knight came and put it on. He thought it was his own helmet."

The Knight looked so solemn about it that Alice did not dare to laugh. "I'm afraid you must have hurt him," she said in a trembling voice, "being on the top of his head."

"I had to kick him, of course," the Knight said, very seriously. "And then he took the helmet off again—but it took hours and hours to get me out. I was as fast as—as lightning, you know."

"But that's a different kind of fastness," Alice objected.

The Knight shook his head. "It was all kinds of fastness with me, I can assure you!" he said. He raised his hands in some excitement as he said this, and instantly rolled out of the saddle, and fell headlong into a deep ditch.

Alice ran to the side of the ditch to look for him. She was rather startled by the fall, as for some time he had kept on very well, and she was afraid that he really *was* hurt this time. However, though she could see nothing but the soles of his feet, she was much relieved to hear that he was talking on in his usual tone. "All kinds of fastness," he repeated: "but it was careless of him to put another man's helmet on— with the man in it, too."

"How *can* you go on talking so quietly, head downwards?" Alice asked, as she dragged him out by the feet, and laid him in a heap on the bank.

The Knight looked surprised at the question. "What does it matter where my body happens to be?" he said. "My mind goes on working all the same. In fact, the more head downwards I am, the more I keep inventing new things."

"Now the cleverest thing that I ever did," he went on after a pause, "was inventing a new pudding during the meat-course."

"In time to have it cooked for the next course?" said Alice. "Well, that *was* quick work, certainly."

"Well, not the *next* course," the Knight said in a slow thoughtful tone: "no, certainly not the next *course*."

"Then it would have to be the next day. I suppose you wouldn't have two pudding-courses in one dinner?"

"Well, not the *next* day," the Knight repeated as before: "not the next *day*. In fact," he went on, holding his head down, and his voice getting lower and lower, "I don't believe that pudding ever *was* cooked! In fact, I don't believe that pudding ever *will* be cooked! And yet it was a very clever pudding to invent."

"What did you mean it to be made of?" Alice asked, hoping to cheer him up, for he seemed quite low-spirited about it.

"It began with blotting-paper," the Knight answered with a groan.

"That wouldn't be very nice, I'm afraid——"

"Not very nice *alone*," he interrupted, quite eagerly: "but you've no idea what a difference it makes, mixing it with other things—such as gunpowder and sealing-wax. And here I must leave you." .

Alice could only look puzzled: she was thinking of the pudding.

"You are sad," the Knight said in an anxious tone: "let me sing you a song to comfort you."

"Is it very long?" Alice asked, for she had heard a good deal of poetry that day.

"It's long," said the Knight, "but it's very, *very* beautiful. Everybody that hears me sing it—either it brings the *tears* into their eyes, or else——"

"Or else what?" said Alice, for the Knight had made a sudden pause.

"Or else it doesn't, you know. The name of the song is called 'Haddocks' Eyes.'"

"Oh, that's the name of the song, is it?" Alice said, trying to feel interested.

"No, you don't understand," the Knight said, looking a little vexed. "That's what the name is *called*. The name really *is* 'The Aged Aged Man.'"

"Then I ought to have said, 'That's what the *song* is called'?" Alice corrected herself.

"No, you oughtn't: that's another thing. The *song* is called 'Ways and Means': but that's only what it's *called*, you know!"

"Well, what *is* the song, then?" said Alice, who was by this time completely bewildered.

"I was coming to that," the Knight said. "The song really

is 'A-sitting on a Gate': and the tune's my own invention."

So saying, he stopped his horse and let the reins fall on its neck: then, slowly beating time with one hand, and with a faint smile lighting up his gentle, foolish face, he began.

Of all the strange things that Alice saw in her journey Through the Looking-glass, this was the one that she always remembered most clearly. Years afterwards she could bring the whole scene back again, as if it had been only yesterday—the mild blue eyes and kindly smile of the Knight—the setting sun gleaming through his hair, and shining on his armour in a blaze of light that quite dazzled her —the horse quietly moving about, with the reins hanging loose on his neck, cropping the grass at her feet—and the black shadows of the forest behind—all this she took in like a picture, as, with one hand shading her eyes, she leant against a tree, watching the strange pair, and listening, in a half-dream, to the melancholy music of the song.

"But the tune *isn't* his own invention," she said to herself: "it's 'I give thee all, I can no more.'" She stood and listened very attentively, but no tears came into her eyes.

> "*I'll tell thee everything I can;*
> *There's little to relate.*
> *I saw an aged aged man,*
> *A-sitting on a gate.*
> *'Who are you, aged man?' I said.*
> *'And how is it you live?'*
> *And his answer trickled through my head*
> *Like water through a sieve.*
>
> "*He said, 'I look for butterflies*
> *That sleep among the wheat:*
> *I make them into mutton pies,*
> *And sell them in the street.*
> *I sell them unto men,' he said,*

'Who sail on stormy seas;
And that's the way I get my bread—
A trifle, if you please.'

"But I was thinking of a plan
To dye one's whiskers green,
And always use so large a fan..
That they could not be seen.
So, having no reply to give
To what the old man said,
I cried, 'Come, tell me how you live!'
And thumped him on the head.

"His accents mild took up the tale:
He said, 'I go my ways,
And when I find a mountain-rill,
I set it in a blaze;
And thence they make a stuff they call
Rowlands' Macassar Oil—
Yet twopence-halfpenny is all
They give me for my toil.'

"But I was thinking of a way
To feed oneself on batter,
And so go on from day to day
Getting a little fatter.
I shook him well from side to side,
Until his face was blue:
'Come, tell me how you live,' I cried,
'And what it is you do!'

"He said, 'I hunt for haddocks' eyes
Among the heather bright,
And work them into waistcoat-buttons
In the silent night.

And these I do not sell for gold
  Or coin of silvery shine,
But for a copper halfpenny,
  And that will purchase nine.

" 'I sometimes dig for buttered rolls,
  Or set limed twigs for crabs;
I sometimes search the grassy knolls
  For wheels of Hansom-cabs.
And that's the way' (he gave a wink)
  'By which I get my wealth—. .
And very gladly will I drink
  Your Honour's noble health.'

"I heard him then, for I had just
  Completed my design
To keep the Menai bridge from rust
  By boiling it in wine.
I thanked him much for telling me

The way he got his wealth,
But chiefly for his wish that he
Might drink my noble health.

"And now, if e'er by chance I put
My fingers into glue,
Or madly squeeze a right-hand foot
Into a left-hand shoe,
Or if I drop upon my toe
A very heavy weight,
I weep, for it reminds me so
Of that old man I used to know—
Whose look was mild, whose speech was slow,
Whose hair was whiter than the snow,
Whose face was very like a crow,
With eyes, like cinders, all aglow,
Who seemed distracted with his woe,
Who rocked his body to and fro,
And muttered mumblingly and low,
As if his mouth were full of dough,
Who snorted like a buffalo—
That summer evening long ago
A-sitting on a gate."

As the Knight sang the last words of the ballad, he gathered up the reins, and turned his horse's head along the road by which they had come. "You've only a few yards to go," he said, "down the hill and over that little brook, and then you'll be a Queen.—But you'll stay and see me off first?" he added as Alice turned away with an eager look. "I shan't be long. You'll wait and wave your handkerchief when I get to that turn in the road? I think it'll encourage me, you see."

"Of course I'll wait," said Alice: "and thank you very much for coming so far—and for the song—I liked it very much."

"I hope so," the Knight said doubtfully: "but you didn't cry so much as I expected."

So they shook hands, and then the Knight rode slowly away into the forest. "It won't take long to see him *off*, I expect," Alice said to herself, as she stood watching him.

"There he goes! Right on his head as usual! However, he gets on again pretty easily—that comes of having so many things hung round the horse——" So she went on talking to herself, as she watched the horse walking leisurely along the road, and the Knight tumbling off, first on one side and then on the other. After the fourth or fifth tumble he reached the turn, and then she waved her handkerchief to him, and waited till he was out of sight.

"I hope it encouraged him," she said, as she turned to run down the hill: "and now for the last brook, and to be a Queen! How grand it sounds!" A very few steps brought her to the edge of the brook. "The Eighth Square at last!" she cried, as she bounded over and threw herself down to rest on a lawn as soft as moss, with little flower-beds dotted all about it here and there. "Oh, how glad I am to get here! And what *is* this on my head?" she exclaimed in a tone of dismay, as she put her hands up to something very heavy, that fitted tight round her head.

"But how *can* it have got there without my knowing it?" she said to herself, as she lifted it off, and set it on her lap to make out what it could possibly be.

It was a golden crown.

CHAPTER IX

QUEEN ALICE

"WELL, this *is* grand!" said Alice. "I never expected I should be a Queen so soon—and I'll tell you what it is, your Majesty," she went on in a severe tone (she was always rather fond of scolding herself), "it'll never do to loll about on the grass like that! Queens have to be dignified, you know!"

So she got up and walked about—rather stiffly just at first, as she was afraid that the crown might come off: but she comforted herself with the thought that there was nobody to see her, "and if I really am a Queen," she said as she sat down again, "I shall be able to manage it quite well in time."

Everything was happening so oddly that she didn't feel a bit surprised at finding the Red Queen and the White Queen sitting close to her, one on each side: she would have liked very much to ask them how they came there, but she feared it would not be quite civil. However, there will be no harm, she thought, in asking if the game was over. "Please, would you tell me——" she began, looking timidly at the Red Queen.

"Speak when you're spoken to!" the Red Queen sharply interrupted her.

"But if everybody obeyed that rule," said Alice, who was always ready for a little argument, "and if you only spoke when you were spoken to, and the other person always waited for *you* to begin, you see nobody would ever say anything, so that——"

"Ridiculous!" cried the Queen. "Why, don't you see, child——" here she broke off with a frown, and, after thinking for a minute, suddenly changed the subject of the conversation. "What do you mean by 'if you really are a Queen'? What right have you to call yourself so? You can't be a Queen, you know, till you've passed the proper examination. And the sooner we begin it, the better."

"I only said 'if'!" poor Alice pleaded in a piteous tone.

The two Queens looked at each other, and the Red Queen remarked, with a little shudder, "She *says* she only said 'if'——"

"But she said a great deal more than that!" the White Queen moaned, wringing her hands. "Oh, ever so much more than that!"

"So you did, you know," the Red Queen said to Alice. "Always speak the truth—think before you speak—and write it down afterwards."

"I'm sure I didn't mean——" Alice was beginning, but the Red Queen interrupted.

"That's just what I complain of! You *should* have meant! What do you suppose is the use of a child without any meaning? Even a joke should have some meaning—and a child's more important than a joke, I hope. You couldn't deny that, even if you tried with both hands."

"I don't deny things with my *hands*," Alice objected.

"Nobody said you did," said the Red Queen. "I said you couldn't if you tried."

"She's in that state of mind," said the White Queen, "that

she wants to deny *something*—only she doesn't know what to deny!"

"A nasty, vicious temper," the Red Queen remarked; and then there was an uncomfortable silence for a minute or two.

The Red Queen broke the silence by saying to the White Queen, "I invite you to Alice's dinner-party this afternoon."

The White Queen smiled feebly, and said, "And I invite *you*."

"I didn't know I was to have a party at all," said Alice; "but if there is to be one, I think *I* ought to invite the guests."

"We gave you the opportunity of doing it," the Red Queen remarked: "but I dare say you've not had many lessons in manners yet?"

"Manners are not taught in lessons," said Alice. "Lessons teach you to do sums, and things of that sort."

"Can you do Addition?" the White Queen asked. "What's one and one and one and one and one and one and one and one and one and one?"

"I don't know," said Alice. "I lost count."

"She can't do Addition," the Red Queen interrupted. "Can you do Subtraction? Take nine from eight."

"Nine from eight I can't, you know," Alice replied very readily: "but——"

"She can't do Substraction," said the White Queen. "Can you do Division? Divide a loaf by a knife—what's the answer to that?"

"I suppose——" Alice was beginning, but the Red Queen answered for her: "Bread-and-butter, of course. Try another Subtraction sum. Take a bone from a dog. What remains?"

Alice considered. "The bone wouldn't remain, of course, if I took it—and the dog wouldn't remain; it would come to bite me—and I'm sure *I* shouldn't remain!"

"Then you think nothing would remain?" said the Red Queen.

"I think that's the answer."

"Wrong, as usual," said the Red Queen; "the dog's temper would remain."

"But I don't see how——"

"Why, look here!" the Red Queen cried. "The dog would lose its temper, wouldn't it?"

"Perhaps it would," Alice replied cautiously.

"Then if the dog went away, its temper would remain!" the Queen exclaimed.

Alice said, as gravely as she could, "They might go different ways." But she couldn't help thinking to herself, "What dreadful nonsense we *are* talking!"

"She can't do sums a *bit!*" the Queens said together, with great emphasis.

"Can *you* do sums?" Alice said, turning suddenly on the White Queen, for she didn't like being found fault with so much.

The Queen gasped and shut her eyes. "I can do Addition," she said, "if you give me time—but I can't do Substraction under *any* circumstances!"

"Of course you know your A B C?" said the Red Queen.

"To be sure I do," said Alice.

"So do I," the White Queen whispered. "We'll often say it over together, dear. And I'll tell you a secret—I can read words of one letter! Isn't *that* grand? However, don't be discouraged. You'll come to it in time."

Here the Red Queen began again. "Can you answer useful questions?" she said. "How is bread made?"

"I know *that!*" Alice cried eagerly. "You take some flour——"

"Where do you pick the flower?" the White Queen asked. "In a garden, or in the hedges?"

"Well, it isn't *picked* at all," Alice explained: "it's *ground*——"

"How many acres of ground?" said the White Queen. "You mustn't leave out so many things."

"Fan her head!" the Red Queen anxiously interrupted. "She'll be feverish after so much thinking." So they set to work and fanned her with bunches of leaves, till she had to beg them to leave off, it blew her hair about so.

"She's all right again now," said the Red Queen. "Do you know Languages? What's the French for fiddle-de-dee?"

"Fiddle-de-dee's not English," Alice replied gravely.

"Who said it was?" said the Red Queen.

Alice thought she saw a way out of the difficulty this time. "If you'll tell me what language 'fiddle-de-dee' is, I'll tell you the French for it!" she exclaimed triumphantly.

But the Red Queen drew herself up rather stiffly, and said, "Queens never make bargains."

"I wish Queens never asked questions," Alice thought to herself.

"Don't let us quarrel," the White Queen said in an anxious tone. "What is the cause of lightning?"

"The cause of lightning," Alice said very decidedly, for she felt quite sure about this, "is the thunder—no, no!" she hastily corrected herself. "I meant the other way."

"It's too late to correct it," said the Red Queen: "when you've once said a thing, that fixes it, and you must take the consequences."

"Which reminds me——" the White Queen said, looking down and nervously clasping and unclasping her hands, "we had *such* a thunderstorm last Tuesday—I mean one of the last set of Tuesdays, you know."

"In *our* country," Alice remarked, "there's only one day at a time."

The Red Queen said, "That's a poor thin way of doing things. Now *here*, we mostly have days and nights two or three at a time, and sometimes in the winter we take as many as five nights together—for warmth, you know."

"Are five nights warmer than one night, then?" Alice ventured to ask.

"Five times as warm, of course."

"But they should be five times as *cold*, by the same rule——"

"Just so!" cried the Red Queen. "Five times as warm, *and* five times as cold—just as I'm five times as rich as you are, *and* five times as clever!"

Alice sighed and gave it up. "It's exactly like a riddle with no answer!" she thought.

"Humpty Dumpty saw it too," the White Queen went on in a low voice, more as if she were talking to herself. "He came to the door with a corkscrew in his hand——"

"What for?" said the Red Queen.

"He said he *would* come in," the White Queen went on, "because he was looking for a hippopotamus. Now, as it happened, there wasn't such a thing in the house, that morning."

"Is there generally?" Alice asked in an astonished tone.

"Well, only on Thursdays," said the Queen.

"I know what he came for," said Alice: "he wanted to punish the fish, because——"

Here the White Queen began again: "It was *such* a thunderstorm, you can't think!" ("She *never* could, you know," said the Red Queen.) "And part of the roof came off, and ever so much thunder got in—and it went rolling round the room in great lumps—and knocking over the tables and things—till I was so frightened, I couldn't remember my own name!"

Alice thought to herself, "I never should *try* to remember my name in the middle of an accident! Where would be the use of it?" But she did not say this aloud for fear of hurting the poor Queen's feelings.

"Your Majesty must excuse her," the Red Queen said to Alice, taking one of the White Queen's hands in her own, and gently stroking it: "she means well, but she can't help saying foolish things, as a general rule."

The White Queen looked timidly at Alice, who felt she *ought* to say something kind, but really couldn't think of anything.

"She never was really well brought up," the Red Queen went on: "but it's amazing how good-tempered she is! Pat her on the head, and see how pleased she'll be!" But this was more than Alice had courage to do.

"A little kindness—and putting her hair in papers—would do wonders with her——"

The White Queen gave a deep sigh, and laid her head on Alice's shoulder. "I *am* so sleepy!" she moaned.

"She's tired, poor thing!" said the Red Queen. "Smooth her hair—lend her your nightcap—and sing her a soothing lullaby."

"I haven't got a nightcap with me," said Alice, as she tried to obey the first direction: "and I don't know any soothing lullabies."

"I must do it myself, then," said the Red Queen, and she began:

"*Hush-a-by lady, in Alice's lap!*
Till the feast's ready, we've time for a nap:
When the feast's over, we'll go to the ball—
Red Queen, and White Queen, and Alice, and all!

"And now you know the words," she added, as she put her head down on Alice's other shoulder, "just sing it through to *me*. I'm getting sleepy too." In another moment both Queens were fast asleep, and snoring loud.

"What *am* I to do?" exclaimed Alice, looking about in great perplexity, as first one round head, and then the other, rolled down from her shoulder, and lay like a heavy lump in her lap. "I don't think it *ever* happened before, that anyone had to take care of two Queens asleep at once! No, not in all the History of England—it couldn't, you know, because there never was more than one Queen at a time. Do wake up, you heavy things!" she went on in an impatient tone; but there was no answer but a gentle snoring.

The snoring got more distinct every minute, and sounded more like a tune: at last she could even make out words, and she listened so eagerly that, when the two great heads suddenly vanished from her lap, she hardly missed them.

She was standing before an arched doorway, over which were the words "QUEEN ALICE" in large letters, and on each side of it there was a bell-handle; one marked "Visitors' Bell," and the other "Servants' Bell."

"I'll wait till the song's over," thought Alice, "and then I'll ring the—the—*which* bell must I ring?" she went on, very much puzzled by the names. "I'm not a visitor, and I'm not a servant. There *ought* to be one marked 'Queen,' you know——"

Just then the door opened a little way, and a creature with a long beak put its head out for a moment and said, "No admittance till the week after next!" and shut the door again with a bang.

Alice knocked and rang in vain for a long time, but at last a very old Frog, who was sitting under a tree, got up and hobbled slowly towards her: he was dressed in bright yellow, and had enormous boots on.

"What is it, now?" the Frog said in a deep, hoarse whisper.

Alice turned round, ready to find fault with anybody. "Where's the servant whose business it is to answer the door?" she began.

"Which door?" said the Frog.

Alice almost stamped with irritation at the slow drawl in which he spoke. "*This* door, of course!"

The Frog looked at the door with his large dull eyes for a minute: then he went nearer and rubbed it with his thumb, as if he were trying whether the paint would come off; then he looked at Alice.

"To answer the door?" he said. "What's it been asking

of?" He was so hoarse that Alice could scarcely hear him.

"I don't know what you mean," she said.

"I speaks English, doesn't I?" the Frog went on. "Or are you deaf? What did it ask you?"

"Nothing!" Alice said impatiently. "I've been knocking at it!"

"Shouldn't do that—shouldn't do that," the Frog muttered. "Wexes it, you know." Then he went up and gave the door a kick with one of his great feet. "You let *it* alone," he panted out, as he hobbled back to his tree, "and it'll let *you* alone, you know."

At this moment the door was flung open, and a shrill voice was heard singing:

"To the Looking-glass world it was Alice that said,
'I've a sceptre in hand, I've a crown on my head;
Let the Looking-glass creatures, whatever they be,
Come and dine with the Red Queen, the White Queen and
  me!'"

And hundreds of voices joined in the chorus:

"Then fill up the glasses as quick as you can
And sprinkle the table with buttons and bran:
Put cats in the coffee, and mice in the tea—
And welcome Queen Alice with thirty-times-three!"

Then followed a confused noise of cheering, and Alice thought to herself, "Thirty times three makes ninety. I wonder if anyone's counting?" In a minute there was silence again, and the same shrill voice sang another verse:

"'O Looking-glass creatures,' quoth Alice, 'draw near!
'Tis an honour to see me, a favour to hear:
'Tis a privilege high to have dinner and tea
Along with the Red Queen, the White Queen, and me!'"

Then came the chorus again:

"Then fill up the glasses with treacle and ink,
Or anything else that is pleasant to drink;
Mix sand with the cider, and wool with the wine—
And welcome Queen Alice with ninety-times-nine!"

"Ninety times nine!" Alice repeated in despair. "Oh, that'll never be done! I'd better go in at once—" and in she went, and there was a dead silence the moment she appeared.

Alice glanced nervously along the table, as she walked up the large hall, and noticed that there were about fifty guests, of all kinds: some were animals, some birds, and there were even a few flowers among them. "I'm glad they've come without waiting to be asked," she thought: "I should never

have known who were the right people to invite!"

There were three chairs at the head of the table; the Red and White Queens had taken two of them, but the middle one was empty. Alice sat down, rather uncomfortable at the silence, and longing for someone to speak.

At last the Red Queen began. "You've missed the soup and fish," she said. "Put on the joint!" And the waiters set a leg of mutton before Alice, who looked at it rather anxiously, as she had never had to carve one before.

"You look a little shy; let me introduce you to that leg of mutton," said the Red Queen. "Alice—Mutton; Mutton —Alice." The leg of mutton got up in the dish and made a little bow to Alice; and she returned the bow, not knowing whether to be frightened or amused.

"May I give you a slice?" she said, taking up the knife and fork, and looking from one Queen to the other.

"Certainly not," the Red Queen said, very decidedly: "It

isn't etiquette to cut anyone you've been introduced to. Remove the joint!" And the waiters carried it off, and brought a large plum-pudding in its place.

"I won't be introduced to the pudding, please," Alice said rather hastily, "or we shall get no dinner at all. May I give you some?"

But the Red Queen looked sulky, and growled, "Pudding—Alice; Alice—Pudding. Remove the pudding!" and the waiters took it away before Alice could return its bow.

However, she didn't see why the Red Queen should be the only one to give orders, so, as an experiment, she called out, "Waiter! Bring back the pudding!" and there it was again in a moment, like a conjuring trick. It was so large that she couldn't help feeling a *little* shy with it, as she had been with the mutton; however, she conquered her shyness by a great effort, and handed a slice to the Red Queen.

"What impertinence!" said the Pudding. "I wonder how you'd like it, if I were to cut a slice out of *you*, you creature!"

Alice could only look at it and gasp.

"Make a remark," said the Red Queen: "it's ridiculous to leave all the conversation to the pudding!"

"Do you know, I've had such a quantity of poetry repeated to me to-day," Alice began, a little frightened at finding that, the moment she opened her lips, there was dead silence, and all eyes were fixed upon her; "and it's a very curious thing, I think—every poem was about fishes in some way. Do you know why they're so fond of fishes, all about here?"

She spoke to the Red Queen, whose answer was a little wide of the mark. "As to fishes," she said, very slowly and solemnly, putting her mouth close to Alice's ear, "her White Majesty knows a lovely riddle—all in poetry—all about fishes. Shall she repeat it?"

"Her Red Majesty's very kind to mention it," the White

Queen murmured into Alice's other ear, in a voice like the cooing of a pigeon. "It would be *such* a treat! May I?"

"Please do," Alice said very politely.

The White Queen laughed with delight, and stroked Alice's cheek. Then she began:

> " *'First the fish must be caught.'*
> *That is easy: a baby, I think, could have caught it.*
> *'Next, the fish must be bought.'*
> *That is easy: a penny, I think, would have bought it.*
>
> " *'Now cook me the fish!'*
> *That is easy, and will not take more than a minute.*
> *'Let it lie in a dish!'*
> *That is easy, because it already is in it.*
>
> " *'Bring it here! Let me sup!'*
> *It is easy to set such a dish on the table.*
> *'Take the dish-cover up!'*
> *Ah, that is so hard that I fear I'm unable!*
>
> *"For it holds it like glue——*
> *Holds the lid to the dish, while it lies in the middle:*
> *Which is easiest to do,*
> *Un-dish-cover the fish, or dishcover the riddle?"*

"Take a minute to think about it, and then guess," said the Red Queen. "Meanwhile, we'll drink your health—Queen Alice's health!" she screamed at the top of her voice, and all the guests began drinking it directly, and very queerly they managed it: some of them put their glasses upon their heads like extinguishers, and drank all that trickled down their faces—others upset the decanters, and drank the wine as it ran off the edges of the table—and three of them (who looked like kangaroos) scrambled into the dish of roast mutton, and began to lap up the gravy, "just like pigs in a trough!" thought Alice.

"You ought to return thanks in a neat speech," the Red Queen said, frowning at Alice as she spoke.

"We must support you, you know," the White Queen whispered, as Alice got up to do it, very obediently, but a little frightened.

"Thank you very much," she whispered in reply, "but I can do quite well without."

"That wouldn't be at all the thing," the Red Queen said very decidedly: so Alice tried to submit to it with a good grace.

("And they *did* push so!" she said afterwards, when she was telling her sister the history of the feast. "You would have thought they wanted to squeeze me flat!")

In fact it was rather difficult for her to keep in her place while she made her speech: the two Queens pushed her so, one on each side, that they nearly lifted her up into the air: "I rise to return thanks——" Alice began: and she really *did* rise as she spoke, several inches; but she got hold of the edge of the table, and managed to pull herself down again.

"Take care of yourself!" screamed the White Queen, seizing Alice's hair with both her hands. "Something's going to happen!"

And then (as Alice afterwards described it) all sorts of things happened in a moment. The candles all grew up to the ceiling, looking something like a bed of rushes with fireworks at the top. As to the bottles, they each took a pair of plates, which they hastily fitted on as wings, and so, with forks for legs, went fluttering about: "and very like birds they look," Alice thought to herself, as well as she could in the dreadful confusion that was beginning.

At this moment she heard a hoarse laugh at her side, and turned to see what was the matter with the White Queen; but, instead of the Queen, there was the leg of mutton sitting in the chair. "Here I am!" cried a voice from the soup-tureen, and Alice turned again, just in time to see the Queen's broad, good-natured face grinning at her for a moment over the edge of the tureen, before she disappeared into the soup.

There was not a moment to be lost. Already several of the guests were lying down in the dishes, and the soup-ladle was walking up the table to Alice, and signing to her to get out of its way.

"I can't stand this any

longer!" she cried, as she seized the table-cloth with both hands: one good pull, and plates, dishes, guests, and candles came crashing down together in a heap on the floor.

"And as for *you*," she went on, turning fiercely upon the Red Queen, whom she considered as the cause of all the mischief—but the Queen was no longer at her side—she had suddenly dwindled down to the size of a little doll, and was now on the table, merrily running round and round after her own shawl, which was trailing behind her.

At any other time, Alice would have felt surprised at this, but she was far too much excited to be surprised at anything *now*. "As for *you*," she repeated, catching hold of the little creature in the very act of jumping over a bottle which had just lighted upon the table, "I'll shake you into a kitten, that I will!"

CHAPTER X

SHAKING

She took her off the table as she spoke, and shook her backwards and forwards with all her might.

The Red Queen made no resistance whatever; only her face grew very small, and her eyes got large and green: and still, as Alice went on shaking her, she kept on growing shorter—and fatter—and softer—and rounder—and——

CHAPTER XI

WAKING

——and it really *was* a kitten, after all.

CHAPTER XII

WHICH DREAMED IT?

"Your Red Majesty shouldn't purr so loud," Alice said,
rubbing her eyes, and addressing the kitten respectfully, yet

with some severity. "You woke me out of—oh! such a nice dream! And you've been along with me, Kitty—all through the Looking-glass world. Did you know it, dear?"

It is a very inconvenient habit of kittens (Alice had once made the remark) that, whatever you say to them, they *always* purr. "If they would only purr for 'yes,' and mew for 'no,' or any rule of that sort," she had said, "so that one could keep up a conversation! But how *can* you talk with a person if they always say the same thing?"

On this occasion the kitten only purred: and it was impossible to guess whether it meant "yes" or "no."

So Alice hunted among the chessmen on the table till she had found the Red Queen: then she went down on her knees on the hearthrug, and put the kitten and the Queen to look at each other. "Now, Kitty!" she cried, clapping her hands triumphantly. "You've got to confess that that was what you turned into!"

("But it wouldn't look at it," she said, when she was explaining the thing afterwards to her sister: "it turned away its head, and pretended not to see it: but it looked a *little* ashamed of itself, so I think it *must* have been the Red Queen.")

"Sit up a little more stiffly, dear!" Alice cried with a merry laugh. "And curtsey while you're thinking what to—what to purr. It saves time, remember!" And she caught it up in her arms, and gave it one little kiss, "just in honour of its having been a Red Queen, you know!"

"Snowdrop, my pet!" she went on, looking over her shoulder at the White Kitten, which was still patiently undergoing its toilet, "when *will* Dinah have finished with your White Majesty, I wonder? That must be the reason you were so untidy in my dream.—Dinah! Do you know that you're scrubbing a White Queen? Really, it's most disrespectful of you, and I'm quite surprised at you!"

"And what did *Dinah* turn to, I wonder?" she prattled on,

as she settled comfortably down, with one elbow on the rug, and her chin in her hand, to watch the kittens. "Tell me, Dinah, did you turn to Humpty Dumpty? I *think* you did—however, you'd better not mention it to your friends just yet, for I'm not sure.

"By the way, Kitty, if only you'd been really with me in my dream, there was one thing you *would* have enjoyed—I had such a quantity of poetry said to me, all about fishes! To-morrow morning you shall have a real treat. All the time you're eating your breakfast, I'll repeat 'The Walrus and the Carpenter' to you; and then you can make believe it's oysters, my dear!

"Now, Kitty, let's consider who it was that dreamed it all.

This is a serious question, my dear, and you should *not* go on licking your paw like that—as if Dinah hadn't washed you this morning! You see, Kitty, it *must* have been either me or the Red King. He was part of my dream, of course—but then I was part of his dream, too! *Was* it the Red King, Kitty? You were his wife, my dear, so you ought to know.—Oh, Kitty, *do* help to settle it! I'm sure your paw can wait!" But the provoking kitten only began on the other paw, and pretended it hadn't heard the question.

Which do *you* think it was?

A TANGLED TALE

TO MY PUPIL

Beloved Pupil! Tamed by thee,
  Addish-, Subtrac-, Multiplica-tion,
Division, Fractions, Rule of Three,
  Attest thy deft manipulation!

Then onward! Let the voice of Fame
  From Age to Age repeat thy story,
Till thou hast won thyself a name
  Exceeding even Euclid's glory.

PREFACE

Tʜɪs Tale originally appeared as a serial in *The Monthly Packet*, beginning in April 1880. The writer's intention was to embody in each Knot (like the medicine so dexterously, but ineffectually, concealed in the jam of our early childhood) one or more mathematical questions—in Arithmetic, Algebra, or Geometry, as the case might be—for the amusement, and possible edification, of the fair readers of that magazine.

L. C.

December 1885.

KNOT I

EXCELSIOR

Goblin, lead them up and down

THE ruddy glow of sunset was already fading into the sombre shadows of night, when two travellers might have been observed swiftly—at a pace of six miles in the hour—descending the rugged side of a mountain; the younger bounding from crag to crag with the agility of a fawn, while his companion, whose aged limbs seemed ill at ease in the heavy chain armour habitually worn by tourists in that district, toiled on painfully at his side.

As is always the case under such circumstances, the younger knight was the first to break the silence.

"A goodly pace, I trow!" he exclaimed. "We sped not thus in the ascent!"

"Goodly, indeed!" the other echoed with a groan. "We clomb it but at three miles in the hour."

"And on the dead level our pace is——?" the younger suggested; for he was weak in statistics, and left all such details to his aged companion.

"Four miles in the hour," the other wearily replied. "Not an ounce more," he added, with that love of metaphor so common in old age, "and not a farthing less!"

" 'Twas three hours past high noon when we left our hostelry," the young man said, musingly. "We shall scarce be back by supper-time. Perchance mine host will roundly deny us all food!"

"He will chide our tardy return," was the grave reply, "and such a rebuke will be meet."

"A brave conceit!" cried the other, with a merry laugh. "And should we bid him bring us yet another course, I trow his answer will be tart!"

"We shall but get our deserts," sighed the elder knight, who had never seen a joke in his life, and was somewhat displeased at his companion's untimely levity. " 'Twill be nine of the clock," he added in an undertone, "by the time we regain our hostelry. Full many a mile shall we have plodded this day!"

"How many? How many?" cried the eager youth, ever athirst for knowledge.

The old man was silent.

"Tell me," he answered, after a moment's thought, "what time it was when we stood together on yonder peak. Not exact to the minute!" he added hastily, reading a protest in the young man's face. "An' thy guess be within one poor half-hour of the mark, 'tis all I ask of thy mother's son! Then will I tell thee, true to the last inch, how far we shall have trudged betwixt three and nine of the clock."

A groan was the young man's only reply; while his convulsed features and the deep wrinkles that chased each other across his manly brow, revealed the abyss of arithmetical agony into which one chance question had plunged him.

KNOT II

ELIGIBLE APARTMENTS

Straight down the crooked lane,
And all round the square.

"LET's ask Balbus about it," said Hugh.

"All right," said Lambert.

"*He* can guess it," said Hugh.

"Rather," said Lambert.

No more words were needed: the two brothers understood each other perfectly.

Balbus was waiting for them at the hotel: the journey down had tired him, he said: so his two pupils had been the round of the place, in search of lodgings, without the old tutor who had been their inseparable companion from their childhood. They had named him after the hero of their Latin exercise-book, which overflowed with anecdotes of that versatile genius —anecdotes whose vagueness in detail was more than compensated by their sensational brilliance. "Balbus has overcome all his enemies" had been marked by their tutor, in the margin of the book, "Successful Bravery." In this way he had tried to extract a moral from every anecdote about Balbus—sometimes one of warning, as in, "Balbus had borrowed a healthy dragon," against which he had written, "Rashness in Speculation"—sometimes of encouragement, as in the words, "Influence of Sympathy in United Action," which stood opposite to the anecdote, "Balbus was assisting his mother-in-law to convince the dragon"—and sometimes it dwindled down to a single word, such as "Prudence," which was all he could extract from the touching record that "Balbus, having scorched the tail of the dragon, went away." His pupils liked the short morals best, as it left them more room for marginal illustrations, and in this instance they required all the space they could get to exhibit the rapidity of the hero's departure.

Their report of the state of things was discouraging. That most fashionable of watering-places, Little Mendip, was "chock-full" (as the boys expressed it) from end to end. But in one Square they had seen no less than four cards, in different houses, all announcing in flaming capitals, "ELIGIBLE APARTMENTS." "So there's plenty of choice, after all, you see," said spokesman Hugh in conclusion.

"That doesn't follow from the data," said Balbus, as he

rose from the easy-chair, where he had been dozing over *The Little Mendip Gazette*. "They may be all single rooms. However, we may as well see them. I shall be glad to stretch my legs a bit."

An unprejudiced bystander might have objected that the operation was needless, and that this long, lank creature would have been all the better with even shorter legs: but no such thought occurred to his loving pupils. One on each side, they did their best to keep up with his gigantic strides, while Hugh repeated the sentence in their father's letter, just received from abroad, over which he and Lambert had been puzzling. "He says a friend of his, the Governor of—*what* was that name again, Lambert?" ("Kgovjni," said Lambert.) "Well, yes. The Governor of—what-you-may-call-it—wants to give a *very* small dinner-party, and he means to ask his father's brother-in-law, his brother's father-in-law, his father-in-law's brother, and his brother-in-law's father: and we're to guess how many guests there will be."

There was an anxious pause. "*How* large did he say the pudding was to be?" Balbus said at last. "Take its cubical contents, divide by the cubical contents of what each man can eat, and the quotient——"

"He didn't say anything about pudding," said Hugh, "—and here's the Square," as they turned a corner and came into sight of the "eligible apartments."

"It *is* a Square!" was Balbus's first cry of delight, as he gazed around him. "Beautiful! Beau-ti-ful! Equilateral! *And* rectangular!"

The boys looked round with less enthusiasm. "Number Nine is the first with a card," said prosaic Lambert; but Balbus would not so soon awake from his dream of beauty.

"See, boys!" he cried. "Twenty doors on a side! What symmetry! Each side divided into twenty-one equal parts! It's delicious!"

"Shall I knock, or ring?" said Hugh, looking in some perplexity at a square brass plate which bore the simple inscription, "RING ALSO."

"Both," said Balbus. "That's an Ellipsis, my boy. Did you never see an Ellipsis before?"

"I couldn't hardly read it," said Hugh evasively. "It's no good having an Ellipsis, if they don't keep it clean."

"Which there is *one* room, gentlemen," said the smiling landlady. "And a sweet room too! As snug a little back-room——"

"We will see it," said Balbus gloomily, as they followed her in. "I knew how it would be! One room in each house! No view, I suppose?"

"Which indeed there *is*, gentlemen!" the landlady indignantly protested, as she drew up the blind, and indicated the back-garden.

"Cabbages, I perceive," said Balbus. "Well, they're green, at any rate."

"Which the greens at the shops," their hostess explained, "are by no means dependable upon. Here you has them on the premises, *and* of the best."

"Does the window open?" was always Balbus's first question in testing a lodging: and, "Does the chimney smoke?" his second. Satisfied on all points, he secured the refusal of the room, and they moved on to Number Twenty-five.

This landlady was grave and stern. "I've nobbut one room left," she told them: "and it gives on the back-gyardin."

"But there are cabbages?" Balbus suggested.

The landlady visibly relented. "There is, sir," she said: "and good ones, though I say it as shouldn't. We can't rely on the shops for greens. So we grows them ourselves."

"A singular advantage," said Balbus: and, after the usual questions, they went on to Fifty-two.

"And I'd gladly accommodate you all, if I could," was

the greeting that met them. "We are but mortal" ("Irrelevant!" muttered Balbus), "and I've let all my rooms but one."

"Which one is a back-room, I perceive," said Balbus: "and looking out on—on cabbages, I presume?"

"Yes, indeed, sir!" said their hostess. "Whatever *other* folks may do, *we* grows our own. For the shops——"

"An excellent arrangement!" Balbus interrupted. "Then one can really depend on their being good. Does the window open?"

The usual questions were answered satisfactorily: but this time Hugh added one of his own invention— "Does the cat scratch?"

The landlady looked round suspiciously, as if to make sure the cat was not listening. "I will not deceive you, gentlemen," she said. "It *do* scratch, but not without you pulls its whiskers! It'll never do it," she repeated slowly, with a visible effort to recall the exact words of some written agreement between herself and the cat, "without you pulls its whiskers!"

"Much may be excused in a cat so treated," said Balbus, as they left the house and crossed to Number Seventy-three, leaving the landlady curtseying on the doorstep, and still murmuring to herself her parting words, as if they were a form of blessing, "—not without you pulls its whiskers!"

At Number Seventy-three they found only a small shy girl to show the house, who said "yes'm" in answer to all questions.

"The usual room," said Balbus, as they marched in: "the usual back-garden, the usual cabbages. I suppose you can't get them good at the shops?"

"Yes'm," said the girl.

"Well, you may tell your mistress we will take the room, and that her plan of growing her own cabbages is simply *admirable!*"

"Yes'm," said the girl, as she showed them out.

"One day-room and three bedrooms," said Balbus, as they returned to the hotel. "We will take as our day-room the one that gives us the least walking to do to get to it."

"Must we walk from door to door, and count the steps?" said Lambert.

"No, no! Figure it out, my boys, figure it out!" Balbus gaily exclaimed, as he put pens, ink, and paper before his hapless pupils, and left the room.

"I say! It'll be a job!" said Hugh.

"Rather!" said Lambert.

KNOT III

MAD MATHESIS

I waited for the train

"WELL, they call me so because I *am* a little mad, I suppose," she said, good-humouredly, in answer to Clara's cautiously worded question as to how she came by so strange a nickname. "You see, I never do what sane people are expected to do nowadays. I never wear long trains (talking of trains, that's the Charing Cross Metropolitan Station—I've something to tell you about *that*), and I never play lawn-tennis. I can't cook an omelette. I can't even set a broken limb! *There's* an ignoramus for you!"

Clara was her niece, and full twenty years her junior; in fact, she was still attending a High School—an institution of which Mad Mathesis spoke with undisguised aversion. "Let a woman be meek and lowly!" she would say. "None of your High Schools for me!" But it was vacation-time just now, and Clara was her guest, and Mad Mathesis was showing her the sights of that Eighth Wonder of the world—London.

"The Charing Cross Metropolitan Station!" she resumed,

waving her hand towards the entrance as if she were introducing her niece to a friend. "The Bayswater and Birming-
ham Extension is just completed, and the trains now run
round and round continuously—skirting the border of Wales,
just touching at York, and so round by the east coast back
to London. The way the trains run is *most* peculiar. The
westerly ones go round in two hours; the easterly ones take
three; but they always manage to start two trains from here,
opposite ways, punctually every quarter of an hour."

"They part to meet again," said Clara, her eyes filling with
tears at the romantic thought.

"No need to cry about it!" her aunt grimly remarked.
"They don't meet on the same line of rails, you know. Talking of meeting, an idea strikes me!" she added, changing
the subject with her usual abruptness. "Let's go opposite
ways round, and see which can meet most trains. No need for
a chaperon—ladies' saloon, you know. You shall go whichever way you like, and we'll have a bet about it!"

"I never make bets," Clara said very gravely. "Our excellent preceptress has often warned us——"

"You'd be none the worse if you did!" Mad Mathesis
interrupted. "In fact, you'd be the better, I'm certain!"

"Neither does our excellent preceptress approve of puns,"
said Clara. "But we'll have a match, if you like. Let me choose
my train," she added after a brief mental calculation, "and
I'll engage to meet exactly half as many again as you do."

"Not if you count fair," Mad Mathesis bluntly interrupted.
"Remember, we only count the trains we meet *on the way*.
You mustn't count the one that starts as you start, nor the
one that arrives as you arrive."

"That will only make the difference of *one* train," said
Clara, as they turned and entered the station. "But I never
travelled alone before. There'll be no one to help me to
alight. However, I don't mind. Let's have a match."

A ragged little boy overheard her remark, and came running after her. "Buy a box of cigar-lights, Miss!" he pleaded, pulling her shawl to attract her attention. Clara stopped to explain.

"I never smoke cigars," she said in a meekly apologetic tone. "Our excellent preceptress——" But Mad Mathesis impatiently hurried her on, and the little boy was left gazing after her with round eyes of amazement.

The two ladies bought their tickets and moved slowly down the central platform, Mad Mathesis prattling on as usual—Clara silent, anxiously reconsidering the calculation on which she rested her hopes of winning the match.

"Mind where you go, dear!" cried her aunt, checking her just in time. "One step more, and you'd have been in that pail of cold water!"

"I know, I know," Clara said dreamily. "The pale, the cold, and the moony——"

"Take your places on the spring-boards!" shouted a porter.

"What are *they* for!" Clara asked in a terrified whisper.

"Merely to help us into the trains." The elder lady spoke with the nonchalance of one quite used to the process. "Very few people can get into a carriage without help in less than three seconds, and the trains only stop for one second." At this moment the whistle was heard, and two trains rushed into the station. A moment's pause, and they were gone again; but in that brief interval several hundred passengers had been shot into them, each flying straight to his place with the accuracy of a Minie bullet—while an equal number were showered out upon the side-platforms.

Three hours had passed away, and the two friends met again on the Charing Cross platform, and eagerly compared notes. Then Clara turned away with a sigh. To young impulsive hearts, like hers, disappointment is always a bitter pill. Mad Mathesis followed her, full of kindly sympathy.

"Try again, my love!" she said cheerily. "Let us vary the experiment. We will start as we did before, but not begin counting till our trains meet. When we see each other, we will say 'One!' and so count on till we come here again."

Clara brightened up. "I shall win *that*," she exclaimed eagerly, "if I may choose my train!"

Another shriek of engine whistles, another upheaving of spring-boards, another living avalanche plunging into two trains as they flashed by: and the travellers were off again.

Each gazed eagerly from her carriage window, holding up her handkerchief as a signal to her friend. A rush and a roar. Two trains shot past each other in a tunnel, and two travellers leaned back in their corners with a sigh—or rather with *two* sighs—of relief. "One!" Clara murmured to herself. "Won! It's a word of good omen. *This* time, at any rate, the victory will be mine!"

But *was* it?

KNOT IV

THE DEAD RECKONING

I did dream of money-bags to-night

NOONDAY on the open sea within a few degrees of the Equator is apt to be oppressively warm; and our two travellers were now airily clad in suits of dazzling white linen, having laid aside the chain-armour which they had found not only endurable in the cold mountain air they had lately been breathing, but a necessary precaution against the daggers of the banditti who infested the heights. Their holiday-trip was over, and they were now on their way home, in the monthly packet which plied between the two great ports of the island they had been exploring.

Along with their armour, the tourists had laid aside the antiquated speech it had pleased them to affect while in knightly disguise, and had returned to the ordinary style of two country gentlemen of the twentieth century.

Stretched on a pile of cushions, under the shade of a huge umbrella, they were lazily watching some native fishermen, who had come on board at the last landing-place, each carrying over his shoulder a small but heavy sack. A large weighing-machine, that had been used for cargo at the last port, stood on the deck; and round this the fishermen had gathered, and, with much unintelligible jabber, seemed to be weighing their sacks.

"More like sparrows in a tree than human talk, isn't it?" the elder tourist remarked to his son, who smiled feebly, but would not exert himself so far as to speak. The old man tried another listener.

"What have they got in those sacks, Captain?" he inquired, as that great being passed them in his never-ending parade to and fro on the deck.

The Captain paused in his march, and towered over the travellers—tall, grave, and serenely self-satisfied.

"Fishermen," he explained, "are often passengers in My ship. These five are from Mhruxi—the place we last touched at—and that's the way they carry their money. The money of this island is heavy, gentlemen, but it costs little, as you may guess. We buy it from them by weight—about five shillings a pound. I fancy a ten-pound note would buy all those sacks."

By this time the old man had closed his eyes—in order, no doubt, to concentrate his thoughts on these interesting facts; but the Captain failed to realise his motive, and with a grunt resumed his monotonous march.

Meanwhile the fishermen were getting so noisy over the weighing-machine that one of the sailors took the precaution of carrying off all the weights, leaving them to amuse themselves with such substitutes in the form of winch-handles, belaying-pins, etc., as they could find. This brought their excitement to a speedy end: they carefully hid their sacks in the folds of the jib that lay on the deck near the tourists, and strolled away.

When next the Captain's heavy footfall passed, the younger man roused himself to speak.

"*What* did you call the place those fellows came from, Captain?" he asked.

"Mhruxi, sir."

"And the one we are bound for?"

The Captain took a long breath, plunged into the word, and came out of it nobly. "They call it Kgovjni, sir."

"K—I give it up!" the young man faintly said.

He stretched out his hand for a glass of iced water which the compassionate steward had brought him a minute ago, and had set down, unluckily, just outside the shadow of the umbrella. It was scalding hot, and he decided not to drink it. The effort of making this resolution, coming close on the fatiguing conversation he had just gone through, was too much for him: he sank back among the cushions in silence.

His father courteously tried to make amends for his nonchalance.

"Whereabouts are we now, Captain?" said he. "Have you any adea?"

The Captain cast a pitying look on the ignorant landsman. "I could tell you *that*, sir," he said, in a tone of lofty condescension, "to an inch!"

"You don't say so!" the old man remarked, in a tone of languid surprise.

"And mean so," persisted the Captain. "Why, what do you suppose would become of My ship, if I were to lose My Longitude and My Latitude? Could *you* make anything of My Dead Reckoning?"

"Nobody could, I'm sure!" the other heartily rejoined.

But he had overdone it.

"It's *perfectly* intelligible," the Captain said, in an offended tone, "to anyone that understands such things." With these words he moved away, and began giving orders to the men, who were preparing to hoist the jib.

Our tourists watched the operation with such interest that neither of them remembered the five money-bags, which in another moment, as the wind filled out the jib, were whirled overboard and fell heavily into the sea.

But the poor fishermen had not so easily forgotten their property. In a moment they had rushed to the spot, and stood uttering cries of fury, and pointing, now to the sea, and now to the sailors who had caused the disaster.

The old man explained it to the Captain.

"Let us make it up among us," he added in conclusion. "Ten pounds will do it, I think you said?"

But the Captain put aside the suggestion with a wave of the hand.

"No, sir!" he said, in his grandest manner. "You will excuse Me, I am sure; but these are My passengers. The accident has happened on board My ship, and under My orders. It is for Me to make compensation." He turned to the angry fishermen. "Come here, my men!" he said, in the Mhruxian dialect. "Tell me the weight of each sack. I saw you weighing them just now."

Then ensued a perfect Babel of noise, as the five natives explained, all screaming together, how the sailors had carried off the weights, and they had done what they could with whatever came handy.

Two iron belaying-pins, three blocks, six holy stones, four winch-handles, and a large hammer, were now carefully weighed, the Captain superintending and noting the results. But the matter did not seem to be settled, even then: an angry discussion followed, in which the sailors and the five natives all joined: and at last the Captain approached our tourists with a disconcerted look, which he tried to conceal under a laugh.

"It's an absurd difficulty," he said. "Perhaps one of you gentlemen can suggest something. It seems they weighed the sacks two at a time!"

"If they didn't have five separate weighings, of course you can't value them separately," the youth hastily decided.

"Let's hear all about it," was the old man's more cautious remark.

"They *did* have five separate weighings," the Captain said, "but—well, it beats *me* entirely!" he added, in a sudden burst of candour. "Here's the result: First and second sack weighed twelve pounds; second and third, thirteen and a half; third and fourth, eleven and a half; fourth and fifth, eight: and then they say they had only the large hammer left, and it took *three* sacks to weigh it down—that's the first, third, and fifth—and *they* weighed sixteen pounds. There, gentlemen! Did you ever hear anything like *that?*"

The old man muttered under his breath, "If only my sister were here!" and looked helplessly at his son. His son looked at the five natives. The five natives looked at the Captain. The Captain looked at nobody: his eyes were cast down, and he seemed to be saying softly to himself, "Contemplate one another, gentlemen, if such be your good pleasure. *I* contemplate *Myself!*"

KNOT V

OUGHTS AND CROSSES

Look here, upon this picture, and on this

"And what made you choose the first train, Goosey?" said Mad Mathesis, as they got into the cab. "Couldn't you count better than *that?*"

"I took an extreme case," was the tearful reply. "Our excellent preceptress always says, 'When in doubt, my dears, take an extreme case.' And I *was* in doubt."

"Does it always succeed?" her aunt inquired.

Clara sighed. "Not *always*," she reluctantly admitted. "And I can't make out why. One day she was telling the little girls —they make such a noise at tea, you know— 'The more noise you make, the less jam you will have, and vice versa.' And I thought they wouldn't know what 'vice versa' meant: so I explained it to them. I said, 'If you make an infinite noise, you'll get no jam: and if you make no noise, you'll get an infinite lot of jam.' But our excellent preceptress said that wasn't a good instance. *Why* wasn't it?" she added plaintively.

Her aunt evaded the question. "One sees certain objections to it," she said. "But how did you work it with the Metropolitan trains? None of them go infinitely fast, I believe."

"I called them hares and tortoises," Clara said—a little timidly, for she dreaded being laughed at. "And I thought there couldn't be so many hares as tortoises on the Line: so I took an extreme case—one hare and an infinite number of tortoises."

"An extreme case, indeed," her aunt remarked with admirable gravity: "and a most dangerous state of things!"

"And I thought, if I went with a tortoise, there would be only *one* hare to meet: but if I went with the hare—you know there were *crowds* of tortoises!"

"It wasn't a bad idea," said the elder lady, as they left the cab, at the entrance of Burlington House. "You shall have another chance to-day. We'll have a match in marking pictures."

Clara brightened up. "I should like to try again, very much," she said. "I'll take more care this time. How are we to play?"

To this question Mad Mathesis made no reply: she was

busy drawing lines down the margins of the catalogue. "See," she said after a minute, "I've drawn three columns against the names of the pictures in the long room, and I want you to fill them with oughts and crosses—crosses for good marks and oughts for bad. The first column is for choice of subject, the second for arrangement, the third for colouring. And these are the conditions of the match: You must give three crosses to two or three pictures. You must give two crosses to four or five——"

"Do you mean *only* two crosses?" said Clara. "Or may I count the three-cross pictures among the two-cross pictures?"

"Of course you may," said her aunt. "Anyone that has *three* eyes, may be said to have *two* eyes, I suppose?"

Clara followed her aunt's dreamy gaze across the crowded gallery, half-dreading to find that there was a three-eyed person in sight.

"And you must give one cross to nine or ten."

"And which wins the match?" Clara asked, as she carefully entered these conditions on a blank leaf in her catalogue.

"Whichever marks fewest pictures."

"But suppose we marked the same number?"

"Then whichever uses most marks."

Clara considered. "I don't think it's much of a match," she said. "I shall mark nine pictures, and give three crosses to three of them, two crosses to two more, and one cross each to all the rest."

"Will you, indeed?" said her aunt. "Wait till you've heard all the conditions, my impetuous child. You must give three oughts to one or two pictures, two oughts to three or four, and one ought to eight or nine. I don't want you to be *too* hard on the R.A.'s."

Clara quite gasped as she wrote down all these fresh conditions. "It's a great deal worse than Circulating Decimals!" she said. "But I'm determined to win, all the same!"

Her aunt smiled grimly. "We can begin *here*," she said,

as they paused before a gigantic picture, which the catalogue informed them was the "Portrait of Lieutenant Brown, mounted on his favourite elephant."

"He looks awfully conceited!" said Clara. "I don't think he was the elephant's favourite Lieutenant. What a hideous picture it is! And it takes up room enough for twenty!"

"Mind what you say, my dear!" her aunt interposed. "It's by an R.A.!"

But Clara was quite reckless. "I don't care who it's by!" she cried. "And I shall give it three bad marks!"

Aunt and niece soon drifted away from each other in the crowd, and for the next half-hour Clara was hard at work, putting in marks and rubbing them out again, and hunting up and down for a suitable picture. This she found the hardest part of all. "I *can't* find the one I want!" she exclaimed at last, almost crying with vexation.

"What is it you want to find, my dear?" The voice was strange to Clara, but so sweet and gentle that she felt attracted to the owner of it, even before she had seen her; and when she turned, and met the smiling looks of two little old ladies, whose round dimpled faces, exactly alike, seemed never to have known a care, it was as much as she could do—as she confessed to Aunt Mattie afterwards—to keep herself from hugging them both. "I was looking for a picture," she said, "that has a good subject—and that's well arranged—but badly coloured."

The little old ladies glanced at each other in some alarm. "Calm yourself, my dear," said the one who had spoken first, "and try to remember which it was. What *was* the subject?"

"Was it an elephant, for instance?" the other sister suggested. They were still in sight of Lieutenant Brown.

"I don't know, indeed!" Clara impetuously replied. "You know it doesn't matter a bit what the subject *is*, so long as it's a good one!"

Once more the sisters exchanged looks of alarm, and one of them whispered something to the other, of which Clara caught only the one word "mad."

"They mean Aunt Mattie, of course," she said to herself—fancying, in her innocence, that London was like her native town, where everybody knew everybody else. "If you mean my aunt," she added aloud, "she's *there*—just three pictures beyond Lieutenant Brown."

"Ah, well! Then you'd better go to her, my dear!" her new friend said soothingly. "*She'll* find you the picture you want. Good-bye, dear!"

"Good-bye, dear!" echoed the other sister. "Mind you don't lose sight of your aunt!" And the pair trotted off into another room, leaving Clara rather perplexed at their manner.

"They're real darlings!" she soliloquised. "I wonder why they pity me so!" And she wandered on, murmuring to herself, "It must have two good marks, and——"

KNOT VI

HER RADIANCY

One piecee thing that my have got,
Maskee [1] *that thing my no can do.*
You talkee you no sabey what?
Bamboo.

They landed, and were at once conducted to the Palace. About half-way they were met by the Governor, who welcomed them in English—a great relief to our travellers, whose guide could speak nothing but Kgovjnian.

[1] "Maskee," in Pigeon-English, means "Without."

"I don't half like the way they grin at us as we go by!" the old man whispered to his son. "And why do they say 'Bamboo' so often?"

"It alludes to a local custom," replied the Governor, who had overheard the question. "Such persons as happen in any way to displease Her Radiancy are usually beaten with rods."

The old man shuddered. "A most objectionable local custom!" he remarked with strong emphasis. "I wish we had never landed! Did you notice that black fellow, Norman, opening his great mouth at us? I verily believe he would like to eat us!"

Norman appealed to the Governor, who was walking at his other side. "Do they often eat distinguished strangers here?" he said, in as indifferent a tone as he could assume.

"Not often—not ever!" was the welcome reply. "They are not good for it. Pigs we eat, for they are fat. This old man is thin."

"And thankful to be so!" muttered the elder traveller. "Beaten we shall be without a doubt. It's a comfort to know it won't be Beaten without the B! My dear boy, just look at the peacocks!"

They were now walking between two unbroken lines of those gorgeous birds, each held in check, by means of a golden collar and chain, by a black slave, who stood well behind, so as not to interrupt the view of the glittering tail, with its network of rustling feathers and its hundred eyes.

The Governor smiled proudly. "In your honour," he said, "Her Radiancy has ordered up ten thousand additional peacocks. She will, no doubt, decorate you, before you go, with the usual Star and Feathers."

"It'll be Star without the S!" faltered one of his hearers.

"Come, come! Don't lose heart!" said the other. "All this is full of charm for me."

"You are young, Norman," sighed his father; "young and light-hearted. For me, it is Charm without the C."

"The old one is sad," the Governor remarked with some anxiety. "He has, without doubt, effected some fearful crime?"

"But I haven't!" the poor old gentleman hastily exclaimed. "Tell him I haven't, Norman!"

"He has not, as yet," Norman gently explained. And the Governor repeated, in a satisfied tone, "Not as yet."

"Yours is a wondrous country!" the Governor resumed, after a pause. "Now here is a letter from a friend of mine, a merchant, in London. He and his brother went there a year ago, with a thousand pounds apiece; and on New Year's Day they had sixty thousand pounds between them!"

"How did they do it?" Norman eagerly exclaimed. Even the elder traveller looked excited.

The Governor handed him the open letter. "Anybody can do it, when once they know how," so ran this oracular document. "We borrowed nought: we stole nought. We began the year with only a thousand pounds apiece: and last New Year's Day we had sixty thousand pounds between us—sixty thousand golden sovereigns!"

Norman looked grave and thoughtful as he handed back the letter. His father hazarded one guess. "Was it by gambling?"

"A Kgovjnian never gambles," said the Governor gravely, as he ushered them through the palace gates. They followed him in silence down a long passage, and soon found themselves in a lofty hall, lined entirely with peacocks' feathers. In the centre was a pile of crimson cushions, which almost concealed the figure of Her Radiancy—a plump little damsel, in a robe of green satin dotted with silver stars, whose pale round face lit up for a moment with a half-smile as the travellers bowed before her, and then relapsed into the exact expression of a wax doll, while she languidly murmured a word or two in the Kgovjnian dialect.

The Governor interpreted: "Her Radiancy welcomes you. She notes the Impenetrable Placidity of the old one, and the Imperceptible Acuteness of the youth."

Here the little potentate clapped her hands, and a troop of slaves instantly appeared, carrying trays of coffee and sweetmeats, which they offered to the guests, who had, at a signal from the Governor, seated themselves on the carpet.

"Sugar-plums!" muttered the old man. "One might as well be at a confectioner's! Ask for a penny bun, Norman!"

"Not so loud!" his son whispered. "Say something complimentary!" For the Governor was evidently expecting a speech.

"We thank Her Exalted Potency," the old man timidly began. "We bask in the light of her smile, which——"

"The words of old men are weak!" the Governor interrupted angrily. "Let the youth speak!"

"Tell her," cried Norman, in a wild burst of eloquence, "that, like two grasshoppers in a volcano, we are shrivelled up in the presence of Her Spangled Vehemence!"

"It is well," said the Governor, and translated this into Kgovjnian. "I am now to tell you," he proceeded, "what Her Radiancy requires of you before you go. The yearly competition for the post of Imperial Scarf-maker is just ended; you are the judges. You will take account of the rate of work, the lightness of the scarves, and their warmth. Usually the competitors differ in one point only. Thus, last year, Fifi and Gogo made the same number of scarves in the trial-week, and they were equally light; but Fifi's were twice as warm as Gogo's and she was pronounced twice as good. But this year, woe is me, who can judge it? Three competitors are here, and they differ in all points! While you settle their claims, you shall be lodged, Her Radiancy bids me say, free of expense—in the best dungeon, and abundantly fed on the best bread and water."

The old man groaned. "All is lost!" he wildly exclaimed. But Norman heeded him not: he had taken out his notebook, and was calmly jotting down the particulars.

"Three they be," the Governor proceeded, "Lolo, Mimi, and Zuzu. Lolo makes 5 scarves while Mimi makes 2; but Zuzu makes 4 while Lolo makes 3! Again, so fairy-like is Zuzu's handiwork, 5 of her scarves weigh no more than one of Lolo's; yet Mimi's is lighter still—5 of hers will but balance 3 of Zuzu's! And for warmth one of Mimi's is equal to 4 of Zuzu's; yet one of Lolo's is as warm as 3 of Mimi's!"

Here the little lady once more clapped her hands.

"It is our signal of dismissal!" the Governor hastily said. "Pay Her Radiancy your farewell compliments—and walk out backwards."

The walking part was all the elder tourist could manage. Norman simply said, "Tell Her Radiancy we are transfixed by the spectacle of Her Serene Brilliance, and bid an agonised farewell to her Condensed Milkiness!"

"Her Radiancy is pleased," the Governor reported, after duly translating this. "She casts on you a glance from Her Imperial Eyes, and is confident that you will catch it!"

"That I warrant we shall!" the elder traveller moaned to himself distractedly.

Once more they bowed low, and then followed the Governor down a winding staircase to the Imperial Dungeon, which they found to be lined with coloured marble, lighted from the roof, and splendidly though not luxuriously furnished with a bench of polished malachite. "I trust you will not delay the calculation," the Governor said, ushering them in with much ceremony. "I have known great inconvenience—great and serious inconvenience—result to those unhappy ones who have delayed to execute the commands of Her Radiancy! And on this occasion she is resolute: she says the thing must and shall be done: and she has ordered up ten thousand additional bamboos!" With these words he left

them, and they heard him lock and bar the door on the outside.

"I told you how it would end!" moaned the elder traveller,
wringing his hands, and quite forgetting in his anguish that
he had himself proposed the expedition, and had never pre-
dicted anything of the sort. "Oh, that we were well out of
this miserable business!"

"Courage!" cried the younger cheerily. "*Hæc olim memi-
nisse juvabit!* The end of all this will be glory!"

"Glory without the L!" was all the poor old man could
say, as he rocked himself to and fro on the malachite bench.
"Glory without the L!"

KNOT VII

PETTY CASH

Base is the slave that pays

"Aunt Mattie!"

"My child?"

"*Would* you mind writing it down at once? I shall be quite
certain to forget it if you don't!"

"My dear, we really must wait till the cab stops. How can
I possible write anything in the midst of all this jolting?"

"But *really* I shall be forgetting it!"

Clara's voice took the plaintive tone that her aunt never
knew how to resist, and with a sigh the old lady drew forth
her ivory tablets and prepared to record the amount that
Clara had just spent at the confectioner's shop. Her expendi-
ture was always made out of her aunt's purse, but the poor
girl knew, by bitter experience, that sooner or later "Mad
Mathesis" would expect an exact account of every penny that
had gone, and she waited, with ill-concealed impatience, while

the old lady turned the tablets over and over, till she had found the one headed "PETTY CASH."

"Here's the place," she said at last, "and here we have yesterday's luncheon duly entered. *One glass lemonade* (Why can't you drink water, like me?), *three sandwiches* (They never put in half mustard enough. I told the young woman so, to her face; and she tossed her head—like her impudence!), *and seven biscuits. Total one-and-twopence.* Well, now for to-day's?"

"One glass of lemonade——" Clara was beginning to say, when suddenly the cab drew up, and a courteous railway-porter was handing out the bewildered girl before she had had time to finish her sentence.

Her aunt pocketed the tablets instantly. "Business first," she said: "petty cash—which is a form of pleasure, whatever *you* may think—afterwards." And she proceeded to pay the driver, and to give voluminous orders about the luggage, quite deaf to the entreaties of her unhappy niece that she would enter the rest of the luncheon account. "My dear, you really must cultivate a more capacious mind!" was all the consolation she vouchsafed to the poor girl. "Are not the tablets of your memory wide enough to contain the record of one single luncheon?"

"Not wide enough! Not half wide enough!" was the passionate reply.

The words came in aptly enough, but the voice was not that of Clara, and both ladies turned in some surprise to see who it was that had so suddenly struck into their conversation. A fat little old lady was standing at the door of a cab, helping the driver to extricate what seemed an exact duplicate of herself: it would have been no easy task to decide which was the fatter, or which looked the more good-humoured of the two sisters.

"I tell you the cab-door isn't half wide enough!" she repeated, as her sister finally emerged, somewhat after the fashion of a pellet from a pop-gun, and she turned to appeal to Clara. "Is it, dear?" she said, trying hard to bring a frown into a face that dimpled all over with smiles.

"Some folks is too wide for 'em," growled the cab-driver.

"Don't provoke me, man!" cried the little old lady, in what she meant for a tempest of fury. "Say another word and I'll put you into the County Court, and sue you for a Habeas Corpus!" The cabman touched his hat, and marched off, grinning.

"Nothing like a little Law to cow the ruffians, my dear!" she remarked confidentially to Clara. "You saw how he quailed when I mentioned the Habeas Corpus? Not that I've any idea what it means, but it sounds very grand, doesn't it?"

"It's very provoking," Clara replied, a little vaguely.

"Very!" the little old lady eagerly repeated. "And we're very much provoked indeed. Aren't we, sister?"

"I never was so provoked in all my life!" the fatter sister assented radiantly.

By this time Clara had recognised her picture-gallery acquaintances, and, drawing her aunt aside, she hastily whispered her reminiscences. "I met them first in the Royal Academy—and they were very kind to me—and they were lunching at the next table to us, just now, you know—and they tried to help me to find the picture I wanted—and I'm sure they're dear old things!"

"Friends of yours, are they?" said Mad Mathesis. "Well, I like their looks. You can be civil to them, while I get the tickets. But do try and arrange your ideas a little more chronologically!"

And so it came to pass that the four ladies found themselves seated side by side on the same bench waiting for the train, and chatting as if they had known one another for years.

"Now this I call quite a remarkable coincidence!" exclaimed the smaller and more talkative of the two sisters—the one whose legal knowledge had annihilated the cab-driver. "Not only that we should be waiting for the same train, and at the same station—*that* would be curious enough—but actually on the same day, and the same hour of the day! That's what strikes *me* so forcibly!" She glanced at the fatter and more silent sister, whose chief function in life seemed to be to support the family opinion, and who meekly responded:

"And me too, sister!"

"Those are not *independent* coincidences——" Mad Mathesis was just beginning, when Clara ventured to interpose.

"There's no jolting here," she pleaded meekly. "*Would* you mind writing it down now?"

Out came the ivory tablets once more. "What was it, then?" said her aunt.

"One glass of lemonade, one sandwich, one biscuit—— Oh, dear me!" cried poor Clara, the historical tone suddenly changing to a wail of agony.

"Toothache?" said her aunt calmly, as she wrote down the items. The two sisters instantly opened their reticules and produced two different remedies for neuralgia, each marked "unequalled."

"It isn't that!" said poor Clara. "Thank you very much. It's only that I *can't* remember how much I paid!"

"Well, try and make it out, then," said her aunt. "You've got yesterday's luncheon to help you, you know. And here's the luncheon we had the day before—the first day we went to that shop—*one glass lemonade, four sandwiches, ten biscuits. Total, one-and-fivepence.*" She handed the tablets to Clara, who gazed at them with eyes so dim with tears that she did not at first notice that she was holding them upside down.

The two sisters had been listening to all this with the deepest interest, and at this juncture the smaller one softly laid her hand on Clara's arm.

"Do you know, my dear," she said coaxingly, "my sister

and I are in the very same predicament! Quite identically the very same predicament! Aren't we, sister?"

"Quite identically and absolutely the very——" began the fatter sister, but she was constructing her sentence on too large a scale, and the little one would not wait for her to finish it.

"Yes, my dear," she resumed; "we were lunching at the very same shop as you were—and we had two glasses of lemonade and three sandwiches and five biscuits—and neither of us has the least idea what we paid. Have we, sister?"

"Quite identically and absolutely——" murmured the other, who evidently considered that she was now a whole sentence in arrears, and that she ought to discharge one obligation before contracting any fresh liabilities; but the little lady broke in again, and she retired from the conversation a bankrupt.

"*Would* you make it out for us, my dear?" pleaded the little old lady.

"You can do Arithmetic, I trust?" her aunt said, a little anxiously, as Clara turned from one tablet to another, vainly trying to collect her thoughts. Her mind was a blank, and all human expression was rapidly fading out of her face.

A gloomy silence ensued.

KNOT VIII

DE OMNIBUS REBUS

This little pig went to market:
This little pig staid at home.

"By Her Radiancy's express command," said the Governor, as he conducted the travellers, for the last time, from the Imperial presence, "I shall now have the ecstasy of escorting you as far as the outer gate of the Military Quarter, where the agony of parting—if indeed Nature can survive the shock—must be endured! From that gate grurmstipths start every quarter of an hour, both ways——"

"Would you mind repeating that word?" said Norman. "Grurm——?"

"Grurmstipths," the Governor repeated. "You call them omnibuses in England. They run both ways, and you can travel by one of them all the way down to the harbour."

The old man breathed a sigh of relief; four hours of courtly ceremony had wearied him, and he had been in constant terror lest something should call into use the ten thousand additional bamboos.

In another minute they were crossing a large quadrangle, paved with marble, and tastefully decorated with a pigsty in each corner. Soldiers, carrying pigs, were marching in all directions: and in the middle stood a gigantic officer giving orders in a voice of thunder, which made itself heard above all the uproar of the pigs.

"It is the Commander-in-Chief!" the Governor hurriedly whispered to his companions, who at once followed his example in prostrating themselves before the great man. The Commander gravely bowed in return. He was covered with gold lace from head to foot: his face wore an expression of deep misery: and he had a little black pig under each arm. Still the gallant fellow did his best, in the midst of the orders he was every moment issuing to his men, to bid a courteous farewell to the departing guests.

"Farewell, O old one!—carry these three to the South corner—and farewell to thee, thou young one—put this fat one on the top of the others in the Western sty—may your shadows never be less—woe is me, it is wrongly done! Empty out all the sties, and begin again!" And the soldier leant upon his sword, and wiped away a tear.

"He is in distress," the Governor explained as they left the court. "Her Radiancy has commanded him to place twenty-four pigs in those four sties, so that, as she goes round the court, she may always find the number in each sty nearer to ten than the number in the last."

"Does she call ten nearer to ten than nine is?" said Norman.

"Surely," said the Governor. "Her Radiancy would admit that ten is nearer to ten than nine is—and also nearer than eleven is."

"Then I think it can be done," said Norman.

The Governor shook his head. "The Commander has been transferring them in vain for four months," he said. "What hope remains? And Her Radiancy has ordered up ten thousand additional——"

"The pigs don't seem to enjoy being transferred," the old man hastily interrupted. He did not like the subject of bamboos.

"They are only *provisionally* transferred, you know," said the Governor. "In most cases they are immediately carried back again: so they need not mind it. And all is done with the greatest care, under the personal superintendence of the Commander-in-Chief."

"Of course she would only go *once* round?" said Norman.

"Alas, no!" sighed their conductor. "Round and round. Round and round. These are Her Radiancy's own words. But oh, agony! Here is the outer gate, and we must part!" He sobbed as he shook hands with them, and the next moment was briskly walking away.

"He *might* have waited to see us off!" said the old man, piteously.

"And he needn't have begun whistling the very *moment* he left us!" said the young one severely. "But look sharp—here are two what's-his-names in the act of starting!"

Unluckily, the sea-bound omnibus was full. "Never mind!"

said Norman cheerily. "We'll walk on till the next one overtakes us."

They trudged on in silence, both thinking over the military problem, till they met an omnibus coming from the sea. The elder traveller took out his watch. "Just twelve minutes and a half since we started," he remarked in an absent manner. Suddenly the vacant face brightened; the old man had an idea. "My boy!" he shouted, bringing his hand down upon Norman's shoulder so suddenly as for a moment to transfer his centre of gravity beyond the base of support.

Thus taken off his guard, the young man wildly staggered forwards, and seemed about to plunge into space: but in another moment he had gracefully recovered himself. "Problem in Precession and Nutation," he remarked—in tones where filial respect only just managed to conceal a shade of annoyance. "What is it?" he hastily added, fearing his father might have been taken ill. "Will you have some brandy?"

"When will the next omnibus overtake us? When? When?" the old man cried, growing more excited every moment.

Norman looked gloomy. "Give me time," he said. "I must think it over." And once more the travellers passed on in silence—a silence only broken by the distant squeals of the unfortunate little pigs, who were still being provisionally transferred from sty to sty, under the personal superintendence of the Commander-in-Chief.

KNOT IX

A SERPENT WITH CORNERS

Water, water, everywhere,
Nor any drop to drink.

"It'll just take one more pebble."
"Whatever *are* you doing with those buckets?"

The speakers were Hugh and Lambert. Place, the beach of Little Mendip. Time, 1:30 P. M. Hugh was floating a bucket in another a size larger, and trying how many pebbles it would carry without sinking. Lambert was lying on his back, doing nothing.

For the next minute or two Hugh was silent, evidently deep in thought. Suddenly he started. "I say, look here, Lambert!" he cried.

"If it's alive, and slimy, and with legs, I don't care to," said Lambert.

"Didn't Balbus say this morning that, if a body is immersed in liquid, it displaces as much liquid as is equal to its own bulk?" said Hugh.

"He said things of that sort," Lambert vaguely replied.

"Well, just look here a minute. Here's the little bucket almost quite immersed: so the water displaced ought to be just about the same bulk. And now just look at it!" He took out the little bucket as he spoke, and handed the big one to Lambert. "Why, there's hardly a teacupful! Do you mean to say *that* water is the same bulk as the little bucket?"

"Course it is," said Lambert.

"Well, look here again!" cried Hugh, triumphantly, as he poured the water from the big bucket into the little one. "Why, it doesn't half fill it!"

"That's *its* business," said Lambert. "If Balbus says it's the same bulk, why, it *is* the same bulk, you know."

"Well, I don't believe it," said Hugh.

"You needn't," said Lambert. "Besides, it's dinner-time. Come along."

They found Balbus waiting dinner for them, and to him Hugh at once propounded his difficulty.

"Let's get you helped first," said Balbus, briskly cutting away at the joint. "You know the old proverb, 'Mutton first, mechanics afterwards'?"

The boys did *not* know the proverb, but they accepted it in perfect good faith, as they did every piece of information, however startling, that came from so infallible an authority as their tutor. They ate on steadily in silence, and, when dinner was over, Hugh set out the usual array of pens, ink, and paper, while Balbus repeated to them the problem he had prepared for their afternoon's task.

"A friend of mine has a flower-garden—a very pretty one, though no great size——"

"How big is it?" said Hugh.

"That's what *you* have to find out!" Balbus gaily replied. "All *I* tell you is that it is oblong in shape—just half a yard longer than its width—and that a gravel-walk, one yard wide, begins at one corner and runs all round it."

"Joining into itself?" said Hugh.

"*Not* joining into itself, young man. Just before doing *that*, it turns a corner, and runs round the garden again, alongside of the first portion, and then inside that again, winding in and in, and each lap touching the last one, till it has used up the whole of the area."

"Like a serpent with corners?" said Lambert.

"Exactly so. And if you walk the whole length of it, to the last inch, keeping in the centre of the path, it's exactly two miles and half a furlong. Now, while you find out the length and breadth of the garden, I'll see if I can think out that sea-water puzzle."

"You said it was a flower-garden?" Hugh inquired, as Balbus was leaving the room.

"I did," said Balbus.

"Where do the flowers grow?" said Hugh. But Balbus thought it best not to hear the question. He left the boys to their problem, and, in the silence of his own room, set himself to unravel Hugh's mechanical paradox.

"To fix our thoughts," he murmured to himself, as, with hands deep-buried in his pockets, he paced up and down the room, "we will take a cylindrical glass jar, with a scale of inches marked up the side, and fill it with water up to the 10-inch mark: and we will assume that every inch depth of jar contains a pint of water. We will now take a solid cylinder, such that every inch of it is equal in bulk to *half* a pint of water, and plunge 4 inches of it into the water, so that the end of the cylinder comes down to the 6-inch mark. Well, that displaces 2 pints of water. What becomes of them? Why, if there were no more cylinder, they would lie comfortably on the top, and fill the jar up to the 12-inch mark. But unfortunately there *is* more cylinder, occupying half the space between the 10-inch and the 12-inch marks, so that only *one* pint of water can be accommodated there. What becomes of the other pint? Why, if there were no more cylinder, it would lie on the top, and fill the jar up to the 13-inch mark. But unfortunately—— Shade of Newton!" he exclaimed, in sudden accents of terror. "When *does* the water stop rising?"

A bright idea struck him. "I'll write a little essay on it," he said.

BALBUS'S ESSAY

"When a solid is immersed in a liquid, it is well known that it displaces a portion of the liquid equal to itself in bulk, and that the level of the liquid rises just so much as it would rise if a quantity of liquid had been added to it, equal in bulk to the solid. Lardner says precisely the same process occurs when a solid is *partially* immersed: the quantity of liquid displaced, in this case, equalling the portion of the solid which is immersed, and the rise of the level being in proportion.

"Suppose a solid held above the surface of a liquid and partially immersed: a portion of the liquid is displaced, and the level of the liquid rises. But, by this rise of level, a little bit more of the solid is of course immersed, and so there is a new displacement of a second portion of the liquid, and a consequent rise of level. Again, this second rise of level causes a yet further immersion, and by consequence another displacement of liquid and another rise. It is self-evident that this process must continue till the entire solid is immersed, and that the liquid will then begin to immerse whatever holds the solid, which, being connected with it, must for the time be considered a part of it. If you hold a stick, six feet long, with its end in a tumbler of water, and wait long enough, you must eventually be immersed. The question as to the source from which the water is supplied—which belongs to a high branch of mathematics, and is therefore beyond our present scope—does not apply to the sea. Let us therefore take the familiar instance of a man standing at the edge of the sea, at ebb-tide, with a solid in his hand, which he partially immerses: he remains steadfast and unmoved, and we all know that he must be drowned. The multitudes who daily perish in this manner to attest a philosophical truth, and whose bodies the unreasoning wave casts sullenly upon our thankless shores, have a truer claim to be called the martyrs of science than a Galileo or a Kepler. To use Kossuth's eloquent phrase, they are the unnamed demigods of the nineteenth century." [1]

"There's a fallacy *somewhere*," he murmured drowsily, as he stretched his long legs upon the sofa. "I must think it over again." He closed his eyes, in order to concentrate his attention more perfectly, and for the next hour or so his slow and regular breathing bore witness to the careful deliberation with which he was investigating this new and perplexing view of the subject.

[1] *Note by the writer.*—For the above essay I am indebted to a dear friend, now deceased.

KNOT X

CHELSEA BUNS

Yea, buns, and buns, and buns!
Old Song.

"How very, very sad!" exclaimed Clara; and the eyes of the gentle girl filled with tears as she spoke.

"Sad—but very curious when you come to look at it arithmetically," was her aunt's less romantic reply. "Some of them have lost an arm in their country's service, some a leg, some an ear, some an eye——"

"And some, perhaps, *all!*" Clara murmured dreamily, as they passed the long rows of weather-beaten heroes basking in the sun. "Did you notice that very old one, with a red face, who was drawing a map in the dust with his wooden leg, and all the others watching? I *think* it was a plan of a battle——"

"The Battle of Trafalgar, no doubt," her aunt interrupted briskly.

"Hardly that, I think," Clara ventured to say. "You see, in that case, he couldn't well be alive——"

"Couldn't well be alive!" the old lady contemptuously repeated. "He's as lively as you and me put together! Why, if drawing a map in the dust—with one's wooden leg—doesn't prove one to be alive, perhaps you'll kindly mention what *does* prove it!"

Clara did not see her way out of it. Logic had never been her forte.

"To return to the arithmetic," Mad Mathesis resumed—the eccentric old lady never let slip an opportunity of driving her niece into a calculation—"what percentage do you suppose must have lost all four—a leg, an arm, an eye, and an ear?"

"How *can* I tell?" gasped the terrified girl. She knew well what was coming.

"You can't, of course, without data," her aunt replied: "but I'm just going to give you——"

"Give her a Chelsea bun, miss! That's what most young ladies likes best!" The voice was rich and musical, and the speaker dexterously whipped back the snowy cloth that covered his basket, and disclosed a tempting array of the familiar square buns, joined together in rows, richly egged and browned, and glistening in the sun.

"No, sir! I shall give her nothing so indigestible! Be off!" The old lady waved her parasol threateningly; but nothing seemed to disturb the good humour of the jolly old man, who marched on, chanting his melodious refrain:

Chel - sea buns! Chel - sea buns hot! Chel - sea buns!

Pi - ping hot! Chel - sea buns hot! Chel - sea buns!

"Far too indigestible, my love!" said the old lady. "Percentages will agree with you ever so much better!"

Clara sighed, and there was a hungry look in her eyes as she watched the basket lessening in the distance; but she meekly listened to the relentless old lady, who at once proceeded to count off the data on her fingers.

"Say that 70 per cent have lost an eye—75 per cent an ear—80 per cent an arm—85 per cent a leg—that'll do it beautifully. Now, my dear, what percentage, *at least*, must have lost all four?"

No more conversation occurred—unless a smothered exclamation of, "Piping hot!" which escaped from Clara's lips as the basket vanished round a corner could be counted as such—until they reached the old Chelsea mansion, where Clara's father was then staying, with his three sons and their old tutor.

Balbus, Lambert, and Hugh had entered the house only a few minutes before them. They had been out walking, and Hugh had been propounding a difficulty which had reduced Lambert to the depths of gloom, and had even puzzled Balbus.

"It changes from Wednesday to Thursday at midnight, doesn't it?" Hugh had begun.

"Sometimes," said Balbus cautiously.

"Always," said Lambert decisively.

"*Sometimes*," Balbus gently insisted. "Six midnights out of seven, it changes to some other name."

"I meant, of course," Hugh corrected himself, "when it *does* change from Wednesday to Thursday, it does it at midnight—and *only* at midnight."

"Surely," said Balbus. Lambert was silent.

"Well, now, suppose it's midnight here in Chelsea. Then it's Wednesday *west* of Chelsea (say in Ireland or America), where midnight hasn't arrived yet: and it's Thursday *east* of Chelsea (say in Germany or Russia), where midnight has just passed by?"

"Surely," Balbus said again. Even Lambert nodded this time.

"But it isn't midnight anywhere else; so it can't be changing from one day to another anywhere else. And yet, if Ireland and America and so on call it Wednesday, and Germany and Russia and so on call it Thursday, there *must* be some place—not Chelsea—that has different days on the two sides of it. And the worst of it is, the people *there* get their days in the wrong order: they've got Wednesday *east* of them, and

Thursday *west*—just as if their day had changed from Thursday to Wednesday!"

"I've heard that puzzle before!" cried Lambert. "And I'll tell you the explanation. When a ship goes round the world from east to west, we know that it loses a day in its reckoning: so that when it gets home and calls its day Wednesday, it finds people here calling it Thursday, because we've had one more midnight than the ship has had. And when you go the other way round you gain a day."

"I know all that," said Hugh, in reply to this not very lucid explanation: "but it doesn't help me, because the ship hasn't proper days. One way round, you get more than twenty-four hours to the day, and the other way you get less: so of course the names get wrong: but people that live on in one place always get twenty-four hours to the day."

"I suppose there *is* such a place," Balbus said, meditatively, "though I never heard of it. And the people must find it very queer, as Hugh says, to have the old day *east* of them, and the new one *west:* because, when midnight comes round to them, with the new day in front of it and the old one behind it, one doesn't see exactly what happens. I must think it over."

So they had entered the house in the state I have described —Balbus puzzled, and Lambert buried in gloomy thought.

"Yes, m'm, Master *is* at home, m'm," said the stately old butler. (N.B.—It is only a butler of experience who can manage a series of three M's together, without any interjacent vowels.) "And the *ole* party is a-waiting for you in the libery."

"I don't like his calling your father an *old* party," Mad Mathesis whispered to her niece, as they crossed the hall. And Clara had only just time to whisper in reply, "He meant the *whole* party," before they were ushered into the library, and the sight of the five solemn faces there assembled chilled her into silence.

Her father sat at the head of the table, and mutely signed

to the ladies to take the two vacant chairs, one on each side of him. His three sons and Balbus completed the party. Writing materials had been arranged round the table, after the fashion of a ghostly banquet: the butler had evidently bestowed much thought on the grim device. Sheets of quarto paper, each flanked by a pen on one side and a pencil on the other, represented the plates—penwipers did duty for rolls of bread—while ink-bottles stood in the places usually occupied by wine-glasses. The *pièce de résistance* was a large green baize bag, which gave forth, as the old man restlessly lifted it from side to side, a charming jingle, as of innumerable golden guineas.

"Sister, daughter, sons—and Balbus——" the old man began, so nervously that Balbus put in a gentle "Hear, hear!" while Hugh drummed on the table with his fists. This disconcerted the unpractised orator. "Sister——" he began again, then paused a moment, moved the bag to the other side, and went on with a rush, "I mean—this being—a critical occasion—more or less—being the year when one of my sons comes of age——" he paused again in some confusion, having evidently got into the middle of his speech sooner than he intended: but it was too late to go back. "Hear, hear!" cried Balbus. "Quite so," said the old gentleman, recovering his self-possession a little: "when first I began this annual custom—my friend Balbus will correct me if I am wrong——" (Hugh whispered, "With a strap!" but nobody heard him except Lambert, who only frowned and shook his head at him) "—this annual custom of giving each of my sons as many guineas as would represent his age—it was a critical time—so Balbus informed me—as the ages of two of you were together equal to that of the third—so on that occasion I made a speech——" He paused so long that Balbus thought it well to come to the rescue with the words, "It was a most——" but the old man checked him with a warning look: "yes, made a speech," he repeated. "A few years after that, Balbus pointed

out—I say pointed out——" ("Hear, hear!" cried Balbus.
"Quite so," said the grateful old man.) "—that it was *an-other* critical occasion. The ages of two of you were together *double* that of the third. So I made another speech—another speech. And now again it's a critical occasion—so Balbus says —and I am making——" (here Mad Mathesis pointedly re-ferred to her watch) "all the haste I can!" the old man cried, with wonderful presence of mind. "Indeed, sister, I'm com-ing to the point now! The number of years that have passed since that first occasion is just two-thirds of the number of guineas I then gave you. Now, my boys, calculate your ages from the data, and you shall have the money!"

"But we *know* our ages!" cried Hugh.

"Silence, sir!" thundered the old man, rising to his full height (he was exactly five-foot five) in his indignation. "I say you must use the data only! You mustn't even assume *which* it is that comes of age!" He clutched the bag as he spoke, and with tottering steps (it was about as much as he could do to carry it) he left the room.

"And *you* shall have a similar *cadeau*," the old lady whis-pered to her niece, "when you've calculated that percentage!" And she followed her brother.

Nothing could exceed the solemnity with which the old couple had risen from the table, and yet was it—was it a *grin* with which the father turned away from his unhappy sons? Could it be—could it be a *wink* with which the aunt aban-doned her despairing niece? And were those—were those sounds of suppressed *chuckling* which floated into the room, just before Balbus (who had followed them out) closed the door? Surely not: and yet the butler told the cook—but no, that was merely idle gossip, and I will not repeat it.

The shades of evening granted their unuttered petition, and "closed not o'er" them (for the butler brought in the lamp): the same obliging shades left them a "lonely bark" (the wail of a dog, in the back-yard, baying the moon) for "a while": but neither "morn, alas," nor any other epoch, seemed likely to "restore" them—to that peace of mind which had once been theirs ere ever these problems had swooped upon them, and crushed them with a load of unfathomable mystery!

"It's hardly fair," muttered Hugh, "to give us such a jumble as this to work out!"

"Fair?" Clara echoed bitterly. "Well!"

And to all my readers I can but repeat the last words of gentle Clara:

FARE-WELL!

APPENDIX

"A knot," said Alice. "Oh, do let me help to undo it!"

ANSWERS TO KNOT I

Problem.—Two travellers spend from 3 o'clock till 9 in walking along a level road, up a hill, and home again: their pace on the level being 4 miles an hour, up hill 3, and down hill 6. Find distance walked: also (within half an hour) time of reaching top of hill.

Answer.—24 miles: half-past 6.

Solution.—A level mile takes ¼ of an hour, up hill ⅓, down hill ⅙. Hence to go and return over the same mile, whether on the level or on the hill-side, takes ½ an hour. Hence in 6 hours they went 12 miles out and 12 back. If the 12 miles out had been nearly all level, they would have taken a little over 3 hours; if nearly all up hill, a little under 4. Hence 3½ hours must be within ½ an hour of the time taken in reaching the peak; thus, as they started at 3, they got there within ½ an hour of ½ past 6.

Twenty-seven answers have come in. Of these, 9 are right, 16 partially right, and 2 wrong. The 16 give the *distance* correctly, but they have failed to grasp the fact that the top of the hill might have been reached at *any* moment between 6 o'clock and 7.

The two wrong answers are from GERTY VERNON and A NIHILIST. The former makes the distance "23 miles," while her revolutionary companion puts it at "27." GERTY VERNON says, "they had to go 4 miles along the plain, and got to the foot of the hill at 4 o'clock." They *might* have done so, I grant; but you have no ground for saying they *did* so. "It was 7½ miles to the top of the hill, and they reached that at ¼ before 7 o'clock." Here you go wrong in your arithmetic, and I must, however reluctantly, bid you farewell. 7½ miles, at 3 miles an hour, would *not* require 2¾ hours. A NIHILIST says, "Let x denote the whole number of miles; y the number of hours to hill-top; $\therefore$ $3y$ = number of miles to hill-top, and $x - 3y$ = number of miles on the other side." You bewilder me. The other side of *what?* "Of the hill," you say. But then, how did they get home again? However, to accommodate your views we will build a new hostelry at the foot of the hill on the opposite side, and also assume (what I grant you is *possible*, though it is not *necessarily* true) that there was no level road at all. Even then you go wrong. You say:

$$\text{``}y = 6 \quad \frac{x - 3y}{6} \quad . \quad . \quad . \quad \text{(i)};$$

$$\frac{x}{4\frac{1}{2}} = 6 \quad . \quad . \quad . \quad . \quad . \quad \text{(ii).''}$$

I grant you (i), but I deny (ii): it rests on the assumption that to go *part* of the time at 3 miles an hour, and the rest at 6 miles an hour, comes to the same result as going the *whole* time at 4½ miles an hour. But this would only be true if the *"part"* were an exact half, *i. e.* if they went up hill for 3 hours, and down hill for the other 3: which they certainly did *not* do.

The sixteen who are partially right, are AGNES BAILEY, F. K., FIFEE, G. E. B., H. P., KIT, M. E. T., MYSIE, A MOTHER'S SON, NAIRAM, A REDRUTHIAN, A SOCIALIST, SPEAR MAIDEN, T. B. C., VIS INERTIÆ, and YAK. Of these, F. K., FIFEE, T. B. C., and VIS INERTIÆ do not attempt the second part at all. F. K. and H. P. give no working. The rest make particular assumptions, such as that there was no level road—that there were 6 miles of level road—and so on, all leading to *particular* times being fixed for reaching the hill-top. The most curious assumption is that of AGNES BAILEY, who says, "Let $x =$ number of hours occupied in ascent; then $\dfrac{x}{2} =$ hours occupied in descent; and $\dfrac{4x}{3} =$ hours occupied on the level." I suppose you were thinking of the relative *rates*, up hill and on the level; which we might express by saying that, if they went x miles up hill in a certain time, they would go $\dfrac{4x}{3}$ miles on the level *in the same time*. You have, in fact, assumed that they took *the same time* on the level that they took in ascending the hill. FIFEE assumes that, when the aged knight said they had gone "four miles in the hour" on the level, he meant that four miles was the *distance* gone, not merely the rate. This would have been—if FIFEE will excuse the slang expression—a "sell," ill-suited to the dignity of the hero.

And now "descend, ye classic Nine!" who have solved the whole problem, and let me sing your praises. Your names are BLITHE, E. W., L. B., A MARLBOROUGH BOY, O. V. L.,

PUTNEY WALKER, ROSE, SEA-BREEZE, SIMPLE SUSAN, and MONEY-SPINNER. (These last two I count as one, as they send a joint answer.) ROSE and SIMPLE SUSAN and Co. do not actually state that the hill-top was reached sometime between 6 and 7, but, as they have clearly grasped the fact that a mile, ascended and descended, took the same time as two level miles, I mark them as "right." A MARLBOROUGH BOY and PUTNEY WALKER deserve honourable mention for their algebraical solutions, being the only two who have perceived that the question leads to *an indeterminate equation*. E. W. brings a charge of untruthfulness against the aged knight—a serious charge, for he was the very pink of chivalry! She says, "According to the data given, the time at the summit affords no clue to the total distance. It does not enable us to state precisely to an inch how much level and how much hill there was on the road." "Fair damsel," the aged knight replies, "—if, as I surmise, thy initials denote Early Womanhood—bethink thee that the word 'enable' is thine, not mine. I did but ask the time of reaching the hill-top as my *condition* for further parley. If *now* thou wilt not grant that I am a truth-loving man, then will I affirm that those same initials denote Envenomed Wickedness!"

CLASS LIST

I

A MARLBOROUGH BOY.	PUTNEY WALKER.

II

BLITHE.	ROSE.
E. W.	SEA-BREEZE.
L. B.	SIMPLE SUSAN.
O. V. L.	MONEY-SPINNER.

BLITHE has made so ingenious an addition to the problem, and SIMPLE SUSAN and Co. have solved it in such tuneful verse, that I record both their answers in full. I have altered a word or two in BLITHE's—which I trust she will excuse; it did not seem quite clear as it stood.

"Yet stay," said the youth, as a gleam of inspiration lighted up the relaxing muscles of his quiescent features. "Stay. Methinks it matters little *when* we reached that summit, the crown of our toil. For in the space of time wherein we clambered up one mile and bounded down the same on our return, we could have trudged the *twain* on the level. We have plodded, then, four-and-twenty miles in these six mortal hours; for never a moment did we stop for catching of fleeting breath or for gazing on the scene around!"

"Very good," said the old man. "Twelve miles out and twelve miles in. And we reached the top sometime between six and seven of the clock. Now mark me! For every five minutes that had fled since six of the clock when we stood on yonder peak, so many miles had we toiled upwards on the dreary mountain-side!"

The youth moaned and rushed into the hostel.

BLITHE.

The elder and the younger knight,
They sallied forth at three;
How far they went on level ground
It matters not to me;
What time they reached the foot of hill,
When they began to mount,
Are problems which I hold to be
Of very small account.

The moment that each waved his hat
Upon the topmost peak—
To trivial query such as this
No answer will I seek.

Yet can I tell the distance well
They must have travelled o'er:
On hill and plain, 'twixt three and nine,
The miles were twenty-four.

Four miles an hour their steady pace
Along the level track,
Three when they climbed—but six when they
Came swiftly striding back
Adown the hill; and little skill
It needs, methinks, to show,
Up hill and down together told,
Four miles an hour they go.

For whether long or short the time
Upon the hill they spent,
Two thirds were passed in going up,
One third in the descent.
Two thirds at three, one third at six,
If rightly reckoned o'er,
Will make one whole at four—the tale
Is tangled now no more.

SIMPLE SUSAN.
MONEY-SPINNER.

ANSWERS TO KNOT II

§ 1. THE DINNER PARTY

Problem.—The Governor of Kgovjni wants to give a very small dinner party, and invites his father's brother-in-law, his brother's father-in-law, his father-in-law's brother, and his brother-in-law's father. Find the number of guests.

Answer.—One.

In this genealogy, males are denoted by capitals, and females by small letters.

The Governor is E and his guest is C.

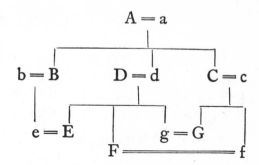

Ten answers have been received. Of these, one is wrong, GALANTHUS NIVALIS MAJOR, who insists on inviting *two* guests, one being the Governor's *wife's brother's father*. If she had taken his *sister's husband's father* instead, she would have found it possible to reduce the guests to *one*.

Of the nine who send right answers, SEA-BREEZE is the very faintest breath that ever bore the name! She simply states that the Governor's uncle might fulfil all the conditions "by intermarriages"! "Wind of the western sea," you have had a very narrow escape! Be thankful to appear in the Class List at all! BOG-OAK and BRADSHAW OF THE FUTURE use genealogies which require 16 people instead of 14, by inviting the Governor's *father's sister's husband* instead of his *father's wife's brother*. I cannot think this so good a solution as one that requires only 14. CAIUS and VALENTINE deserve special mention as the only two who have supplied genealogies.

CLASS LIST

I

| BEE. | M. M. | OLD CAT. |
| CAIUS. | MATTHEW MATTICKS. | VALENTINE. |

II

BOG-OAK.   BRADSHAW OF THE FUTURE.

III

SEA-BREEZE.

§ 2. The Lodgings

Problem.—A Square has 20 doors on each side, which contains 21 equal parts. They are numbered all round, beginning at one corner. From which of the four, Nos. 9, 25, 52, 73, is the sum of the distances, to the other three, least?

Answer.—From No. 9.

Let A be No. 9, B No. 25, C No. 52, and D No. 73.

Then $AB = \sqrt{(12^2 + 5^2)} = \sqrt{169} = 13$;

$AC = 21$;

$AD = \sqrt{(9^2 + 8^2)} = \sqrt{145} = 12 +$

(N.B. *i. e.* "between 12 and 13")

$BC = \sqrt{(16^2 + 12^2)} = \sqrt{400} = 20$;

$BD = \sqrt{(3^2 + 21^2)} = \sqrt{450} = 21 +$;

$CD = \sqrt{(9^2 + 13^2)} = \sqrt{250} = 15 +$;

```
            A
        ┌──────────┐
        │ 9 .  12 5│
        │ 8        │
        │ .      . │ B
     D  │ .        │
        │ 13    16 │
        │ 9.    12 │
        └──────────┘
            C
```

Hence sum of distances from A is between 46 and 47; from B, between 54 and 55; from C, between 56 and 57; from D, between 48 and 51. (Why not "between 48 and 49"? Make this out for yourselves.) Hence the sum is least for A.

Twenty-five solutions have been received. Of these, 15 must be marked "zero," 5 are partly right, and 5 right. Of the 15, I may dismiss Alphabetical Phantom, Bog-Oak, Dinah Mite, Fifee, Galanthus Nivalis Major (I fear the cold spring has blighted our Snowdrop), Guy, H.M.S. Pinafore, Janet, and Valentine with the simple remark that they insist on the unfortunate lodgers *keeping to the pavement.* (I used the words "crossed to Number Seventy-three" for the special purpose of showing that *short cuts* were possible.) Sea-Breeze does the same, and adds that "the result would be the same" even if they crossed the Square, but gives no proof of this. M. M. draws a diagram, and says that No. 9 is the house, "as the diagram shows." I cannot see *how* it does so. OLD CAT assumes that the house *must* be No. 9 or No. 73. She does not explain how she estimates the distances. BEE's Arithmetic is faulty: she makes $\sqrt{169} + \sqrt{442} + \sqrt{130} = 741$. (I suppose you mean $\sqrt{741}$, which would be a little nearer the truth. But roots cannot be added in this manner. Do you think $\sqrt{9} + \sqrt{16}$ is 25, or even $\sqrt{25}$?) But AYR's state is more perilous still: she draws illogical conclusions with a frightful calmness. After pointing out (rightly) that AC is less than BD, she says, "therefore the nearest house to the other three must be A or C." And again, after pointing out (rightly) that B and D are both within the half-square containing A, she says, "therefore" AB + AD must be less than BC + CD. (There is no logical force in either "therefore." For the first, try Nos. 1, 21, 60, 70: this will make your premiss true, and your conclusion false. Similarly, for the second, try Nos. 1, 30, 51, 71.)

Of the five partly-right solutions, RAGS AND TATTERS and MAD HATTER (who send one answer between them) make No. 25 6 units from the corner instead of 5. CHEAM, E. R. D. L., and MEGGY POTTS leave openings at the corners of the Square, which are not in the data: moreover CHEAM gives values for the distances without any hint that they are only *approximations*. CROPHI AND MOPHI make the bold and unfounded assumption that there were really 21 houses on each side, instead of 20 as stated by Balbus. "We may assume," they add, "that the doors of Nos. 21, 42, 63, 84, are invisible from the centre of the Square"! What is there, I wonder, that CROPHI AND MOPHI would *not* assume?

Of the five who are wholly right, I think BRADSHAW OF THE FUTURE, CAIUS, CLIFTON C., and MARTREB deserve special praise for their full *analytical* solutions. MATTHEW MATTICKS picks out No. 9, and proves it to be the right house in two ways, very neatly and ingeniously, but *why* he picks it out does not appear. It is an excellent *synthetical* proof, but lacks the analysis which the other four supply.

CLASS LIST

I

BRADSHAW OF THE FUTURE.   CLIFTON C.
CAIUS.   MARTREB.

II

MATTHEW MATTICKS.

III

CHEAM.   MEGGY POTTS.
CROPHI AND MOPHI.   { RAGS AND TATTERS.
E. R. D. L.   { MAD HATTER.

A remonstrance has reached me from SCRUTATOR on the subject of Knot I, which he declares was "no problem at all." "Two questions," he says, "are put. To solve one there is no data: the other answers itself." As to the first point, SCRUTATOR is mistaken; there *are* (not "is") data sufficient to answer the question. As to the other, it is interesting to know that the question "answers itself," and I am sure it does the question great credit: still I fear I cannot enter it on the list of winners, as this competition is only open to human beings.

ANSWERS TO KNOT III

Problem.—(1) Two travellers, starting at the same time, went opposite ways round a circular railway. Trains start each way every 15 minutes, the easterly ones going round in 3 hours, the westerly in 2. How many trains did each meet on the way, not counting trains met at the terminus itself?

(2) They went round, as before, each traveller counting as "one" the train containing the other traveller. How many did each meet?

Answers.—(1) 19. (2) The easterly traveller met 12; the other 8.

The trains one way took 180 minutes, the other way 120. Let us take the l.c.m., 360, and divide the railway into 360 units. Then one set of trains went at the rate of 2 units a minute and at intervals of 30 units; the other at the rate of 3 units a minute and at intervals of 45 units. An easterly train starting has 45 units between it and the first train it will meet: it does ⅖ of this while the other does ⅗, and thus meets it at the end of 18 units, and so all the way round. A westerly train starting has 30 units between it and the first train it will meet: it does ⅗ of this while the other does ⅖, and thus meets it at the end of 18 units, and so all the way round. Hence if the railway be divided, by 19 posts, into 20 parts, each containing 18 units, trains meet at every post, and, in (1), each traveller passes 19 posts in going round, and so meets 19 trains. But, in (2), the easterly traveller only begins to count after traversing ⅖ of the journey, *i. e.* on reaching the 8th post, and so counts 12 posts: similarly the other counts 8. They meet at the end of ⅖ of 3 hours, or ⅗ of 2 hours, *i. e.* 72 minutes.

Forty-five answers have been received. Of these, 12 are beyond the reach of discussion, as they give no working. I can but enumerate their names. ARDMORE, E. A., F. A. D., L. D., MATTHEW MATTICKS, M. E. T., Poo-Poo, and THE RED QUEEN are all wrong. BETA and ROWENA have got (1) right and (2) wrong. CHEEKY BOB and NAIRAM give the right answers, but it may perhaps make the one less cheeky, and induce the other to take a less inverted view of things, to be informed that, if this had been a competition for a prize, they would have got no marks. (N.B.—I have not ventured to put E. A.'s name in full, as she only gave it provisionally, in case her answer should prove right.)

Of the 33 answers for which the working is given, 10 are wrong; 11 half-wrong and half-right; 3 right, except that they cherish the delusion that it was *Clara* who travelled in the easterly train—a point which the data do not enable us to settle; and 9 wholly right.

The 10 wrong answers are from Bo-Peep, Financier, I. W. T., Kate B., M. A. H., Q. Y. Z., Sea-Gull, Thistle-down, Tom-Quad, and an unsigned one. Bo-Peep rightly says that the easterly traveller met all trains which started during the 3 hours of her trip, as well as all which started during the previous 2 hours, *i. e.* all which started at the commencements of 20 periods of 15 minutes each; and she is right in striking out the one she met at the moment of starting; but wrong in striking out the *last* train, for she did not meet this at the terminus, but 15 minutes before she got there. She makes the same mistake in (2). Financier thinks that any train, met for the second time, is not to be counted. I. W. T. finds, by a process which is not stated, that the travellers met at the end of 71 minutes and 26½ seconds. Kate B. thinks the trains which are met on starting and on arriving are *never* to be counted, even when met elsewhere. Q. Y. Z. tries a rather complex algebraical solution, and succeeds in finding the time of meeting correctly: all else is wrong. Sea-Gull seems to think that, in (1), the easterly train *stood still* for 3 hours; and says that, in (2), the travellers met at the end of 71 minutes 40 seconds. Thistledown nobly confesses to having tried no calculation, but merely having drawn a picture of the railway and counted the trains; in (1) she counts wrong; in (2) she makes them meet in 75 minutes. Tom-Quad omits (1): in (2) he makes Clara count the train she met on her arrival. The unsigned one is also unintelligible; it states that the travellers go "¹/₂₄ more than the total distance to be traversed"! The "Clara" theory, already referred to, is adopted by 5 of these, viz. Bo-Peep, Financier, Kate B., Tom-Quad, and the nameless writer.

The 11 half-right answers are from Bog-Oak, Bridget, Castor, Cheshire Cat, G. E. B., Guy, Mary, M. A. H., Old Maid, R. W., and Vendredi. All these adopt the "Clara" theory. Castor omits (1). Vendredi gets (1) right, but in (2) makes the same mistake as Bo-Peep. I notice in your solution a marvellous proportion-sum: "300 miles : 2 hours :: one mile : 24 seconds." May I venture to advise your acquiring, as soon as possible, an utter disbelief in the possibility of a ratio existing between *miles* and *hours?* Do not be disheartened by your two friends' sarcastic remarks on your "roundabout ways." Their short method, of adding 12 and 8, has the slight disadvantage of bringing the answer wrong: even a "roundabout" method is better than *that!* M. A. H., in (2), makes the travellers count "one" *after* they met, not *when* they met. Cheshire Cat and Old Maid get "20" as answer for (1), by forgetting to strike out the train met on arrival. The others all get "18" in various ways. Bog-Oak, Guy, and R. W. divide the trains which the westerly traveller has to meet into 2 sets, viz. those already on the line, which they (rightly) make "11," and those which started during her 2 hours' journey (exclusive of train met on arrival), which they (wrongly) make "7"; and they make a similar mistake with the easterly train. Bridget (rightly) says that the westerly traveller met a train every 6 minutes for 2 hours, but (wrongly) makes the number "20"; it should be "21." G. E. B. adopts Bo-Peep's method, but (wrongly) strikes out (for the easterly traveller) the train which started at the *commencement* of the previous 2 hours. Mary thinks a train met on arrival must not be counted, even when met on a *previous* occasion.

The 3 who are wholly right but for the unfortunate "Clara" theory, are F. Lee, G. S. C., and X. A. B.

And now "descend, ye classic ten!" who have solved the whole problem. Your names are AIX-LES-BAINS, ALGERNON BRAY (thanks for a friendly remark, which comes with a heart-warmth that not even the Atlantic could chill), ARVON, BRADSHAW OF THE FUTURE, FIFEE, H. L. R., J. L. O., OMEGA, S. S. G., and WAITING FOR THE TRAIN. Several of these have put Clara, provisionally, into the easterly train: but they seem to have understood that the data do not decide that point.

CLASS LIST

I

AIX-LES-BAINS.
ALGERNON BRAY.
BRADSHAW OF THE FUTURE.
FIFEE.

H. L. R.
OMEGA.
S. S. G.
WAITING FOR THE TRAIN.

II

ARVON. J. L. O.

III

F. LEE. G. S. C. X. A. B.

ANSWERS TO KNOT IV

Problem.—There are 5 sacks, of which Nos. 1, 2, weigh 12 lbs.; Nos. 2, 3, 13½ lbs.; Nos. 3, 4, 11½ lbs.; Nos. 4, 5, 8 lbs.; Nos. 1, 3, 5, 16 lbs. Required the weight of each sack.

Answer.—5½, 6½, 7, 4½, 3½.

The sum of all the weighings, 61 lbs., includes sack No. 3 *thrice* and each other *twice*. Deducting twice the sum of the

1st and 4th weighings, we get 21 lbs. for *thrice* No. 3, *i. e.* 7 lbs. for No. 3. Hence, the 2nd and 3rd weighings give 6½ lbs., 4½ lbs. for Nos. 2, 4; and hence again, the 1st and 4th weighings give 5½ lbs., 3½ lbs., for Nos. 1, 5.

Ninety-seven answers have been received. Of these, 15 are beyond the reach of discussion, as they give no working. I can but enumerate their names, and I take this opportunity of saying that this is the last time I shall put on record the names of competitors who give no sort of clue to the process by which their answers were obtained. In guessing a conundrum, or in catching a flea, we do not expect the breathless victor to give us afterwards, in cold blood, a history of the mental or muscular efforts by which he achieved success; but a mathematical calculation is another thing. The names of this "mute inglorious" band are COMMON SENSE, D. E. R., DOUGLAS, E. L., ELLEN, I. M. T., J. M. C., JOSEPH, KNOT I, LUCY, MEEK, M. F. C., PYRAMUS, SHAH, VERITAS.

Of the eighty-two answers with which the working, or some approach to it, is supplied, one is wrong: seventeen have given solutions which are (from one cause or another) practically valueless: the remaining sixty-four I shall try to arrange in a Class List, according to the varying degrees of shortness and neatness to which they seem to have attained.

The solitary wrong answer is from NELL. To be thus "alone in the crowd" is a distinction—a painful one, no doubt, but still a distinction. I am sorry for you, my dear young lady, and I seem to hear your tearful exclamation, when you read these lines, "Ah! This is the knell of all my hopes!" Why, oh why, did you assume that the 4th and 5th bags weighed 4 lbs. each? And why did you not test your answers? However, please try again: and please don't change your *nom-de-plume:* let us have NELL in the First Class next time!

The seventeen whose solutions are practically valueless are ARDMORE, A READY RECKONER, ARTHUR, BOG-LARK, BOG-OAK, BRIDGET, FIRST ATTEMPT, J. L. C., M. E. T., ROSE, ROWENA, SEA-BREEZE, SYLVIA, THISTLEDOWN, THREE-FIFTHS ASLEEP, VENDREDI, and WINIFRED. BOG-LARK tries it by a sort of "rule of false," assuming experimentally that Nos. 1, 2, weigh 6 lbs. each, and having thus produced 17½, instead of 16, as the weight of 1, 3, and 5, she removes "the superfluous pound and a half," but does not explain how she knows from which to take it. THREE-FIFTHS ASLEEP says that (when in that peculiar state) "it seemed perfectly clear" to her that, "3 out of the 5 sacks being weighed twice over, ⅗ of 45 = 27, must be the total weight of the 5 sacks." As to which I can only say, with the Captain, "it beats me entirely!" WINIFRED, on the plea that "one must have a starting-point," assumes (what I fear is a mere guess) that No. 1 weighed 5½ lbs. The rest all do it, wholly or partly, by guess-work.

The problem is of course (as any algebraist sees at once) a case of "simultaneous simple equations." It is, however, easily soluble by arithmetic only; and, when this is the case, I hold that it is bad workmanship to use the more complex method. I have not, this time, given more credit to arithmetical solutions; but in future problems I shall (other things being equal) give the highest marks to those who use the simplest machinery. I have put into Class I those whose answers seemed specially short and neat, and into Class III those that seemed specially long or clumsy. Of this last set, A. C. M., FURZE-BUSH, JAMES, PARTRIDGE, R. W., and WAITING FOR THE TRAIN, have sent long wandering solutions, the substitutions have no definite method, but seeming to have been made to see what would come of it. CHILPOME and DUBLIN BOY omit some of the working. ARVON MARLBOROUGH BOY only finds the weight of *one* sack.

CLASS LIST

I

B. E. D.
C. H.
Constance Johnson.
Greystead.
Guy.
Hoopoe.
J. F. A.
M. A. H.

Number Five.
Pedro.
R. E. X.
Seven Old Men.
Vis Inertiæ.
Willy B.
Yahoo.

II

American Subscriber.
An Appreciative Schoolma'am.
Ayr.
Bradshaw of the Future.
Cheam.
C. M. G.
Dinah Mite.
Duckwing.
E. C. M.
E. N. Lowry.
Era.
Euroclydon.
F. H. W.
Fifee.
G. E. B.
Harlequin.
Hawthorn.
Hough Green.
J. A. B.
Jack Tar.

J. B. B.
Kgovjni.
Land Lubber.
L. D.
Magpie.
Mary.
Mhruxi.
Minnie.
Money-Spinner.
Nairam.
Old Cat.
Polichinelle.
Simple Susan.
S. S. G.
Thisbe.
Verena.
Wamba.
Wolfe.
Wykehamicus.
Y. M. A. H.

III

A. C. M.	JAMES.
ARVON MARLBOROUGH BOY.	PARTRIDGE.
CHILPOME.	R. W.
DUBLIN BOY.	WAITING FOR THE TRAIN.
FURZE-BUSH.	

ANSWERS TO KNOT V

Problem.—To mark pictures, giving 3 X's to 2 or 3, 2 to 4 or 5, and 1 to 9 or 10; also giving 3 o's to 1 or 2, 2 to 3 or 4, and 1 to 8 or 9; so as to mark the smallest possible number of pictures, and to give them the largest possible number of marks.

Answer.—10 pictures; 29 marks; arranged thus:

```
X  X  X  X  X  X  X  X  X  o
X  X  X  X  X        o  o  o  o
X  X  o  o  o  o  o  o  o  o
```

Solution.—By giving all the X's possible, putting into brackets the optional ones, we get 10 pictures marked thus:

```
X  X  X  X  X  X  X  X  X  (X)
X  X  X  X  (X)
X  X  (X)
```

By then assigning o's in the same way, beginning at the other end, we get 9 pictures marked thus:

```
                              (o)  o
                         (o)  o  o  o
            (o)  o  o  o  o  o  o  o  o
```

All we have now to do is to run these two wedges as close together as they will go, so as to get the minimum number of pictures—erasing optional marks where by so doing we can run them closer, but otherwise letting them stand. There are 10 necessary marks in the 1st row, and in the 3rd; but only 7 in the 2nd. Hence we erase all optional marks in the 1st and 3rd rows, but let them stand in the 2nd.

Twenty-two answers have been received. Of these, 11 give no working; so, in accordance with what I announced in my last review of answers, I leave them unnamed, merely mentioning that 5 are right and 6 wrong.

Of the eleven answers with which some working is supplied, 3 are wrong. C. H. begins with the rash assertion that under the given conditions "the sum is impossible. For," he or she adds (these initialed correspondents are dismally vague beings to deal with: perhaps "it" would be a better pronoun), "10 is the least possible number of pictures" (granted): "therefore we must either give 2 ×'s to 6, or 2 o's to 5." Why "must," O alphabetical phantom? It is nowhere ordained that every picture "must" have 3 marks! FIFEE sends a folio page of solution, which deserved a better fate: she offers 3 answers, in each of which 10 pictures are marked, with 30 marks; in one she gives 2 ×'s to 6 pictures; in another to 7; in the 3rd she gives 2 o's to 5; thus in every case ignoring the conditions. (I pause to remark that the condition "2 ×'s to 4 or 5 pictures" can only mean "*either* to 4 *or else* to 5": if, as one competitor holds, it might mean *any* number not less than 4, the words "*or 5*" would be superfluous.) I. E. A. (I am happy to say that none of these bloodless phantoms appear this time in the class-list. Is it IDEA with the "D" left out?) gives 2 ×'s to 6 pictures. She then takes me to task for using the word "ought" instead of "nought." No doubt, to one who thus rebels against the rules laid down for her guidance, the word must be distasteful. But does not I. E. A. remember the parallel case of "adder"? That creature was originally "a nadder": then the two words took to bandying the poor "n" backwards and forwards like a shuttlecock, the final state of the game being "an adder." May not "a nought" have similarly become "an ought"? Anyhow, "oughts and crosses" is a very old game. I don't think I ever heard it called "noughts and crosses."

In the following Class List, I hope the solitary occupant of III will sheathe her claws when she hears how narrow an escape she has had of not being named at all. Her account of the process by which she got the answer is so meagre that, like the nursery tale of "Jack-a-Minory" (I trust I. E. A. will be merciful to the spelling), it is scarcely to be distinguished from "zero."

CLASS LIST

I

Guy.　　　　Old Cat.　　　　Sea-Breeze.

II

Ayr.　　　　　　　　　　　　F. Lee.
Bradshaw of the Future.　　H. Vernon.

III

Cat.

ANSWERS TO KNOT VI

Problem 1.—*A* and *B* began the year with only £1000 apiece. They borrowed nought; they stole nought. On the next New Year's Day they had £60,000 between them. How did they do it?

Solution.—They went that day to the Bank of England. *A* stood in front of it, while *B* went round and stood behind it.

Two answers have been received, both worthy of much honour. Addlepate makes them borrow "zero" and steal "zero," and uses both cyphers by putting them at the right-hand end of the £1000, thus producing £100,000, which is well over the mark. But (or to express it in Latin) AT SPES INFRACTA has solved it even more ingeniously: with the first cypher she turns the "1" of the £1000 into a "9," and adds the result to the original sum, thus getting £10,000: and in this, by means of the other "zero," she turns the "1" into a "6." thus hitting the exact £60,000.

CLASS LIST

I

AT SPES INFRACTA.

II

ADDLEPATE.

Problem 2.—*L* makes 5 scarves, while *M* makes 2: *Z* makes 4, while *L* makes 3. Five scarves of *Z*'s weigh one of *L*'s; 5 of *M*'s weigh 3 of *Z*'s. One of *M*'s is as warm as 4 of *Z*'s: and one of *L*'s as warm as 3 of *M*'s. Which is best, giving equal weight in the result of rapidity of work, lightness, and warmth?

Answer.—The order is *M, L, Z*.

Solution.—As to rapidity (other things being constant), *L*'s merit is to *M*'s in the ratio of 5 to 2: *Z*'s to *L*'s in the ratio of 4 to 3. In order to get one set of 3 numbers fulfilling these conditions, it is perhaps simplest to take the one that occurs *twice* as unity, and reduce the others to fractions: this gives, for *L, M,* and *Z*, the marks 1, $\frac{2}{5}$, $\frac{4}{3}$. In estimating for *lightness*, we observe that the greater the weight, the less the merit, so that *Z*'s merit is to *L*'s as 5 to 1. Thus the marks for *lightness* are $\frac{1}{5}$, $\frac{5}{3}$, 1. And similarly, the marks for warmth are 3, 1, $\frac{1}{4}$. To get the total result, we must *multiply* *L*'s 3 marks together, and do the same for *M* and for *Z*. The final numbers are $1 \times \frac{1}{5} \times 3$, $\frac{2}{5} \times \frac{5}{3} \times 1$, $\frac{4}{3} \times 1 \times \frac{1}{4}$; *i. e.* $\frac{3}{5}$,

⅔, ⅓; *i. e.* multiplying throughout by 15 (which will not alter the proportion), 9, 10, 5; showing the order of merit to be *M, L, Z.*

Twenty-nine answers have been received, of which five are right, and twenty-four wrong. These hapless ones have all (with three exceptions) fallen into the error of *adding* the proportional numbers together, for each candidate, instead of *multiplying.* *Why* the latter is right, rather than the former, is fully proved in textbooks, so I will not occupy space by stating it here: but it can be *illustrated* very easily by the case of length, breadth, and depth. Suppose *A* and *B* are rival diggers of rectangular tanks: the amount of work done is evidently measured by the number of *cubical feet* dug out. Let *A* dig a tank 10 feet long, 10 wide, 2 deep: let *B* dig one 6 feet long, 5 wide, 10 deep. The cubical contents are 200, 300; *i. e. B* is best digger in the ratio of 3 to 2. Now try marking for length, width, and depth, separately; giving a maximum mark of 10 to the best in each contest, and then *adding* the results!

Of the twenty-four malefactors, one gives no working, and so has no real claim to be named; but I break the rule for once, in deference to its success in Problem 1: he, she, or it, is ADDLEPATE. The other twenty-three may be divided into five groups.

First and worst are, I take it, those who put the rightful winner *last;* arranging them as "Lolo, Zuzu, Mimi." The names of these desperate wrong-doers are AYR, BRADSHAW OF THE FUTURE, FURZE-BUSH, and POLLUX (who send a joint answer), GREYSTEAD, GUY, OLD HEN, and SIMPLE SUSAN. The latter was *once* best of all; the Old Hen has taken advantage of her simplicity, and beguiled her with the chaff which was the bane of her own chickenhood.

Secondly, I point the finger of scorn at those who have put the worst candidate at the top; arranging them as "Zuzu,

Mimi, Lolo." They are GRÆCIA, M. M., OLD CAT, and
R. E. X. " 'Tis Greece, but——"

The third set have avoided both these enormities, and
have even succeeded in putting the worst last, their answer
being "Lolo, Mimi, Zuzu." Their names are AYR (who also
appears among the "quite too too"), CLIFTON C., F. B.,
FIFEE, GRIG, JANET, and MRS. SAIREY GAMP. F. B. has not
fallen into the common error; she *multiplies* together the
proportionate number she gets, but in getting them she goes
wrong, by reckoning warmth as a *de*-merit. Possibly she is
"Freshly Burnt," or comes "From Bombay." JANET and
MRS. SAIREY GAMP have also avoided this error: the method
they have adopted is shrouded in mystery—I scarcely feel
competent to criticise it. MRS. GAMP says, "If Zuzu makes 4
while Lolo makes 3, Zuzu makes 6 while Lolo makes 5 [bad
reasoning], while Mimi makes 2." From this she concludes,
"Therefore Zuzu excels in speed by 1" (*i. e.* when compared
with Lolo? but what about Mimi?). She then compares the
3 kinds of excellence, measured on this mystic scale. JANET
takes the statement that "Lolo makes 5 while Mimi makes
2," to prove that "Lolo makes 3 while Mimi makes 1 and
Zuzu 4" (worse reasoning than MRS. GAMP's), and thence
concludes that "Zuzu excels in speed by ⅛"! JANET should
have been ADELINE, "mystery of mysteries!"

The fourth set actually put Mimi at the top, arranging
them as "Mimi, Zuzu, Lolo." They are MARQUIS AND CO.,
MARTREB, S. B. B. (first initial scarcely legible: *may* be
meant for "J"), and STANZA.

The fifth set consists of AN ANCIENT FISH and CAMEL.
These ill-assorted comrades, by dint of foot and fin, have
scrambled into the right answer, but, as their method is
wrong, of course it counts for nothing. Also AN ANCIENT
FISH has very ancient and fishlike ideas as to *how* numbers
represent merit: she says, "Lolo gains 2½ on Mimi." Two
and a half *what?* Fish, fish, art thou in thy duty?

Of the five winners I put Balbus and The Elder Traveller slightly below the other three—Balbus for defective reasoning, the other for scanty working. Balbus gives two reasons for saying that *addition* of marks is *not* the right method, and then adds, "It follows that the decision must be made by *multiplying* the marks together." This is hardly more logical than to say, "This is not Spring: *therefore* it must be Autumn."

CLASS LIST

I

Dinah Mite.   E. B. D. L.   Joram.

II

Balbus.   The Elder Traveller.

With regard to Knot V, I beg to express to Vis Inertiæ and to any others who, like her, understood the condition to be that *every* marked picture must have *three* marks, my sincere regret that the unfortunate phrase "*fill* the columns with oughts and crosses" should have caused them to waste so much time and trouble. I can only repeat that a *literal* interpretation of "fill" would seem to *me* to require that *every* picture in the gallery should be marked. Vis Inertiæ would have been in the First Class if she had sent in the solution she now offers.

ANSWERS TO KNOT VII

Problem.—Given that one glass of lemonade, 3 sandwiches, and 7 biscuits, cost 1s. 2d.; and that one glass of lemonade, 4 sandwiches, and 10 biscuits, cost 1s. 5d.: find the cost of (1) a glass of lemonade, a sandwich, and a biscuit; and (2) 2 glasses of lemonade, 3 sandwiches, and 5 biscuits.

Answer.—(1) 8d.; (2) 1s. 7d.

Solution.—This is best treated algebraically. Let $x =$ the cost (in pence) of a glass of lemonade, y of a sandwich, and z of a biscuit. Then we have $x + 3y + 7z = 14$, and $x + 4 + 10z = 17$. And we require the values of $x + y + z$, and of $2x + 3y + 5z$. Now, from *two* equations only, we cannot find, *separately*, the values of *three* unknowns: certain *combinations* of them may, however, be found. Also we know that we can, by the help of the given equations, eliminate 2 of the 3 unknowns from the quantity whose value is required, which will then contain one only. If, then, the required value is ascertainable at all, it can only be by the 3rd unknown vanishing of itself: otherwise the problem is impossible.

Let us then eliminate lemonade and sandwiches, and reduce everything to biscuits—a state of things even more depressing than "if all the world were apple-pie"—by subtracting the 1st equation from the 2nd, which eliminates lemonade, and gives $y + 3z = 3$, or $y = 3 - 3z$; and then substituting this value of y in the 1st, which gives $x - 2z = 5$, *i. e.* $x = 5 + 2z$. Now if we substitute these values of x, y, in the quantities whose values are required, the first becomes $(5 + 2z) + (3 - 3z) + z$, *i. e.* 8: and the second becomes $2(5 + 2z) + 3(3 - 3z) + 5z$, *i. e.* 19. Hence the answers are (1) 8*d.*, (2) 1*s.* 7*d.*

The above is a *universal* method: that is, it is absolutely certain either to produce the answer, or to prove that no answer is possible. The question may also be solved by combining the quantities whose values are given, so as to form those whose values are required. This is merely a matter of ingenuity and good luck: and as it *may* fail, even when the thing is possible, and is of no use in proving it *im*possible, I cannot rank this method as equal in value with the other. Even when it succeeds, it may prove a very tedious process. Suppose the 26 competitors who have sent in what I may call *accidental* solutions, had had a question to deal with where every number contained 8 or 10 digits! I suspect it would have been a case of "silvered is the raven hair" (see *Patience*) before any solution would have been hit on by the most ingenious of them.

Forty-five answers have come in, of which 44 give, I am happy to say, some sort of *working*, and therefore deserve to be mentioned by name, and to have their virtues, or vices, as the case may be, discussed. Thirteen have made assumptions to which they have no right, and so cannot figure in the Class List, even though, in 10 of the 12 cases, the answer is right. Of the remaining 28, no less than 26 have sent in *accidental* solutions, and therefore fall short of the highest honours.

I will now discuss individual cases, taking the worst first, as my custom is.

FROGGY gives no working—at least this is all he gives: after stating the given equations, he says, "Therefore the difference, 1 sandwich $+$ 3 biscuits, $=$ 3*d*.": then follow the amounts of the unknown bills, with no further hint as to how he got them. FROGGY has had a *very* narrow escape of not being named at all!

Of those who are wrong, VIS INERTIÆ has sent in a piece of incorrect working. Peruse the horrid details, and shudder! She takes x (call it "y") as the cost of a sandwich, and concludes (rightly enough) that a biscuit will cost $\dfrac{3-y}{3}$. She then subtracts the second equation from the first, and deduces $3y + 7 \times \dfrac{3-y}{3} - 4y + 10 \times \dfrac{3-y}{3} = 3$. By making two mistakes in this line, she brings out $y = \dfrac{3}{2}$. Try it again, O VIS INERTIÆ! Away with INERTIÆ:

infuse a little more Vis: and you will bring out the correct (though uninteresting) result, o = o! This will show you that it is hopeless to try to coax any one of these 3 unknowns to reveal its *separate* value. The other competitor who is wrong throughout, is either J. M. C. or T. M. C.: but, whether he be a Juvenile Mis-Calculator or a True Mathematician Confused, he makes the answers 7*d.* and 1*s.* 5*d.* He assumes, with Too Much Confidence, that biscuits were ½*d.* each, and that Clara paid for 8, though she only ate 7!

We will now consider the 13 whose working is wrong, though the answer is right: and, not to measure their demerits too exactly, I will take them in alphabetical order. ANITA finds (rightly) that "1 sandwich and 3 biscuits cost 3*d.*" and proceeds, "therefore 1 sandwich = 1½*d.*, 3 biscuits = 1½*d.*, 1 lemonade = 6*d.*" DINAH MITE begins like ANITA: and thence proves (rightly) that a biscuit costs less than 1*d.*: whence she concludes (wrongly) that it *must* cost ½*d.* F. C. W. is so beautifully resigned to the certainty of a verdict of "guilty," that I have hardly the heart to utter the word, without adding a "recommended to mercy owing to extenuating circumstances." But really, you know, where *are* the extenuating circumstances? She begins by assuming that lemonade is 4*d.* a glass, and sandwiches 3*d.* each (making with the 2 given equations, *four* conditions to be fulfilled by *three* miserable unknowns!). And, having (naturally) developed this into a contradiction, she then tries 5*d.* and 2*d.* with a similar result. (N.B.—*This* process might have been carried on through the whole of the Tertiary Period, without gratifying one single Megatherium.) She then, by a "happy thought," tries halfpenny biscuits, and so obtains a consistent result. This may be a good solution, viewing the problem as a conundrum: but it is *not* scientific. JANET identifies sandwiches with biscuits! "One sandwich + 3 biscuits" she makes equal to "4." Four *what?* MAYFAIR makes the astounding assertion that the equation, $s + 3b = 3$, "is evidently only satisfied by $s = \frac{3}{2}, b = \frac{1}{2}$"! OLD CAT believes that the assumption that a sandwich costs $1\frac{1}{2}d.$ is "the only way to avoid unmanageable fractions." But *why* avoid them? Is there not a certain glow of triumph in taming such a fraction? "Ladies and gentlemen, the fraction now before you is one that for years defied all efforts of a refining nature: it was, in a word, hopelessly vulgar. Treating it as a circulating decimal (the treadmill of fractions) only made matters worse. As a last resource, I reduced it to its lowest terms, and extracted its square root!" Joking apart, let me thank OLD CAT for some very kind words of sympathy, in reference to a correspondent (whose name I am happy to say I have now forgotten) who had found fault with me as a discourteous critic. O. V. L. is beyond my comprehension. He takes the given equations as (1) and (2): thence, by the process $[(2) - (1)]$, deduces (rightly) equation (3), viz. $s + 3b = 3$: and thence again, by the process $[\times 3]$ (a hopeless mystery), deduces $3s + 4b = 4$. I have nothing to say about it: I give it up. SEA-BREEZE says, "It is immaterial to the answer" (why?) "in what proportion $3d.$ is divided between the sandwich and the 3 biscuits": so she assumes $s = 1\frac{1}{2}d.$, $b = \frac{1}{2}d.$ STANZA is one of a very irregular metre. At first she (like JANET) identifies sandwiches with biscuits. She then tries two assumptions ($s = 1, b = \frac{2}{3}$, and $s = \frac{1}{2}, b = \frac{5}{6}$), and (naturally) ends in contradictions. Then she returns to the first assumption, and finds the 3 unknowns separately: *quod est absurdum.* STILETTO identifies sandwiches and biscuits, as "articles." Is the word ever used by confectioners? I fancied, "What is the next article, ma'am?" was limited to linendrapers. Two SISTERS first assume that biscuits are 4 a penny, and then that they are 2 a penny, adding that "the answer will of course be the same in both cases." It is a dreamy remark, making one feel something like Macbeth grasping at the spectral dagger. "Is this a statement that I see before me?" If you were to say, "We both walked the same way this morning," and *I* were to say, "*One* of you walked the same way, but the other didn't," which of the three would be the most hopelessly confused? Turtle Pyate (what *is* a Turtle Pyate, please?) and Old Crow, who send a joint answer, and Y. Y., adopt the same method. Y. Y. gets the equation $s + 3b = 3$: and then says, "This sum must be apportioned in one of the three following ways." It *may* be, I grant you: but Y. Y. do you say "must"? I fear it is *possible* for Y. Y. to be *two* Y's. The other two conspirators are less positive: they say it "can" be so divided: but they add "either of the three prices being right"! This is bad grammar and bad arithmetic at once, O mysterious birds!

Of those who win honours, The Shetland Snark must have the Third Class all to himself. He has only answered half the question, viz. the amount of Clara's luncheon: the two little old ladies he pitilessly leaves in the midst of their "difficulty." I beg to assure him (with thanks for his friendly remarks) that entrance-fees and subscriptions are things unknown in that most economical of clubs, "The Knot-Untiers."

The authors of the 26 "accidental" solutions differ only in the number of steps they have taken between the data and the answers. In order to do them full justice I have arranged the Second Class in sections, according to the number of steps. The two Kings are fearfully deliberate! I suppose walking quick, or taking short cuts, is inconsistent with kingly dignity: but really, in reading Theseus' solution, one almost fancied he was "marking time," and making no advance at all! The other King will, I hope, pardon me for having altered "Coal" into "Cole." King Coilus, or Coil, seems to have reigned soon after Arthur's time. Henry of Huntingdon identifies him with the King Coël who first built walls round Colchester, which was named after him. In the Chronicle of Robert of Gloucester we read:

> *Aftur Kyng Aruirag, of wam we habbeth y told,*
> *Marius ys sone was kyng, quoynte mon & bold.*
> *And ys sone was aftur hym,* Coil *was ys name,*
> *Bothe it were quoynte men, & of noble fame.*

BALBUS lays it down as a general principle that "in order to ascertain the cost of any one luncheon, it must come to the same amount upon two different assumptions." (*Query*. Should not "it" be "we"? Otherwise the *luncheon* is represented as wishing to ascertain its own cost!) He then makes two assumptions—one, that sandwiches cost nothing; the other, that biscuits cost nothing (either arrangement would lead to the shop being inconveniently crowded!)—and brings out the unknown luncheons as 8*d.* and 19*d.* on each assumption. He then concludes that this agreement of results "shows that the answers are correct." Now I propose to disprove his general law by simply giving *one* instance of its failing. One instance is quite enough. In logical language, in order to disprove a "universal affirmative," it is enough to prove its contradictory, which is a "particular negative." (I must pause for a digression on Logic, and especially on Ladies' Logic. The universal affirmative, "Everybody says he's a duck," is crushed instantly by proving the particular negative, "Peter says he's a goose," which is equivalent to "Peter does *not* say he's a duck." And the universal negative, "Nobody calls on her," is well met by the particular affirmative, "*I* called yesterday." In short, either of two contradictories disproves the other: and the moral is that, since a particular proposition is much more easily proved than a universal one, it is the wisest course, in arguing with a lady, to limit one's *own* assertions to "particulars," and leave *her* to prove the "universal" contradictory, if she can. You will thus generally secure a *logical* victory: a *practical* victory is not to be hoped for, since she can always fall back upon the crushing remark, "*That* has nothing to do with it!"—a move for which Man has not yet discovered any satisfactory answer. Now let us return to Balbus.) Here is my "particular negative," on which to test his rule: Suppose the two recorded luncheons to have been "2 buns, one queen-cake, 2 sausage-rolls, and a bottle of Zoëdone: total, one-and-ninepence," and "one bun, 2 queen-cakes, a sausage-roll, and a bottle of Zoëdone: total, one-and-fourpence." And suppose Clara's unknown luncheon to have been "3 buns, one queen-cake, one sausage-roll, and 2 bottles of Zoëdone": while the two little sisters had been indulging in "8 buns, 4 queen-cakes, 2 sausage-rolls, and 6 bottles of Zoëdone." (Poor souls, how thirsty they must have been!) If Balbus will kindly try this by his principle of "two assumptions," first assuming that a bun is 1*d*. and a queen-cake 2*d*., and then that a bun is 3*d*. and a queen-cake 3*d*., he will bring out the other two luncheons, on each assumption, as "one-and-ninepence" and "four-and-tenpence" respectively, which harmony of results, he will say, "shows that the answers are correct." And yet, as a matter of fact, the buns were 2*d*. each, the queen-cakes 3*d*., the sausage-rolls 6*d*., and the Zoëdone 2*d*. a bottle: so that Clara's third luncheon had cost one-and-sevenpence, and her thirsty friends had spent four-and-fourpence!

Another remark of Balbus I will quote and discuss: for I think that it also may yield a moral for some of my readers. He says, "It is the same thing in substance whether in solving this problem we use words and call it arithmetic, or use letters and signs and call it algebra." Now this does not appear to me a correct description of the two methods: the arithmetical method is that of "synthesis" only; it goes from one known fact to another, till it reaches its goal: whereas the algebraical method is that of "analysis"; it begins with the goal, symbolically represented, and so goes backwards, dragging its veiled victim with it, till it has reached the full day-light of known facts, in which it can tear off the veil and say, "I know you!"

Take an illustration: Your house has been broken into and robbed, and you appeal to the policeman who was on duty that night. "Well, mum, I did see a chap getting out over your garden wall: but I was a good bit off, so I didn't chase him, like. I just cut down the short way to the 'Chequers,' and who should I meet but Bill Sykes, coming full split round the corner. So I just ups and says, 'My lad, you're wanted.' That's all I says. And he says, 'I'll go along quiet, Bobby,' he says, 'without the darbies,' he says." There's your *Arithmetical* policeman. Now try the other method: "I seed somebody a-running, but he was well gone or ever *I* got nigh the place. So I just took a look round in the garden. And I noticed the footmarks, where the chap had come right across your flower-beds. They was good big footmarks sure-ly. And I noticed as the left foot went down at the heel, ever so much deeper than the other. And I says to myself, 'The chap's been a big hulking chap: and he goes lame on his left foot.' And I rubs my hand on the wall where he got over, and there was soot on it, and no mistake. So I says to myself, 'Now where can I light on a big man, in the chimbley-sweep line, what's lame of one foot?' And I flashes up permiscuous: and I says, 'It's Bill Sykes!' says I." There is your *Algebraical* policeman—a higher intellectual type, to my thinking, than the other.

LITTLE JACK's solution calls for a word of praise, as he has written out what really is an algebraical proof *in words*, without representing any of his facts as equations. If it is all his own, he will make a good algebraist in the time to come. I beg to thank SIMPLE SUSAN for some kind words of sympathy, to the same effect as those received from OLD CAT.

HECLA and MARTREB are the only two who have used a method *certain* either to produce the answer, or else to prove it impossible: so they must share between them the highest honours.

CLASS LIST

I

HECLA.	MARTREB.

II

§ 1 (2 *steps*)
ADELAIDE.
CLIFTON C. . . .
E. K. C.
GUY.
L'INCONNU.
LITTLE JACK.
NIL DESPERANDUM.
SIMPLE SUSAN.
YELLOW-HAMMER.
WOOLLY ONE.

§ 2 (3 *steps*)
A. A.
A CHRISTMAS CAROL.
AFTERNOON TEA.
AN APPRECIATIVE SCHOOL-
MA'AM.
BABY.
BALBUS.
BOG-OAK.

§ 2 (3 *steps*)—continued
THE RED QUEEN.
WALL-FLOWER.

§ 3 (4 *steps*)
HAWTHORN.
JORAM.
S. S. G.

§4 (5 *steps*)
A STEPNEY COACH.

§ 5 (6 *steps*)
BAY LAUREL.
BRADSHAW OF THE FUTURE.

§ 6 (9 *steps*)
OLD KING COLE.

§ 7 (14 *steps*)
THESEUS.

ANSWERS TO CORRESPONDENTS

I HAVE received several letters on the subjects of Knots II and VI, which lead me to think some further explanation desirable.

In Knot II, I had intended the numbering of the houses to begin at one corner of the Square, and this was assumed by most, if not all, of the competitors. TROJANUS, however, says, "Assuming, in default of any information, that the street enters the square in the middle of each side, it may be supposed that the numbering begins at a street." But surely the other is the more natural assumption?

In Knot VI, the first Problem was, of course, a mere *jeu de mots*, whose presence I thought excusable in a series of Problems whose aim is to entertain rather than to instruct: but it has not escaped the contemptuous criticisms of two of my correspondents, who seem to think that Apollo is in duty bound to keep his bow always on the stretch. Neither of them has guessed it: and this is true human nature. Only the other day—the 31st of September, to be quite exact—I met my old friend Brown, and gave him a riddle I had just heard. With one great effort of his colossal mind, Brown guessed it. "Right!" said I. "Ah," said he, "it's very neat—very neat. And it isn't an answer that would occur to everybody. Very neat indeed." A few yards farther on, I fell in with Smith, and to him I propounded the same riddle. He frowned over it for a minute, and then gave it up. Meekly I faltered out the answer. "A poor thing, sir!" Smith growled, as he turned away. "A very poor thing! I wonder you care to repeat such rubbish!" Yet Smith's mind is, if possible, even more colossal than Brown's.

The second Problem of Knot VI is an example in ordinary Double Rule of Three, whose essential feature is that the result depends on the variation of several elements, which are so related to it that, if all but one be constant, it varies as that one: hence, if none be constant, it varies as their product. Thus, for example, the cubical contents of a rectangular tank vary as its length, if breadth and depth be constant, and so on; hence, if none be constant, it varies as the product of the length, breadth, and depth.

When the result is not thus connected with the varying elements, the problem ceases to be Double Rule of Three and often becomes one of great complexity.

To illustrate this, let us take two candidates for a prize, *A* and *B*, who are to compete in French, German, and Italian:

(*a*) Let it be laid down that the result is to depend on their *relative* knowledge of each subject, so that, whether their marks, for French, be "1, 2" or "100, 200," the result will be the same: and let it also be laid down that, if they get equal marks on 2 papers, the final marks are to have the same ratio as those of the 3rd paper. This is a case of ordinary Double Rule of Three. We multiply *A*'s 3 marks together, and do the same for *B*. Note that, if *A* gets a single "zero," his final mark is "zero," even if he gets full marks for 2 papers while *B* gets only one mark for each paper. This of course would be very unfair on *A*, though a correct solution under the given conditions.

(*b*) The result is to depend, as before, on *relative* knowledge; but French is to have twice as much weight as German or Italian. This is an unusual form of question. I should be inclined to say, "The resulting ratio is to be nearer to the French ratio than if we multiplied as in (*a*), and so much nearer that it would be necessary to use the other multipliers *twice* to produce the same result as in (*a*)": *e. g.* if the French ratio were $\frac{9}{10}$, and the others $\frac{4}{9}$, $\frac{1}{9}$, so that the ultimate ratio, by method (*a*), would be $\frac{4}{45}$, I should multiply instead by $\frac{2}{3}$, $\frac{1}{3}$, giving the result, $\frac{1}{5}$, which is nearer to $\frac{9}{10}$ than if we had used method (*a*).

(*c*) The result is to depend on *actual* amount of knowledge of the 3 subjects collectively. Here we have to ask two questions: (1) What is to be the "unit" (*i. e.* "standard to measure by") in each subject? (2) Are these units to be of equal, or unequal, value? The usual "unit" is the knowledge shown by answering the whole paper correctly; calling this "100," all lower amounts are represented by numbers between "zero," and "100." Then, if these units are to be of equal value, we simply add A's 3 marks together, and do the same for B.

(*d*) The conditions are the same as (*c*), but French is to have double weight. Here we simply double the French marks, and add as before.

(*e*) French is to have such weight that, if other marks be equal, the ultimate ratio is to be that of the French paper, so that a "zero" in this would swamp the candidate: but the other two subjects are only to affect the result collectively, by the amount of knowledge shown, the two being reckoned of equal value. Here I should add A's German and Italian marks together, and multiply by his French mark.

But I need not go on: the problem may evidently be set with many varying conditions, each requiring its own method of solution. The Problem in Knot VI was meant to belong to variety (*a*), and to make this clear, I inserted the following passage:

"Usually the competitors differ in one point only. Thus, last year, Fifi and Gogo made the same number of scarves in the trial week, and they were equally light; but Fifi's were twice as warm as Gogo's, and she was pronounced twice as good."

What I have said will suffice, I hope, as an answer to BAL-BUS, who holds that (*a*) and (*c*) are the only possible varieties of the problem, and that to say, "We cannot use addition, therefore we must be intended to use multiplication," is "no more illogical than, from knowledge that one was not born in the night, to infer that he was born in the daytime"; and also to FIFEE, who says, "I think a little more consideration will show you that our 'error of *adding* the proportional numbers together for each candidate instead of *multiplying*' is no error at all." Why, even if addition *had* been the right method to use, not one of the writers (I speak from memory) showed any consciousness of the necessity of fixing a "unit" for each subject. "No error at all"! They were positively steeped in error!

One correspondent (I do not name him, as the communication is not quite friendly in tone) writes thus: "I wish to add, very respectfully, that I think it would be in better taste if you were to abstain from the very trenchant expressions which you are accustomed to indulge in when criticising the answer. That such a tone must not be" ("be not"?) "agreeable to the persons concerned who have made mistakes may possibly have no great weight with you, but I hope you will feel that it would be as well not to employ it, *unless you are quite certain of being correct yourself.*" The only instances the writer gives of the "trenchant expressions" are "hapless" and "malefactors." I beg to assure him (and any others who may need the assurance: I trust there are none) that all such words have been used in jest, and with no idea that they could possibly annoy anyone, and that I sincerely regret any annoyance I may have thus inadvertently given. May I hope that in future they will recognise the distinction between severe language used in sober earnest, and the "words of unmeant bitterness," which Coleridge has alluded to in that lovely passage beginning, "A little child, a limber elf"? If the writer will refer to that passage, or to the Preface to *Fire, Famine, and Slaughter,* he will find the distinction, for which I plead, far better drawn out than I could hope to do in any words of mine.

The writer's insinuation that I care not how much annoyance I give to my readers I think it best to pass over in silence; but to his concluding remark I must entirely demur. I hold that to use language likely to annoy any of my correspondents would not be in the least justified by the plea that I was "quite certain of being correct." I trust that the knot-untiers and I are not on such terms as those!

I beg to thank G. B. for the offer of a puzzle—which, however, is too like the old one, "Make four 9's into 100."

ANSWERS TO KNOT VIII

§ 1. THE PIGS

Problem.—Place twenty-four pigs in four sties so that, as you go round and round, you may always find the number in each sty nearer to ten than the number in the last.

Answer.—Place 8 pigs in the first sty, 10 in the second, nothing in the third, and 6 in the fourth: 10 is nearer ten than 8; nothing is nearer ten than 10; 6 is nearer ten than nothing; and 8 is nearer ten than 6.

This problem is noticed by only two correspondents. BAL-BUS says, "It certainly cannot be solved mathematically, nor do I see how to solve it by any verbal quibble." NOLENS VOLENS makes Her Radiancy change the direction of going round; and even then is obliged to add, "the pig must be carried in front of her"!

§ 2. THE GRURMSTIPTHS

Problem.—Omnibuses start from a certain point, both ways, every 15 minutes. A traveller, starting on foot along with one of them, meets one in 12½ minutes: when will he be overtaken by one?

Answer.—In 6¼ minutes.

Solution.—Let "*a*" be the distance an omnibus goes in 15 minutes, and "*x*" the distance from the starting-point to where the traveller is overtaken. Since the omnibus met is due at the starting-point in 2½ minutes, it goes in that time as far as the traveller walks in 12½, *i. e.* it goes 5 times as fast. Now the overtaking omnibus is "a" behind the traveller when he starts, and therefore goes "$a + x$" while he goes "x." Hence $a + x = 5x$; *i. e.* $4x = a$, and $x = \dfrac{a}{4}$. This distance would be traversed by an omnibus in $\dfrac{15}{4}$ minutes, and therefore by the traveller in $5 \times \dfrac{15}{4}$. Hence he is overtaken in $18\frac{3}{4}$ minutes after starting, *i. e.* in $6\frac{1}{4}$ minutes after meeting the omnibus.

Four answers have been received, of which two are wrong. DINAH MITE rightly states that the overtaking omnibus reached the point where they met the other omnibus 5 minutes after they left, but wrongly concludes that, going 5 times as fast, it would overtake them in another minute. The travellers are 5 minutes' walk ahead of the omnibus, and must walk ¼ of this distance farther before the omnibus overtakes them, which will be ⅕ of the distance traversed by the omnibus in the same time: this will require 1¼ minutes more. NOLENS VOLENS tries it by a process like "Achilles and the Tortoise." He rightly states that, when the overtaking omnibus leaves the gate, the travellers are ⅕ of "a" ahead, and that it will take the omnibus 3 minutes to traverse this distance; "during which time" the travellers, he tells us, go ⅟₁₅ of "a" (this should be ⅟₂₅). The travellers being now ⅟₁₅ of "a" ahead, he concludes that the work remaining to be done is for the travellers to go ⅟₆₀ of "a," while the omnibus goes ⅟₁₂. The *principle* is correct, and might have been applied earlier.

CLASS LIST

I

BALBUS.   DELTA.

ANSWERS TO KNOT IX

§ 1. THE BUCKETS

Problem.—Lardner states that a solid, immersed in a fluid, displaces an amount equal to itself in bulk. How can this be true of a small bucket floating in a larger one?

Solution.—Lardner means, by "displaces," "occupies a space which might be filled with water without any change in the surroundings." If the portion of the floating bucket, which is above the water, could be annihilated, and the rest of it transformed into water, the surrounding water would not change its position: which agrees with Lardner's statement.

Five answers have been received, none of which explains the difficulty arising from the well-known fact that a floating body is the same weight as the displaced fluid. HECLA says that "Only that portion of the smaller bucket which descends below the original level of the water can be properly said to be immersed, and only an equal bulk of water is displaced." Hence, according to HECLA, a solid whose weight was equal to that of an equal bulk of water, would not float till the whole of it was below "the original level" of the water: but, as a matter of fact, it would float as soon as it was all under water. MAGPIE says the fallacy is "the assumption that one body can displace another from a place where it isn't," and that Lardner's assertion is incorrect, except when the containing vessel "was originally full to the brim." But the question of floating depends on the present state of things, not on past history. OLD KING COLE takes the same view as HECLA. TYMPANUM and VINDEX assume that "displaced" means "raised above its original level," and merely explain how it comes to pass that the water, so raised, is less in bulk than the immersed portion of bucket, and thus land themselves—or rather set themselves floating—in the same boat as HECLA.

I regret that there is no Class List to publish for this Problem.

§ 2. BALBUS'S ESSAY

Problem.—Balbus states that if a certain solid be immersed in a certain vessel of water, the water will rise through a series of distances, two inches, one inch, half an inch, etc., which series has no end. He concludes that the water will rise without limit. Is this true?

Solution.—No. This series can never reach 4 inches, since, however many terms we take, we are always short of 4 inches by an amount equal to the last term taken.

Three answers have been received—but only two seem to me worthy of honours.

TYMPANUM says that the statement about the stick "is merely a blind, to which the old answer may well be applied, *solvitur ambulando*, or rather *mergendo*." I trust TYMPANUM will not test this in his own person, by taking the place of the man in Balbus's Essay! He would infallibly be drowned.

OLD KING COLE rightly points out that the series, 2, 1, etc., is a decreasing geometrical progression: while VINDEX rightly identifies the fallacy as that of "Achilles and the Tortoise."

CLASS LIST

I

OLD KING COLE.   VINDEX.

§ 3. THE GARDEN

Problem.—An oblong garden, half a yard longer than wide, consists entirely of a gravel walk, spirally arranged, a yard wide and 3630 yards long. Find the dimensions of the garden.

Answer.—60, 60½.

Solution.—The number of yards and fractions of a yard traversed in walking along a straight piece of walk, is evidently the same as the number of square yards and fractions of a square yard contained in that piece of walk: and the distance traversed in passing through a square yard at a corner, is evidently a yard. Hence the area of the garden is 3630 square yards: *i. e.* if x be the width, $x(x + \frac{1}{2}) = 3630$. Solving this quadratic, we find $x = 60$. Hence the dimensions are 60, 60½.

Twelve answers have been received—seven right and five wrong.

C. G. L., Nabob, Old Crow, and Tympanum assume that the number of yards in the length of the path is equal to the number of square yards in the garden. This is true, but should have been proved. But each is guilty of darker deeds. C. G. L.'s "working" consists of dividing 3630 by 60. Whence came this divisor, O Segiel? Divination? Or was it a dream? I fear this solution is worth nothing. Old Crow's is shorter, and so (if possible) worth rather less. He says the answer "is at once seen to be 60 × 60½"! Nabob's calculation is short, but "as rich as a Nabob" in error. He says that the square root of 3630, multiplied by 2, equals the length plus the breadth. That is 60·25 × 2 = 120½. His first assertion is only true of a *square* garden. His second is irrelevant, since 60·25 is *not* the square root of 3630! Nay, Bob, this will *not* do! Tympanum says that, by extracting the square root of 3630, we get 60 yards with a remainder of $\frac{30}{60}$, or half a yard, which we add so as to make the oblong 60 × 60½. This is very terrible: but worse remains behind. TYMPANUM proceeds thus: "But why should there be the half-yard at all? Because without it there would be no space at all for flowers. By means of it, we find reserved in the very centre a small plot of ground, two yards long by half a yard wide, the only space not occupied by walk." But Balbus expressly said that the walk "used up the whole of the area." O TYMPANUM! My tympa is exhausted: my brain is num! I can say no more.

HECLA indulges, again and again, in that most fatal of all habits in computation—the making *two* mistakes which cancel each other. She takes x as the width of the garden, in yards, and $x + \frac{1}{2}$ as its length, and makes her first "coil" the sum of $x - \frac{1}{2}$, $x - \frac{1}{2}$, $x - 1$, $x - 1$, *i. e.* $4x - 3$: but the fourth term should be $x - 1\frac{1}{2}$, so that her first coil is $\frac{1}{2}$ a yard too long. Her second coil is the sum of $x - 2\frac{1}{2}$, $x - 2\frac{1}{2}$, $x - 3$, $x - 3$: here the first term should be $x - 2$ and the last $x - 3\frac{1}{2}$: these two mistakes cancel, and this coil is therefore right. And the same thing is true of every other coil but the last, which needs an extra half-yard to reach the *end* of the path: and this exactly balances the mistake in the first coil. Thus the sum-total of the coils comes right though the working is all wrong.

Of the seven who are right, DINAH MITE, JANET, MAGPIE, and TAFFY make the same assumption as C. G. L. AND Co. They then solve by a quadratic. MAGPIE also tries it by arithmetical progression, but fails to notice that the first and last "coils" have special values.

ALUMNUS ETONÆ attempts to prove what C. G. L. assumes by a particular instance, taking a garden 6 by 5½. He ought to have proved it generally: what is true of one number is not always true of others. OLD KING COLE solves it by an arithmetical progression. It is right, but too lengthy to be worth as much as a quadratic.

VINDEX proves it very neatly, by pointing out that a yard

of walk measured along the middle represents a square yard of garden, "whether we consider the straight stretches of walk or the square yards at the angles, in which the middle line goes half a yard in one direction and then turns a right angle and goes half a yard in another direction."

CLASS LIST

I

VINDEX.

II

ALUMNUS ETONÆ.   OLD KING COLE.

III

DINAH MITE.   MAGPIE.
JANET.   TAFFY.

ANSWERS TO KNOT X

§ I. THE CHELSEA PENSIONERS

Problem.—If 70 per cent have lost an eye, 75 per cent an ear, 80 per cent an arm, 85 per cent a leg: what percentage, *at least*, must have lost all four?

Answer.—Ten.

Solution.—(I adopt that of POLAR STAR, as being better than my own.) Adding the wounds together, we get 70 + 75 + 80 + 85 = 310, among 100 men; which gives 3 to each, and 4 to 10 men. Therefore the least percentage is 10.

Nineteen answers have been received. One is "5," but, as no working is given with it, it must, in accordance with the rule, remain "a deed without a name." JANET makes it "35⁷⁄₁₀." I am sorry she has misunderstood the question, and has supposed that those who had lost an ear were 75 per cent *of those who had lost an eye;* and so on. Of course, on this supposition, the percentages must all be multiplied together. This she has done correctly, but I can give her no honours, as I do not think the question will fairly bear her interpretation. THREE SCORE AND TEN makes it "19⅜." Her solution has given me—I will not say "many anxious days and sleepless nights," for I wish to be strictly truthful, but—some trouble in making any sense at all of it. She makes the number of "pensioners wounded once" to be 310 ("per cent," I suppose!): dividing by 4, she gets 77½ as "average percentage": again dividing by 4, she gets 19⅜ as "percentage wounded four times." Does she suppose wounds of different kinds to "absorb" each other, so to speak? Then, no doubt, the data are equivalent to 77 pensioners with one wound each, and a half-pensioner with a half-wound. And does she then suppose these concentrated wounds to be *transferable,* so that ¾ of these unfortunates can obtain perfect health by handing over their wounds to the remaining ¼? Granting these suppositions, her answer is right; or rather, *if* the question had been, "A road is covered with one inch of gravel, along 77½ per cent of it. How much of it could be covered 4 inches deep with the same material?" her answer *would* have been right. But alas, that *wasn't* the question! DELTA makes some most amazing assumptions: "let every one who has not lost an eye have lost an ear," "let every one who has not lost both eyes and ears have lost an arm." Her ideas of a battlefield are grim indeed. Fancy a warrior who would continue fighting after losing both eyes, both ears, and both arms! This is a case which she (or "it"?) evidently considers *possible.*

Next come eight writers who have made the unwarrantable assumption that, because 70 per cent have lost an eye, *therefore* 30 per cent have *not* lost one, so that they have *both* eyes. This is illogical. If you give me a bag containing 100 sovereigns, and if in an hour I come to you (my face *not* beaming with gratitude nearly so much as when I received the bag) to say, "I am sorry to tell you that 70 of these sovereigns are bad," do I thereby guarantee the other 30 to be good? Perhaps I have not tested them yet. The sides of this illogical octagon are as follows, in alphabetical order: ALGERNON BRAY, DINAH MITE, G. S. C., JANE E., J. D. W., MAGPIE (who makes the delightful remark, "Therefore 90 per cent have two of something," recalling to one's memory that fortunate monarch with whom Xerxes was so much pleased that "he gave him ten of everything"!), S. S. G., and TOKIO.

BRADSHAW OF THE FUTURE and T. R. do the question in a piecemeal fashion—on the principle that the 70 per cent and the 75 per cent, though commenced at opposite ends of the 100, must overlap by *at least* 45 per cent; and so on. This is quite correct working, but not, I think, quite the best way of doing it.

The other five competitors will, I hope, feel themselves sufficiently glorified by being placed in the first class, without my composing a Triumphal Ode for each!

CLASS LIST

I

OLD CAT.   POLAR STAR.
OLD HEN.   SIMPLE SUSAN.
                    WHITE SUGAR.

II

BRADSHAW OF THE FUTURE.   T. R.

III

ALGERNON BRAY.   J. D. W.
DINAH MITE.   MAGPIE.
G. S. C.   S. S. G.
JANE E.   TOKIO.

§ 2. CHANGE OF DAY

I must postpone, *sine die*, the geographical problem—partly because I have not yet received the statistics I am hoping for, and partly because I am myself so entirely puzzled by it; and when an examiner is himself dimly hovering between a second class and a third, how is he to decide the position of others?

§ 3. THE SONS' AGES

Problem.—At first, two of the ages are together equal to the third. A few years afterwards, two of them are together double of the third. When the number of years since the first occasion is two-thirds of the sum of the ages on that occasion, one age is 21. What are the other two?

Answer.—15 and 18.

Solution.—Let the ages at first be x, y, $(x+y)$. Now, if $a + b = 2c$, then $(a - n) + (b - n) = 2(c - n)$, whatever be the value of n. Hence the second relationship, if *ever* true, was *always* true. Hence it was true at first. But it cannot be true that x and y are together double of $(x + y)$. Hence it must be true of $(x + y)$, together with x or y; and it does not matter which we take. We assume, then, $(x + y) + x = 2y$; *i. e.* $y = 2x$. Hence the three ages were, at first, x, $2x$, $3x$; and the number of years since that time is two-thirds of $6x$, *i. e.* is $4x$. Hence the present ages are $5x$, $6x$, $7x$. The ages are clearly *integers*, since this is only "the year when one of my sons comes of age." Hence $7x = 21$, $x = 3$, and the other ages are 15, 18.

Eighteen answers have been received. One of the writers merely asserts that the first occasion was 12 years ago, that the ages were then 9, 6, and 3; and that on the second occasion they were 14, 11, and 8! As a Roman father, I *ought* to withhold the name of the rash writer; but respect for age makes me break the rule: it is THREE SCORE AND TEN. JANE E. also asserts that the ages at first were 9, 6, 3: then she calculates the present ages, leaving the *second* occasion unnoticed. OLD HEN is nearly as bad; she "tried various numbers till I found one that fitted *all* the conditions"; but merely scratching up the earth, and pecking about, is *not* the way to solve a problem, O venerable bird! And close after OLD HEN prowls, with hungry eyes, OLD CAT, who calmly assumes, to begin with, that the son who comes of age is the *eldest*. Eat your bird, Puss, for you will get nothing from me!

There are yet two zeroes to dispose of. MINERVA assumes that, on *every* occasion, a son comes of age; and that it is only such a son who is "tipped with gold." Is it wise thus to interpret, "Now, my boys, calculate your ages, and you shall have the money"? BRADSHAW OF THE FUTURE says "let" the ages at first be 9, 6, 3, then assumes that the second occasion was 6 years afterwards, and on these baseless assumptions brings out the right answers. Guide *future* travellers, an thou wilt; thou art no Bradshaw for *this* Age!

Of those who win honours, the merely "honourable" are two. DINAH MITE ascertains (rightly) the relationship between the three ages at first, but then *assumes* one of them to be "6," thus making the rest of her solution tentative. M. F. C. does the algebra all right up to the conclusion that the present ages are $5z$, $6z$, and $7z$; it then assumes, without giving any reason, that $7z = 21$.

Of the more honourable, DELTA attempts a novelty—to discover *which* son comes of age by elimination: it assumes, successively, that it is the middle one, and that it is the youngest; and in each case it *apparently* brings out an absurdity. Still, as the proof contains the following bit of algebra: "$63 = 7x + 4y$; $\therefore 21 = x + \frac{4}{7}$ of y," I trust it will admit that its proof is not *quite* conclusive. The rest of its work is good. MAGPIE betrays the deplorable tendency of her tribe—to appropriate any stray conclusion she comes across, without having any *strict* logical right to it. Assuming A, B, C, as the ages at first, and E as the number of the years that have elapsed since then, she finds (rightly) the 3 equations, $2A = B$, $C = B + A$, $D = 2B$. She then says, "Supposing that $A = 1$, then $B = 2$, $C = 3$, and $D = 4$. Therefore for A, B, C, D, four numbers are wanted which shall be to each other as $1 : 2 : 3 : 4$." It is in the "therefore" that I detect the unconscientiousness of this bird. The conclusion *is* true, but this is only because the equations are "homogeneous" (*i. e.* having one "unknown" in each term), a fact which I strongly suspect had not been grasped—I beg pardon, clawed —by her. Were I to lay this little pitfall: "$A + 1 = B$, $B + 1 = C$; supposing $A = 1$, then $B = 2$, and $C = 3$. *Therefore* for A, B, C, three numbers are wanted which shall be to one another as $1 : 2 : 3$," would you not flutter down into it, O MAGPIE! as amiably as a Dove? SIMPLE SUSAN is anything but simple to *me*. After ascertaining that the 3 ages at first are as $3 : 2 : 1$, she says, "Then, as two-thirds of their sum, added to one of them, $= 21$, the sum cannot exceed 30, and consequently the highest cannot exceed 15." I suppose her (mental) argument is something like this: "Two-thirds of sum, $+$ one age, $= 21$; $\therefore$ sum, $+$ 3 halves of one age, $= 31\frac{1}{2}$. But 3 halves of one age cannot be less than $1\frac{1}{2}$ [here I perceive that SIMPLE SUSAN would on no account present a guinea to a new-born baby!]; hence the sum cannot exceed 30." This is ingenious, but her proof, after that, is (as she candidly admits) "clumsy and roundabout." She finds that there are 5 possible sets of ages, and eliminates four of them. Suppose that, instead of 5, there had been 5 million possible sets? Would SIMPLE SUSAN have courageously ordered in the necessary gallon of ink and ream of paper?

The solution sent in by C. R. is, like that of SIMPLE SUSAN, partly tentative, and so does not rise higher than being Clumsily Right.

Among those who have earned the highest honours, ALGERNON BRAY solves the problem quite correctly, but adds that there is nothing to exclude the supposition that all the ages were *fractional*. This would make the number of answers infinite. Let me meekly protest that I *never* intended my readers to devote the rest of their lives to writing out answers! E. M. RIX *points* out that, if fractional ages be admissible, any one of the three sons might be the one "come of age"; but she rightly rejects this supposition on the ground that it would make the problem indeterminate. WHITE SUGAR is the only one who has detected an oversight of mine: I had forgotten the possibility (which of course ought to be allowed for) that the son who came of age that *year*, need not have done so by that *day*, so that he *might* be only 20. This gives a second solution, viz. 20, 24, 28. Well said, pure Crystal! Verily, thy "fair discourse hath been as sugar"!

CLASS LIST

I

ALGERNON BRAY.	S. S. G.
AN OLD FOGEY.	TOKIO.
E. M. RIX.	T. R.
G. S. C.	WHITE SUGAR.

II

C. R.	MAGPIE.
DELTA.	SIMPLE SUSAN.

III

DINAH MITE.	M. F. C.

I have received more than one remonstrance on my assertion, in the Chelsea Pensioners' problem, that it was illogical to assume, from the datum, "70 per cent have lost an eye," that 30 per cent have *not*. ALGERNON BRAY states, as a parallel case, "Suppose Tommy's father gives him 4 apples, and he eats one of them, how many has he left?" and says, "I think we are justified in answering, 3." I think so too. There is no "must" here, and data are evidently meant to fix the answer *exactly:* but, if the question were set me, "How many *must* he have left?" I should understand the data to be that his father gave him 4 *at least,* but *may* have given him more.

I take this opportunity of thanking those who have sent, along with their answers to the Tenth Knot, regrets that there are no more Knots to come, or petitions that I should recall my resolution to bring them to an end. I am most grateful for their kind words; but I think it wisest to end what, at best, was but a lame attempt. "The stretched metre of an antique song" is beyond my compass; and my puppets were neither distinctly *in* my life (like those I now address), nor yet (like Alice and the Mock Turtle) distinctly *out* of it. Yet let me at least fancy, as I lay down the pen, that I carry with me into my silent life, dear reader, a farewell smile from your unseen face, and a kindly farewell pressure from your unfelt hand! And so, good night! Parting is such sweet sorrow, that I shall say "good night!" till it be morrow.

THE HUNTING OF THE SNARK

AN AGONY IN EIGHT FITS

INSCRIBED TO A DEAR CHILD:
IN MEMORY OF GOLDEN SUMMER HOURS
AND WHISPERS OF A SUMMER SEA.

Girt with a boyish garb for boyish task,
   Eager she wields her spade: yet loves as well
Rest on a friendly knee, intent to ask
   The tale he loves to tell.

Rude spirits of the seething outer strife,
   Unmeet to read her pure and simple spright,
Deem, if you list, such hours a waste of life,
   Empty of all delight!

Chat on, sweet Maid, and rescue from annoy
   Hearts that by wiser talk are unbeguiled.
Ah, happy he who owns that tenderest joy,
   The heart-love of a child!

Away, fond thoughts, and vex my soul no more!
   Work claims my wakeful nights, my busy days—
Albeit bright memories of that sunlit shore
   Yet haunt my dreaming gaze!

PREFACE

If—and the thing is wildly possible—the charge of writing nonsense were ever brought against the author of this brief but instructive poem, it would be based, I feel convinced, on the line (in p. 403):

Then the bowsprit got mixed with the rudder sometimes.

In view of this painful possibility, I will not (as I might) appeal indignantly to my other writings as a proof that I am incapable of such a deed: I will not (as I might) point to the strong moral purpose of this poem itself, to the arithmetical principles so cautiously inculcated in it, or to its noble teachings in Natural History—I will take the more prosaic course of simply explaining how it happened.

The Bellman, who was almost morbidly sensitive about appearances, used to have the bowsprit unshipped once or twice a week to be revarnished, and it more than once happened, when the time came for replacing it, that no one on board could remember which end of the ship it belonged to. They knew it was not of the slightest use to appeal to the Bellman about it—he would only refer to his Naval Code, and read out in pathetic tones Admiralty Instructions which none of them had ever been able to understand—so it generally ended in its being fastened on, anyhow, across the rudder. The helmsman [1] used to stand by with tears in his eyes: *he* knew it was all wrong, but alas! Rule 42 of the Code, "No one shall speak to the Man at the Helm," had

[1] This office was usually undertaken by the Boots, who found in it a refuge from the Baker's constant complaints about the insufficient blacking of his three pair of boots.

been completed by the Bellman himself with the words, "and the Man at the Helm shall speak to no one." So remonstrance was impossible, and no steering could be done till the next varnishing day. During these bewildering intervals the ship usually sailed backwards.

As this poem is to some extent connected with the lay of the Jabberwock, let me take this opportunity of answering a question that has often been asked me, how to pronounce "slithy toves." The "i" in "slithy" is long, as in "writhe"; and "toves" is pronounced so as to rhyme with "groves." Again, the first "o" in "borogoves" is pronounced like the "o" in "borrow." I have heard people try to give it the sound of the "o" in "worry." Such is Human Perversity.

This also seems a fitting occasion to notice the other hard words in that poem. Humpty Dumpty's theory, of two meanings packed into one word like a portmanteau, seems to me the right explanation for all.

For instance, take the two words "fuming" and "furious." Make up your mind that you will say both words, but leave it unsettled which you will say first. Now open your mouth and speak. If your thoughts incline ever so little towards "fuming," you will say "fuming-furious"; if they turn, by even a hair's breadth, towards "furious," you will say "furious-fuming"; but if you have that rarest of gifts, a perfectly balanced mind, you will say "frumious."

Supposing that, when Pistol uttered the well-known words:

Under which king, Bezonian? Speak or die!

Justice Shallow had felt certain that it was either William or Richard, but had not been able to settle which, so that he could not possibly say either name before the other, can it be doubted that, rather than die, he would have gasped out, "Rilchiam!"?

FIT THE FIRST

THE LANDING

"Just the place for a Snark!" the Bellman cried,
  As he landed his crew with care;
Supporting each man on the top of the tide
  By a finger entwined in his hair.

"Just the place for a Snark! I have said it twice:
  That alone should encourage the crew.
Just the place for a Snark!—I have said it thrice:
  What I tell you three times is true."

The crew was complete: it included a Boots—
  A maker of Bonnets and Hoods—
A Barrister, brought to arrange their disputes—
  And a Broker, to value their goods.

A Billiard-marker, whose skill was immense,
  Might perhaps have won more than his share—
But a Banker, engaged at enormous expense,
  Had the whole of their cash in his care.

There was also a Beaver, that paced on the deck,
  Or would sit making lace in the bow:
And had often (the Bellman said) saved them from wreck,
  Though none of the sailors knew how.

There was one who was famed for the number of things
  He forgot when he entered the ship:
His umbrella, his watch, all his jewels and rings,
  And the clothes he had bought for the trip.

He had forty-two boxes, all carefully packed,
  With his name painted clearly on each:
But, since he omitted to mention the fact,
  They were all left behind on the beach.

The loss of his clothes hardly mattered, because
  He had seven coats on when he came,
With three pair of boots—but the worst of it was,
  He had wholly forgotten his name.

He would answer to "Hi!" or to any loud cry,
  Such as "Fry me!" or "Fritter my wig!"
To "What-you-may-call-um!" or "What-was-his-name!"
  But especially "Thing-um-a-jig!"

While, for those who preferred a more forcible word,
  He had different names from these:
His intimate friends called him "Candle-ends,"
  And his enemies "Toasted-cheese."

"His form is ungainly—his intellect small——"
  (So the Bellman would often remark)
"But his courage is perfect! And that, after all,
  Is the thing that one needs with a Snark."

He would joke with hyænas, returning their stare
  With an impudent wag of the head:
And he once went a walk, paw-in-paw, with a bear,
  "Just to keep up its spirits," he said.

He came as a Baker: but owned when too late—
  And it drove the poor Bellman half-mad—
He could only bake Bridecake—for which, I may state,
  No materials were to be had.

"Supporting each man on the top of the tide"

The last of the crew needs especial remark,
 Though he looked an incredible dunce:
He had just one idea—but, that one being "Snark,"
 The good Bellman engaged him at once.

He came as a Butcher: but gravely declared,
 When the ship had been sailing a week,
He could only kill Beavers. The Bellman looked scared,
 And was almost too frightened to speak:

But at length he explained, in a tremulous tone,
 There was only one Beaver on board;
And that was a tame one he had of his own,
 Whose death would be deeply deplored.

The Beaver, who happened to hear the remark,
 Protested, with tears in its eyes,
That not even the rapture of hunting the Snark
 Could atone for that dismal surprise!

It strongly advised that the Butcher should be
 Conveyed in a separate ship:
But the Bellman declared that would never agree
 With the plans he had made for the trip:

Navigation was always a difficult art,
 Though with only one ship and one bell:
And he feared he must really decline, for his part,
 Undertaking another as well.

The Beaver's best course was, no doubt, to procure
 A second-hand dagger-proof coat—
So the Baker advised it—and next, to insure
 Its life in some Office of note:

"He had wholly forgotten his name"

This the Banker suggested, and offered for hire
   (On moderate terms), or for sale,
Two excellent Policies, one Against Fire,
   And one Against Damage from Hail.

Yet still, even after that sorrowful day,
   Whenever the Butcher was by,
The Beaver kept looking the opposite way,
   And appeared unaccountably shy.

FIT THE SECOND

THE BELLMAN'S SPEECH

THE Bellman himself they all praised to the skies—
   Such a carriage, such ease and such grace!
Such solemnity, too! One could see he was wise,
   The moment one looked in his face!

He had bought a large map representing the sea,
   Without the least vestige of land:
And the crew were much pleased when they found it to be
   A map they could all understand.

"What's the good of Mercator's North Poles and Equators,
   Tropics, Zones, and Meridian Lines?"
So the Bellman would cry: and the crew would reply,
   "They are merely conventional signs!

"Other maps are such shapes, with their islands and capes!
   But we've got our brave Captain to thank"
(So the crew would protest) "that he's bought us the best—
   A perfect and absolute blank!"

"The Beaver kept looking the opposite way"

This was charming, no doubt: but they shortly found out
  That the Captain they trusted so well
Had only one notion for crossing the ocean,
  And that was to tingle his bell.

He was thoughtful and grave—but the orders he gave
  Were enough to bewilder a crew.
When he cried, "Steer to starboard, but keep her head lar-
      board!"
  What on earth was the helmsman to do?

Then the bowsprit got mixed with the rudder sometimes:
  A thing, as the Bellman remarked,
That frequently happens in tropical climes,
  When a vessel is, so to speak, "snarked."

But the principal failing occurred in the sailing,
  And the Bellman, perplexed and distressed,
Said he *had* hoped, at least, when the wind blew due East
  That the ship would *not* travel due West!

But the danger was past—they had landed at last,
  With their boxes, portmanteaus, and bags:
Yet at first sight the crew were not pleased with the view,
  Which consisted of chasms and crags.

The Bellman perceived that their spirits were low,
  And repeated in musical tone
Some jokes he had kept for a season of woe—
  But the crew would do nothing but groan.

He served out some grog with a liberal hand,
  And bade them sit down on the beach:
And they could not but own that their Captain looked grand,
  As he stood and delivered his speech:

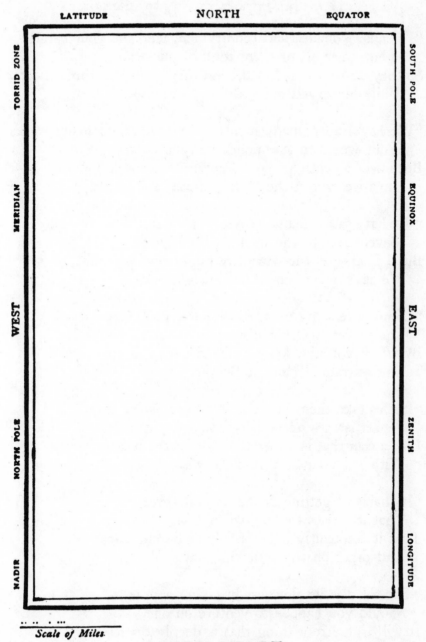

LATITUDE NORTH EQUATOR

TORRID ZONE

SOUTH POLE

MERIDIAN

EQUINOX

WEST

EAST

NORTH POLE

ZENITH

NADIR

LONGITUDE

Scale of Miles.

OCEAN-CHART

"Friends, Romans, and countrymen, lend me your ears!"
  (They were all of them fond of quotations:
So they drank to his health, and they gave him three cheers,
  While he served out additional rations).

"We have sailed many months, we have sailed many weeks
  (Four weeks to the month you may mark),
But never as yet ('tis your Captain who speaks)
  Have we caught the least glimpse of a Snark!

"We have sailed many weeks, we have sailed many days
  (Seven days to the week I allow),
But a Snark, on the which we might lovingly gaze,
  We have never beheld until now!

"Come, listen, my men, while I tell you again
  The five unmistakable marks
By which you may know, wheresoever you go,
  The warranted genuine Snarks.

"Let us take them in order. The first is the taste,
  Which is meagre and hollow, but crisp:
Like a coat that is rather too tight in the waist,
  With a flavour of Will-o'-the-wisp.

"Its habit of getting up late you'll agree
  That it carries too far, when I say
That it frequently breakfasts at five-o'clock tea,
  And dines on the following day.

"The third is its slowness in taking a jest;
  Should you happen to venture on one,
It will sigh like a thing that is deeply distressed:
  And it always looks grave at a pun.

"The fourth is its fondness for bathing-machines,
  Which it constantly carries about,
And believes that they add to the beauty of scenes—
  A sentiment open to doubt.

"The fifth is ambition. It next will be right
  To describe each particular batch:
Distinguishing those that have feathers, and bite,
  From those that have whiskers, and scratch.

"For, although common Snarks do no manner of harm,
  Yet, I feel it my duty to say,
Some are Boojums——" The Bellman broke off in alarm,
  For the Baker had fainted away.

FIT THE THIRD

THE BAKER'S TALE

THEY roused him with muffins—they roused him with ice—
  They roused him with mustard and cress—
They roused him with jam and judicious advice—
  They set him conundrums to guess.

When at length he sat up and was able to speak,
  His sad story he offered to tell;
And the Bellman cried, "Silence! not even a shriek!"
  And excitedly tingled his bell.

There was silence supreme! Not a shriek, not a scream,
  Scarcely even a howl or a groan,
As the man they called "Ho!" told his story of woe
  In an antediluvian tone.

"My father and mother were honest, though poor——"
   "Skip all that!" cried the Bellman in haste.
"If it once becomes dark, there's no chance of a Snark—
   We have hardly a minute to waste!"

"I skip forty years," said the Baker, in tears,
   "And proceed without further remark
To the day when you took me aboard of your ship
   To help you in hunting the Snark.

"A dear uncle of mine (after whom I was named)
   Remarked, when I bade him farewell——"
"Oh, skip your dear uncle!" the Bellman exclaimed,
   As he angrily tingled his bell.

"He remarked to me then," said that mildest of men,
   " 'If your Snark be a Snark, that is right:
Fetch it home by all means—you may serve it with greens,
   And it's handy for striking a light.

" 'You may seek it with thimbles—and seek it with care;
   You may hunt it with forks and hope;
You may threaten its life with a railway-share;
   You may charm it with smiles and soap——' "

("That's exactly the method," the Bellman bold
   In a hasty parenthesis cried,
"That's exactly the way I have always been told
   That the capture of Snarks should be tried!")

" 'But oh, beamish nephew, beware of the day,
   If your Snark be a Boojum! For then
You will softly and suddenly vanish away,
   And never be met with again!'

"But oh, beamish nephew, beware of the day"

"It is this, it is this that oppresses my soul,
    When I think of my uncle's last words:
And my heart is like nothing so much as a bowl
    Brimming over with quivering curds!

"It is this, it is this——" "We have had that before!"
    The Bellman indignantly said.
And the Baker replied, "Let me say it once more.
    It is this, it is this that I dread!

"I engage with the Snark—every night after dark—
    In a dreamy delirious fight:
I serve it with greens in those shadowy scenes,
    And I use it for striking a light;

"But if ever I meet with a Boojum, that day,
    In a moment (of this I am sure),
I shall softly and suddenly vanish away—
    And the notion I cannot endure!"

FIT THE FOURTH

THE HUNTING

THE Bellman looked uffish, and wrinkled his brow.
    "If only you'd spoken before!
It's excessively awkward to mention it now,
    With the Snark, so to speak, at the door!

"We should all of us grieve, as you well may believe,
    If you never were met with again—
But surely, my man, when the voyage began,
    You might have suggested it then?

"It's excessively awkward to mention it now—
  As I think I've already remarked."
And the man they called "Hi!" replied, with a sigh,
  "I informed you the day we embarked.

"You may charge me with murder—or want of sense
  (We are all of us weak at times):
But the slightest approach to a false pretence
  Was never among my crimes!

"I said it in Hebrew—I said it in Dutch—
  I said it in German and Greek;
But I wholly forgot (and it vexes me much)
  That English is what you speak!"

" 'Tis a pitiful tale," said the Bellman, whose face
  Had grown longer at every word;
"But, now that you've stated the whole of your case,
  More debate would be simply absurd.

"The rest of my speech" (he explained to his men)
  "You shall hear when I've leisure to speak it.
But the Snark is at hand, let me tell you again!
  'Tis your glorious duty to seek it!

"To seek it with thimbles, to seek it with care;
  To pursue it with forks and hope;
To threaten its life with a railway-share;
  To charm it with smiles and soap!

"For the Snark's a peculiar creature, that won't
  Be caught in a commonplace way.
Do all that you know, and try all that you don't:
  Not a chance must be wasted to-day!

"For England expects—I forbear to proceed:
    'Tis a maxim tremendous, but trite:
And you'd best be unpacking the things that you need
    To rig yourselves out for the fight."

Then the Banker endorsed a blank cheque (which he
        crossed),
    And changed his loose silver for notes.
The Baker with care combed his whiskers and hair,
    And shook the dust out of his coats.

The Boots and the Broker were sharpening a spade—
    Each working the grindstone in turn;
But the Beaver went on making lace, and displayed
    No interest in the concern:

Though the Barrister tried to appeal to its pride,
    And vainly proceeded to cite
A number of cases, in which making laces
    Had been proved an infringement of right.

The maker of Bonnets ferociously planned
    A novel arrangement of bows:
While the Billiard-marker with quivering hand
    Was chalking the tip of his nose.

But the Butcher turned nervous, and dressed himself fine,
    With yellow kid gloves and a ruff—
Said he felt it exactly like going to dine,
    Which the Bellman declared was all "stuff."

"Introduce me, now there's a good fellow," he said,
    "If we happen to meet it together!"
And the Bellman, sagaciously nodding his head,
    Said, "That must depend on the weather."

"To pursue it with forks and hope"

The Beaver went simply galumphing about,
  At seeing the Butcher so shy:
And even the Baker, though stupid and stout,
  Made an effort to wink with one eye.

"Be a man!" said the Bellman in wrath, as he heard
  The Butcher beginning to sob.
"Should we meet with a Jubjub, that desperate bird,
  We shall need all our strength for the job!"

FIT THE FIFTH

THE BEAVER'S LESSON

THEY sought it with thimbles, they sought it with care;
  They pursued it with forks and hope;
They threatened its life with a railway-share;
  They charmed it with smiles and soap.

Then the Butcher contrived an ingenious plan
  For making a separate sally;
And had fixed on a spot unfrequented by man,
  A dismal and desolate valley.

But the very same plan to the Beaver occurred:
  It had chosen the very same place;
Yet neither betrayed, by a sign or a word,
  The disgust that appeared in his face.

Each thought he was thinking of nothing but "Snark"
  And the glorious work of the day;
And each tried to pretend that he did not remark
  That the other was going that way.

But the valley grew narrow and narrower still,
  And the evening got darker and colder,
Till (merely from nervousness, not from goodwill)
  They marched along shoulder to shoulder.

Then a scream, shrill and high, rent the shuddering sky,
  And they knew that some danger was near:
The Beaver turned pale to the tip of its tail,
  And even the Butcher felt queer.

He thought of his childhood, left far, far behind—
  That blissful and innocent state—
The sound so exactly recalled to his mind
  A pencil that squeaks on a slate!

" 'Tis the voice of the Jubjub!" he suddenly cried
  (This man, that they used to call "Dunce").
"As the Bellman would tell you," he added with pride,
  "I have uttered that sentiment once.

" 'Tis the note of the Jubjub! Keep count, I entreat;
  You will find I have told it you twice.
'Tis the song of the Jubjub! The proof is complete,
  If only I've stated it thrice."

The Beaver had counted with scrupulous care,
  Attending to every word:
But it fairly lost heart, and outgrabe in despair,
  When the third repetition occurred.

It felt that, in spite of all possible pains,
  It had somehow contrived to lose count,
And the only thing now was to rack its poor brains
  By reckoning up the amount.

"Two added to one—if that could but be done,"
　　It said, "with one's fingers and thumbs!"
Recollecting with tears how, in earlier years,
　　It had taken no pains with its sums.

"The thing can be done," said the Butcher, "I think.
　　The thing must be done, I am sure.
The thing shall be done! Bring me paper and ink,
　　The best there is time to procure."

The Beaver brought paper, portfolio, pens,
　　And ink in unfailing supplies:
While strange creepy creatures came out of their dens,
　　And watched them with wondering eyes.

So engrossed was the Butcher, he heeded them not,
　　As he wrote with a pen in each hand,
And explained all the while in a popular style
　　Which the Beaver could well understand:

"Taking Three as the subject to reason about—
　　A convenient number to state—
We add Seven, and Ten, and then multiply out
　　By One Thousand diminished by Eight.

"The result we proceed to divide, as you see,
　　By Nine Hundred and Ninety and Two:
Then subtract Seventeen, and the answer must be
　　Exactly and perfectly true.

"The method employed I would gladly explain,
　　While I have it so clear in my head,
If I had but the time and you had but the brain—
　　But much yet remains to be said.

"The Beaver brought paper, portfolio, pens"

"In one moment I've seen what has hitherto been
    Enveloped in absolute mystery,
And without extra charge I will give you at large
    A Lesson in Natural History."

In his genial way he proceeded to say
    (Forgetting all laws of propriety,
And that giving instruction, without introduction,
    Would have caused quite a thrill in Society),

"As to temper, the Jubjub's a desperate bird,
    Since it lives in perpetual passion:
Its taste in costume is entirely absurd—
    It is ages ahead of the fashion:

"But it knows any friend it has met once before:
    It never will look at a bribe:
And in charity-meetings it stands at the door,
    And collects—though it does not subscribe.

"Its flavour when cooked is more exquisite far
    Than mutton, or oysters, or eggs:
(Some think it keeps best in an ivory jar,
    And some, in mahogany kegs:)

"You boil it in sawdust: you salt it in glue:
    You condense it with locusts and tape:
Still keeping one principal object in view—
    To preserve its symmetrical shape."

The Butcher would gladly have talked till next day,
    But he felt that the Lesson must end,
And he wept with delight in attempting to say
    He considered the Beaver his friend;

While the Beaver confessed, with affectionate looks
   More eloquent even than tears,
It had learnt in ten minutes far more than all books
   Would have taught it in seventy years.

They returned hand-in-hand, and the Bellman, unmanned
   (For a moment) with noble emotion,
Said, "This amply repays all the wearisome days
   We have spent on the billowy ocean!"

Such friends as the Beaver and Butcher became,
   Have seldom if ever been known;
In winter or summer, 'twas always the same—
   You could never meet either alone.

And when quarrels arose—as one frequently finds
   Quarrels will, spite of every endeavour—
The song of the Jubjub recurred to their minds,
   And cemented their friendship for ever!

FIT THE SIXTH

THE BARRISTER'S DREAM

THEY sought it with thimbles, they sought it with care;
   They pursued it with forks and hope;
They threatened its life with a railway-share;
   They charmed it with smiles and soap.

But the Barrister, weary of proving in vain
   That the Beaver's lace-making was wrong,
Fell asleep, and in dreams saw the creature quite plain
   That his fancy had dwelt on so long.

He dreamed that he stood in a shadowy Court,
    Where the Snark, with a glass in its eye,
Dressed in gown, bands, and wig, was defending a pig
    On the charge of deserting its sty.

The Witnesses proved, without error or flaw,
    That the sty was deserted when found:
And the Judge kept explaining the state of the law
    In a soft under-current of sound.

The indictment had never been clearly expressed,
    And it seemed that the Snark had begun,
And had spoken three hours, before anyone guessed
    What the pig was supposed to have done.

The Jury had each formed a different view
    (Long before the indictment was read),
And they all spoke at once, so that none of them knew
    One word that the others had said.

"You must know——" said the Judge: but the Snark ex-
        claimed, "Fudge!
    That statute is obsolete quite!
Let me tell you, my friends, the whole question depends
    On an ancient manorial right.

"In the matter of Treason the pig would appear
    To have aided, but scarcely abetted:
While the charge of Insolvency fails, it is clear,
    If you grant the plea 'never indebted.'

"The fact of Desertion I will not dispute:
    But its guilt, as I trust, is removed
(So far as relates to the costs of this suit)
    By the Alibi which has been proved.

"*"You must know—*" *said the Judge: but the Snark exclaimed '*Fudge!*'*"

"My poor client's fate now depends on your votes."
    Here the speaker sat down in his place,
And directed the Judge to refer to his notes
    And briefly to sum up the case.

But the Judge said he never had summed up before;
    So the Snark undertook it instead,
And summed it so well that it came to far more
    Than the Witnesses ever had said!

When the verdict was called for, the Jury declined,
    As the word was so puzzling to spell;
But they ventured to hope that the Snark wouldn't mind
    Undertaking that duty as well.

So the Snark found the verdict, although, as it owned,
    It was spent with the toils of the day:
When it said the word, "GUILTY!" the Jury all groaned,
    And some of them fainted away.

Then the Snark pronounced sentence, the Judge being quite
    Too nervous to utter a word:
When it rose to its feet, there was silence like night,
    And the fall of a pin might be heard.

"Transportation for life" was the sentence it gave,
    "And *then* to be fined forty pound."
The Jury all cheered, though the Judge said he feared
    That the phrase was not legally sound.

But their wild exultation was suddenly checked
    When the jailer informed them, with tears,
Such a sentence would not have the slightest effect,
    As the pig had been dead for some years.

The Judge left the Court, looking deeply disgusted:
    But the Snark, though a little aghast,
As the lawyer to whom the defence was entrusted,
    Went bellowing on to the last.

Thus the Barrister dreamed, while the bellowing seemed
    To grow every moment more clear:
Till he woke to the knell of a furious bell,
    Which the Bellman rang close at his ear.

FIT THE SEVENTH

THE BANKER'S FATE

THEY sought it with thimbles, they sought it with care;
    They pursued it with forks and hope;
They threatened its life with a railway-share;
    They charmed it with smiles and soap.

And the Banker, inspired with a courage so new
    It was matter for general remark,
Rushed madly ahead and was lost to their view
    In his zeal to discover the Snark.

But while he was seeking with thimbles and care,
    A Bandersnatch swiftly drew nigh
And grabbed at the Banker, who shrieked in despair,
    For he knew it was useless to fly.

He offered large discount—he offered a cheque
    (Drawn "to bearer") for seven-pounds-ten:
But the Bandersnatch merely extended its neck
    And grabbed at the Banker again.

Without rest or pause—while those frumious jaws
   Went savagely snapping around—
He skipped and he hopped, and he floundered and flopped,
   Till fainting he fell to the ground.

The Bandersnatch fled as the others appeared:
   Led on by that fear-stricken yell:
And the Bellman remarked, "It is just as I feared!"
   And solemnly tolled on his bell.

He was black in the face, and they scarcely could trace
   The least likeness to what he had been:
While so great was his fright that his waistcoat turned
     white—
   A wonderful thing to be seen!

To the horror of all who were present that day,
   He uprose in full evening dress,
And with senseless grimaces endeavoured to say
   What his tongue could no longer express.

Down he sank in a chair—ran his hands through his hair—
   And chanted in mimsiest tones
Words whose utter inanity proved his insanity,
   While he rattled a couple of bones.

"Leave him here to his fate—it is getting so late!"
   The Bellman exclaimed in a fright.
"We have lost half the day. Any further delay,
   And we shan't catch a Snark before night!"

"So great was his fright that his waistcoat turned white"

FIT THE EIGHTH

THE VANISHING

THEY sought it with thimbles, they sought it with care;
    They pursued it with forks and hope;
They threatened its life with a railway-share;
    They charmed it with smiles and soap.

They shuddered to think that the chase might fail,
    And the Beaver, excited at last,
Went bounding along on the tip of its tail,
    For the daylight was nearly past.

"There is Thingumbob shouting!" the Bellman said.
    "He is shouting like mad, only hark!
He is waving his hands, he is wagging his head,
    He has certainly found a Snark!"

They gazed in delight, while the Butcher exclaimed,
    "He was always a desperate wag!"
They beheld him—their Baker—their hero unnamed—
    On the top of a neighbouring crag,

Erect and sublime, for one moment of time.
    In the next, that wild figure they saw
(As if stung by a spasm) plunge into a chasm,
    While they waited and listened in awe.

"It's a Snark!" was the sound that first came to their ears,
    And seemed almost too good to be true.
Then followed a torrent of laughter and cheers:
    Then the ominous words, "It's a Boo——"

"Then, silence"

Then, silence. Some fancied they heard in the air
   A weary and wandering sigh
That sounded like "—jum!" but the others declare
   It was only a breeze that went by.

They hunted till darkness came on, but they found
   Not a button, or feather, or mark,
By which they could tell that they stood on the ground
   Where the Baker had met with the Snark.

In the midst of the word he was trying to say,
   In the midst of his laughter and glee,
He had softly and suddenly vanished away——
   For the Snark *was* a Boojum, you see.

NONSENSE FROM LETTERS

THE THREE CATS [1]

A VERY curious thing happened to me at half-past four, yesterday. Three visitors came knocking at my door, begging me to let them in. And when I opened the door, who do you think they were?

You'll never guess.

Why, they were three cats! Wasn't it curious? However, they all looked so cross and disagreeable that I took up the first thing I could lay my hand on (which happened to be the rolling-pin) and knocked them all down as flat as pancakes!

That was fair, wasn't it?

Of course I didn't leave them lying flat on the ground, like dried flowers: no, I picked them up, and I was as kind as I could be to them. I lent them the portfolio for a bed—they wouldn't have been comfortable in a real bed, you know: they were too thin—but they were *quite* happy between the sheets of blotting-paper—and each of them had a pen-wiper for a pillow. Well, then I went to bed: but first I lent them the three dinner-bells to ring if they wanted anything in the night.

You know I have *three* dinner-bells—the first (which is the largest) is rung when dinner is *nearly* ready; the second (which is rather larger) is rung when it is quite ready; and the third (which is as large as the other two put together) is rung all the time I am at dinner. And I told them they must ring if they happened to want anything. And, as they

---

[1] This delightful fantasy is extracted from a series of letters written by Lewis Carroll to two little acquaintances of his, Agnes and Amy Hughes. Merely by omitting some extraneous matter, a little masterpiece of nonsense has been preserved, and one typical of Lewis Carroll's genius.

rung *all* the bells *all* night, I suppose they did want something or other, only I was too sleepy to attend to them.

In the morning I gave them some rat-tail jelly and buttered mice for breakfast and they were as discontented as they could be. And, do you know, when I had gone out for a walk, they got *all* my books out of the bookcase, and opened them on the floor to be ready for me to read. They opened them at page 50, because they thought that would be a nice useful page to begin at. It was rather unfortunate, though: because they took my bottle of gum and tried to gum pictures upon the ceiling (which they thought would please me). They accidentally spilt a quantity of it all over the books. So when they were shut up and put by, the leaves all stuck together, and I can never read page 50 again in any of them!

However, they meant it very kindly, so I wasn't angry. I gave them each a spoonful of ink as a treat; but they were ungrateful for that and made the most dreadful faces. But, of course, as it was given them for a treat, they had to drink it. One of them has turned black since: it was a white cat to begin with.

They wanted some boiled pelican, but, of course, I knew it wouldn't be good for them. So all I said was "Go to Agnes Hughes, and if it's *really* good for you she'll give you some."

Then I shook hands with them all, and wished them good-bye, and drove them up the chimney. They seemed very sorry to go.

A FEW OF THE THINGS I LIKE [1]

I MAY as well just tell you a few of the things I like, and then whenever you want to give me a birthday present (my

[1] From a letter to Miss Jessie Sinclair, 1878.

birthday comes once every seven years on the fifth Tuesday in April) you will know what to give me.

Well, I like *very* much indeed, a little mustard with a bit of beef spread thinly under it; and I like brown sugar—only it should have some apple pudding mixed with it to keep it from being too sweet; but perhaps what I like best of all is salt, with some soup poured over it. The use of the soup is to hinder the salt from being too dry; and it helps to melt it. Then there are three other things I like; for instance, pins—only they should always have a cushion put round them to keep them warm. And I like two or three handfuls of hair; only they should always have a little girl's head beneath them to grow on, or else whenever you open the door they get blown all over the room and then they get lost, you know.

MYSELF AND ME [1]

My dear Magdalen,

I want to explain to you why I did not call yesterday. I was sorry to miss you, but you see I had so many conversations on the way. I tried to explain to the people in the street that I was going to see you, but they wouldn't listen; they said they were in a hurry, which was rude.

At last I met a wheelbarrow that I thought would attend to me, but I couldn't make out what was in it. I saw some features at first, then I looked through a telescope, and found it was a countenance; then I looked through a telescope and it was a face! I thought it was rather like me, so I fetched a large looking-glass to make sure, and then to my great joy I found it was me. We shook hands, and were just beginning to talk, when myself came up and joined us, and

---

[1] This letter written to a child friend in 1875 is such a pure example of Carroll's metaphysical humour that it can well be included with his immortal "Alice."

we had quite a pleasant conversation. I said, "Do you re-member when we all met at Sandown?" and myself said, "It was very jolly there; there was a child called Magdalen," and me said, "I used to like her a little; not much, you know —only a little."

Then it was time for us to go to the train, and who do you think came to the station to see us off? You would never guess. They were two very dear friends of mine, who happen to be here just now, and beg to be allowed to sign this letter as your affectionate friends,

LEWIS CARROLL and C. L. DODGSON.

THE TWO CLOCKS

WHICH is better, a clock that is right only once a year, or a clock that is right twice every day? "The latter," you reply, "unquestionably." Very good, now attend.

I have two clocks: one doesn't go *at all*, and the other loses a minute every day: which would you prefer? "The losing one," you answer, "without a doubt." Now observe: the one which loses a minute a day has to lose twelve hours, or seven hundred and twenty minutes, before it is right again, consequently it is only right once in two years, whereas the other is evidently right as often as the time it points to comes round, which happens twice a day.

So you've contradicted yourself *once*.

"Ah, but," you say, "what's the use of its being right twice a day, if I can't tell when the time comes?"

Why, suppose the clock points to eight o'clock, don't you see that the clock is right *at* eight o'clock? Consequently, when eight o'clock comes round your clock is right.

"Yes, I see *that*," you reply.

Very good, then you've contradicted yourself *twice*: now

get out of the difficulty as best you can, and don't contradict yourself again if you can help it.

You *might* go on to ask, "How am I to know when eight o'clock *does* come? My clock will not tell me." Be patient: you know that when eight o'clock comes your clock is right; very good; then your rule is this: keep your eye fixed on your clock, and *the very moment it is right* it will be eight o'clock. "But——," you say. There, that'll do; the more you argue, the farther you get from the point, so it will be as well to stop.

PHOTOGRAPHY EXTRAORDINARY

(From "The Rectory Umbrella")

THE recent extraordinary discovery in Photography, as applied to the operations of the mind, has reduced the art of novel-writing to the merest mechanical labour. We have been kindly permitted by the artist to be present during one of his experiments; but as the invention has not yet been given to the world, we are only at liberty to relate the results, suppressing all details of chemicals and manipulation.

The operator began by stating that the ideas of the feeblest intellect, when once received on properly prepared paper, could be "developed" up to any required degree of intensity. On hearing our wish that he would begin with an extreme case, he obligingly summoned a young man from an adjoining room, who appeared to be of the very weakest possible physical and mental powers. On being asked what we thought of him, we candidly confessed that he seemed incapable of anything but sleep; our friend cordially assented to this opinion.

The machine being in position, and a mesmeric rapport established between the mind of the patient and the object glass, the young man was asked whether he wished to say anything; he feebly replied, "Nothing." He was then asked what he was thinking of, and the answer, as before, was "Nothing." The artist on this pronounced him to be in a most satisfactory state, and at once commenced the operation.

After the paper had been exposed for the requisite time, it was removed and submitted to our inspection; we found it to be covered with faint and almost illegible characters. A closer scrutiny revealed the following:

"The eve was soft and dewy mild; a zephyr whispered in the lofty glade, and a few light drops of rain cooled the thirsty soil. At a slow amble, along the primrose-bordered path rode a gentle-looking and amiable youth, holding a light cane in his delicate hand; the pony moved gracefully beneath him, inhaling as it went the fragrance of the road-side flowers; the calm smile, and languid eyes, so admirably harmonising with the fair features of the rider, showed the even tenor of his thoughts. With a sweet though feeble voice, he plaintively murmured out the gentle regrets that clouded his breast:

'Alas, she would not hear my prayer!
Yet it were rash to tear my hair;
Disfigured, I should be less fair.

'She was unwise, I may say blind;
Once she was lovingly inclined;
Some circumstance has changed her mind.'

There was a moment's silence; the pony stumbled over a stone in the path, and unseated his rider. A crash was heard among the dried leaves; the youth arose; a slight bruise on his left shoulder, and a disarrangement of his cravat, were the only traces that remained of this trifling accident."

"This," we remarked, as we returned the paper, "belongs apparently to the milk-and-water School of Novels."

"You are quite right," our friend replied, "and, in its present state, it is, of course, utterly unsaleable in the present day: we shall find, however, that the next stage of development will remove it into the strong-minded or Matter-of-Fact School." After dipping it into various acids, he again submitted it to us: it had now become the following:

"The evening was of the ordinary character, barometer at 'change'; a wind was getting up in the wood, and some rain was beginning to fall; a bad look-out for the farmers. A gentleman approached along the bridle-road, carrying a stout knobbed stick in his hand, and mounted on a serviceable nag, possibly worth some £40 or so; there was a settled business-like expression on the rider's face, and he whistled as he rode; he seemed to be hunting for rhymes in his head, and at length repeated, in a satisfied tone, the following composition:

> *'Well! so my offer was no go!*
> *She might do worse, I told her so;*
> *She was a fool to answer "No."*

> *'However, things are as they stood;*
> *Nor would I have her if I could,*
> *For there are plenty more as good.'*

At this moment the horse set his foot in a hole, and rolled over; his rider rose with difficulty; he had sustained several severe bruises and fractured two ribs; it was some time before he forgot that unlucky day."

We returned this with the strongest expression of admiration, and requested that it might now be developed to the highest possible degree. Our friend readily consented, and shortly presented us with the result, which he informed us belonged to the Spasmodic or German School. We perused it with indescribable sensations of surprise and delight:

"The night was wildly tempestuous—a hurricane raved through the murky forest—furious torrents of rain lashed the groaning earth. With a headlong rush—down a precipitous mountain gorge—dashed a mounted horseman armed to the teeth—his horse bounded beneath him at a mad gallop, snorting fire from its distended nostrils as it flew. The rider's knotted brows—rolling eyeballs—and clenched teeth —expressed the intense agony of his mind—weird visions loomed upon his burning brain—while with a mad yell he poured forth the torrent of his boiling passion:

> *'Firebrands and daggers! hope hath fled!*
> *To atoms dash the doubly dead!*
> *My brain is fire—my heart is lead!*
>
> *'Her soul is flint, and what am I?*
> *Scorched by her fierce, relentless eye,*
> *Nothingness is my destiny!'*

There was a moment's pause. Horror! his path ended in a fathomless abyss. . . . A rush—a flash—a crash—all was over. Three drops of blood, two teeth, and a stirrup were all that remained to tell where the wild horseman met his doom."

The young man was now recalled to consciousness, and shown the result of the workings of his mind; he instantly fainted away.

In the present infancy of the art we forbear from further comment on this wonderful discovery; but the mind reels as it contemplates the stupendous addition thus made to the powers of science.

Our friend concluded with various minor experiments, such as working up a passage of Wordsworth into strong, sterling poetry: the same experiment was tried on a passage of Byron, at our request, but the paper came out' scorched and blistered all over by the fiery epithets thus produced.

As a concluding remark: *could* this art be applied (we put the question in the strictest confidence)—*could* it, we ask, be applied to the speeches in Parliament? It may be but a delusion of our heated imagination, but we will still cling fondly to the idea, and hope against hope.

.   .   .   .

CHRIST CHURCH, OXFORD,
March 8, 1880.

MY DEAR ADA,—(Isn't that your short name? "Adelaide" is all very well, but you see when one is *dreadfully* busy one hasn't time to write such long words—particularly when it takes one half an hour to remember how to spell it—and even then one has to go and get a dictionary to see if one has spelt it right, and of course the dictionary is in another room, at the top of a high bookcase—where it has been for months and months, and has got all covered with dust—so one has to get a duster first of all, and nearly choke oneself in dusting it—and when one *has* made out at last which is dictionary and which is dust, even *then* there's the job of remembering which end of the alphabet "A" comes—for one feels pretty certain it isn't in the *middle*—then one has to go and wash one's hands before turning over the leaves—for they've got so thick with dust one hardly knows them by sight—and, as likely as not, the soap is lost, and the jug is empty, and there's no towel, and one has to spend hours and hours in finding things—and perhaps after all one has to go off to the shop to buy a new cake of soap—so, with all this

bother, I hope you won't mind my writing it short and saying, "My dear Ada".) You said in your last letter you would
like a likeness of me: so here it is, and I hope you will like
it—I won't forget to call the next time I'm in Wallington.

Your very affectionate friend,

LEWIS CARROLL.

A letter to Miss Adelaide Paine.

CHRIST CHURCH, OXFORD,
October 28, 1876.

MY DEAREST GERTRUDE,—You will be sorry, and surprised, and puzzled, to hear what a queer illness I have had
ever since you went. I sent for the doctor, and said, "Give
me some medicine, for I'm tired." He said, "Nonsense and
stuff! You don't want medicine: go to bed!" I said, "No; it
isn't the sort of tiredness that wants bed. I'm tired in the
face." He looked a little grave, and said, "Oh, it's your *nose*
that's tired: a person often talks too much when he thinks he
nose a great deal." I said, "No; it isn't the nose. Perhaps
it's the *hair.*" Then he looked rather grave, and said, "*Now*
I understand: you've been playing too many hairs on the
pianoforte." "No, indeed I haven't!" I said, "and it isn't
exactly the *hair:* it's more about the nose and chin." Then
he looked a good deal graver, and said, "Have you been
walking much on your chin lately?" I said, "No." "Well!"
he said, "it puzzles me very much. Do you think that it's
in the lips?" "Of course!" I said. "That's exactly what it is!"
Then he looked very grave indeed, and said, "I think you
must have been giving too many kisses." "Well," I said, "I
did give *one* kiss to a baby child, a little friend of mine."
"Think again," he said; "are you sure it was only *one?*" I
thought again, and said, "Perhaps it was eleven times." Then
the doctor said, "You must not give her *any* more till your
lips are quite rested again." "But what am I to do?" I said,